PARTY GIRLS

PARTY GIRLS

ROZ BAILEY

Kensington Books
http://www.kensingtonbooks.com

KENSINGTON BOOKS are published by

Kensington Publishing Corp.
850 Third Avenue
New York, NY 10022

All Kensington titles, imprints and distributed lines are available at special quantity discounts for bulk purchases for sales promotion, premiums, fund-raising, educational or institutional use.

Special book excerpts or customized printings can also be created to fit specific needs. For details, write or phone the office of the Kensington Special Sales Manager: Kensington Publishing Corp., 850 Third Avenue, New York, NY 10022. Attn. Special Sales Department. Phone: 1-800-221-2647.

Kensington and the K logo Reg. U.S. Pat. & TM Off.

ISBN 0-7582-0196-6

First Trade Printing: July 2002
10 9 8 7 6 5 4 3

Printed in the United States of America

Part One

Don't Let Them See You Cry

1

Some things never change.
Like New York City.

Corny phrases from songs played in Zoey's head as the train plunged into the dark tunnel in its approach to Penn Station. A hell of a town. The city that never sleeps. If I can make it there, I'll make it anywhere.

Let's hope so.

Zoey McGuire stared at her reflection in the train window. Long brown hair with gold highlights. Round brown eyes, not too red since she'd managed to avoid a crying jag today. Youthful skin, not too pale, thanks to a brighter shade of blush, and a turned-up Irish nose that would probably have people thinking she was cute well into her fifties, despite her quest for sophistication.

The real question was, did she look like a divorcing person? A lost soul? Well, even if she did, that was one of the benefits of Manhattan. The island had plenty of room for losers of every persuasion; she would fit right in.

When she'd phoned her mother about her plans, Lila Mc-

Guire Carter had told her she sounded like an adolescent who was running away from home. "Believe me, I'm not defending Nick, but aren't you showing a lack of maturity by trying to escape your problems? Men have had affairs since the beginning of time, and some women stay and wage a war for their men."

Or they look the other way, Zoey thought, thinking back to the many business trips her father had taken when she was a child. Dad's infidelity had never been a topic of conversation, not with her father before he died, and never with her mother, who still maintained a flawless facade of happy suburban wife. These days the husband (Harve Carter) and the house (Florida condo) were new, but the dynamic remained, and Zoey was determined not to duplicate her parents' mistakes.

"I can't control Nick's behavior, Mom," Zoey had told her, repeating the phrase she'd heard countless times from her therapist. Fortunately, Harve had insisted that Lila retire from teaching so that she would be available to vacuum and make grilled cheese sandwiches on a full-time basis in far-off Florida. From there the only damage Mom could do was over the phone, and although those fiber optics could be loaded, Zoey had call screening.

Zoey felt an odd rush as the train screeched to a stop inside Penn Station. Maybe it was nerves, or anticipation, or panic, or all of the above. In a way Mom was right; she wasn't supposed to be here. An interlude in New York City was not part of the master plan for Zoey McGuire's happiness; at least, it wasn't until her husband Nick Satamian had started feeding the blueprints for happily-ever-after through the shredder. The bastard. He had forced Zoey to come up with a Plan B. And C. And D.

Sweat was forming on her brow, and she lifted her hair and unbuttoned the top of her shearling coat, which was going to be way too heavy for March in the city. Still, she couldn't bear to leave it behind, worrying that Nick, in a fit of spite over losing a point in the divorce agreement, would give it to charity or loan it to his new girlfriend. And that would really kill me, Zoey thought, twisting her hair up and clamping it there with a clip from her pocket. It seemed like the past few months had been chock-full of new and improved ways for Nick to hurt, insult, and devastate Zoey. Nick proclaiming passion for his girlfriend. Nick freezing the joint bank account. Nick putting Zoey on a $700 per month allowance. Well, Nick the Prick had enjoyed a long, successful run, but his show was ending, as of today. As of now.

She pulled her bags close to squeeze through the train door and stepped onto the platform, right into something sticky. Wincing, she lifted her heel to find chewing gum stretching from the sole of her shoe. Her brand-new brown suede Rockport lace-up. She'd thought it was a practical choice for walking in the city, but apparently she'd been a little too optimistic. Converse high-tops would have worked. Or maybe she should have invested in a few pairs of those plastic shoe covers that the guys at the Mercedes dealership wore, where she took Nick's car in for servicing.

Taking the car in. Running to the cleaners. God, her life really had changed. Once upon a time she was a Manhattan girl turned young novelist on the *New York Times* best-seller list before she hit thirty. When had she turned all that in for valet parking at Lord and Taylor's and a membership to Blockbuster?

It had been five years since she and Nick had left New York. Five years of big changes like success and marriage and mergers and mortgages. Fortunately, New York hadn't changed much at all. The odor of burnt grease still filled the corridors of Penn Station. The noise of a compressor split the air as she reached the top of the escalator, and that warred with the hysterical lecture of a man trying to hand out flyers warning of some god-awful atrocity—the Apocalypse? Or was it the rising price of fuel oil? Hard to tell with the noise of car horns coming from Seventh Avenue.

Scurrying away from the noise, Zoey hitched up the strap of her overstuffed Coach bag and rolled her suitcase toward the que for cabs. The line of uninterested people, most of them talking on cell phones, stretched halfway down the block. She'd have to take the subway to Skye's apartment on East 22nd Street. She paused to pull out her cell phone and hit the speed-dial for Mouse.

"I'm here."

"Get out! Where are you?"

"Just outside Penn Station. The line for cabs is insane so I'm walking over to the N and the R train." Zoey darted left to avoid a man dressed in soiled clothes and oversized flip-flops who seemed to be harassing anyone who got too close.

"Can you manage everything on the subway? If I had to pack up, I would have bags and bags of things. When my friend Sonia left her husband, she needed three moving vans to haul her collection of garden statues and . . ."

"I just packed the basics," Zoey cut her off, not wanting to get into the treacherous territory of divorce while dragging her belongings up Seventh Avenue. "I tried to pretend I was going on *Survivor,* my luxury item being my computer." Actually, that was a lie. Her true luxury item was a bottle of Cabernet she'd swiped from Nick's collection. Nick had always droned on about the excellence of the grape crop in that year, producing a full-bodied bouquet with subtle undertones of cherry and peanut brittle. Or something like that. Bottom line, he'd been saving this sucker for a special occasion, and Zoey had big plans to toast him with it from the safe distance of a hundred or so miles.

"You always were so practical," Mouse was saying. "And you sound way too calm for everything that's going on. How do you feel?"

"I'm alternating between numb and scared to death."

"Scared to be back in the city?"

"Scared over life in general. The city is great. I need a little peace and lunacy and . . . noise," Zoey finished as a groaning vehicle on the corner dumped construction debris into a huge container. She tried to veer away from it but was stuck waiting for the light. "Hold on!" she coughed to Mouse as a cloud of dust wafted toward her.

Yes, some things never changed.

Thank God.

"Your timing is so perfect!" Mouse was saying.

"Not that I had much choice." You couldn't really plan on the exact moment when you discover that your husband is sleeping with a legal secretary at the firm. Scratch that—sleeping with any available warm body, but "deeply in love" with a legal secretary at the firm. The extent of Nick's betrayal had been that much worse because Zoey had trusted him. When he'd said he was working late, she'd believed him. When he said was working with a client in Pittsburgh or Boston or Philly, she imagined him in a conference room, his shirtsleeves rolled up, his Cross pen moving rapidly over a yellow legal pad, his eyes a bit red from reading over contracts.

He had sold her on his stoic work ethic, and she had taken care of the house and cars and thrown her arms around him for an enthusiastic kiss each time he returned.

Shame on me, thought Zoey.

"But really, this is great!" Mouse went on. "I just got back from the road and I am ready to party." Mouse, whose legal and stage name was Marielle Griffin, had been touring with the road production of *The Sound of Music*. She'd been cast as one of the children, though she'd understudied for the role of Maria. Unfortunately for Mouse, the principal actress had been healthy as a horse—no pesky laryngitis or debilitating ankle sprains. "And right now, I just happen to be working in the hottest spot in Manhattan. Girl, you're gonna love Club Vermillion. Great music, outrageously expensive drinks, and there's always a long line outside. Actually, there's a line to get in, plus a line of ambulances for the stupid kids who O.D., but we won't go there now. Are you lucky or what?"

"Discount drinks," Zoey said distractedly. "And a fleet of EMS trucks at my fingertips. Now that's a reason to end my marriage and return to New York."

"I just want to come right down and welcome you properly, but I've got to drop some papers by my agent before work. Where are you again? What is it, forty-second?"

"Twenty-second," Zoey said clearly. "But don't sweat it, we'll get together soon."

"Tonight! You have to come tonight."

"I don't think so."

"Come on, Zoey. It's just what you need."

What I need? I need my husband back. My life back. Zoey bit
her lower lip, trying to stay focused. "Look, Mouse, don't count
on me to show at the club anytime soon. The way I'm feeling
now, I'd ruin the party."

"No, no, no! You've got to come tonight. Jade is going to be
there, and I'm going to call Merlin as soon as we hang up. That
boy's gonna freak to hear you're back."

Steering her suitcase around a foul-smelling puddle, Zoey
wondered if it was true. Merlin Chong, one of her best friends
from college, was the person she'd missed most during her stint
as suburban wife and reclusive writer. Over the past few years
she'd met him for lunch occasionally in the city, but he'd never
made the trip out to Connecticut for Christmas parties or barbe-
cues. And sometimes, because of Nick's tedious clients, he wasn't
even invited. "I'm not sure Merlin is going to throw confetti at
the sight of me."

"Why wouldn't he? Just because of Nick? Actually, what's the
story with that? Did Nick and Merlin actually have a fight or
something, or was it just Nick's attitude?"

"Can you spell 'homophobic'?"

"Oh . . . really?" The line got quiet, then Mouse plunged on.
"Once I was in a show with a guy like that. Totally scared of gay
guys, like they were going to attack him or something. He didn't
get along with anybody. I think he moved back to Kansas or
Kalamazoo or something. One of those 'K' places."

"All righty, then," Zoey said, heading toward the subway entrance. "I'm going underground, so the connection's going to
go."

"So I'll see you later!" Mouse's enthusiasm gushed through
the phone, reminding Zoey of why they had stayed friends for so
long. You could count on Mouse, any place, any time. "It's gonna
be like old times, girlfriend—NYU all over again."

"Without the exams and tedious papers," Zoey added. "And
now we have to pay our own room and board." Which was a big
deal in Manhattan, the city where buildings and real estate
climbed sky-high. Jade had mentioned that some of her one-

bedrooms were listed for three thousand dollars. Three grand. At that rate, Zoey might be able to sublet a closet out in Queens or Brooklyn.

Slipping her phone into her bag, Zoey hoped that Skye had remembered to clear everything with the doorman of her building. It would be just like her to forget to make one tiny call and leave Zoey stranded while Skye was off in some author's Tuscany palazzo romancing a book out of him. Not that Zoey didn't appreciate her editor's offer. So far Skye Blackwell was one of the few people who knew about the breakup with Nick, and she knew only because she had extracted it with all the efficiency of a medical technician drawing blood. "So what's the deal with this writer's block?" Skye had asked. "Personal crisis? Breakdown? Honey, we've all been there. I can get you numbers for a few lovely therapists."

"Been there, done that," Zoey had told her. "But thanks."

"So it's the husband. Divorce? Or is it too early to tell?"

At that point Zoey had been unable to answer over the sobs that ballooned in her throat. She hadn't told her family or most of her friends yet, somehow hoping that if she sucked it up and didn't talk about it, the devastating situation would vanish.

But Skye had pried the truth out of her. In her usual take-charge manner, Skye had offered her apartment as a place to hole up for awhile, and Zoey had seen the therapeutic value instantly. The Connecticut house she'd painstakingly decorated was a quotidian reminder of the beautiful life she'd planned. The hand-stenciled walls, the pickled pine floors, the ceramic tiled swimming pool—all the features of the house she'd loved now surrounded her with a voice of their own, a constant reminder that she had failed. And then there were the memories, of dinner parties she'd thrown for Nick's law firm, of evenings spent sipping sherry by the fire, of mornings spent making love in the light that flooded through the French doors of their master bedroom.

She had to get out of that place.

Determined to put the ghosts of her once beautiful life on the cul-de-sac out of her mind, she hoisted her suitcase and descended the stairs at the subway entrance. Manhattan was the perfect escape.

Halfway down the stairs Zoey paused as the man in front of her leaned over to spit on the dirty concrete landing. God, it was good to be back in New York.

2

"Why would you want to ruin a great relationship by making it legal?" Merlin Chong sat up in bed and pulled the smooth sheet over his naked legs. He usually cherished these interludes at the hotel, a few hours of wild sex, sweet romance, and delicious back rubs, but today Josh's restlessness was seeping into the magic.

Beside him, Josh lay back on the gold brocade pillow in a soft pool of light, the smoke from his cigarette curling gracefully. Merlin hated the habit, knowing it could only hurt Josh in the long run, but he had to admit there was something sexy about the way the boy held a cigarette, stabbing it at the air to make a point, then bringing it to his lips, still swollen from kissing. . . .

"It's not about conforming to government standards, so just get the whole institutional angle out of your head," Josh said, snubbing his cigarette out in the ashtray. "This is supposed to be an incredibly special time for us. I mean, how long have we been together, Merl? What, six years? In Merlin time, that's like twenty."

Merlin folded his arms, thinking of the days when commitment meant deciding whether to drink Coronas or margaritas that night. True, when he'd met Josh he'd been falling in love with someone new nearly every month. Ha! Every week. And at that point in his life Merlin had managed to hook any guy he wanted.

The only child of a Chinese father and a Swedish mother, Merlin had always stood out in the crowd. Something about his almond-shaped blue eyes, square jaw, and jet-black hair. Throughout high school most of the kids in his lily-white class had considered him an oddity—whether because of his looks or his sexual identity, he wasn't really sure. But in his first year of college he'd discovered that guys were drawn to him for those exact same reasons. That was when he'd decided to make the most of his unusual features by purchasing deep blue contact lenses and cutting his hair in a spike with the front part high-lighted as if dipped in gold. He still remembered walking into Club Iguana after his self-styled makeover, stopping guys dead with his killer look. Suddenly, he was hot, and he took advantage of that. Not that he'd been reckless—he'd always practiced safe sex. He just had trouble "practicing" with the same person night after night.

His friends always told him he had impossibly high standards, and they were probably right. It was as if Merlin could see through people to their essence—a psychic gift, one of his as-trology teachers told him—and very often he didn't see any-thing of substance. Consequently, Merlin got bored with people very quickly. Bored with their shallow view of the world or their selfishness or their idiosyncracies like a snorty laugh or a silly swagger or a tendency to undertip.

Then Josh came along and blew everyone else out of the water. Josh with the waif-like brown eyes and wholesome smile and preppy khaki pants. Josh the Gemini, a sign with neither positive nor negative polarity, ruled by Mercury. Like quicksilver, the metal of Gemini, Josh was elusive and contradictory. Try to hold quicksilver in your hands and it flows through your fingers. Same with Josh.

Back then the boy Josh was a cool breath of Midwestern wholesomeness on the outside, a maze of complexity within, a maze dark and intricate and compelling. Despite his wholesome Minnesota twang, Josh was born of trouble, a teen runaway. His mother had died when he was young and his father had abused him, first mentally, then physically. Merlin had heard enough of the horror stories, of Josh coming home from school to pick up his bleeding and drunk father from the floor, Josh the mender, Josh the caretaker. The boy had brought out fierce caregiving instincts in Merlin, who had never felt paternal toward anyone. Merlin had begun to accept that he would never fathom the inner essence of Josh. Ah, but the challenge, the challenge was sweet.

So why the sudden push for commitment? Somehow it didn't mesh with what Merlin knew of his partner. He would have to check Josh's chart again. Maybe this was some kind of a transit he was going through.

Josh lifted his arms and tucked them under his head with a sigh. "I can't even believe we're having this conversation after all this time. That you wouldn't want to do this with me. Where's your sense of romance?"

"Don't talk to me about romance." Merlin pinged his partner's shoulder. "Who's the one that arranges this romantic rendezvous once a month? Most guys don't have a lover who books them a suite at the Royale Hotel."

"Now don't get all pissy about it." Josh swept his dark hair out of his eyes, at once handsome and boyish as he smirked at Merlin. "God. Propose to a guy and he starts right in with the finger wagging."

Merlin pulled his knees up to his chest and hugged them defensively.

"Oh, and the body language . . ."

"Just stop," Merlin said. "Things are great with us now. We've got a subscription to the Roundabout Theatre, we belong to the same gym, and now we even work together. We've been partners for a long time, and I hate to lose the . . . the ease of our relationship. Ten years down the road, I don't want to be stuck in the kitchen wearing an apron, waiting for you to storm in and yell, 'Hey, Lucy, I'm home!'"

Josh scrunched his face into a scowl to screech: "Aaaww, Rickeee!"

Laughter bubbled out of Merlin as he sank down in the bed, pulling the covers over his head. "That's it! That's exactly what I'm afraid of!"

"Rickee! Come back, sweetie! I know you're in there!" Josh squealed, plunging under the sheet after him. "And Little Ricky's got chicken pox!" He tickled Merlin's ribs, and Merlin pulled him close as they laughed together, their bare chests rumbling against each other.

Merlin felt secure in the warmth of Josh's body as their laughter subsided. Their breathing slowed, their heartbeats calmed, as if in unison. How rare was it to find another person that was such a perfect match—physically, psychologically, emotionally? Merlin knew he had to protect what they had.

He slid his hands over Josh's shoulders, cupping the curve of his biceps. "I love you. You know that."

Josh nodded, his eyes alight with the pain that Merlin felt he could never completely soothe. "All I'm asking is that you let the world know it too." He kissed Merlin softly, tugging on his lower lip. Then, leaning back, he whispered: "I want you forever. And I want you to want me."

"I do," Merlin whispered, feeling a newfound tenderness as Josh ran a finger along his jawline. "I do."

3

What the hell am I doing here? Zoey wondered as she rolled her luggage down the sidewalk of West 16th Street, the uptown end of Union Square. First, she had not pictured herself returning to her old college stomping grounds this way. Second, she had never imagined that her life could fly so completely off track. Crash and burn. And third, she wasn't able to get off at the right subway station.

She had been unable to take the subway directly to 23rd Street since the downtown platform of the station was closed for short-term construction. So she'd ended up at Union Square, unwilling to make another transfer just to go ten or so blocks. She was walking over to Park Avenue to hail a cab when she passed the window of a men's shop. Soft flannel shirts, the kind Nick loved for weekends and after work, were displayed in an array of colors: buttery yellow, pearl, cornflower blue. Zoey paused. Maybe she should pick one up for him while she was here.

Her shoulder bag began to slip, a hard tug of reality.

The voice of her conscience railed at her: You moved out of the house this morning! Your husband left two months ago.

Your relationship is so over. How many ways does it have to be spelled out for you?

But it's hard to give up, so impossible to abandon your heart's desire, she thought, closing her eyes against a cold, bracing wind. She would go through long sessions with herself, deciding to let go and move on, convincing herself that it was all for the best and that her life would be a peaceful, aesthetically roomy place without Nick. But hours of solid resolution were constantly displaced in moments like these—the memory of soft flannel, the smell of shaving cream, the clinking of wine glasses, all connections that sent her mind sliding back to Nick.

They'd met in college, when she was majoring in English, he in history. He'd been pre-law all the way, and his singular vision had cured Zoey of any desire to take the LSAT and apply to law schools herself. At the time she'd been floundering for a vocation, thinking law might be the way to go, but her interest in logic and rules paled beside Nick's burning determination. And Nick had excelled in law school. He was able to speed-read textbooks and hold the information in his mind. He remembered the details of every case and tort. He quickly learned how to analyze and organize facts, how to talk the talk and argue like a pro. In the end, he had graduated summa cum laude and received offers from a handful of choice Manhattan firms.

That was the Nick she had fallen in love with: determined, fiery, so sure of himself in school, at work, in bed.

She missed that Nick. For the past two months she'd been operating on low energy, realizing that something crucial was missing. Diminished capacity. Now she had only half a life, half a brain, half a heart.

Pulling up her shoulder bag, she turned to the street and hailed a cab. Just get your butt over to Skye's and take it from there. One step at a time. Minute by minute.

Ten minutes later Zoey slammed the door of the taxi and rolled her luggage up the ramp of Skye's building, a twenty-story tower of blond brick and glass. Nothing spectacular from the outside, but the neighborhood was nice, with plenty of delis, fruit markets, and small restaurants lining Second Avenue.

The doorman pulled open the glass door as an elderly woman with a small, ratlike dog exited gingerly. "Have a nice day, Mrs. VanHone." He held the door for Zoey, eyeing her with the seasoned discernment of someone who spent his life sizing up people. "Can I help you?"

Moment of truth. "I'm Zoey McGuire, Skye's friend," Zoey said, trying to remember the specifics of Skye's email:

> Tell him you're a friend. Don't mention that you're pay-
> ing rent! Sublets need board approval, and the co-op peo-
> ple are a royal pain in the ass.

"Skye Blackwell," Zoey went on when the man's eyes didn't soften at all. "In seventeen-oh-two. I'm going to be visiting for awhile."

The doorman scratched his graying beard, still doubtful. "Let me look in the book." He went behind the reception desk and pulled out a large log book from a lower shelf. As he leafed through the crimped pages, Zoey tried to fight the voice of insecurity, the one that kept coming up every time she sat at her computer. *You think you can write!* it mocked as the cursor blinked, nudging her like a schoolyard bully. *Go ahead! Try it! Go ahead!* Only now the voice was saying, *You think you can breeze into someone else's apartment? Live someone else's life! Escape from the fraud you really are? Just try it! Try it! Try—*

"Zoey McGuire, the writer." He smiled up from the book. "You look too young and pretty to be a famous writer. Ms. Blackwell says you're to have the keys and the red carpet treatment."

"Hey, I'll take any perks I can get," Zoey said, feeling some of the tension dissipate. She was in.

"You should! We don't have any other famous writers in the building." He stood up and came around the desk to hand her the keys. "Maybe I read something you wrote? Name some of the books."

It was Zoey's turn to assess the man in his crisp white shirt, navy tie with red dots, and dark pants. Late forties, five-foot six, salt-and-pepper hair and beard, kind blue eyes. Was this the sort of man who might have read her book? Zoey wasn't sure. In fact, every time she heard Skye crowing about the millions of copies sold ("And honey, with those numbers it's got to be women *and* men!"), she worked hard to paint a mental picture. A million people reading her books. But who? Her mother's friends? Her cousin's book club? The price checker at the grocery store? The tennis pro at the club? This middle-aged, slightly Hispanic looking man?

"*His Daughter's Keeper*," she said, trying to ignore the usual feeling of embarrassment over discussing her work with strangers. It was always difficult to take something so profoundly personal and treat it with total detachment. Sort of like waving her skimpiest underwear in front of her tenth-grade English teacher's nose. It didn't help that readers and reviewers had always considered *Keeper* to be autobiographical despite the fact that it was not, not really, and Zoey was sick of going through and pointing out which parts were fiction and which parts were inspired by real-life events.

The doorman nodded, but the distant look in his eyes told her that this was not a man interested in what *Newsweek* had summarized as "the difficult bond between a father and his daughter that outlived the man and drove his daughter to the brink of suicide in the quest for his approval."

"I also wrote two others," Zoey went on, mostly to fill the empty space and make herself feel less like a fraud posing as a writer. "*Custodian of the Soul.* And *River Light.*"

"*River Light*? Isn't that the one with Sean Connery?" Now the doorman seemed genuinely impressed.

Zoey wiped the sheen of oil from her forehead as she pushed back her hair. "He's supposed to be in the film version." Another writer's lament. Why did films get so much attention, even before they opened, while the source book sat quietly on library shelves?

"Yeah, I knew that one sounded familiar," the doorman said

proudly. "Anyway, I'm Bobby if you need anything, Ms. McGuire. And they're doing some work up there, sort of intermittently. Did Ms. Blackwell mention it?"

"Right," Zoey said slowly, thinking back to the email. Something about electricians and wiring.

Bobby added, "There's an intercom button by the door, if you have any questions."

Zoey took the keys, noticing that the ring was attached to a fat, heart-shaped crystal carved out of green glass. Flashy and romantic, just like Skye.

God bless Skye, Zoey thought as she rode the elevator up to the seventeenth floor. Without her, I'd be . . . I don't know. Moving in with Mom? Dodging elderly drivers in the parking lots of strip malls. Joining Mom and Harve for the early-bird special. Donning a sweater to ward off the chill of relentless air-conditioning. With a shudder, she stepped off the elevator and rolled her luggage down the hall.

Skye's door swung open into an airy mirrored hallway. Straight ahead, a small white modern kitchen gleamed in the winter light. Zoey dropped her bags, slipped off her coat and Rockports, and wandered into the living room area on her left. By Manhattan standards it was huge—large enough to have a separate dining room area and living room, delineated by a sectional sofa covered by drop cloths. The wall at the far end was all windows—Manhattan under glass.

Wow.

Twisting her hair up over her head, Zoey stepped close to the plants that lined the floor there and took it all in with a deep breath. The apartment was light and airy, as if hanging in the sky, and she wondered if she would be able to write here. Already she missed her office at home, the smooth oak floors covered by an Oriental rug in deep shades of magenta. Often her mind wandered through those colors and patterns as light moved across the room. She'd called it her thinking rug, with its mazes and patterns a roadmap of her characters' innermost thoughts and feelings.

She remembered the day she talked Nick into buying it. There had been a carpet sale at his parents' Armenian church in Queens, and Zoey had insisted that they browse through the auditorium, not intending to buy but hoping to score a few points with her future in-laws for being courteous and interested in the cultural exchange. The men selling the rugs were kind, but obviously were not comfortable speaking English, and Zoey knew only a few words of Armenian. While Nick's parents were swept into a heated conversation with two merchants, Zoey wandered off to a corner where more modestly sized rugs were laid out. That was when she saw it, the soft rug patterned with magenta, cherry, burgundy, black and pink. A little girl with dark, springy curls around her head sat on the rug, reciting something as she patted the magenta swirls.

Zoey touched Nick's arm. "What's she doing?"

"Counting in Armenian," Nick answered, unmoved. He looked to the door, anxious to leave.

Zoey smiled down at the little girl, who couldn't be more than six, in her tights and patent-leather shoes. A flicker of prescience lit her mind, and she wondered if she was seeing their future together. Could this be a glimmer of their own little girl, the child they would have, with Nick's dark hair and her quick mind?

"Let's get this one," she'd told Nick.

"Are you nuts? We can't buy a rug. Do you have any idea how much one of these things costs?" he'd asked, scratching his head.

"Please?" At the time, Zoey was earning a pittance by day as a contract assistant for an insurance consultant—a job she hated. By night, she had begun a first draft of her novel, but there was no banking on ever selling the manuscript. Still, she saw the rug as an investment. A gesture toward Nick's parents, an investment in their future. As long as the rug existed, they would want to be together to share it.

"Please?" she repeated. "Oh, Nick, it's so lovely and there's something special about it. Mystical powers, maybe, or at least good luck."

"I don't believe in luck," Nick said coldly. "People make their own fortune and misfortune."

"Oh, come on, Nick. I'm paying for it. Can't you just say it's nice and let me be happy?"

Nick glanced back at the rug, his eyes dark and sulky. "It's a waste of money. A total waste."

His words had stuck with Zoey even after his parents had joined them, negotiated a price, and helped load the rug into Nick's BMW. The rug warmed Zoey's bedroom in Greenwich Village, then was moved to the office of their Connecticut home, a dear old friend by now. Zoey always cherished it, and in her mind she downplayed Nick's reaction to it. Granted, it was just a rug, but it was the beginning of a pattern that she chose to ignore, for when it came time to pick out an engagement ring, choose a house, buy a car, Nick always found a way to slight Zoey's opinion and bully her into accepting his decision.

Maybe the rug was a message and I didn't listen. . . .

Letting her hair drop to her shoulders, she stared at the skyline. *Get a grip. You are in New York City, a writer's haven, and you've landed in a pretty swell apartment. This is the perfect opportunity to start over, though there is still the question of just what to start.*

When she was attending NYU, she'd shared a tiny basement apartment with Mouse and Jade. The place was a moldy dive, but they scraped together enough cash to rip up the smelly rug and install commercial carpeting. They talked the landlord into replacing the leaky windows that were painted shut, and by the time sophomore year rolled around they were living in cramped subterranean comfort. But Skye's apartment was no collegiate crib. This was a place with a "spectacular view" as she'd heard Jade tell clients on the phone. Although it was a one-bedroom, it stretched from north to south, and from where she stood Zoey could make out the spires of the Empire State Building, the Chrysler Building, and that tall building on East 34th where her publisher used to have offices before they moved to the Flatiron Building. And when she looked directly down, East 22nd looked so orderly, the yellow cabs moving gently into traffic framed by straight, clean lines of black asphalt and white sidewalks. The marvelous illusion of order from seventeen stories.

She dropped her jaw and smacked her face repeatedly. Why don't I feel lucky to be here? She turned away from the view. The walls that weren't mirrored were painted in a light shade of peach, though a few holes had been poked through the sheet rock. Actually, now that she looked at it, the entire ceiling was dotted with holes, as if a family of groundhogs had burrowed tunnels above the apartment. What had Skye's email said?

One of the track lights caught fire, so I need new wiring throughout. But don't worry—the electrician is already done and I've hired some men to plug up the holes.

Apparently the repairmen hadn't gotten to the patchwork yet.

Zoey picked up an art book from the coffee table, then caught her own movement in the mirrored wall that ran a good thirty feet to the kitchen. She adjusted her pearl pink cashmere sweater and turned sideways to suck in her abdomen until her jeans fell against her hip bones. Thank God she'd kept up her routine at the gym, working her butt off on the Stairmaster and clanking the weights of the Nautilus machines. At least she could be sure that Nick hadn't left her because she'd gotten fat and flabby.

Ordinarily Zoey was not a fan of mirrors, but somehow they worked here, opening up the long, narrow room and painting the walls with a brilliant reflection of the skyline. Yes, she could see herself staying in Skye's apartment for a while. Considering Skye's flair for the exotic and outlandish, the place was surprisingly comfortable.

So why do I feel so miserable?

Sinking onto the sofa, Zoey dropped the book on the floor and buried her face in her hands and started to cry. She hated crying. The McGuires were a family who held their emotions in check, and Zoey had always prided herself on taking control of her life. But lately, she couldn't control the sobs that made her curl up in a fetal position like the five-year-old Zoey reduced to tears over a scraped knee in a bike accident.

What the hell was she doing here?

Oh, yeah. Escape. Breathing room. And maybe, just maybe, some healing.

4

It was nearly eight and Jade was still in the office with a client, but she didn't mind at all. There were few highs to match the euphoria of closing a real estate deal. The aura of power, the promise of money, the smell of the future wafting into grand terraced duplex penthouses with shiny parquet floors, ornate crown moldings, and panoramic views of the city. Jade Cohen loved her job. The only thing that came close was sex, but for Jade there was no challenge in that. Not even the most gorgeous, connected, sweet-talking man could compare to the thrill of sweeping a client up in an elevator and opening the door to three hundred square feet of prime real estate.

"Okay, then, Mr. Takiyama. Just two more signatures and you are on your way to owning that spectacular Fifth Avenue penthouse. Let's see." Jade leaned across her glass desk, low enough to reveal cleavage as she showed her client where to sign. "This simply states the address of the property, that it's a duplex, full dining room and three master bedrooms."

His thin lips formed a smile, though she wasn't sure whether it was because he was pleased to be acquiring the Fifth Avenue

duplex with great park views or just delighted over a more im-
mediate view—the one down her blouse.

Jade waved the pen in the air. "Mr. Takiyama? Did I lose you in
the details?"

His gaze lifted from her breasts and he bowed his head, somewhat reverently. "Not at all, Jade." He signed the contract on the
proper lines as he continued to speak. "It's simply that I have observed that your energy seems to be a little . . . how you say? . . .
trapped. Not flowing properly, if you don't mind my saying this.
I have some familiarity with acupressure and meridians, and that
is why I speak of this."

"Really?" Jade straightened in her chair, her breasts aimed at
her target. Although Jade had been born with a lean, shapely
physique, she considered her breasts to be her best asset, well
worth the money she'd paid for those saline implants. She might
be pushing thirty-five, but her breasts were still firm, high, and
perky as a teenager's. She tucked a strand of her straight black
hair behind her ear in a coy, "Come get me, Handsome," gesture.

Mr. Takiyama stood up, his body a lean line before her. "Am I
offending?"

"No, no, please go on."

He held up one hand then pressed his fingertips down the
center of his chest. "There is a meridian here—the stress meridian. And you do seem rather tight there."

"I do?" Jade touched the area between her breasts, wondering
if she'd underestimated Mr. Takiyama. Some clients were all
business, and she'd assumed he'd belonged in that category.
Now that familiar scent of attraction suggested that she might
have been wrong. Lust! She could smell it a mile away.

Nodding, Mr. Takiyama came around her desk and stood behind her chair. "Yes," he said, nudging her hand gently to place
his hand between her breasts. "Right here, this is the meridian of
stress, and you are very tight." As he spoke he ran his hand down
her chest along the center of her rib cage.

"Very tight?" Jade wanted to laugh as she leaned back in her
chair, letting her head loll against him. She'd had plenty of men

tell her she was tight before, just not in this context. Hmm. And he called this acupressure? The explanation had some solid foundation and his touch was gentle and warm. This was either a free lesson in Eastern medicine or the best pickup line she'd ever heard.

"Please stand up," he said, suddenly lifting her out of the chair.

Feeling like a rag doll, Jade leaned against him as his hands slid down to her tummy. "This, your lower abdomen, is the center of your energy source. Do you feel the energy there?"

"Yes," Jade whispered, wishing his hands would move just a few inches lower. She wasn't usually big on the tease, but so far Mr. Takiyama was handling it so beautifully.

He pressed on her abdomen. "Do you feel it? Feel the heat there?"

"Definitely. I am getting very hot." In my panties, she wanted to add. Should she move his hand down? Slip it under her skirt? Or would that scare the man off?

"Excellent." His hands dropped away as he stepped back.

What? Jade swung around, feeling let down.

"If you like, you can return to my hotel with me and we will work on your energy flow." Mr. Takiyama bowed graciously, ever the diplomat.

"Of course." Jade bowed, trying to hide her grin. "I am . . . your humble student," she said, hoping it didn't sound too much like a low-budget martial arts flick. Hey, she'd done sexual role playing before, and if Mr. Takiyama wanted to be the teacher, she could always be his submissive Grasshopper.

As she grabbed her purse she saw Mouse's name on her calendar for the evening. She'd planned to hit Club Vermillion tonight, but the club scene could always wait. After all, life was hectic. Sometimes you needed to take a little time for a good, slow fuck.

5

"Paradise!" the rock singer shrieked. "Paradise! Paradise!" A crowd of kids shrieked along with him, jumping and shaking and bouncing against each other in a big group slam-dance. The lights of Club Vermillion flashed red across the dance floor like a rapid-fire Uzi. Mouse scanned the dance floor, watching for the next kid to drop like a smashed fly. Drug overdoses were beginning to be a nightly event at Club Vermillion, where casual cocaine and marijuana had taken a backseat to Ecstasy, a stimulant with hallucinogenic properties, and GHB, or gamma hydroxybutyrate, a depressant.

Behind the bar, Marielle Griffin was having an epiphany that was not brought on by the music or the crowd or the high-speed delusion of Ecstasy or the fact that it was after eleven and all of her friends had failed to show. The problem: No more clean glasses. The solution: Quit this job.

She was an actress. A singer. A performer masquerading as a cocktail waitress. And she was reaching the limits of this role.

"What's the story?" she asked Elvis, the other bartender, who wore his dark sideburns long to play up his resemblance to the King. "Is the dishwasher broken?"

Elvis rolled his eyes. "You got me. Last time I complained, Vince told me he's got bigger things to worry about than dishes."

"If I were a clean glass, where would I be?" Mouse asked, scooping back her beaded baby dreads to peer into the storage bins under the bar. She reached the end of the bar, where Vince Gambetti, the club's manager, leaned casually, toothpick in teeth.

"Hey, Vince! We need glasses. Desperately."

"Talk to Jimmy," Vince said, not looking away from the crowd on the dance floor. "Look at dat! They love this band! People love this stuff." Manager of Club Vermillion by default—his brother owned the place—Vince was always saying how great the club was. Oh, to be dumb and happy like Vince, Mouse thought as she turned on the blender and poured a glass of wine. "Paradise!" Vince sang along.

"If this is paradise, send me to hell," Mouse said under her breath. She slid two beers across the bar, turned off the blender, and set up two glasses in one fluid motion. Customers served, money collected, bar wiped. The job had become second nature to her, but that didn't make it any easier to deal with the ego deflation. The clientele was getting younger and more obnoxious by the minute. All night long kids barked orders and abusive comments, which were no reflection on the service but simply a sign of the times—the new entitlement that twentyish college grads possessed. For some reason they thought the world owed them everything.

Still, the real ego damage came in the early morning hours when she fell into bed, exhausted. She hadn't experienced that bone-weary ennui when she was on Broadway in the cast of *Ragtime* or touring with *The Sound of Music*. Waitressing sucked the life out of her. It used up all the energy she needed to shine at auditions and land new parts. She had to quit. Tonight. Right now.

She swung around toward Vince, then paused. What about

this month's rent? She was still a few hundred short, and at the moment there were no lead roles in sight, despite the fact that she attended an audition every other day. Maybe she could make the rent in tips over the weekend. If only the club would start drawing an older crowd, the expense-account guys who added an extra digit to the "tip" section of the credit card receipt.

"Hey! Hey, bead girl!" a young woman shouted from down the bar.

Mouse lifted her head with a scathing look. She didn't have a persecution complex about being African-American, but she could not let rudeness bordering on racism go unpunished. At five-three and only 105 pounds, Mouse was slight, but she could pack a wallop with The Look. Elvis held up his hands, indicating, She's all yours! Good. Mouse would enjoy this one.

The young blond woman leaned across the bar to shout: "Where's our fancy glasses? We ordered Manhattans, but all we got were these things."

Mouse stood behind the fluted glasses and used The Voice—that cool, detached tone airport announcers use to warn passengers that cars must not be parked in the red zone. "I'm so very sorry. Those are the only glasses that are clean at the moment, and if you want 'fancy' maybe you should try Tiffany's."

The blond woman turned to her friend, who adjusted her ultra-cool rectangular eyeglasses. Perry Ellis. Mouse knew, because she'd almost got them for herself until she realized they were outrageously expensive, and besides, she didn't need to wear glasses, they just looked cool. "Tiffany's," Blondie said. "Is that a new club?"

Designer Glasses shrugged and whined, "But I want a special glass!"

Mouse walked away from them to take an order at the other end of the bar. She was dropping olives into wineglasses when her cell phone began to vibrate against her thigh. She whipped it out of her apron pocket, turned away from Vince, and flipped it open.

"Mouse, it's me. Jade."

"What happened to you? And why are you all whispery?"

"I can't talk now," Jade said, stretching her naked body out on the soft straw mat of Mr. Takiyama's suite. "He's in the shower. But I hooked up with a Japanese lover, and he's performing some sort of ancient kinetic ritual that is heaven."

"Me, too!" Mouse said enthusiastically. "My guy's taking me to Tokyo for the weekend on his private jet. Then it's off to Hollywood to star in my own feature film. Which he's financing."

"I don't mean to rub it in," Jade said. "I just wanted to let you know what happened. Why I didn't show."

"Yeah, yeah," Mouse said, trying not to sound as annoyed as she felt. "Actually, I guess I should feel honored. A phone call from you is a rarity." During college Jade used to disappear for days, driving Zoey completely bonkers. "Look," Zoey had told Jade, "we're not your mommy, and we don't care if you want to be superslut, but a phone call is necessary. Just let us know you're alive." Mouse smiled at the memory, then it occurred to her that Zoey had blown her off, too. And where was Merlin?

"Forgive me?" Jade asked.

"Yeah. You and Zoey and Merlin. But at least you have a good excuse. What's that poker saying? Four fucking kings beats a full house of friends?"

"Thanks." Jade cocked her head as she heard the shower turn off. "I think he's coming. Gotta go." She closed her phone and tucked it into her bag beside the painted silk screen. When he'd said his "hotel," Jade hadn't realized that he had his own suite on the top floor. After the reception they received, with about a dozen bowing concierges and other staff members, Jade had to wonder why he'd want to leave this place for a Fifth Avenue duplex. Maybe for privacy. Possibly for the investment. Hmm . . . Jade was wondering if he might be interested in some other real estate investment properties when Taki reappeared nude and pale in the dim light. Beads of water glistened on his chest, and his penis was still fully erect, white and pink and proud.

Jade sat up, hugging her legs as she smiled up at him.

He bowed before her, his dark hair and square shoulders shining. Taki wasn't much to look at, not buff or muscular, but the man did know a thing or two about erogenous zones. "Are you ready for the next lesson?" he asked.

"I am so ready!" She leaned back on the mat and stroked her hands over her body. She caressed her hard pink nipples, then slid her hands between her legs, where she was already hot and moist with anticipation.

He kneeled at her feet and lifted her legs onto his lap. "A foot massage," he said, squeezing the toe of her right foot, then moving his fingers between the toes to the next. Jade groaned.

As he moved to the other foot, Jade felt herself floating off, as if disconnected from her body. It was something she did all the time—"a gift" her friends said. Even without a meditation guide like Taki, she had the ability to empty her mind and go off to a world of sensation, a world of sensual pleasure and erotic delight. The gift made sex so easy and satisfying. It also allowed her to disengage from her partner and focus on her own pleasure, her own orgasm. Yes, the gift was handy when she hooked up with Mr. Not-So-Right, which happened eight times out of ten.

"You like the foot massage?" he asked.

"Mmm." His touch was so erogenous, inciting a vivid craving to have him. She wanted his cock, and she wanted it now.

"Honey," she said softly, "that feels delicious, but I've got to have you. Now."

He smiled, moving the warm pressure of his hands down to the tender arches of her feet. "Are you familiar with tantra?" he asked. "The formula for converting sex energy—whether you call it your soul or vital force or your chi—into a state of divinity?" He slid his hands up her legs, making each part tremble at his touch. Ankles, calves, knees, thighs, she was quivering with anticipation. Delicately, he touched her between the legs, his fingers skilled and artful.

"I must pay homage to your yoni," he said, somewhere in the distance.

Eyes closed, Jade spent the next few moments savoring sweet sensation rising to an ecstatic peak. She sucked air between her teeth.

"That feels divine." Jade moaned. "You know, honey, I've read about tantric sex, but I don't think it's for me." She sat up and ran a finger over his hard dick. "The thing is, I just can't wait that long for an orgasm. I want it now. And then again later . . . and maybe again after that. I know how to come and I'm very good at it."

"We shall see," he told her, spreading his legs wide. "Come. Sit on my lap."

The sight of him straddling the straw mat, his cock still erect and standing tall, almost made her cream again. She moved closer and straddled his legs, her thighs over his, her hands on his shoulders. His skin felt smooth and warm to the touch. "Oh, please," she whispered, longing to feel him inside her. "Please, please, please . . ."

"You are very impatient." He smiled, pushing his penis down. She lifted her hips to take him in. "Give it to me," she begged. "Give me your cock." Jade gasped as she felt the head slide against her. Then she rocked against him and he plunged inside.

"Ahhh!" she screamed as he finally gave her what she wanted. "Aahhh!" Forget about energy flow and meridians. Orgasm was energy!

6

"If I listened long enough to you," Zoey sang, her voice strong and brilliant as it echoed from the green marble tiles of Skye's bathroom. "I'd find a way to believe that it's all true. . . ." She leaned back into the bubbles and sighed. She'd never really liked that song until tonight when she came across the Rod Stewart CD in Skye's collection, but then she'd never really been in a position to understand it. She lifted her wineglass to belt out the line about how Nick had "lied, straight-faced, while I cried!"

So true. So deeply insightful.

"Now I get it," she said, toasting the air and taking a sip. She had the song set on "repeat" mode on the living room stereo so that it would play over and over again while she soaked in the bathtub, sipping Nick's prized bottle of Cabernet. The twinkling flames of candles surrounded her, casting fascinating shadows over everything in the room: the faucets, the soap bottle, the basket of washcloths. Even the commode had an interesting shadow, sinister and huddled against the toilet paper dispenser.

"Fascinating," Zoey said to no one. Her hair was pinned atop her head, but one fat strand had fallen, trailing into the water.

She tucked it behind her ear, then lifted the Waterford cut-crystal goblet and finished off a third glass of wine. Not bad, but not particularly stupendous either. She would have to tell Nick that his extremely rare, extremely expensive Cabernet was a bit of a bust. Yes, she would have to tell him . . . just as soon as she decided to speak to him again.

Not that she wasn't a reasonable person. No, she did not cut people off without a fair trial. But Nick had gone over the line. Okay, any guy could make a mistake. Any guy could have an affair by accident. Sort of. She rubbed her nose, wondering how Eileen had accidentally gotten her dress off at the firm's Christmas party. Hmm. And how did Nick's thing find its way into . . .

No, no, she wasn't going to think about that again. Because she actually forgave Nick that affair, the big jerk. It was only after New Year's when Zoey surprised Nick in his office and found a pair of woman's panties in his desk drawer . . . that was when she couldn't forgive him. Because he didn't want forgiveness; he wanted Eileen. *And* Zoey. "You'd really like her if you got to know her," Nick had told Zoey as he squeezed her hands. The bastard.

She grabbed the Waterford goblet and slugged back another drink.

No, no, Nick couldn't live without Eileen, or her sexy briefs, apparently.

She leaned back into the soothing water and stared at the ceiling. "Unbelievable." The bathroom ceiling was mirrored, too. Ooh, and showing a tantalizing view of Zoey between the bubbles. Although Zoey couldn't imagine who else but her gynecologist would be privy to that view anytime in the next millennium. She would have to thank Skye again for the use of her apartment. That afternoon, as soon as she'd plugged in her computer, she had emailed Skye in Tuscany or Florence or wherever she was.

Can't thank you enough for letting me use your place.
I've already made friends with the doorman and watered

the plants. It's lovely and I feel at home already and most of all, I can tell that I'll be able to write here. Which is a backhanded way of saying that, no, I don't have the concept for my next novel finished yet. In fact, I haven't quite nailed it down. Not exactly sure what direction I want to go in. Major crossroads. But then you guessed that, didn't you? Sorry to be late—you know I've never missed a deadline before.

Never. Zoey had always been on top of her game, a true professional, until Nick took that away too.

The electronic whir of the cell phone made her flinch. "Oh, who could be calling me here!" she lamented. She reached a hand out of the tub then paused. Let it ring. It could wait. Besides, who could it possibly . . . ?

Nick.

Her heart thudded in her chest. "Oh my God, Nick!" she gasped. He wanted her to come home. He missed her. He couldn't believe that this separation thing had gone on this long and . . .

Zoey bolted up in the tub and snatched the phone with one wet hand, but the caller ID panel didn't display SATAMIAN, NICHOLAS. Instead, it read GRIFFIN, MARIELLE. Mouse.

"Hello," Zoey said.

"Where the hell are you?" Loud music nearly drowned out Mouse's voice. "It's almost midnight and I am standing here alone like a total loser."

"Mouse, you're tending bar. You're supposed to stand there alone."

"Merlin called to say he was too tired and Jade hooked up with some Zen Guide to Booty Call. And what's your problem?"

"Problem?" Zoey had to squint to focus on the question. The very expensive wine was beginning to fuzz her brain. "It's hard to articulate everything that's gone wrong in my life in . . . in one brief topic sentence."

"Well, get your butt over here and I'll help you articulate."

"I can't," Zoey said helplessly. "I just can't, Mouse. I'm in the tub and it's way past my bedtime. Besides, I'm too drunk to drive."

"You don't have a car. You're in Manhattan."

"Esactly. And, if you didn't notice, Mouse, I'm old. Thirty-four. That's middle age if I live to be sixty-eight. Time for fiber and plenty of sleep."

"You want fiber? I'll make you a pina colada with a banana."

"Mouse, sweetie, my head's exploding."

"All right, all right. I'll just weave through the crowd and find some friends who know how to party."

Zoey rested her head against the side of the tub. "Good luck weaving. I mean, is there really anyone there over thirty?"

"Hardly. And the whole scene is different from when we went to school. The Village scene has lost its bohemian feel. No more NYU rebels. Now NYU stands for Not Yet Upstanding. These kids are graduating into corporate jobs with stock options and country club memberships. But don't get me started."

"Okay. I won't."

"Hey! Over here!" a girl called, waving a twenty-dollar bill at Mouse. Blondie was back.

Pretending not to notice, Mouse lifted a tub of dirty glasses. "Be right back," she told Elvis. "I'm going for glasses." She stepped into the back hallway, trying not to breathe in the stench of rotted booze. The narrow space was already cluttered with two carts loaded with bins of dirty glasses. No wonder there were no fancy glasses for fancy drinks.

"Jimmy!" Mouse shouted, trying to raise the busboy.

"Yeeouch!" Zoey complained over the phone. "You just pufforated my eardrums. God, these fiber options are too good. Or is it digital now? Why don't you call tomorrow and we'll do something."

"Okay, whatever." Mouse clicked the phone off and dropped it into her apron pocket. "Jimmy!"

Chandra, one of the cocktail waitresses, stuck her head out the kitchen door. "What?"

"I need clean glasses!" Mouse said, flicking her beaded dreads back over one shoulder. "Have you seen Jimmy?"

"He's in the cooling-off room," Chandra said, tossing her cigarette on the floor and grinding it out with her platform shoe. "Helping some girl."

Now the busboy was sucking up to the druggies? Mouse couldn't take it. Furious, she marched to the cooling-off room, which was basically a sick room for the idiots who got overheated on Ecstasy. The club's owner had allowed patrons to use the room in the hopes that it would prevent more overdoses—and stop the police from investigating the fact that clubs like Vermillion were becoming a haven for illegal drug use.

Mouse flung open the door and put her hands on her hips, ready to throw a tantrum. Jimmy sat on the couch, barely noticing her.

"Would you get your butt out here?" Mouse asked. "If we don't get glasses soon we're going to have to start doing navel shooters."

He gave her an apologetic look as he stroked the dark hair of the girl sobbing on his lap. "She's having a bad time." Despite the harsh appearance of his shaved head and multi-pierced ear, Jimmy looked very vulnerable at the moment. He was scared.

Mouse bit her lower lip, feeling annoyed by the delay. "Does she feel hot?"

Jimmy nodded, asking the girl, "Can you sit up, Donna? Do you want some ice?"

"I don't want anything!" she shouted, springing up to her feet.

Mouse blinked as she recognized the rectangular Perry Ellis glasses. She usually avoided the cooling-off room, sure that it was full of twentyish brats who blew Dad's money on too many nasty drugs, but as she watched Donna start to pace she felt oddly distant from this room, this club, this whole scene.

It was a place to die, and Mouse found herself unable to care.

Donna was talking to herself, flushed bright red, sweating, and tugging at her clothes. Mouse knew she needed to get Donna to the hospital.

"She's got to go," Mouse told Jimmy, nodding her head toward the rear exit where a private ambulance always waited.

He frowned. "Are you sure? Vince wanted her to cool off. He

said we should try to avoid sending kids to the hospital unless it's absolutely necessary."

Donna's sweater was stained with sweat and her face was flushed. "This is not the picture of good health," Mouse said sarcastically.

"Yeah, but . . ." Jimmy shrugged. "Vince said—"

"Jimmy, you and I know shit about this stuff. Go get the ambulance attendant."

"On fire!" Donna cried, rubbing her hands over her head as she paced. "Fire, fire, fire!"

"Donna . . ." Jimmy tried to touch her shoulders, but she swatted him away.

"Go!" Mouse told him. "Now!"

He ran out of the room, but Donna turned to follow him, shrieking: "No! No! I can't take it! I can't . . ." She grabbed at the sleeves of her sweater, pulling them up, ripping one in the process. "I'm burning!" She collapsed onto the floor, tearing at her clothes.

Kneeling on the floor beside Donna, Mouse realized that the girl before her might die. And she didn't really care.

Oh, Lord, how could I not care?

She had never taken this overdose stuff too seriously, always assuming that the kids who were carted off to the hospital got an IV ride to Stomach Pump Land before they were sent home in a cab, only to return to the scene of the crime the next night. And honestly, Mouse was not happy to see the spoiled brats back. Would the world be a worse place without this girl in it? Would she ever get beyond her snooty entitlement attitude to contribute anything, any glimmer of positive energy to society?

But it's a human life from God, and I shouldn't judge, she told herself. Censor those thoughts, that was easy enough. Still, she wasn't sure how to address the lack of feeling for this girl and all the others who willingly popped or snorted or injected something.

Suddenly Donna crouched forward in Mouse's arms. A stream of brown vomit flew out of her mouth onto the carpeting. Then her head dropped onto her chest, heavy and lifeless.

Swallowing back a sick feeling of her own, Mouse tried to drag Donna away from the mess. She wanted to dump the girl in a chair and hightail it back to the bar. Who would know? This whole situation seemed unreal, wrought with ugliness that had nothing to do with her, and she didn't want any part of it.

But she stayed. Trying not to breathe in the stench, she glanced away from the girl and tried to feel the Lord's presence. Dear Jesus, save me from this ship of fools. Get my ass out of here, Lord.

7

The whirring noise in Zoey's head was unrelenting. She turned over in bed and realized this was not her bed or her bedroom. The light was brighter, the sheets stiffer, and the noise . . .

Her head pounded. How much wine had she drunk? She did remember pouring some of it down the toilet, its cherry-red stream tinkling into the porcelain bowl in a ritualistic ceremony that she could title "The dumping of the soon-to-be-ex husband's naughty but amusing cabernet." Much like the dumping of the naughty but amusing husband. She rubbed her eyes as the whirring noise began again. Real noise, not hangover head-pounding. What was going on?

She slid out of Skye's four-poster bed and padded across the parquet floors to the hall. A young man with jet-black hair was perched on a ladder, drilling into the ceiling. Drilling so intently that he didn't notice her standing there in her Joe Boxer T-shirt and panties. Should she get dressed first? That might be the proper thing to do, but she would have to close the door and his drill was plugged into the outlet of her room, blocking the door from closing.

Oh, God, what would Martha Stewart do? Zoey pulled back her hair, feeling proprietary. It was her apartment, sort of. And it was also—she turned to check the digital alarm clock by the bed—7:44 in the morning. She felt her palms begin to sweat from nerves and from the heat that had come up during the night. Suddenly the apartment felt too warm and much too crowded, but Skye had warned her about the workers. Time to confront.

"Hello?" she said, but the drill was too loud. She covered her ears, waiting for it to stop before she tried again. "Hello? I take it you're the carpenter?"

The man looked down at her and flinched. Actually he was a boy, with the unformed jawline of a puppy and wide, frightened eyes. He shouted down the hall in a foreign language—maybe Portuguese. Zoey knew Spanish and French and a little bit of Armenian from Nick's family, and it wasn't any of those tongues, though from his tone she was sure he was crying for help. Another man popped his head out from behind the living room wall and nodded at Zoey. He was an older version of the boy on the ladder, also with jet black hair and wide, dark eyes.

"Good morning, Meez. I am Carlos. We are here to correct the damage from the wires. Wires burned." He pointed up to the track lighting. "We are hired by Meez Blackwell."

"Okay." She rubbed her sweaty palms on her T-shirt, suddenly embarrassed. Why was it that you could parade around in the beach in a thong and feel great about yourself, but let someone catch you in your pajamas and you felt like a naked wood nymph? "Okay, but can I ask you what time you usually start work?"

The man nodded furiously. "Always on time. Always."

"Okay, so you always start at . . ." she shrugged, "seven-thirty?"

Again, the bobbing nods. "Always. Sometimes not."

"Look, seven-thirty is a little too early. Can you make it eight-thirty? Or even closer to nine. Nine would be better."

"Nine is good." Carlos nodded. "We start at nine?"

"Nine is great," Zoey said. Folding her arms, she circled the ladder and headed toward the bathroom. Although the thought of these two men standing in the hallway listening to her pee was not the most comfortable wake-up call in the world, nature was indeed calling. "Okay, nine is perfect. Thanks, Carlos," she said, then pulled the door shut behind her.

In one fluid motion she locked the door, flicked on the light, scraped down her panties and sat. Sigh. She was almost finished when she turned to the vanity and gasped.

The creature.

It sat on the marble shelf around the sink, its fat body poised menacingly. A water bug. A huge water bug.

Zoey squeezed her eyes shut and covered her head with her hands. Flashbacks to a hairy centipede crawling up her arm. The ticklish pull of a spider web she'd walked into at her aunt's cottage. The sting of red ants some neighborhood kids had tricked her into exploring. And roaches . . . dirty, fat, lazy things, roaches were at the top of her list of Most Hated Urban Things.

Okay, she was insect-phobic. She opened one eye for another look. The creature was surreal, its translucent wings and oversized head a true model for the type of aliens she had always imagined invading the earth. Truly, this was the dominant species of the future. It could manipulate her on fear alone!

Its huge eyes watched her even as its antennae swept suspiciously over the shiny marble, sensing an intruder in its path.

Zoey was no entomologist, but she had endured standoffs with insects before. She knew it was preparing for attack.

"Eeeeeh!" She bolted out of the bathroom, grabbed her purse, and ran out the front door of the apartment into the cheerful art deco corridor of the seventeenth floor. It wasn't until it swung closed behind her that she realized she had nowhere to go. She rooted through her purse for her cell phone.

The door opened behind her. "Is there a problem, Meez?" Carlos asked.

Stop shaking already! she told herself, forcing a smile for

Carlos. "Actually, there's a huge water bug in the bathroom, and I just have this, this *thing* about insects."

"Oh." He nodded sagely. "Don't worry. I will smash it for you, Meez."

Zoey closed her eyes and tried not to picture a giant smashed insect. "Thanks," she said, punching in Jade's number. "Thank you, Carlos."

He nodded and disappeared as the connection clicked on. "Hello?"

"I'm sorry to call you so early and I know you sleep late because you don't go into work until later but I couldn't help it because this is an emergency."

"Honey, slow down." Jade sounded sleepy. "Where are you?"

"In the hall outside Skye's apartment, and that's why I'm calling. I need your help."

"What time is it, anyway?"

"You don't want to know." Zoey tucked her hair behind one ear and rested her forehead against the wall. "The thing is, you've got to find me a new apartment. Today. I . . . I can't go back in there. I can't, Jade."

Silence. "Honey, do you remember the housing market when you and Nick left Manhattan and I told you to hold on to your apartment?"

Zoey nodded. "Yes, yes, it was wild. A seller's market, and Nick insisted on getting the profit while we could."

"Well . . ." Jade yawned. "Today's market is like . . . I don't know, a zillion times worse. So you're out of that gorgeous apartment standing in the hall . . . what could have possibly driven you out?" Zoey listened to her own heartbeat in the silence that followed. "Did you see some sort of insect in Skye's apartment?" Jade asked. All of Zoey's close friends knew of her insect-phobia.

"Just a water bug." Zoey's heart pounded at the image in her head. "It was the size of a small dog."

Jade sighed again. "Hold on a second, honey, and I'll talk you back in. Just let me get the coffee on."

8

As Merlin went through the motions of playing concierge at the reception desk of the Royale Hotel, his mind was elsewhere. That was the upside of his job. For seven years he had juggled staff, coaxed various computer systems, and catered to a large roster of guests with varying demands. Now his job was a no-brainer, which left him time to worry about Zoey.

Not that he'd be allowed *not* to worry about Zoey, at least not with Mouse on the case. She had left him three messages, then called the hotel and tracked him down at the reception desk, and now that she had him hooked on the line she was prattling through Zoey's endless list of woes.

"She's broke. Nick has her on some piss-poor allowance. And she's suffering from writer's block so she can't even write a book or article to make some money. And she's subletting this apartment but who knows for how long, and guess what happened this morning?"

Merlin clicked into work mode as Dave, his supervisor, passed behind the desk and paused nearby. "I'm sorry, but we are completely booked that night," he told Mouse. "Can I try another date for you?"

"I'll tell you what happened. She woke up this morning and found a bug in the apartment and nearly ran down the fire escape," Mouse said. "The girl's got problems, and it's up to us to band together and let her know her friends are going to stick by her no matter what."

"That sounds excellent," Merlin said distractedly. Through the glass wall he could see a party arriving—it looked like Mr. Chenowitz. The billionaire owner of a successful dot com, he always came in on a low-cost airport van service and usually dressed in jeans and T-shirts with corporate logos—the kind given away as gifts at trade shows.

"So you'll be there, right?" Mouse pressed. She gave him the address again. "It's on the seventeenth floor. Are you writing this down?"

"I have a photogenic memory," he joked.

"So don't tell me you forgot. I'll bring the beer and we'll order Chinese when we get there."

Dave leaned in next to Merlin to bring up something on the computer screen built into the paneled console. But after a few taps he just stared at the screen. Probably spying, checking up on me, Merlin realized.

"Excellent, sir," Merlin told Mouse.

"I know your supervisor is there now, but you'd better show up tonight. Zoey needs you. If you screw up this reunion I swear I will hunt you down and kill you."

"I look forward to it. Have a wonderful evening!" Merlin hung up, then took in a deep breath to greet Mr. Chenowitz.

"Merlin! Buddy! Am I glad to see you here! I almost changed my reservations when I read that the hotel changed hands back in January." Mr. Chenowitz slid his slim laptop onto the reception desk and reached across to shake Merlin's hand.

Beside him, Merlin felt Dave beam with approval. Good, maybe he'd get that raise next month. Dave patted Merlin's shoulder then headed toward the back room.

"No need to worry, Mr. Chenowitz," Merlin said, launching into the corporate line he'd been reciting for months. "The change in ownership will only be better for all of us! There will be upgraded facilities in the gym and health spa, new furnishings, a four-star chef in our dining room, and the new owners were wise enough to retain the fine staff members who have always provided you with superior service—like me."

"Glad to hear it," Mr. Chenowitz said, reaching into his pocket. "I guess I'd better check in."

"I've taken care of that already," Merlin said. "Your assistant called ahead with all the details. The only thing you need is this, sir." He handed the man a gold-edged folder with two plastic keys inside. "You've got the Ambassador Suite, as usual. I can have Abdul take you up to your room, but I remember you prefer to navigate alone."

"Still do." Chenowitz peeled a fifty-dollar bill from a money clip and handed it across the counter. "Thanks, Merlin."

"Thank you, and welcome back, sir."

As Chenowitz walked off toward the elevator, Merlin realized it was almost five, time to end his shift. He started going through the roster of VIP check-ins, making notations on preferences and special requests. He checked in two other customers and fielded a few calls before his shift ended at five-thirty.

"Hey, gorgeous," a familiar voice called from behind the desk.

"Hey, yourself."

Merlin didn't need to look up to know that Josh had arrived; that familiar feeling still sparked in his chest whenever Josh was near. Thank God. Maybe it was because they worked opposite shifts and didn't have time to get sick of each other. Overwhelming ennui had always been one Merlin's biggest problem in relationships, as he quickly tired of other people's idiosyncracies.

It was only a few months ago that Josh had begun to work the evening shift. When the new regime of the Royale Hotel needed to hire staff back in January, Merlin had encouraged Josh to apply, and then had managed to use his influence to get Josh into a front desk position working with guests. Josh had the ability to sublimate his dark side and put on a sunny appearance, which worked well with the public.

"What's cooking, lover?" Josh joined Merlin beside the computer and pinched his butt while looking the other way.

"I'll let you get away with that only because no one is waiting for my services," Merlin said, puckering his mouth to keep from smiling. "Actually, if you're nice to me I may let you do it again."

This time Josh gave his butt a tender squeeze, moving his hand down for a slight caress before anyone could see. Then he lifted his hands and folded them on the counter. "Love you," Josh whispered, his brown eyes mellow as he faced Merlin.

"I love you, too." Merlin cleared off a few scribbled notes and tossed them into the trash. "How was your day?"

"Okay. I made it to the gym, then got rooked into getting groceries for old lady Birnbaum." Sophie Birnbaum, the upstairs tenant in their Greenwich Village apartment, claimed to be eighty-eight years old and going strong. Josh enjoyed doing little errands to help her out, then complaining about her endlessly. "Oh, and you have a voice mail message, which I saved. Mouse is staging a hangout at Zoey's for all you NYU snobs. Tonight. What's going on with Zoey?"

"Her husband left." Not wanting to get into it, Merlin brushed a piece of lint from the sleeve of Josh's navy blazer. On Josh the concierge attire had all the charm of a British prep school uniform, and Merlin loved to see his partner looking like a schoolboy dressed for church.

"I figured that much," Josh said, straightening his tie. "What was that relationship about? Did she marry him for the money, or did she really believe his act?"

"I think she was a believer." Merlin felt a little sick at the thought of what Zoey must be going through right now. He'd been there when she fell in love with Nick, and he remembered the endless debates over whether an individual had to surrender his or her identity and control in order to engage in a romantic partnership. Zoey had been reticent to make that lifetime commitment. She had struggled with it for years. Funny, he was struggling with the same issues now.

Merlin tapped the computer screen. "Mr. Chenowitz checked into the Ambassador Suite, and I didn't get a chance to make a run for his stuff."

Josh nodded. "What is he . . . Stolichnaya and M&Ms?"

"Peanut M&Ms," Merlin said, writing it out on a notepad just in case. "Don't forget the peanuts." He prided himself on perfection, which made him an excellent concierge. Over the years he'd seen a few guests become unglued when other concierges didn't follow their instructions to the letter. "And remember, Mrs. Van Cleef's parakeet needs to be fed. Oh, and there's a crew from Platter Air on the fifth floor." For some reason, the pilots on that particular airline always employed the services of local prostitutes. Not that their behavior bothered Merlin and Josh, but other guests sometimes complained about the steady stream of hookers parading into the hotel.

"Great," Josh said sarcastically. "What, do those guys think they're filming *Pretty Woman II?*"

Merlin signed off on the computer, then snapped his fingers in the air with a flourish. "I am out of here."

"Wait." Josh touched his arm, a strange intensity in his eyes. "Are you going tonight? To Zoey's?"

"I don't know." Merlin tried to sound casual; he knew what was coming next.

"Please don't." Josh picked up a pen from the desk and clicked it on and off nervously. "Not that I don't like Zoey. Honestly, I think she's a sweet girl. But you can't be best friends with her again, you know that, Merlin. The position is filled, by a beautiful yet mysterious young lover . . . who can't wait to come home tonight and find you wrapped in cellophane or decked out in whipped cream or something equally delicious."

Merlin smiled. Their chemistry was stronger than ever. "I was leaning toward chocolate syrup tonight."

"One of my personal favorites." Josh's face softened as he grinned.

Merlin stepped into the room behind the desk and checked his hair in the mirror. The highlighted spike stood up straight, the gold a striking contrast to his jet black hair. His eyes glittered deep blue with the enhancement of colored contacts.

"So, really," Josh called from the desk. "Are you going to see Zoey?"

"No, not tonight," Merlin answered, catching a look in his own eyes. Lying eyes.

9

"I can't get over this place!" Jade said as she walked through the rooms of Skye's apartment one more time, ever the peripatetic broker. "Even with water bugs, it's a treasure. Two major exposures, doorman, wide-open airy feel, parquet floors . . . and the square footage! What's Skye charging you?"

"Seven hundred a month," Zoey called from the kitchen. "But that's a secret, because the co-op board doesn't know she's subletting." She came into the living room, waving the bottle opener. "Found it!"

"Seven? You know I could rent this place for three thousand . . . maybe more! Honey, you've got such a deal! And where is this Skye person?"

"She's my editor, Skye Blackwell. She's off in Italy, staying in some writer's palazzo. Apparently she has to hold his hand and stay by his side, his inspiration. She's got to stay to extract a manuscript from him, page by page."

"Really?" Mouse opened a Corona and handed it to Zoey. "And who is this famous writer?"

Zoey took a sip. "Mmm . . . not sure and she won't say. But it's got to be a best-selling author for the publisher to send her to the palazzo for a few months." She stepped closer to Mouse and reached up to touch her hair. "Look at you in baby dreads with beads. Beautiful beads."

"Straight from India. Don't you love them? Took nine hours to get it done, and it better be worth the sore butt. I wanted to look connected to my roots for this audition tomorrow." Mouse cocked her head, squinting at Zoey. "And what's with your hair? Don't tell me it's streaked from the sun?"

"Do ya think?" Zoey pretended to preen as she lifted her long hair and flung it back. "Just two hundred dollars' worth of foiling. I'm still not sure about it. That frosted look always turned me off, but I needed to do something to cover the gray." She had wanted to cut it, but Nick wouldn't allow it. A few years ago she'd had it trimmed to shoulder length for the summer, and Nick had greeted her with a devastated look. He'd spent the summer singing a fairly obscure Beach Boys song that lamented, "Where did your long hair go? Where is the girl I used to know?" That was the last time Zoey got her hair cut.

"These windows look relatively new, and the track lighting is being repaired. . . ." Still the real estate agent, Jade paced in front of the windows, her high-heeled Prada shoes clicking on the parquet floor. "This place is a little gem. If it was on the market I'd snatch it up for myself. Well, God bless Skye . . ." she said, "and the difficult Italian writer for giving you a great apartment when you really need it. The market is insane out there, honey, and even if I found something, you'd have to sign at least a one-year lease. I say you hire an exterminator for the bugs and enjoy Casa Skye until she throws you out."

"The doorman said an exterminator comes around every two weeks, and I signed up." Zoey rubbed her arms, shivering at the thought of seeing another insect.

"And you know, water bugs aren't really dirty, not like roaches," Mouse reassured Zoey. "They're attracted to the water, actually. They may live right in the pipes of this building." She opened a Corona and handed it to Jade.

"Are you trying to give me nightmares?" Zoey hugged herself

harder. "I'll never be able to pee again. I'll always be watching for some fat, boogly bug to swim up from the bowl and bite my tush."

Mouse and Jade exchanged a look, then burst out laughing. When Zoey flashed them an indignant look, Mouse swatted at her arm. "Oh, come on, sister girl. That is one funny picture."

"Go on, have a good laugh." Zoey dropped onto the sofa and held the glass beer bottle against her cheek. "Pick on the pitiful bug-phobic, but I'm telling you, someday when I am successful I'm going to start a society for people who share my affliction."

Mouse pointed a maroon-lacquered, rhinestone-embedded finger at her. "You *are* successful."

"Ya think so?" Zoey took a slug of beer. "Then why am I broke, busted, and blocked?"

Just then the door intercom buzzed. "That must be Merlin," Zoey said, jumping up and skidding down the hall on her socks.

"Well, hold that thought," Jade called, "because I can see that we've got a lot of work to do here, toots." To Mouse, she added, "She's just lost two hundred pounds of loser and she's acting as if she lost her grip on life."

"I heard that," Zoey called from the hall. "And thank you, Jade. I knew I could rely on you for a total lack of sympathy." The doorman said that Merlin Chong had arrived, and Zoey told him to send him up. Merlin had been her first college friend and had remained one of her closest. They'd met at the beginning of freshman year when everything was new and scary, sitting in the back row of the huge lecture hall in Economics 101. The room was hot and crowded and it was impossible to hear and the teaching assistant at the front didn't seem to care. Merlin borrowed a pen, but never wrote anything down. He had brought along a bag of pistachios, which they shared during the lecture. By the end of the first lecture, they were friends. By the end of the week they were taking Economics Pass/Fail and spending the class session in the student center playing hearts. It had been an important relationship for both of them—their first connection in a school where many students passed through without connecting at all.

Zoey picked a piece of lint off her black sweater, actually nervous about seeing him now. They'd had lunch together back in November, but that was different. Back then she'd been a respectable married woman meeting with an old college friend during a day trip to the city. Today she was a mere shell of her former self, as if an army of insects had come through and eaten away all the flesh and features, leaving just a dull skeleton to rattle around.

Oooh! She shivered again. She had to stop thinking of bugs.

"I'm starved. Let's order the food now," Mouse said, sticking her half-empty beer bottle on Skye's knickknack shelf. "Where are we ordering from?"

"There are a couple of menus in the kitchen drawer," Zoey said, pulling them out. "Three Chinese, one Thai . . . and here are a couple Mexican and Italian."

"The United Nations of fast food," Jade said, leaning on the kitchen doorjamb. "I'm up for Chinese."

"Me too," Zoey said. "You can't get good Chinese in Connecticut."

"You can't get good *anything* in Connecticut," Mouse insisted. "Except for insurance and traffic. Lots of traffic every time I drive through Connecticut." Mouse grew up in Rhode Island and still traveled north occasionally for holidays and family functions.

There was a tap on the door, and Zoey slid across the parquet to welcome Merlin. She pulled open the door and threw her arms out. "Hey, hi! It's good to see you."

He smiled and gave her a stiff hug. "You've run away from home, I hear?"

Although he said it with the right mixture of concern and amusement, Zoey felt her throat go tight with emotion. "Yes," she said hoarsely. Oh, why did it hit her at the worst times? The letdown of total failure. The jagged edge of pain.

"I'm on the lam," she finished, turning away before he could see her face pucker up froggy-fashion. She squeezed past Jade into the kitchen and hid her head inside the fridge while Jade and Mouse said hello to Merlin. "We've got Sam Adams and

Corona," she called to Merlin. "Or seltzer, if you're feeling the need to maintain your purity."

"Sam Adams," he said as Jade tugged him into the bedroom to show him the apartment.

With a deep, composing breath, Zoey pulled out a cold beer and joined Mouse, who was frantically circling things on the menu.

"Fried rice with shrimp. Veggie dumplings. Ribs. But we've got to find out if they use dark meat in the chicken dishes. I hate dark meat. And no MSG. Do you want white rice or brown?"

"Brown," Zoey said, heading out of the kitchen. "And I officially leave the ordering up to you. Surprise me."

"Okay, guys," Mouse called down the hall. "I'm calling in the order, so speak now or forever hold your egg rolls."

"Get something spicy with tofu," Merlin shouted.

"And some ribs," Jade added.

Zoey joined the apartment tour, which wrapped up in the living room, where they all grabbed their beers and plotzed on the sofa.

"Your timing was perfect," Jade told Merlin. "We were just about to put Zoey under the microscope and psychoanalyze her life."

"Oh, were we?" Zoey took a swig of beer, squinting at Jade. "Well, you'd better look fast because there won't be much left after Nick's lawyers get through with me."

"Nick the Prick," Jade said.

Mouse let out a laugh.

Merlin grinned, his blue eyes giddy.

"Oh, didn't you know we had a nickname for him?" Jade added.

Zoey tucked her feet under her. "I didn't, but it's rather descriptive and so appropriate, too."

"I told you she'd like it," Merlin said, his blue eyes flashing as he teased Jade and Mouse. "So . . . what's your next move, Zo?"

"It's time for me to move on, I guess. I've filed for divorce, but apparently Nick beat me to the punch. His lawyer froze all of our savings and our assets and my next royalty payments, making it sort of impossible for me to operate. I mean, Nick gets a fat salary every two weeks, I get a tiny monthly stipend—seven hundred dollars. Which would have been fine, if I were still living in the Connecticut house."

"How could he do that to you?" Mouse was indignant. "It's your money, too!"

"Nick claims that he's been carrying me financially for years. Since he paid the mortgage, he thinks he owns the house. Forget that I used my royalties for the down payment. And since he came into the marriage with family money, which we all know I certainly didn't have, he says that our assets belong to him."

"Assets, my ass!" Jade insisted. "You put up with that windbag for years; you deserve more than half for that alone."

Merlin started to peel the label off his Samuel Adams. "You're fighting this, I hope?" he said casually.

"Through my lawyer, of course I am. But I've got to leave it up to her since I don't have the energy to deal with Nick anymore. I've got to focus on . . . the rest of my life." Zoey threw her head back against the couch as the blank highway of "the rest of her life" expanded before her eyes. "For starters, I've got to earn some money. I'll need to find a real place to live for when I get booted out of here. Then I've got to figure out what to do with the rest of my life."

"What you want to do when you grow up? I've been working on that one for thirty-three years," Mouse said. "You don't want to go there."

The intercom buzzed and Zoey jumped up, relieved to have a break from the strain of looking inward. "Saved by the bell."

"It's not that easy," Jade said as she stood up and stretched, her hair shining like the fur of a black jaguar. "You're not off the hook until we hear every last detail about Nick the Prick."

"Great," Zoey said, accepting a ten-dollar bill from Mouse for the food. "Nothing like bearing your soul over moo shoo pork."

10

Within minutes Skye's dining room table was covered with bags, paper containers, and foil trays of steaming hot food. Zoey helped herself to an egg roll and steamed vegetables and chicken with peanuts. Merlin made her try some spicy tofu, which was delicious when mixed with steamed veggies. They decided to abandon the food on the table and kneel around the coffee table, true Chinese style.

"My father would be proud," Merlin said as he rubbed his chopsticks together. "Though the only resemblance this meal has to real Chinese cuisine is probably the fact that both contain rice."

"You know, sometimes I envy you," Zoey told Merlin.

He rolled his eyes. "Oh, do tell."

"Just that your roots are so definitive and you're so . . . connected to your ethnic background. I barely know what my heritage is, and nobody in my family seems to care about the few facts about the family tree that we do know. When my father was alive I asked him about the Irish side of his family and he said something about being a descendant of the criminal McGuires. Murderers. It was like a dagger in my twelve-year-old heart. I don't know whether he was trying to shock me or if he really knew something, but after that I stopped asking him."

"You want to be steeped in heritage, come to my parents' house for Passover," Jade said, rolling up a moo shoo pancake. "My father still insists on saying all the prayers despite the fact that the man doesn't believe in God, and the damned dinner goes on for hours."

"I *have* been to Passover dinner at your parents'," Zoey said. "The brisket was great."

Merlin lifted a cube of tofu between the chopsticks. "Hey, anytime you want to celebrate Swedish-Chinese-American day with me, you are more than welcome."

"Thanks." Zoey smiled over a mouthful of chicken with peanuts.

"I hate to break up this ethnic lovefest," Mouse said, "but let's cut the bullshit and get to the point. How the hell are you really doing, Zoey? How are you handling this?"

Zoey struggled to swallow a mouthful, then took a sip of beer to wash it past the new tightness in her throat. "I'm okay, I guess."

"So it's really over with Nick," Mouse said, shaking her head as if she never saw that one coming.

"Yes." Zoey stabbed at a piece of chicken as that sinking feeling returned. "No. I don't know. I want it to be over, but I don't. I mean, after everything he's done, my head is saying that this man is a bastard and he doesn't love me or even know the meaning of love."

Mouse nodded. "That's right, girl. And you've got to watch out for yourself. Take care of number one. Don't let him step all over you."

But Zoey just sank down and rested her head on the table. "Oh, God, I am so not over him."

"Oh, no!" Mouse grabbed Zoey's shoulders and gave her a gentle shake. "No, no, don't say it! Don't tell me you still love him."

"I do," Zoey murmured against the table. "Call me an idiot, but I do."

"It happens." Merlin sounded calm, accepting.

"Love." Jade's voice was loaded with distaste. "What the hell is that? My therapist won't let me use the word during our sessions and you know, she's right. What the hell does love mean? Attraction? Lust? The fact that you can live with someone for more than a year and not kill them? Or the desire to see yourself paired with someone, as in an accessory, as in, Don't I look great with this hat? Love means nothing, and the sooner you accept that, the sooner you'll be able to have equal relationships without guilt or emotional baggage or some guy leaving the toilet seat up and filling your closet with his collection of baseball cards."

"But I believe in love," Zoey said.

"And you've got the emotional baggage to prove it," Mouse cut in.

Zoey lifted her head. The concerned faces of her friends surrounded her, a triad of support. "Yes, I'm in a lot of pain, most of it probably self-inflicted, but I can't seem to make it go away. It's so clear to me that Nick has been operating on another astral plane, not being honest about his feelings and lying about where he's been and totally cheating on me. Intellectually I know our relationship is over, but it's so hard to abandon my . . . my heart's desire. Like an idiot I wrapped my entire future into my life with Nick, and with him out of the picture I'm afraid that it's totally over for me when it comes to relationships."

"Don't be so sure, honey," Jade said. "You're attractive, bright, and even a minor celebrity. You'll meet someone else. I can give you a few phone numbers tonight."

"It's not about sex or dating," Zoey said. "It's more about blowing my big chance. I've always had this theory that true lovers are star-crossed; that there's one person for every person and if you're lucky enough to find your match you need to hold onto him and cherish him. And look at me: I found my one person and he turned out to be a jerk."

"That's not your fault," Merlin said. "You can't control Nick's behavior."

"But maybe I could have." Zoey wound her hair up into a bun, then stuck a spare set of chopsticks through to keep it in place. "Maybe if I'd been more accessible, less withdrawn while I was writing. Maybe if we'd stayed in the city instead of taking the yuppy track to suburbia. Or if I'd been more aggressive in bed . . ."

"You can second-guess yourself forever," Merlin said. "How about if you'd never met Nick in the first place? That would have changed your life, too."

"And what's this star-crossed theory about?" Jade waved a spare rib at Zoey. "I think you're confusing lust with the romantic notion of love. Which is no more than a myth that makes for good headlines on the cover of *Cosmo.*"

"But it's not the same." Zoey rose onto her knees to defend herself. "Think about all the guys you meet. Attractive guys. They have great jobs, great teeth, nice laughs, good sense of humor. But it's so awkward to date most of them because you need a special chemistry—the perfect mixture of sexual attraction and intellectual melding, not to mention a basic compatibility so that you can live side by side without killing each other. How often do you find that magical attraction? For me it was only twice in my life, and the first guy, Brian Massiello, doesn't really count because I was in tenth grade and he fit into my fantasies of teen rebellion. Besides, we never lived together. The closest we came was when I pretended to be at my girlfriend's sleepover and we spent the night in his car down by the foundation of the overpass. God, what made me think of him?"

"Magical attraction," Mouse said. "And I think I know what you mean. It's the reason why I haven't had a date since the demolition of the Berlin Wall. I mean, I'm around guys all the time, in shows, at the club, at the gym, in workshops, but most of the theater guys are gay, and the ones at the club are way too young. What is it about guys in their twenties? It's amazing that they can function at all with their heads up their asses."

Merlin laughed over a mouthful of rice, then started to cough.

"Don't take it personally, honey," Jade told him.

"I'm not offended," he said. "I was actually thinking how true it is. Ten years ago I was so into the club scene, if I missed one night at Limelight or a show at the Palladium, I'd go into withdrawal."

Jade licked the bare rib bone and tossed it onto her plate. "I don't buy the star-crossed crap at all. When you look at humans as a species, it's a wonder that marriage exists at all. With all the varieties of behaviors and the possibility that we're each evolving, who could expect two human beings to agree on what they want for dinner, let alone life choices? And to limit sexual partners?" She swung her head back, her dark hair flying over one shoulder. "Why would I want a vanilla sundae every night? Maybe I want Rocky Road or Raspberry Almond. Maybe I want nuts or hot fudge or caramel. Or maybe I don't want a sundae at all and I'm in the mood for pie or cake or crème brûlée."

Merlin wiped his mouth with a napkin and turned to Zoey. "Got any ice cream in your freezer?"

But Jade was on a roll. "And don't go blaming yourself for your failed marriage," she said with a stern look for Zoey. "Your only mistake was that you invested time in that loser. But you're free now, thanks to Nick the Prick. Try to think of it as your liberation, the beginning of endless possibilities. Your days won't be so predictable and dull anymore."

"I do well with predictable," Zoey said.

"Anything is possible now," Jade went on. "And best of all, you can have sex with anyone you want. Any time, any place."

"Oooh, you make it sound so juicy," Mouse said. "Bring it on, baby!"

"Really." Merlin took a sip of beer. "You know, Jade, we always thought you'd outgrow the slut thing. Who knew you'd make a career out of it."

Jade lifted her chin with a contented smile. "Sex is empowering. When are you girls going to drop your romantic notions and enjoy sex for all it's worth?"

"I am ready, sister!" Mouse clapped her hands and shook her head, her beads jingling wildly. "All aboard on the love train." She turned to squint at Zoey. "You comin' along, honey? Because a good, solid rebound relationship is exactly what you need. A tall, dark, and hard—"

"Stop it!" Zoey giggled. "Really, guys, I'd love a distraction, but at the moment I can't imagine ever having sex again or even getting naked with another male in the room—excluding my gynecologist, and that's only because the female doctor left the practice to have a baby."

"Mm-hmm." Mouse nodded knowingly. "Just you wait, Zoey. Things will change as soon as you get that husband out of your head. Your karma will change."

Merlin snapped his fingers. "I should do your chart. It might be helpful to see what you're going through astrologically."

"Maybe . . ." Zoey raised her shoulders, cowering. "You know that stuff always makes me nervous. I'm just sure you're going to look at my chart and see me getting run down by a cab or hit by a falling satellite or something."

"So you'd rather not know?" Merlin teased. "Ignorance is bliss."

When Zoey didn't answer, Mouse cut in, "Why don't you take a look at my chart and find out when my big break is coming? And is tomorrow a good day? Because I have this really important audition for a new musical. One of the writers is a hit-machine, and it's all loaded with juicy roles for gorgeous African-American girls like myself."

"Really?" Zoey raised her hands to applaud. "Break a leg, Mouseburger. This could be really huge for you."

"Please!" Mouse dabbed at her smooth, dark mouth with a napkin. "I am so through with tending bar for the Not Yet Upwardly Mobile crowd. Spoiled brats with a false sense of entitlement, as if they deserve to have everything from great apartments to designer drugs handed to them on a silver platter."

"You're just sick of being on the wrong end of the club scene," Jade pointed out. "We were party girls once. Some of us still are."

Mouse lifted her shoulders, puffing up with a knowing look.

"Nah-ah. We never acted out the way these brats do, and we managed to work our way through the drug scene without too much damage. But this Ecstasy is some bad-assed shit, and kids don't seem to care that it kills some of them because they're always sure it won't happen to them. That 'it'll never happen to me' bullshit. I saw a girl OD on it last night—totally freaked and overheated." Mouse covered her eyes with her manicured fingers. "I can't take it anymore. She might have died, and you know what? I really didn't care."

"Aren't we getting calloused?" Merlin said.

Mouse nodded. "I'm scaring myself. We sent her to the hospital in an ambulance, out of my hands, one-two-three. We're just the meat processors, sending in a few fresh bodies each night. And the club owner doesn't even want them going in unless they're totally strung out because once they go to the ER it's on record. Which means the police can start keeping track of the illegal drug use at Club Vermillion. Which means they might eventually go after the owner for operating a drug-prone establishment."

"We had that rap star at the hotel, he OD'd in one of the suites," Merlin said, his voice detached and even. "I didn't see it, thank God, but I'm glad it didn't happen on my shift. And I will never assign that room to anyone I know. Just the idea that some guy died there gives me the creeps, like his spirit still lingers."

Jade wiped her fingers on a napkin, tossed it onto the table, then leaned back against the couch. "You guys read way too much into everything. If these people are killing themselves— whether kids or rap stars—there's nothing you can do to stop them. And shame on them for their irresponsible behavior. I don't feel sorry for them at all, and you shouldn't either, honey," she told Mouse. "You need to focus on your own shit."

"It just scares me to look inside and find nothing. No compassion, no feeling at all for these people," said Mouse.

"Don't waste your energy on it," Jade said. "Think of the club as one more stage and your role is to be the detached bartender. Oh, and speaking of focus, I just had the most amazing sex with this man who's all into breathing and massage and relaxation. I think he's into that tantric-sex thing, but we did some basic things like focusing on abdominal muscles and breathing. He called it my sex energy, but whatever you call it, it totally blew me away." Jade's black hair splayed against the white couch as she leaned her head back. "Actually, I blew him first, but that's another story."

"Not another Jade sex story!" Merlin made a show of checking his watch. "Can you keep it short? I have to work in the morning."

"Don't start that again." Jade got up and stood behind Merlin to take him by the shoulders. "You will listen and you will love it," she said, shaking him gently. "My sex life is fascinating stuff."

"Mmm . . . a little to the left," Merlin said, closing his eyes.

"You are working on the wrong guy," Mouse told Jade. "He's got Josheepoo to take care of his little aches and pains."

"That's right." Jade pulled her hands away. "I forgot that Merlin is the only one of us with a steady partner."

"And Josh does give excellent massages," Merlin said. "I finally talked him into going to masseuse school. He started last fall."

"They have schools for that?" Mouse raised her hand. "I volunteer to be his homework assignment."

"They have partners for that." Merlin stood up and stretched. "I'd better go. Thanks for including me in the Nick-the-Prick-bashing session."

"You're not getting off so easy," Mouse said. "We are meeting at the club one night this week. You guys owe me."

"After all the charming things we've heard about that place?" Jade rolled her eyes. "Can't wait."

"Come on, Jade," Mouse said, "you've never turned down a night of free drinks and no cover charge."

"Guilty," Jade admitted, raising her hand. "How about Thursday?"

"This Thursday?" Zoey pretended to think. "I think my calendar's clear. At least, till the next millennium."

"Good." Mouse pointed a finger at Merlin. "And no backing out this time."

Merlin held his hands up in surrender as he walked to the

door. He'd learned years ago that it was no use arguing with Mouse; she always won.

Zoey followed him to the door while Jade went to the window and Mouse chose a CD to pop into the stereo. Merlin seemed a little stiff now, his shoulders squared off, his gait hesitant. Something was bothering him, Zoey could tell.

"What's up with you?" She squinted at him. "If you went before a jury now the verdict would be guilty as charged."

"Guilty." He closed his eyes and sighed. "Yes, I am guilty. I told Josh I wasn't coming here tonight. The thing is, he's jealous of you."

"What?" Zoey blinked. "Of me? Where is he getting that from? Or have you decided to make a major life change? Oh, your mother will be so happy. She always liked me."

"Still does. It's me she can't stand." Merlin shook his head. "Josh knows we had a special relationship, something he can't compete with, and that bothers him."

"I see. So you would have been better off if I'd stayed married happily ever after in Connecticut."

Merlin seemed to consider that, then shook his head. "Nope. I missed you." He opened his arms and gave Zoey a warm hug, and she could feel his tension draining away. "I'll talk to Josh. He'll come around."

"I sure hope so. I hate to think that he'd get mad at you for cheating on him without really cheating on him at all."

"You know, I'm following that. Pretty scary." He leaned back, his blue eyes flickering with the humor she'd grown so accustomed to during those years of college. "Welcome back. You're like one of those heroes on *Survivor.* You managed to escape the domestic prison of a suburban marriage."

Zoey smiled. "God, I hope you're right."

11

That night while rinsing plates and sealing up leftover Chinese food in the kitchen Zoey felt a strange sensation—the prickle on the back of the neck that told her she was not alone. Hmm. She glanced over toward the door of the apartment, but it was double-bolted shut. Strange.

She reached over to open the dishwasher door . . . and then she saw it. Another water bug, poised on the kitchen floor.

"Ughughugh!" She lunged back into the doorway. Okay, okay, she had to get a grip here. What had Jade told her? "You are alone but not indefensible. You are bigger than the bug." She couldn't smash it and didn't have the nerve to get close enough to touch it. But she could strand it, right? Hold it there until someone else came along to kill the damned thing.

Containment was the thing.

Opening a kitchen cabinet she found a large metal bowl that could be used to trap the thing against the floor. If only it didn't hop up or jump in her face or fly away. Oh, God, did water bugs jump? Could they fly?

"Just stay right there," she spoke to it quietly, edging closer.

"Don't move and you'll be just fine." She had to bite back revulsion over the fat, black, big-eyed creature as she leaned over it . . .

Then dropped the bowl over it. "Wong, wong, wong . . ." the rim of the bowl sang as it rotated on the floor, finally coming to a safe stop over the insect.

Zoey sucked in her breath, relieved. The first battle was won. Now she needed to find a hit man to finish the job. She headed toward the phone, then came back and put a fat book on top of the bowl for good measure. No telling how strong this insect could be and she didn't want it slithering out from under the rim.

Neither Jade nor Mouse answered their phones, perhaps because it was after midnight. Zoey imagined that Mouse was asleep with the phone turned off, but she managed to reach Jade on her cell phone. "Call the doorman and ask him to send up the porter," Jade told her. "Skye must give them all a big fat tip at Christmastime, and they'll probably love the whole damsel-in-distress angle."

"You think so?" Zoey asked, watching the trapped insect from her post outside the kitchen doorway. "I just hate to make waves, being an illegal sublet and all."

"They don't know that! Get on the phone and tell them your sob story. Don't forget the part about . . . oh, hold on," Jade said, calling to someone. "Yes, honey. One minute and I'll . . . woof!" She giggled.

"Jade? Are you alone? Stupid question. Who is it, your Japanese Tantra Master?"

"No, it's Chuck, my friend from the sixth floor. What is that?" Jade asked him, then laughed into the phone. "Whipped cream! Clever you. Look, Zo, I gotta go. I'll . . . ooh, that's so nice. Listen, Zoey, I'll talk to you in the morning."

"Okay," Zoey said, and Jade's end of the line clicked off before she could say good-bye.

Following Jade's advice, Zoey called the doorman, who promised to send up the night porter as soon as he was free. Well, that was easier than I expected, Zoey thought as she quickly changed into sweatpants and her nightshirt to wait for the man.

Two hours and four follow-up calls later, she was parked in the hallway, her laptop plugged into the hall outlet and set on the floor outside the kitchen. She had planned to work tonight and didn't want to slack off, but she couldn't bear to leave her watch post for fear that the enemy would break loose in the apartment and destroy her chances of ever sleeping again.

Before her the keyboard was a blank mist framed by the word processing toolbar.

Why couldn't she write anymore?

Put anything down. Gibberish. You can edit yourself later.

She typed in a sentence about the weather. God, you know you're desperate when you're writing about the weather. Next she would be describing Muzak or writing about two people trapped in an elevator.

She backspaced over the whole damned sentence, back to an empty screen.

Empty.

Blank.

Oh, why am I so blocked? Because I have no life. Nothing left to say. Nick took it all, damn him. No wonder he wanted out of the marriage; he had married an empty shell of a woman.

The cursor blinked at her mockingly, as if to say, Ha! Ha! Ha! Your career is over. Better get a job scanning groceries at Waldbaum's; you're going to need the money.

It was nearly three A.M. when the porter showed up and took care of Zoey's little monster. By then she was slumped over her computer playing solitaire, having abandoned trying to come up with a story concept for her next novel.

Something will come to me while I'm sleeping, she thought as she locked the front door behind the porter, a heavyset man in his fifties badly in need of dental work. Now I'm safe and I'll get a restful, blissful night of sleep and wake up with formed characters and concept, with pivotal plot points and a few eloquent details. It had worked so well for her in college when she'd been at a loss as to how to end a short story or what direction to take in a

thesis summary. Her mind worked best while the conscious part
was turned off.

Slipping between the smooth sheets, she hugged the pillow
and squirmed until she felt settled in and relaxed. Her body was
shot, if only she could quiet her mind and welcome sleep . . . the
last great escape.

12

Her eyes were still closed when Jade rolled over feeling cold and sticky. The red digits of the clock blared 4:23. She must have dozed off, which wasn't like her. Ordinarily after a quick romp in bed she was dressed and gone within minutes, never one to hang around for cuddling and kissing once she'd gotten her satisfaction.

She glanced down over her naked body, her legs partly twisted in the sheets of Chuck's bed. The sticky feeling was from the orgy of Cool Whip he'd spread over her thighs, licking his way to the creamy center. That was Chuck—fun-loving, creative in bed, totally noncommitted, and conveniently located in the same apartment building.

Sitting up in bed, she squinted, trying to find her clothes in the dark disorder. There was her shirt, draped over the handle-bars of Chuck's bike. Her skirt was in a puddle on the floor; her Prada heels dropped in a trail from the door. Jade never felt guilty about her occasional flings with Chuck—or with any man, for that matter. But tonight, as she dressed, she was aware of an unusual sense of emptiness, a void that was almost painful.

What was that about?

It had been a near perfect night. Another apartment leased at work, an evening with her oldest, closest friends, a sexual encounter with two orgasms and a whipped cream garnish. What was not to like?

The bad feeling prevailed as she let herself out of Chuck's place and rode the elevator down to her apartment. Tears streamed down her face as the doors opened and she rushed out on the sixth floor. By the time she'd unlocked her door she could barely hold back the sobs. She slammed it shut behind her and collapsed in the hallway, hugging her knees as the pain overtook her. The low-pad commercial carpeting felt rough under her cheek, and in the dim light she noticed the uneven line of the baseboards in the hall. This place was a dump, and she deserved better. As one of the top real estate agents in New York City she could certainly score a better place to live. Why wasn't she taking care of herself the way she took care of other people?

She felt cold and hollow, and although she hated to admit it she missed Mr. Takiyama. Not his personality so much, but the sexual contact they'd made had tapped a source deeper in Jade, answering a need she'd never realized she possessed.

That was it, she thought, sucking in a jagged breath. By comparison, tonight's sex with Chuck was lackluster and routine. Orgasm was like a basic knee-jerk reaction, a quick fix. True satisfaction was in that deeper connection.

Jade pulled herself up to her knees, wiping her tears. She had a feeling Mr. Takiyama was married, but that had never stopped her before. And now her quest was motivated by a stronger, deeper desire.

Cosmic sex.

The buzzing noise went right through Zoey like the dentist's drill grinding into a tooth. Zoey opened one eye, still not sure where she was.

Sunlight was just beginning to seep through the miniblinds of the bedroom window—Skye's bedroom window. The digital clock said 7:42.

Again, the buzzing noise, and Zoey sat up in bed. The workers?

She threw back the covers and padded out to the hallway, where Carlos stood on a ladder drilling something into brackets in the ceiling.

"Good morning," he said, nodding.

"Not really. Not this early at least. Carlos . . ." She pointed to her wrist, pretending there was a watch there. "It's too early. You said you would start at nine o'clock, remember?"

"Nine o'clock." He nodded, then went on to explain his side of the situation in great detail. The only problem was that the explanation was in Portuguese.

Zoey raked her hair back, realizing she must look like hell. "I'm sorry, but I don't understand a word you're saying."

He frowned, then answered, "Meez Skye Blackwell hired us."

"Right, yes, that I know. But can't you start work a little later?"

"We work on the ceiling."

"Right." Turning away, Zoey rubbed her eyes and marched back to bed. She slid under the covers and pulled the pillow over her head—her fuzzy-brained, empty head. A brilliant plot had not taken shape in her mind that night, but what could you expect with four hours' sleep?

She breathed in, sucking the soft cotton pillowcase against her nostrils. With any luck, she'd suffocate by the time the guys breaked for coffee.

13

Oh, dear Jesus, this is it, Mouse prayed as she waited for the light to change at 49th and Broadway. I know this is the moment you've been leading me to. Jesus, Lord, let your brilliance shine through me at this audition. Make me a tool of your greatness, Lord.

With a dramatic sweep of her hand she pushed back her black velvet cape to check her belt buckle, a swirl shape studded with glittering turquoise rhinestones, which matched her turquoise v-necked sweater, which matched the beads in her hair. Hey, when you had a few minutes to make an impression, you had to make color work for you. And the short black skirt that hugged her perfectly curved butt didn't hurt, either. Granted, she was petite, but the Lord didn't pass her over when he was doling out boobs and bootie. She had it goin' on, and she knew how to make the most of it.

A crowd of tourists closed around her as traffic poured through the intersection then stopped, blocking the crosswalk. Horns blared and someone shoved close to her, but Mouse ignored it all. She needed to stay focused and ready to shine at this audition.

Jesus, this could be one of the most important roles of my life, and I thank you, Lord, for bringing me this far in your love and . . .

Someone rubbed up against her butt—with something hard and firm.

"What the fuck do you think you're doing?" she yelled, whirling around to face the pervert.

A large woman in a quilted coat winced, her heavily made-up eyes full of fright. "Sorry, miss," she said, nervously grabbing the dangling buckle on her coat that must have poked Mouse. "I didn't mean to bump into you."

"Oh." Mouse took a deep breath, glad that she hadn't been groped on the way to an important audition. "No harm done, honey." She stepped off the curb, making sure to stay on the white lines for good luck. That morning she'd eaten instant oatmeal with apples and cinnamon for breakfast—her lucky breakfast. And she was wearing her smooth, black Barely There panties, the ones she'd been wearing the day she got the role in *The Sound of Music*. Not that she was superstitious or anything, but it didn't hurt to pad your chances.

Smoke stung her throat as she cut through a cluster of nervous actors sucking down cigarettes outside the rehearsal studio. Not recognizing any friendly faces, Mouse tugged the door open and slipped from the sunny day into the dark, musty corridor. In the distance she heard the clatter of tap shoes as some poor actor tried to hoof his or her way into a part. Mouse frowned. She hadn't brought her tap shoes, but dancing was not her expertise, and besides, who would expect to see tap routines in a musical about the Underground Railroad?

"This is perfect for you! It's like the show was written with you in mind," her agent, Mel Lansky, had told her when she returned his page. "It's about heartbreak, social injustice, and liberation—sort of *Showboat* meets *Hair!*"

Whatever that meant. "Great!" she'd told him, reminding him

that she had played Abe Lincoln in the European revival tour of *Hair*. Granted, she was the shortest and blackest Abe Lincoln in the history of theater, but that was part of the fun of a show that played against types.

This show was probably more straightforward, she guessed as she beamed a huge smile at one of the people in charge and signed in on a clipboard at the table in the hall.

"Do you have your headshots?" the kid asked.

Mouse took a turquoise envelope out of her bag. "Two headshots and my credits," she said, making eye contact with him. "And how is your day going?"

"Just barely," he answered, frowning. "Take a seat. We'll get you in in a few minutes."

Two other actors were seated in folding chairs there, since only production staff was allowed in the rehearsal room while someone was auditioning, and Mouse tried not to size them up as she sat and pulled out the two songs she'd prepared—one from *Ragtime* and one from *Porgy and Bess*. But she couldn't help but notice that the dark-skinned woman had a diamond stud in her nose. A pierced nose. That could wreak havoc on a sinus infection. And the other woman kept shifting her legs and nudging Mouse's foot. Was she deliberately trying to be annoying, or was it a natural gift?

"Sorry," the woman said, and Mouse flashed her a smile that said, "Don't bother, I'm out of your league."

Actors. They had to be the most self-centered human beings on the planet. Thank God I'm not like that, Mouse thought.

The door opened and a young woman in a leopard-print jumpsuit strutted out, her large breasts bobbing against the fabric. Talk about flaunting it.

Oh, dear Jesus, please don't reward her for that gauche display, Mouse prayed, trying to block out the scene around her. Lord, you know how hard I've worked for this and I know you won't let me down. I trust in you.

While she waited, Mouse divided her time between prayer and studying her music. At last, she was called in. Immediately she tried to single out Eli Gray from publicity photos, but he wasn't there. Plan B—try to identify who's really in power. She scanned the three people at the table, a black man with striking silver hair, a coco-skinned woman with schoolmarm glasses, and a white man with a large head that would rival a Neanderthal's.

Schoolmarm caught her staring, and Mouse quickly smiled, imagining hearts and flowers and glitter flying out of her mouth to float around the room and captivate the producers.

"Your name?" Neanderthal man asked as she handed the pianist her music.

"Marielle Griffin, and I just want to congratulate you on the buzz over this show," she said quickly, determined to make an impression with her sparkling personality. Besides, people liked praise, even important producer people. "Everyone's excited about it."

Silver Hair smiled. Schoolmarm checked her notes. Neanderthal cocked his head to the side. "And what might that buzz be?" Neanderthal asked.

Oooh, think fast! She hadn't expected him to quiz her. "That it . . . it makes powerful statements about black culture and liberation." Her heart beat hard in her chest as she tried to remember Mel's bullshit. "That it's bound to be *Showboat* meets *Hair* . . . and you'll see from my credits that I toured Europe with that recent production of *Hair.* It's an amazing show."

"'*Hair?*'" Neanderthal scratched his head, then looked down the table at Silver Hair, who shrugged.

Oh, shit! I said the wrong thing. Mouse was about to retract the statement when Schoolmarm cued the pianist, who started the intro to "Summertime."

She had to sing! Oh, dear Jesus Lord, let your Spirit shine through me! she prayed. Pulling her head up, shoulders back, spine straight, Mouse filled her lungs with air and belted out the bittersweet melody.

That made Schoolmarm sit up and take notice. Well, at least her voice wasn't failing her. Clear, steady, strong—Mouse's voice caressed the notes as her body swayed in rhythmic dramatic interpretation. As soon as she finished they had her go directly to the song from *Ragtime,* and she nailed that one, too. She was sure of it.

"Thank you so much for your time," she said, stepping up to the table and shaking each producer's hand. As she looked each person in the eye, she tried to strike that delicate balance between confidence and humility, something there was not enough of in this business of big egos and bigger idiots.

"I know you have a lot of actors to audition, but let me just say that I know in my heart that I am the best for the role you're casting, and I look forward to working with producers with your reputation and learning from your talents. Thank you so much for seeing me." Her voice oozed sincerity as she nodded goodbye, then confidently marched out the door.

I am the best, dear Jesus, please let them feel it now.

The best, the best, the best . . . she repeated to herself with each step down the street, across Times Square. It was her mantra as she stood on the N train platform.

I am the best, the best, the best.

Oh, God, please let them choose me.

14

"I didn't get the part." It was the first thing Mouse said when Zoey picked up the phone one evening from her new working spot atop Skye's four-poster bed. Zoey's mind was in another world, engrossed in the sadness of a boy who had lost his saxophone in a snowstorm, thus ending a promising career as a musician and his only form of self-expression.

Zoey blinked in the shadowed room. "Who is this, and what time is it, anyway?"

"It's me," Mouse said, "and I'm not in the *Underground Railroad* musical."

"Don't say that," Zoey said as she'd said so often over the last few days. She picked up a pencil and tapped it against the quilted red and pink bedspread. "Maybe they didn't make a decision yet. Just because they haven't called, doesn't mean—"

"They cast one of the other girls my agent represents. And somehow he managed to get the entire cast list, and I'm not on it. He had his assistant call to tell me, can you imagine? He couldn't even take the time to call me himself."

Zoey wiped her palms on her jeans. "I'm so sorry, Mouse.

God, it's entirely unfair. I don't know how you deal with the rejection and blatant criticism in that business. You're a stronger
person than I am."

"Right now I am a very angry person. Those people made the
wrong choice, and it's going to be bad for them and for me. Do
you know how many parts there are for tiny African-American
women?"

"Oh, Mouse . . ." They'd covered this territory a million times
before. "Where are you?"

"At the club. Can you come down tonight?"

"Tonight?" Biting her lower lip, Zoey glanced down at her
NYU sweatshirt and blue jeans, her slum-around-and-write outfit. She hated to leave when she was on a roll at the computer.

"Please?" Mouse begged. "I'm feeling dangerously close to
vaulting over the bar and telling all the party brats exactly how I
feel about their daddies' beamers and their piss-poor attitudes."

Reluctantly, Zoey clicked on the "Save" icon and slid off the
bed. Time to save her girlfriend's butt. "Ignore the brats and
start chilling the Cosmopolitan glasses; I'll be there in a half
hour."

Over the weeks Zoey fell into a steady routine of quiet despair.
Each morning she was rousted from bed by hammering or
drilling. She quickly dressed inside Skye's walk-in closet and
spent the morning drinking way too much coffee while she
stared at her computer screen and began countless story out-
lines about distant characters in situations that held no interest
for her. Some of them she deleted by lunchtime; others survived
long enough to receive names and a place in her "Documents"
file, which was turning into an impressively long list.

Too bad that none of the story ideas had legs. Reading back
over them, Zoey would see the merit and think, yes, that would
make an interesting novel . . . for someone else to write. She just
couldn't bring herself to care about these people or the dilem-
mas they faced.

Afternoons were punctuated by more construction noises,
total lack of privacy, and the feeling that the world was coming to

an end here in some stranger's apartment. A few evenings a week she forced herself out to meet her friends at Club Vermillion, where the deafening noise and youthful crowd reminded her that she was too old for the dating scene, though Mouse always argued that Vermillion was no way to gauge date-ability since it attracted a young, rowdy crowd.

"Was the music this loud when we were in college?" Zoey shouted one night over a round of Cuervo Gold margaritas expertly prepared by the Mouster.

Merlin nodded, stepping over to slip an arm around Josh's waist. Somehow—Zoey wasn't sure of the details—Merlin had convinced Josh not to be jealous of Zoey and managed to drag him along for the occasional crew meeting at the bar. To Zoey's surprise, Josh seemed to relax with the group, listening with concern when she went through her tales of insect invasion and sharing anecdotes about Merlin that amused everyone. "I can't believe you actually jumped into the pond in Central Park," Zoey told Merlin. "Did you make sure all your shots are updated?"

That was the night that Jade had snuck into the back room of the bar for a quickie with Elvis, the bartender/impersonator. "He ain't nothin' but a hound dog," Zoey had sung in Jade's ear, but Jade waved off the warning as usual. Or was that the night that Jade had left early with a cigar-smoking guy in his twenties who'd been cruising the city in a limousine with his bachelor-party crew? Jade's sex life was so hard to keep track of, Zoey had begun jotting down notations on her calendar, just out of curiosity. Certainly it would be liberating to have Jade's sex drive and total lack of guilt and commitment, but lately Zoey had noticed Jade stalking her men with a new hunger and precision. Change was stirring on Jade's sexual landscape, but Zoey wasn't sure exactly where the new weather front was headed.

In terms of her own sexual landscape, Zoey wasn't even looking. She didn't talk to strangers, didn't make eye contact with anyone in the clubs aside from her own friends, and to be honest, she didn't miss sex. Oh, there were those occasional twinges when she caught a glimpse of a couple kissing on the street or a titillating close-up of flesh in a movie, but otherwise she was resigning herself to the chaste existence of a prudish matron sequestered in her seventeenth-story tower.

A tower that was still quite vulnerable to enemy invaders.

Every few nights, despite professional extermination and the purchase of a can of Raid that totally stunk up the apartment, Zoey was visited by a surreal creature from the bowels of the plumbing system, its antennae waving, probing, undermining all feelings of independence. "These bugs love you," the porter said one night as he headed off with the latest casualty in a paper bag. "You're like a magnet."

"That's me," Zoey said, forcing a smile. She hated when the night porter teased her about being afraid of insects, but she didn't want to lash out at him and take the chance of alienating him. Who else would make the trip up to the apartment in the middle of the night to annihilate the enemy?

And so it looked like March was going to end as dismally as it started, and Zoey was clueless as to how to insulate her world from the little things—like carpenters, writer's block, and bugs—that were steadily destroying what was left of her peace of mind.

She had complained to Skye in a few delicately worded emails, and Skye had responded with impressions of Tuscany, raves over the gourmet dishes created by her unnamed author, and descriptions of the sun setting over the hills. Finally, Zoey sent an email that bordered on complaint-land, and Skye responded with glib amusement.

Leave it to you and your fertile writer's imagination to turn a few insects into an invasion from another dimension! I do enjoy your descriptions of the little pests. By all means, get the exterminator in more often. Personally, I just smashed them with a fat book and left them for the maid to clean up. Which, considering your phobia, might be a good reason for you to avoid handling my copy of *War and Peace*—the cover might still be stained with bug juice.

And isn't Carlos a riot? Don't even try to communicate

with him unless you're taking a crash course in Portuguese. The thing with Carlos is he's dirt cheap but not board approved, but the doormen think he's on the list, so don't spill, okay?

As far as writer's block goes, maybe you need some time off? No, forget I said that. We have a deadline, my dear! Okay, let's talk marketing. If you look at the numbers, your best bet is a personal story involving romance, since your other novels haven't come close to the monster sales of *His Daughter's Keeper*, which ended so happily with that nice romance at the rehab center. So go for romance, and sex it up if the spirit moves you. On the other hand, if that doesn't inspire you, forget I said it. I button my lip and invite you to follow your muse.

Zoey stared at the screen, which mocked her yet again.

Write something romantic and sexy? Oh, right, just when she was the poster child of the brokenhearted. All those rolling hills and glorious sunsets were turning Skye's brain to mush. Or maybe it was the red wine, which the Italians dispensed like water. In any case, Skye was way off target; romantic fiction was out of the question for Zoey.

So, then, what would she write?

"What would I write? What could I write? What should I write on a boring night?" Zoey stood up and turned away from the computer. "Certainly not Dr. Seuss."

Zoey paced down the hall past Skye's photos of herself with celebrity authors and opened the door of the refrigerator. Rule number 238 in dealing with writer's block: When in doubt, snack.

15

"Tell me again, why are we doing this?" Zoey asked Merlin as they leaned over their stockinged feet and contemplated two pair of ice skates with tongues out and laces gaping open like large angry mouths. Josh, who had already laced up his skates, was already out on the ice making a virgin run.

"Josh likes to do active things," Merlin said, pushing one foot into a skate. "Tennis, swimming, skiing . . ."

"Good for him. But when I said I'd meet you guys, I thought he meant for drinks or dinner. I haven't worn a pair of ice skates since I was fourteen, and even then it was only a poorly conceived plan to get Brian Massiello to catch me when I fell on the ice." The smells and sounds here at Chelsea Piers sent her back to that time—the echoing noise in the rink, the cold air tweaking your nose, the freezer smell of the ice as the Zamboni turned it into a smooth sheet.

"You'll be fine. Actually, consider yourself lucky. If the weather was nicer we'd probably be biking down from here to Battery Park. Maybe next month."

"Oh, great. Something to look forward to." Zoey shoved her

foot into a skate and pulled up the tongue. It felt heavy and awkward, and she hoped she would have the strength to move with these clunkers on.

"Hey, how's it going?" Josh called, swaggering over on his skates. His dark eyes were bright with exhilaration, his cheeks a healthy pink.

"Zoey hasn't been on skates for awhile," Merlin explained, lacing his second skate.

How had he done that so fast? And he seemed so limber as he leaned over his ankles. "You guys must come here all the time," Zoey said as it finally hit her. "Oh, God, you're secret skating pros. What, are you trying out for the Ice Dancing Event in the next Olympics?"

Josh laughed. "I still have my doubts about that event. Call me a purist, but there's nothing like classic figure skating." He kneeled at Zoey's feet and began tightening her laces, firmly but gently. "And we come here as often as we can, though the ice is often monopolized by hockey teams and professional figure skaters. The open sessions get edged out all the time."

"Really?" Zoey was surprised to see Josh lacing up her skates the way she'd imagined Brian Massiello would have done it if he'd been a decent boyfriend. The gesture was so personal, so . . . helpful. This was a side of Josh she'd never seen.

"Tell me if it's too tight," Josh said, pulling the laces taut.

"But you want it a little tight for support," Merlin advised.

"It feels fine, and I am totally in your hands," Zoey said gratefully. "Just promise me you won't leave me marooned out there if I fall and can't get up. I'd hate to get scraped up by the Zamboni."

Josh laughed as Merlin led the way to the ice. "It's easier than you remember," Josh said, touching her shoulder gently. Another first. What exactly had Merlin told the boy about her to warm him up this way?

Knees wobbling, Zoey held tight to the side board and moved onto the ice. The first step seemed a little slippery, but then she began to get used to gliding. Think of it as sliding along a wood floor in your socks, she told herself. "It's not so bad," she said.

In front of her, Josh was skating backwards, his hands out-stretched in encouragement. "You're doing great!"

Merlin glided beside her, not as skilled as Josh but certainly steady on his feet.

The rink wasn't too crowded tonight, but the skaters seemed to know what they were doing. Couples circled hand-in-hand, experts practiced in the center, and two groups of teenagers hung in clusters, talking and laughing.

Zoey gritted her teeth, plodding ahead. "Okay, I'm skating. So when does it begin to be fun?"

"You do have a great sense of humor!" Josh said with a huge grin. "No wonder you're a writer." With that he turned and dashed ahead, looping around a slower skater and hotdogging into a twirl and a jump.

"Oh my God, Merlin, you're dating Brian Boitano."

Merlin arched an eyebrow. "Only cuter."

It took Zoey a few minutes but she began to get the hang of it. The rock music lilting through the air helped her forget the mechanics and she started loosening up a bit, despite her shaky legs. A teenaged boy in a hockey jersey whipped in front, almost knocking her off balance. Zoey lashed out at him, "Take it easy, Speedo!" To her surprise, he turned back to apologize.

Merlin laughed as the boy skated off. "You're starting to resemble a city girl again. A real loud-mouth, fast-walking, take-no-prisoners chick. It's good to have you back."

"And I'm finally beginning to feel at home. Maybe it's because I'm sleeping again, thanks to Tylenol PM and the fact that the workers aren't waking me up at dawn anymore."

"You finally talked some sense into them?"

"Hardly. They just stopped showing up one morning, though the job is far from finished. Bob the doorman says that the co-op found out they weren't licensed and refused to let them in, which is fine with me. I emailed Skye to ask about it, but haven't heard back from her."

"A temporary peace," Merlin said. Zoey noticed how his royal blue scarf matched his eyes, making him look so tranquil, like a

Caribbean beach at dawn. He had always given off a zen vibe, comforting and placid amid hellacious turmoil.

Then the music stopped abruptly and an announcer's voice came on.

"Ladies and gentleman, we have interrupted our music to direct your attention to the signboard where there's an important message from Tom to Celia."

Zoey teetered back as she turned toward the board between the hockey scoreboards. It read, "Will you marry me, Celia? Love, Tom."

Most of the skaters paused, whether out of respect or curiosity, Zoey wasn't sure. Across the ice, a woman skated over to her guy and kissed him on the lips. He lifted her off the ice, then waved to everyone.

"Looks like the answer is yes!" the announcer boasted. "Congratulations and best of luck to our happy couple."

"Bad move, Celia." Merlin rolled his eyes. "Who would marry a jerk who pours his money into renting a signboard?"

"When did you get so jaded?" Josh asked him. "I think it's kind of romantic."

That closed look came over Merlin's face, as if he'd checked out emotionally. "If you can buy romance, yeah. I don't know, maybe it's just the negative polarity of a Capricorn. It's easy for me to withdraw."

"Don't use that as an excuse. With the duality of your Capricorn personality you should be able to jump from cerebral to passionate to party-ready just like that," Josh said, snapping his fingers.

Merlin shrugged. "I think not. Capricorn is ruled by Saturn, planet of contracted, concentrated energy. We require more time to change than other people."

Zoey was still watching the couple, who now skated off the ice. Probably going off to party and have sex and sew together their delicate dreams.

"Sometimes I wish I could be stupid and happy," she said, the words coming out before she thought about what they meant.

"Not to judge anyone, but I do think it would be nice not to worry about fulfilling my creative vision or pleasing other people or missing a one-time art exhibit. Dumb and happy. Dinner at five and a night on the couch watching *Millionaire.*"

Both Josh and Merlin were silent as the rock music started again.

"I guess we're all cursed," Merlin said. "Not that we can't ever be happy, but for us it will be in the form of momentary events. Brief glimpses of satisfaction or pleasure or even bliss. Because . . ." He slipped an arm over Zoey's shoulders. ". . . you are far from stupid. And that is your curse."

"Well, I wouldn't mind receiving a singing telegram or finding a message to me in a Macy's window display," Josh said, skating backwards. "You don't have to be stupid to enjoy life." He turned and skated off, making Zoey wonder if she'd offended him.

"Is he mad?" Zoey asked.

"Probably at me. He has his moods, but he usually gets through them quickly. Blink and he'll be on to something else."

Zoey was glad that Merlin was secure in his relationship with Josh.

"How long have you guys been together?" she asked.

"Six years."

"Really? You're like an old married couple."

"Exactly what I'm afraid of."

Zoey was about to push the topic further, but Merlin got a page from work and stepped off the ice to call in. Watching him go, Zoey became conscious of her shaky thigh muscles. She felt like a child doing baby steps across the globe.

The ice ripped as Josh skated up from behind her. "You're really getting the hang of it," he said, his dark eyes flashing.

"So why do I feel like an elephant on roller skates?"

He smiled. "I'm glad you came along. I've been wanting to talk to you about Merlin for awhile. He's in a slump, stuck in the mud, head in the sand—whatever you want to call it. I know he loves me, but he won't commit." Josh clasped his face in his hands and raised his voice. "Oh, what should I do, Dr. Zoey?"

Zoey laughed. Was this the man who'd snagged Merlin with his deep, dark side? The boy in pain whom Merlin had saved from the depths of hell? "Josh, I have never seen this side of you."

"I only bring it out for tourists and hotel guests," Josh said. "But really, I need your help. Can't you work on Merlin for me? Persuade him that I'm the best thing that ever happened to him?"

"He knows that."

"So why won't he act on it? Every time I bring up marriage, he pulls a Marlene Dietrich on me." Josh tossed back his head and gave Zoey a sulking look.

She smiled, suddenly beginning to understand what Merlin saw in this guy. She'd never known that Josh could be so determined and eager to please. "He's scared. Not because of you, I think, but because of his own feelings, his own reservations about commitment and how complacency might change your relationship."

"But he respects you, and you know him so well, Zoey. Talk to him. Tell him marriage can be a good thing. That commitments are not only for the criminally insane."

"You know, Josh . . ." Zoey shook her head. "I'm not sure how much you know about me, but suffice it to say I'm going through a difficult divorce. I do believe in love and marriage. All the notions of star-crossed love and that there's one true partner for each person in the universe . . . it's still part of my belief system, and that's the problem. I believe in something that doesn't exist for me anymore. My marriage is over, which hardly qualifies me to go to Merlin and campaign for lifetime commitment."

Josh waved off her logic. "Everyone knows Nick was a prick. Will you talk to Merlin?"

Zoey stopped skating and took a breath. Oh, why not? "I'll do my best, but please don't have great expectations. I think you two belong together, but his issues about commitment have nothing to do with you."

"Thanks, Zoey!" Josh lowered his head, his brown eyes full of warmth. "You are a good friend, and I know you'll always be there for us. And if everything works out, you would be the perfect mother for our child."

"What?" Zoey's foot slipped and she danced on the ice, trying to get her balance. It didn't work, and she landed on her butt with a grunt.

Josh leaned down, extending a hand, but the sight of his face freaked her out again. Was he really thinking about having a baby with Merlin? And that they would ask her to be the mother . . . she'd had her share of maternal fantasies, though none of those included herself as a surrogate.

"Tell me you're joking," she said.

"Of course." Josh grinned. "Gotcha!"

16

"So you've gone from being the proper Connecticut wife of a starched-shirt lawyer to possibly carrying the love child of a gay couple in what—a month or so? Not bad for an evolving person," Jade said when Zoey managed to reach her in the office the next day.

"He said he was joking," Zoey said, pulling her feet into the lotus position atop Skye's bed. From here she could see the Zeckendorf Towers at Union Square, and it made her wonder when the spring farmer's market was going to start up at the edge of the park there. It would be fun to load up the kitchen with fresh apples, flowers, pies, and cheeses. At last, she was beginning to feel at home in the city.

"I think that Merlin better—Oh, sorry. Hold on, honey," Jade said, cutting away. It was the downside of talking to Jade when she was at work; she had to divide her conversation between you and half a dozen barking clients.

The line clicked on again, and Jade said, "Yes, Mr. Swersky, I'd be delighted to show you that one-of-a-kind penthouse this afternoon at—"

"Jade, it's me . . . Zoey."

"Oh, sorry, honey, I've got a gazillion people on hold here. Hold on."

Zoey was still on hold when the door buzzer rang, and she skidded down the hall in her socks.

"There's a Scott Peterson on his way up to you," said Bobby. "He's a contractor, to finish off the work for Ms. Blackwell."

"Oh, okay," Zoey said, her head lolling to the side. Just when she'd been enjoying a little privacy! She had gotten an email from Skye about a new guy, but she'd hoped that with Skye so far away it might take a few weeks to set everything up. No such luck.

"I'm back, but I have to run," Jade said. "But before I forget, are you free tonight? I thought you could go apartment hunting with me. Totally for myself, since I've been talking about getting a new place for ages but can never find the time. Of course, if you see something you like in the meantime, it's gravy."

"Sounds like fun," Zoey said, fantasizing about a place of her own free of waterbugs and contractors. "Want me to meet you at the office?"

"Sure. We'll grab a bite after we hit a few places."

The doorbell rang, and Zoey pulled the pencil out of her hair and shook it out, which was about as much primping as she was going to do for this loser. "Someone's at my door, so I'll see you later," she told Jade, swinging the door open.

A pair of startling blue eyes and broad shoulders greeted her on the other side.

Zoey felt her face heat up as the man smiled and extended his hand.

"Hi, I'm Scott Peterson, the new contractor," he said. His hand was warm and strong, with none of the calluses and grease stains that marked the hands of Carlos and his son.

"Hi." Zoey could barely glance away as he stepped in and turned to close the door behind him. He wore a blue satin baseball jacket with "Scott Peterson Carpentry" emblazoned across the back. When he turned to face her again, he tilted his head casually, embracing her with a friendly look that made her feel as if they were old friends.

"I imagine you're less than thrilled to have someone working in the apartment, but I promise you I'll be as quiet and neat as possible. If you let me know what hours work for you, I'll work around your schedule, since I'm always juggling jobs and estimates."

Zoey wanted to hug him. "That's . . . that's great," she mumbled like a teenager. "The thing is, I'm a writer and I really value my creative solitude."

"A writer." Scott beamed. "That's awesome. My kids will be thrilled. They always get excited when I'm working for a celebrity, though the best was when I installed new doors for the actor who played Steve in *Blue's Clues.*"

Zoey shook her head. "I don't even know who he is."

"You will when you have kids of your own," Scott said, stepping around her. "Do you mind if I take a look at the job first? I know it's sort of last minute, but—"

"Sure, no problem," Zoey said, holding out her arm like Vanna White. "Do you want some coffee or something?" she asked, hoping he'd say no since she didn't have any in the apartment. A Starbucks run was part of her morning ritual.

"No, thanks," he said, breezing past her, all gorgeous six feet of him. His thick blond hair was cut short around his perfect ears. His skin was slightly tanned, probably from working on rooftops in the sun, she thought, enjoying the image of this man swinging down a ladder.

Just stop it right now, Zoey, she told herself. Stop the fantasy. This guy is married and here to do a job, so stop your sex-starved libido from going there.

"Okay, this is fine," he said, nodding. "If it's all right with you, I'll run downstairs, get my tools, and get under way. The sooner I start, the sooner I'll be out of your way."

"No problem," Zoey said again, feeling a rush of energy as he brushed past her on his way out the door. She leaned against the doorjamb, her eyes on Scott's blue-jeaned butt as he swaggered toward the elevator. Okay, he was totally off-limits. Out of bounds. Hands off.

But a girl could dream.

17

"Honey, it's healthy to have a good sex fantasy once in a while," Jade told Zoey as they sped up Eighth Avenue in a yellow cab. "Personally, I wouldn't stop at the fantasy. Especially if he's filling the air of your apartment with all that testosterone. Who could resist?"

"He's married," Zoey reminded her friend and herself. "With kids."

Jade shrugged. "All the better. He won't expect you to give up your friends and move to the boondocks of Connecticut."

Zoey smiled. "Touché." Jade had such a different notion of the perfect relationship. And apparently Skye had a very different notion of the perfect carpenter. In her last email Skye had made it quite obvious that she was upset about losing Carlos and pissed off at the co-op for interfering:

> I'm going with a guy the co-op recommended, but he's expensive and I'm leaving it up to you to make sure he works while he's there. The co-op loves to hire losers who

can't find work elsewhere; their little mission to lower the unemployment rate. Anyway, please keep an eye on this Scott person. Make sure he doesn't steal my jewelry or walk off with the VCR. And how'd the exterminator work out? Those water bugs are persistent.

Actually, the exterminator's latest visit seemed to have warded off the enemy for now. At least Zoey could enjoy the evening with Jade not having to face the sure probability of meeting a repulsive arthropod when she returned home.

"So where are we going first?" asked Zoey.

"A rarely available condo with soaring views in the prime Lincoln Center area. Two master bedrooms, two and a half baths, just reduced to two and a half million."

"Million?" Zoey's jaw dropped. "Oh my God! Is that your price range?"

"No, but I need to check this place out for a client, and since we're going to be in the neighborhood looking at a fourth-floor one-bedroom walk-up with a limited view and a nonworking fireplace, I figured we could drool and dream."

Glancing out the window, Zoey noticed a man following his leashed cocker spaniel into an apartment lobby of beveled glass. Beside it a brownstone with a cherry red door had a light on in the front room, illuminating a baby grand piano. "I've always wondered what it was like inside other people's homes, other people's lives," said Zoey. Even as a kid, whenever she'd traveled long distances with her parents, for summer vacations to the cool, friendly lakes of Michigan where her father grew up, or to Florida to visit the grandparents, Zoey had studied every passing house, wishing for x-ray vision into the internal workings of each home. What emotions ruled those places where women hung wash in the yards and men mowed lawns and children circled the block on bicycles and in wagons?

"Trust me," Jade said, taking a ten-dollar bill out of her purse, "it's never as pleasant as you imagine it to be. Even some of the wealthiest people let their places go. Doris Duke had a penthouse with cranky old air conditioners hanging in the windows. And you'd be amazed at the worn carpeting and peeling paint in some celebrities' homes. People can be such pigs." She leaned forward and told the driver, "You can let us out on the right-hand corner here."

The Lincoln Center condo did indeed have a soaring view, but the unfinished apartment was so sterile with its stucco ceiling, bare white walls, and gray, commercial-carpeted floors. Zoey couldn't imagine feeling at home here, nestling on the couch to finish reading a novel or sipping coffee in the morning sunshine.

By contrast, the fourth-floor walk-up was a glorified closet.

"This was probably a maid's quarters in the eighteen hundreds, before the building was divided into apartments," Jade said as she walked through the small rooms quickly, dismissing it immediately. "I had a feeling from the listing, but none of the other agents had taken a look at this place." She held the door for Zoey. "Chop chop. We've got a few more to squeeze in tonight."

Next was a Fifth Avenue duplex divided into two apartments. The bathrooms were brand-new, with shiny gold fixtures and speckled blue tiles, but Jade found the rooms to be too small and boxy. A two-bedroom condo across town at the United Nations Plaza had "all the charm of a college dormitory," as Jade put it, grimacing over the questionable odor coming from the kitchen.

Downtown, Jade immediately dismissed a Tribeca loft and a Chelsea basement with exposed brick as "havens for aging hippies."

The varied dimensions and views and locations became a blur in her mind as Zoey rubbed her temples and sat on the window seat of the basement apartment. Instead of the cozy nooks and inspiring views of her expectations she'd been assaulted by hideous wallpaper, leaky windows, and odd smells. "Compared to the listings, everything is so disappointing," she told Jade. "Call me an optimist, but I just expected more."

"You are definitely an optimist, but I won't hold it against you." Jade tugged at Zoey's hand to raise her from the window seat. "Back on your feet. We've got one more space to check out, this one for a client of mine."

"I need food," Zoey complained. "Nachos. Shrimp. Cosmos. Margaritas."

"Delay gratification," Jade ordered. "It's not far from here. We can walk. Then I'll buy you dinner at Vermillion. Mouse is working tonight."

"Okay," Zoey said, "but just one more."

Jade enjoyed the click of her heels as she led Zoey into the paneled cherrywood lobby of the Chelsea building. Gorgeous Prada heels and Isaac Mizrahi mules and snake-embossed leather pumps and sexy slingbacks had been a part of Jade's identity since the day she started showing apartments. The sound of her own footsteps on tile or parquet reminded her of her power, her control of any space she ventured into. Jade loved her job, though she hadn't imagined that this would be her calling when she'd been temping for a realtor twelve years ago. After all, few little girls dreamed of multiple listings and commissions. And as her mother always reminded her, "What can you do with a sociology major in this day and age? Sociology? What—social work? I can't see it, Bubalah."

Nor could Jade.

The doorman gave them the key, and they rode up to the twelfth floor in a wood-paneled elevator with gleaming brass rails. "This will just take a minute," Jade said, turning the key. "I've got a client from L.A. who wants to be bicoastal but keeps holding out for the perfect match. Sort of your theory of romance if you applied it to apartment hunting."

"I hope he's luckier than I am," said Zoey.

Jade pushed the door open and felt a rush. Above her the gold-leafed dome of the entry beckoned, majestic, welcoming, soothing. "Wow. I didn't expect anything this elaborate in this building." Stepping inside was like entering another world. A circular staircase led up to a windowed haven lined by wood banisters. The living room had a working fireplace with blue and white tiles imported from the Netherlands. Warm, smooth shelves of African mahogany lined the walls of the library. The kitchen had been recently renovated with pearwood cabinets and stainless appliances. There were parquet floors, two master bedrooms that felt both cozy and luxurious, and details, details, details, like crown moldings and beveled windows and airy skylights.

"Now this is nice," Zoey said, touching a leather-tooled book in the library. "It's one of those places that feels like home the first time you visit."

"It's lovely." Jade measured her footsteps across the Chinese rug, remembering a room so similar from her childhood. "It reminds me of my grandfather's study in Boston. My parents were fools to sell the place, but by the time my grandfather passed away my father was deeply enmeshed in the business here." Funny how the smell of lemon wax and pipe tobacco could bring back so many memories. As a child Jade had listened to Grandfather's outlandish stories seated on an Oriental rug like this one. She had napped on a couch by the fire and had tea parties with her grandmother using tiny demitasse cups with rosebuds. "If I had three million, I'd buy it myself."

And she meant it. This place had strong vibrations, something Jade didn't usually find. Well, good for her L.A. client, tough luck for her. "Let's go get some dinner," she told Zoey. With a wistful good-bye, she closed the door and locked it.

Club Vermillion wasn't too crowded yet, and Mouse was able to clear a corner of the bar for their impromptu dinner of nachos, cocktail shrimp, and Caesar salads. In between courses, while Zoey told Mouse all about the apartments they'd seen, Jade slipped off to the ladies' lounge to call a few clients and make appointments for the next day.

Then she paged Mr. Takiyama—again. She had been paging him once a day since their last meeting, a poignant session of sex that had lasted from night until dawn. In the morning Taki had tried to end the relationship, admitting that his wife was coming from Japan.

"That doesn't matter to me," she had told him, relaxed and sated.

But he had simply bowed, then turned and let himself out of her apartment.

Oooh, he was ruining her life, spoiling her disposition. She'd thought that apartment hunting would get her back on track again, remind her that every day was a new start, every man a new prospect, but so far it wasn't working.

Checking her cell phone to make sure it was on, Jade cursed him again. He had to call her back. She couldn't lose Taki. Not that she wanted him, per se, but the sex was so amazing. Trudging back to the bar, she bit her lower lip.

"What's up with you?" Mouse asked from across the bar as she poured two fresh Cosmopolitans in y-shaped glasses.

Jade sat on the stool and lifted her chin. "Nothing. Absolutely nothing." She wasn't ready to air her problems, certainly not here in the open forum of a twenty-something dance club.

"Don't worry," Mouse said. "You'll find an apartment eventually. God, you'll actually get the first look, being the broker and all. You've got an edge over the competition." Mouse dropped the shaker into the sink and moved down the bar to a large party of girls.

"Looks like Ladies' Night," Zoey said, pushing her hair over one shoulder.

Jade tried to mutter an answer, but her voice was caught in her throat, caught over the feeling of panic that swelled there. Oh, God, she hadn't felt this way for years. What was happening to her?

He's just a man, just a man. And you don't love him or find him devastatingly good-looking. It's all about sex, and you can have sex with anyone.

Anyone. So why did she miss him so much? Why did she worry that she would never feel really good—truly satisfied, totally fulfilled—again?

"Jade?" Zoey swung around and looked her in the eye. "Oh, whoa. Something is wrong. What is it?"

Somehow Zoey's concern made Jade's emotions sharper,

stronger, and before she realized what was happening a wave of despair swept over her.

"I . . . I can't . . ." Jade felt tears well in her eyes as the sobs rocked her. "It's just that, I have this terrible feeling that . . . that my life is over."

18

The sight of Jade, her red face bowed beneath a curtain of silky black hair to hide the fact that she was whimpering at the Vermillion bar with its backdrop of flickering lights, raucous dancers, and clubby brats struck Zoey as totally incongruous.

Jade never cried. Breakups with guys didn't really bother her, usually because she was the one initiating the split, and with the help of a trust fund from her grandparents Jade didn't even have to sweat paying the rent. Thinking back to college days, Zoey remembered the pregnancy tests and the AIDS scares and the time their apartment had been robbed, all of which Jade had faced with total composure bordering on callousness.

"Oh, Jade . . ." Zoey put her hand on Jade's back and rubbed between the shoulder blades. She honestly didn't have a clue as to why Jade was so upset, which was probably testimony to her total absorption in her own problems. Jade was falling apart before her eyes. "It's okay, really. Whatever is going on, it's . . . it's okay."

"It's not," Jade whimpered, dark tears of mascara running down her cheeks.

Zoey handed her a cocktail napkin. "Am I an idiot or what? So wrapped up in my own shit. I didn't know you were feeling this way."

"It's all about Taki," Jade said, dabbing at her cheeks. "He broke it off, but I can't let him go, and that scares me." She shook her head. "What am I becoming, a stalker? The man wants out but I'm afraid to let him go. And it's not that I love him or anything. It's all about sex."

"This is the tantric sex guy?"

Jade nodded.

"He's that good?"

Jade nodded again as fresh tears rolled down her cheeks.

"Okay, okay, wait." Zoey held up her hands, trying to get a grip on the situation. "Let's think about this. Didn't you say that he's kind of skinny? Skinny and aloof? Sounds like that philosophy professor we used to have."

Jade laughed through her tears. "I didn't say it made sense."

"No, no, that's okay," Zoey insisted. "I'm just wondering if there are other guys out there who know the same rodeo tricks in bed. I mean, I don't know much about tantric sex—just what I've read about celebrity couples who tried it and liked it. Isn't it a three-day ritual? You have to wait three days to come?"

"Three days would never fly in New York, but yes, it's slow and meditative . . . and incredibly satisfying. He spent like an hour just focusing on me, touching me. My yoni, he called it." Jade looked up, tears sparkling in her eyes. "I know you guys think I'm on the slutty side—"

"No, really—"

"It's okay, because I've always felt comfortable with my own actions." She sat up straight, lifting her chin. "I like sex, Zoey, and there's nothing wrong with that. But this obsession with one man scares me. Not that I even want him. I want sex with him. Oh, God, is this how stalkers start out?"

"No, no, you're not a slut and you're not a stalker. My feeling is that you're focusing on the wrong aspect of this new . . . interest, for lack of a better word. You're trying to get the man, but it seems to me that it's not so much him but this new method of sex that really interests you. And that's what you need to pursue. Research it. Take a class or hit the bookstore or join an I-Love-Tantric-Sex support group."

Jade's head tilted to the side. "I guess I could try that."

Zoey handed Jade her drink. "And think about it this way: once you research it, you can become a teacher to every guy you have sex with. Think about it. If you become the tantric sex expert, that's something you can take into every relationship. You can train men to be better sex partners. Jade, you can become the Tantric Sex Guru of Manhattan." She lifted her drink in a toast. "Whaddaya think?"

Jade sniffed. "I like it." She touched her glass to Zoey's, then downed her Cosmopolitan in one long sip.

Sipping her own drink, Zoey hoped she'd given her friend responsible advice. "You know, I should look into tantric sex myself. Not that I'm ever going to have any form of sex again in my life, but it could make for good material."

"I'll let you know what I turn up," Jade said. She tossed the crumpled napkin on the bar and slid off her stool. "Be right back."

As Jade headed off to the ladies' room, Zoey stared blankly over the crowd. A few couples were kissing. A guy seemed to be arguing with Elvis, and a group of girls stood off to the side of the dance floor, looking like a line of dateless debs at the prom. Zoey's eyes returned to the couples, who would no doubt be having sex before dawn. She'd always considered herself to be prudent, but maybe she was downright repressed. Most of the people in this room were probably getting regular sex. Some of them might already be into the pain of sado-masochism or the wonders of tantric sex.

"You are so naive," she said to herself as Mouse returned.

"Where's Jade?" Mouse asked.

"Making some calls." Zoey reached for her bag and dug inside for a pen. A story idea was forming, and she didn't want to lose it.

"Want another round?"

"Sure." As Mouse cleared the drinks, Zoey turned over a cocktail napkin and wrote

Tantric Sex—Main characters driven by sex
Sex as a basic need, like food, oxygen
People have sex, you moron!
(Just not you)

"What's that?" Mouse asked.

"Some notes for a book." I hope, thought Zoey.

"Really? How's the writing going?"

"It's not, not really. But I figure, any day . . ." Zoey swung her arm out, like a jet taking off. "Breakthrough. It's going to happen. It's got to."

"I read a case study once about an artist who completely lost it. He couldn't even pick up a brush again, he was so blocked."

"And?" Zoey prodded, hoping for a happy ending.

"Oh, that was the end of his career," Mouse said, dropping a scoop of ice into the shaker. "Or maybe he was the one who switched hands." She pointed a blue-polished fingernail at Zoey. "That's it. He picked up the brush with his other hand and started painting beautifully. And I think this guy was famous. Maybe it was Michelangelo?"

"Uh-huh." Zoey shoved the napkin into her pocket, still contemplating the issue of sex. Everyone did it. So why couldn't she write about it?

19

Two weeks later, Zoey had almost two hundred pages of a lusty, musky relationship between a blind woman and her neighbor, a skilled physical therapist. The woman, a former concert pianist named Armine Nakashian who had always defined herself by her voracious sexual appetite, had lost her sight in a tragic car accident, which had immediately sent her into hiding in her Brooklyn apartment. Enter Quinn Carroll, an earnest young physical therapist who'd recently returned to take care of his ailing mother after a teaching stint at the University of Kansas. Quinn starts visiting Armine, both to help her learn to cope with her blindness and to escape the tedium of his mother's world.

There's something here, Zoey thought as she scrolled through the file. Each page was laced with the physical chemistry between Armine and Quinn. Of course, there were a few glaring gaps, starting from page five. So far there were a lot of intense cravings and therapeutic touching, leading up to sex scenes that were to be filled in later. Yes, many steamy, erotic scenes were in order. Yes, indeed, something far more graphic than the sweet intellectual romance she had worked into the conclusion of *His Daughter's Keeper.* But every time she tried to write a sex scene, the censors in her head kept hitting the delete button.

What if Mom decided to read this, which she inevitably would. How would Mom handle it with her book club in Boca?

And what about the nuns and the parish priests back at St. Rose of Lima, where Zoey had attended Catholic school? Okay, the nuns had all retired or passed away, but there were still a few nice Catholic girls from eighth grade whom Zoey kept in touch with, and many of them had young children. Think of the aunts and uncles at family reunions, Bobby the doorman's kids, the creepy men bound to look up your name in the phone book to read choice passages to you over the phone.

So Zoey had left a series of stars where each love scene should be and continued on with the emotional story of these characters. The writing was going so well she didn't want to stop, but after a solid week of work punctuated only by Starbucks runs, take-out deliveries, and the polite, methodic noise of Scott at work, Zoey couldn't put Mouse off any longer. Especially when the order came in Mouse's subtle shorthand: "Get your ass dressed and get uptown."

She met Mouse for a late lunch at the Vinyl Diner on West 54th, just uptown from the theater district where Mouse was auditioning for an off-Broadway show. Mouse got there first. Probably not a good sign, thought Zoey, as Mouse waved from a booth in the center island of the restaurant. Some ambitious waiter had opened the windows, no doubt hoping for an early spring, and the April afternoon sun cast its lazy yellow glow over a few of the stained-glass tables. Unfortunately the wind was whipping in, making the napkins flap under the forks as Zoey leaned over the table to Mouse.

"Look at you! Your hair is beautiful . . . like Rapunzel."

Today Mouse's hair was styled in long, luxuriant curls angled down over her shoulders. She struck a princess pose, her long curls bouncing. "Hair extensions. Five hundred dollars and about five hours in the chair for this one."

"Well, I'm sure it turned heads at the audition. How did it go?" Zoey asked, sliding into the booth. "Did you knock 'em dead?"

"Those guys were dead long before I got there," Mouse said. "The part was all wrong for me, and the casting people barely looked up from contemplating their navels to check me out, but that's all my agent's fault. He shouldn't be wasting my time sending me out for parts I'm never going to get. I have half a mind to fire him right now."

"But he did get you the part in *Sound of Music,*" Zoey pointed out. "And it's been such a dry season on Broadway. What, with only four new musicals opening before the Tony season ends?"

"Someone's been reading the *Times.*"

"Religiously." Zoey flipped open the old album cover containing her menu. She had a Linda Ronstadt, Mouse had Elton John's "Yellow Brick Road." "So what's good here?"

"Pretty much everything. And right now it fits my budget, since I haven't been on stage since February." Mouse tossed her head and silky hair cascaded over one shoulder. "I don't know, Ms. Zoey, I just don't know. I'm trying to get my taxes done, and it looks like almost half of my income is from waitressing. And this was a good year. You know that space on your tax return that says 'Occupation'? Pretty soon I'm going to tell my accountant to change it from 'actress' to 'waitress,' because that's what I'm going to be."

"Oh, Mouse . . ." Zoey hesitated, not sure whether she should play her usual role of cheerleader or just commiserate and validate Mouse's feelings. "It's been bad before, right? Everybody has dry spells. Look at me. How many weeks did that writer's block last when I wasn't able to write my way out of a closet? It happens."

Mouse looked up, as if the answer were dangling from the art deco chandelier on the ceiling. "It's just that it's easier to endure a dry spell when you're twenty-five, and you can explain it away by saying that your talent hasn't been discovered yet. Then you get discovered and a couple of dynamite reviews, but nobody has parts for you. Then you get a few roles, but they're secondary parts or a stint as one of the chorus kids. Then you hit thirty and people give you this look like, 'When the hell are you going to figure out that if you haven't made it by now, it's not happening for you?'"

"You know you're talented," Zoey said. "Nobody's got a voice like you. A real stage voice that can blow people right out of their seats."

"It's a gift from God, and I know He blessed me with a purpose in mind," Mouse said. "But sometimes He throws a lot of shit my way, too. Not that I'm complaining."

"God forbid." Zoey lifted her menu. "We never complain." Although they were joking, Zoey was aware of the underlying sense of defeat in Mouse's tone. Once again she wondered what it would take for Mouse to get the break she needed, the role that would boost her into prominence, higher paying roles, frequent roles, and a rooftop garden penthouse on the Upper West Side. There was no doubt about the scope of Mouse's talents. She'd been born with a face that could telegraph emotions across Times Square at rush hour, a voice that was rich, booming, and sassy. And the girl had been blessed with natural beauty, body and soul.

So why wasn't her phone bleeping with constant calls from producers and casting agents? Zoey wasn't sure. A reviewer had once said that Mouse had "the voice of a vixen with the body of a debutante," something that stuck in Zoey's head and left her wondering if that was Mouse's problem: Was her petite, girlish physique incongruous with her mature, sensuous voice?

Zoey ordered Butternut Squash Soup and the quesadilla of the day, while Mouse got Chickpea Curry with Tofu. The soup was warm and rich, and Zoey wondered if she was doing herself a disservice dining on low-fat muffins, fruit, and take-out Thai. Her creativity could only benefit from a more diverse diet, not to mention the sheer act of getting out, striking a new path up a street she rarely traveled and just observing New Yorkers as they hurried through their busy lives.

"I really need to get out more," Zoey said.

"I'll say. We haven't seen you at Club Vermillion for weeks.

Jade thinks you're depressed. Merlin says you're licking your wounds."

"Maybe a little of both, though it hasn't been that long, Mouse." Zoey leaned back and shivered as the waiter started closing windows. It was one of those in-between days, too warm for her shearling, too cold for the white cable-knit sweater she wore over her black cashmere sweater and jeans. "Honestly, I've been working, strong and steadily. I told you that the early-morning carpenters were replaced, right? But the guy who replaced them has been really great for me. Quiet and considerate. He works around my schedule, and sometimes he even brings me coffee."

"He brings you coffee?" The corner of Mouse's lips lifted in a wicked grin. "That sounds highly suspicious. Tell me he's attractive and I'll understand why you haven't left the apartment for days."

"He's gorgeous," Zoey said, thinking of her last view of Scott as she'd left the apartment today, his tool belt slung around his lean hips like a carpenter-cowboy, his blue eyes flashing from behind safety goggles, his biceps straining against his T-shirt as he reached into the ceiling. "I'm glad you're getting out today," he'd told her, "because I've got to cut out a lot of this drywall and it's bound to be messy." At the start of the job he had set up some sort of air-filtering machine, and he often used a fan pointed toward the window to suck out dust-filled air. Every morning he set up drop cloths in his work area, and every night he folded them up, leaving the apartment neat and very habitable. Yes, Scott was the ideal worker to have around, considerate, cheerful, and oh-so-fun to watch.

Mouse smiled smugly as she chewed a mouthful of curried tofu. "Well, that explains it. No wonder you've become a hermit. How long has this been going on?"

"He's been working for a little more than two weeks, but it's not what you think. He's married, so that kind of relationship is out. But I do like watching him work. In his goggles and coated gloves, with the miter box and nail gun and table saw and tape measure . . ." The way he worked with such precision, cutting wedges to hold things in place and nailing up perfectly shaped, smooth pieces of Sheetrock to cover the ceiling, as if he were filling in the pieces of a complicated jigsaw puzzle.

"Really?" Mouse seemed surprised. "Who knew a hammer could be so sexy? I'll have to watch more carefully next time the cable guy comes around."

"Okay, maybe it says more about my sex life or lack thereof, but I do like to watch him. And we talk. Not much, but every day there's a little conversation about the weather or the most recent annoying thing the mayor's done or the skyrocketing price of fuel and the diminishing polar ice caps. Sometimes he talks about his kids, and twice he left early to see them in a school show or take them to the doctor. He never asks about my writing, which is great, and I don't ask about what he's doing and why Carlos took so long to accomplish nothing, since it's not my apartment."

"Which reminds me," Mouse said, her fork poised in the air, "how *is* the writing going?"

"Actually, it's rolling along, which is hard to believe since I feel like I spend so much of my time watching Scott. But he's been good for me. Having him around keeps me on my toes." Zoey chewed on a wedge of spinach quesadilla, recalling one afternoon at the computer while Scott was working out in the hall. She'd kept stealing looks at him, then finally gave up writing to watch as he'd worked on the ladder, his abdomen curving as he curled down to reach for nails or screws or something. The hair on his arms was smooth and pale, catching the light from outside. And his hands . . .

"His hands are fascinating," she told Mouse. "Really strong, but not covered with the calluses and scars I'd expect. His fingers are long and tapered, and sometimes he wears these cool gloves with the fingers covered in tacky green plastic. The way his fingers move, gently circling a high hat or bracing a piece of lumber." She laughed. "I like watching him, and I think he might enjoy the attention, too. It's a little flattering. Friendly flirting, that's all."

"Mm-hhm." Mouse cocked an eyebrow, teasing, "You definitely need to get out more. And if you're looking for a quick thrill, they're doing construction on the next block. A whole army of men in hard hats with heavy machinery, cranes and riveters and metal beams. Hell, with tools like that you'll be turned on for hours."

Zoey laughed.

"Maybe I'll go check them out with you," Mouse said. "It's been awhile."

"Whatever happened to Shane?" Over the years Mouse had been seeing a record producer with a slow, easy smile and a totally nocturnal lifestyle. They had met when Mouse was tending bar at the Underground, and for awhile Mouse had enjoyed stealing moments to talk with Shane while she worked the bar, then spending the early morning hours talking and rolling in bed with him.

"His old lady reeled him in. I think he's back with his wife and kids for good."

"That's too bad."

"Naw, Shane was sexy in a rubber-band man sort of way, but that was going nowhere. He was on the run from reality, and I always knew I'd want more someday. Well, someday is here, isn't it?"

"It is," Zoey said definitively. "Let's go do something totally impulsive. We can sign up for a health club and get the free yoga class, then cancel our membership."

Mouse pulled a cluster of curls over one shoulder. "This is not health club hair, honey. This is 'Go on the Dave Letterman Show and break into song' hair."

She knew Mouse was kidding, but it did seem like a fun idea. "Let's see if we can get tickets! He's only a few blocks from here and he tapes this time of day, right?" Zoey read the check, then reached into her jeans pocket for a twenty-dollar bill. Why did everything in the world seem to cost twenty dollars these days? Dinner, lunch, dry cleaning. Put twenty on your subway card and you get a bonus. Give the cabdriver or the kid making your cappuccino a twenty and you seemed to get a quarter back. At this rate the source of the twenties was going to dry up fairly soon.

"Now that's a little higher on the 'wild' barometer," Mouse

said, sliding out of the booth. Under her bronze cable-knit tank sweater she wore shiny leopard-print spandex leggings that looked sexy without being sleazy. Zoey had always marveled at how Mouse could give class to the K-Mart special of the week: take the same outfit that could get a tourist from Cleveland kicked out of the Four Seasons, put it on Mouse, and she would sparkle as an usher at the Tony Awards or a featured performer at a gala event in Bryant Park.

Walking along 54th Street they passed a noisy construction site, and Mouse teased Zoey mercilessly for two blocks until they spotted the blue and yellow marquis on Broadway. "Let's find out where the studio audience lines up," Mouse said, heading for one of the doors.

The audience was already seated, but an usher told Mouse that they could get in line and hope for a standby seat. "Standby? It's like flying to L.A.," Mouse told Zoey, and they decided to keep moving.

"Let's just walk," Zoey said, pulling the sleeves of her sweater over her hands. She wanted to get back to work, but she sensed that Mouse needed a little lift. She knew Mouse would get a charge out of cutting through the lobbies and roaming the halls of some of the Rockefeller buildings that housed studios. Lots of news shows and morning talk shows were filmed there. Sometimes the mere ambience of a place so steeped in history and energy was inspiring—not to mention the probability of running into a celebrity or two.

"Your hair *is* stunning and you should be seen around town," Zoey insisted. "Sometimes we forget that we're in the hub of everything. Theater and television, and lately they're making so many films here, too. I say we head over to Rock Center and soak up some of the communications vibrations."

Cocking her head to the side so that her hair dangled demurely, Mouse smiled. "Suddenly I'm remembering why we're girlfriends, girlfriend." She put on her sunglasses and walked down Broadway, shoulder to shoulder with Zoey.

Here we are, two chicks in Manhattan, walking through midtown in the chill of fake spring, Zoey thought as the wind whirled a newspaper past their boots. She glanced up at the clear blue sky, a tiny patch between spiring buildings, and realized the power of the city.

"I love this city," she told Mouse, still gazing up like a tourist. "It holds us together, all of us, when we fail and when we succeed."

"That's beautiful," Mouse said, steering Zoey away from a turning cab. "Even though I don't know what the hell you're talking about."

Part Two

Hello, Big O!

20

"How did I get myself sucked into this?" Zoey asked aloud as she glanced at Skye's bedside clock. Five-thirty, and she was supposed to be uptown at the Metropolitan Museum by seven. She shoved a chewed pencil back in her mouth and dug her fingers into her hair, which was coming loose from its chopstick bun. She needed a shower, she needed something to wear . . . and she needed to finish this damned thing.

Zoey's fingers tapped the computer keys rapidly.

It had been such a productive day. She'd discovered a few endearing qualities in her characters and a plot thread that provided some impetus for Armine's withdrawal from society . . . all in one day. Her new manuscript, *Pleasure Points,* was coming together, despite the many holes that would be love scenes, and she was eager to get the entire first draft off to Skye. Zoey bit her lip when she thought of Skye, who was expecting only an outline and would be thrilled to see how much more Zoey had accomplished away from Nick's stifling stranglehold.

She had to get this out.

But Mouse was performing a few songs tonight at this fundraiser, and she had finagled free tickets for all the friends. Even Merlin and Josh were coming. How could Zoey not show?

The phone rang, and Zoey grabbed it with her right hand while her left continued typing. "Hello?"

"I hope you're on your way out the door," Mouse said.

"Any minute. But I got held up today by—"

"Don't even think about weaseling out," Mouse interrupted. "Be there by seven, otherwise the good appetizers disappear." The line clicked off.

"Well, that solves that. Hold that thought," Zoey told Armine the character as she clicked on the "Save" icon, then rolled off the bed. Out in the living room Scott was working with hammer and saw, the sounds of the tools a rhythmic backdrop to her work. Zoey usually didn't shower while he was here, but she always felt she needed that extra edge before a formal event—the shower, the midday tooth brushing and gargle—all the ablutions to wipe away any trace of real human odor. Inside Skye's walk-in closet she pulled the door closed and quickly stripped off her jeans and NYU sweatshirt, and socks. Pulling on her short white terry robe, she belted it at the waist and skidded out the door.

You can go to the benefit and have fun with your friends, she told herself, feeling like her own fairy godmother. But keep your characters in your head. Carry them with you and let them speak to you. When you sit at the computer tomorrow, their words will still be in your fingertips.

Reciting her new creed, she padded down the hall and into the bathroom. What would Mouse be singing tonight? Had Josh agreed to marry Merlin yet? And she wondered if Jade had made any progress on her sex research. . . .

Her mind was elsewhere as she hit the light switch, stepped up to the sink . . . and backed away with a frenzied shriek.

Adrenaline shot through her veins as she backed into the door, the knob poking her in the ribs. Her heart pounded in her ears, pounding, pounding. . . . "Oh, God!"

"What is it?" Scott paused beside her, touching her shoulder gently. Then he followed Zoey's gaze to the insect. "Little bastard," he said, closing in on it.

Backing out into the hall, Zoey heard a slam, then the toilet was flushing. The water was running in the sink, and she peeked in to see Scott leaning forward to wash his hands, his broad shoulders so capable in light of his heroic act. She eyed the tool belt that was slung low on his hips, wondering which implement had finished off the insect.

She swallowed, barely able to find her voice. "I have this . . . this thing about insects."

"Can't blame you." He turned off the water and wiped his hands on Skye's gray and burgundy art deco towels. "Those things are monsters."

Zoey held her hands to her temples as the adrenaline rush evened out.

"Are you okay?" He touched her shoulders. "You look like you're going to pass out."

Her hands slid down over his arms as she swayed against him. No, she wasn't going to faint but was only trying to get her bearings, and somehow it helped to hold on to Scott's arms. But her terry robe was falling open at the top, the belt slipping down. His eyes passed down from her face, over her neck and lower. And before she knew what was happening he was pushing her robe completely open and gently cupping one breast.

"Oooh!" she sucked air in through her teeth, feeling a thrill at his touch.

His eyes studied her face again, searching for an answer.

Yes, she thought, pressing her body against him. Yes. She couldn't speak but leaned forward to kiss him, and his mouth felt soft and moist. He nipped at her lips gently, then pressed his tongue into her mouth. She moaned, loving the feeling of his body against hers. His chest was as hard as she'd always imagined, solid and sweet-smelling, like a baby's fabric softener.

And his hands elicited tingling cravings as he smoothed the skin of her shoulders, the curve of her breasts, her taut nipples. "Oh . . ." she moaned, giving herself up to the incredible sensations.

He slid his hands around her waist and hoisted her onto his body. She straddled him and locked her knees around him, tool belt and all, and she sort of liked the way his leather nail pouch pushed up into her thigh. Feeling as if she were disembodied and watching the whole scene, she heard herself moan as he carried her into the bedroom. How could she want him so much? How could it be . . . a guy she barely knew?

It doesn't matter, came the answer as he placed her on the bed and unfastened his tool belt. He's a man and you're a woman and this is how the sex thing goes. People have sex, a hell of a lot more often than you do, and if it's just this one time and you want him so much and he obviously wants you. . . .

Oh, turn the damn censors off and go for it.

His belt and boots and pants were off, and Zoey stared respectfully at his erect penis. He was bigger than Nick and pinker, too, and at the moment he was sliding on a condom that was even pinker—a sort of marbelized hot pink.

"Don't worry," he said, "it's ribbed and flavored."

"Flavored?" She blinked. Before this moment she wasn't even aware that such things existed. She slid off the bed, her robe falling completely open as she knelt in front of him and licked his cock. He groaned, pulling up his T-shirt to watch her.

"That's it," he whispered. "Take a taste, baby."

"Mmm. Raspberry." She actually liked licking him, not feeling any sense of obligation. She pulled the head into her mouth, making him groan. One hand wrapped around his hips to his buttocks, smooth and hairless, and she let her fingers take hold. The cheeks were firm, tensing even more as she touched him, and she loved the feeling of control as she held him steady with one hand while her head dipped down and up, her lips and cupped hand caressing him.

He pushed back her terry robe and she felt a tickle as it dropped off her shoulders, dangling from her elbows. "That's it," he said, stroking her shoulders. "Gotta feel good." His hands— his beautiful, strong hands—ran over her shoulders, down her back, then over her shoulders again to her breasts, massaging her as if she were a fine piece of lumber ready for refinishing. She couldn't take it anymore.

She lifted her head and kissed his hip bone. "I have to," she whispered, letting her robe drop to the floor. "I have to have you inside me."

Suddenly he grabbed her under the arms and lifted her off the floor. "Whoo," she gasped, smiling as he placed her on the bed and leaned over her. She was ready for him, hot and wet, dripping wet. The feel of his taut genitalia rubbing against hers was excruciatingly delicious. She wanted to laugh, amazed and proud that she could feel so open to a man she barely knew.

"Come on," he said, moving his hips, searching for her opening. "Let's do it."

"Let's," she said, lifting her legs and clamping her feet over his butt.

At last, he found his way in. Zoey groaned as he slid inside her, filling her so completely. She began to close her eyes, then opened them, wanting to see the passion and pleasure on Scott's face as he rocked her hard, deep, and steady.

Oh, so steady.

21

"You're late because you fucked the carpenter?" Mouse's voluminous voice echoed through one of the gothic-styled vestibules of the Metropolitan Museum of Art.

Zoey winced, imagining the entire party stopping—wineglasses poised in the air, ensemble musicians frozen, revelers silent and waiting for the naughty girl's answer to that even naughtier "F" word. But when she opened her eyes, the party was flowing as usual, a new line of patrons pushing into the hors d'oeuvre table for cocktail shrimp and tiny new potatoes stuffed with sour cream and caviar.

Merlin and Josh began to clap, and it took Zoey a moment to realize they were applauding her.

"Brava!" Josh's eyes were alight with giddiness.

"That's our Zo," Merlin said. "Taking good care of the hired help. I always knew a good working stiff could count on you."

"Did you get to see my songs?" Mouse asked, annoyed at Zoey's nonverbal answer. "I finagle passes to this huge charity event— an event that none of us can come close to affording, by the way—and you miss my performance because you want to play hide the salami with the handyman?"

"Oh, please!" Zoey clasped her hands over her eyes, shielding herself from the party at large. "I don't even know how I feel about this yet and I'm certainly not ready to be the target of your jokes."

Jade dropped a shrimp tail onto a waiter's silver tray, giving him the once-over as he passed by. "Honey, if we have to tell you how to feel, he was doing something wrong."

"No, no, that part felt fine. It's just that he's married and, legally, so am I, and the relationship can't go anywhere." Trying to gather her scattered thoughts, Zoey smoothed down the chemise shoulder of her black dress and grabbed at the diamond heart pendant that dangled over her breasts. The diamond from soon-to-be-ex husband. She squeezed it hard, wondering how much it would bring in if she sold it to a diamond broker. "Not that there's really a relationship between Scott and me," she rambled on. "I mean, we'll never have sex again; it was just a momentary fluke. He saved me from a bug and I was grateful and . . . well, I guess my gratitude got out of control. But it's my Catholic guilt and his family that I'm struggling with."

"Catholic guilt? Really?" Josh seemed intrigued. "When was the last time you went to church?"

Zoey shrugged. "I don't know—the day after my Confirmation? I'm not devout, but it's in there, ingrained on my psyche or my soul. And I was never one to sleep around, even before Nick. I've always been a little conservative when it comes to sex."

Jade grabbed two glasses of white wine from a waiter's tray and handed one to Zoey. "Honey, the Republican Whip is conservative. You are downright prudish."

Zoey put her hands on her hips. "And who just nailed the carpenter?"

Jade waved her off. "Don't even start. The real point is, was he any good?"

All eyes were on Zoey as she considered the question. "We shouldn't even be talking about this." She pressed her lips together and felt the fullness there. Lips still swollen from kisses. Her entire body was still humming, as if the act of lovemaking was an exercise in tuning up an idle instrument. "It's personal."

"Not always," Jade said. "I've had some very public sex and it's just fine. On the beach in Southampton. In the bathroom of a commercial airline. In the reading room at the library."

"You've been inside a library?" Josh feigned amazement. "I didn't think you'd ever read a book, Jade."

"I didn't think you ever remembered my name, Josh," sniped Jade.

Josh blinked, and Merlin put a hand on his shoulder. "All righty, then, let me reintroduce you two," said Merlin. "Josh, you remember Jade, the bitchy one."

"Actually I'd forgotten, but the word bitch brings it all rushing back," Josh said.

"Oh, can it, you queens," Mouse said impatiently. "Let's stop sniping at each other and get the real dirt on Zoey and the handyman." She turned to Zoey. "So how was it? Did you come?"

With the wineglass pressed to her lips, Zoey nearly did a spit-take. She swallowed hard, tried to think of a way to avoid this line of questioning, then realized it was impossible. "Did I? Well, of course. Actually, twice, if you have to know . . ."

Josh and Merlin applauded again, until Zoey glared at them.

Lowering her voice, she continued, ". . . though I think that's far more information than any girl should have to reveal, especially at a public affair."

"Twice. . . ." One hand on the hip of her red Vera Wang gown, Mouse raised her glass thoughtfully. "I used to come twice, even three times, back in the good old days when I had someone to have sex with."

Jade rolled her eyes. "There's always someone around to have sex with; the problem is that you girls always want more than a purely physical relationship. Commitment. Marriage. Mortgage and babies." She turned to Zoey. "Thank God you stopped short of the baby trap. Once you squeeze out one of those little buggers you lose your membership in Party Girls Incorporated. If you had a baby now, you wouldn't . . ." She paused, her blue eyes flashing in interest as she studied Zoey. "Wait a minute." Lifting the jeweled hem of her square-cut ivory gown, she circled Zoey suspiciously.

"What? What is it? Toilet paper on my shoes? Or did someone tape an idiot sign to my backside?"

"There's just something different," Jade said. "A different vibe . . ."

"I know what you mean." Merlin nodded, staring at Zoey with equal intensity. "Our Zoey is a changed woman somehow."

Slyly, Jade took a sip of wine, then smiled. "I know what it is," she sang as if reciting a child's rhyme. "That's the look of contentment. True female satisfaction."

Zoey felt a tingle of embarrassment—or was that residual sensation from the way Scott had played her body? From the first thrust—which alone was somewhat orgasmic for Zoey—they had been in sync, moving and breathing together. She had been aware of his mounting pleasure, and he seemed to sense hers as their rhythm slowed with each tantalizing stroke. She remembered the feel of his soft, warm hands on her shoulders, the press of his solid chest against hers, the swell of pleasure rising up from within her, filling her body with warmth and light and sweetness. . . .

"Look at her, she's blushing," Mouse said of Zoey.

"I was just remembering, thinking back to . . . oh, hell." Zoey tossed back the rest of her wine and handed the empty glass to Josh. "More, please. Lots more, if we're going to keep talking about this stuff. Sober Catholic girls do not discuss sex and orgasms." She turned to her other friends, adding, "If you must know, Scott was great. More than great. The guy totally blew me away." She thought of the surging rush of sensation she'd felt in Scott's arms. "It was never that way with Nick. I mean, I used to come, but—"

"It's called an orgasm," Jade interrupted. "Hello, Big O!"

Her friends laughed, but Zoey felt her face heat up again. She had read magazine articles and stories about people who could discuss their sex lives and sexual needs openly, but she had always considered them to be a different class of people, far removed from her middle-class mores.

The only one who wasn't laughing was Merlin, who'd left Josh's side to stand beside Zoey under the gargoyle-strewn corner post. "It's okay," he said quietly. "It's okay to not want to discuss it. Not everyone is like Jade. And it's okay to do it." When Zoey shook her head, he went on. "Really. Isn't sex a normal, healthy part of life? You have lungs to breathe, a stomach to digest food, and genitalia to bring pleasure. Of course, some people prefer to use them for reproduction, but that's their mistake."

"You're right, you're right, I know you are," Zoey told him. "I guess my head is stuck in that adolescent morality of the pre-Nick days." She shook her head, taking in the finely dressed crowd, candlelit tables, and low conversation around her. "Am I like, the most sexually naive person you've ever met, or what?"

"Well, it's about time you had a walloping rebound relationship," Mouse said. "I'm just sorry you missed my performance. They let me do one of the songs from *Ragtime,* and it really worked."

"She was spectacular," Josh admitted as Mouse gathered her full satin skirt into her white gloves and curtsied.

"Sorry I missed it, Mouse," Zoey said sincerely. "I'll bet you were the best person on stage."

"By far," Jade agreed, toasting Mouse with her glass. As her eyes traveled past Mouse's shoulder, her smile grew. "Don't look now, but I think we have Donald Tarrant, millionaire investor, heading our way."

Zoey turned to glance at the man, who seemed taller and ruddier than his photos in the newspaper.

"I said don't look!" Jade snapped.

"Like he doesn't know he's famous," Mouse said, grabbing a cheese puff. "Like people don't turn to stare at him every day, hoping that he might shake the money tree and let a few bills land in their pockets."

"Hmm." Jade smiled, turning slightly as Tarrant and his entourage of men, one of whom was obviously a public relations person from the fundraising committee, passed by.

"How are you this evening?" Donald Tarrant's teeth glimmered with a brilliance that Zoey was sure came from bleaching.

"Just fine," Jade answered, unofficial spokesperson for their party. "And how are you?" She lowered her head toward his to confide: "How is Anita doing?" Anita Tarrant, a youngish, blondish woman from Palm Springs was confined to bed rest until the birth of the couple's first child.

"She's doing well, thanks for asking," Donald said.

Jade touched Donald's shoulder. "Give her my best, will you?"

"I will, thanks," Donald said, nodding before the PR guy swept him onward.

"I don't believe it!" Mouse was aghast. "You know Donald Tarrant?"

Jade shrugged. "Only what I've read in the papers, but I can bullshit with the best of them." She turned to watch Tarrant's entourage disappear up a staircase. "Too bad he's expecting a child. He'd be a good conquest, but men get so sentimental when their wives are expecting."

"I can't believe you'd even go after a family man," Zoey said.

Everyone turned to look at her.

"Wait a second," Josh said, holding up his hands. "I'm getting confused. Just who gets to wear the scarlet 'A' next?"

Zoey felt her jaw drop. "Okay, guilty," she confessed. "Totally guilty. But it's not going to happen again. Ever. Really!"

22

It happened the next day.

Zoey had decided not to even mention previous day's sexual encounter to Scott, the theory being that they were both swept away with the feelings of the moment and she didn't want him to have to explain himself or apologize. So she greeted him with her usual smile and he asked if she wanted coffee, and he returned with two steaming cups of Starbucks' house blend and they proceeded to do their usual everyday tasks. He went out to the living room to apply tape to the ceiling; she settled in on Skye's bed to get back to the developing relationship between Armine and Quinn.

Everything was business as usual . . . except that Zoey couldn't get down to business. She couldn't stop thinking about Scott.

Leaning over to the bedside table, Zoey grabbed a clip and started twisting her hair up in a knot. Outside, clouds draped the sky like ethereal curtains hung by Zoey's mother-in-law, who insisted on hanging some sort of window dressing over every portal of the world. Well, there were some positive points about saying good-bye to Nick. She wouldn't miss his clinging, stubborn family.

Outside she heard a ripping noise as Scott worked. Sexy Scott. No, scratch that. She scratched her nose, turning back to the screen. Time to settle in and concentrate.

No such luck.

She grabbed her coffee cup and passed through the hall, stealing a glimpse of his lean abs as he reached up to test something on the ceiling. That chest had felt so strong and hot under her palms, that body had felt so good against her bare breasts.

Ooh, stop it! She told herself, ducking into the kitchen, pretending to add more sweetener to her coffee. It was a fluke, a total fluke.

Outside, the scratching noise of the tape stopped. Zoey looked up from stirring her coffee to find Scott standing in the doorway.

He took one step into the kitchen and she dropped the spoon and reached around his waist and pressed her hips against his.

"Mmm." The pleasant moan escaped his lips as she felt the hardness under his jeans. She lifted her chin to kiss him, and his lips felt pleasantly moist. His mouth tasted of coffee as she ran her tongue over his smooth teeth and pulled back.

"Do you want to?" she asked, fairly sure of the answer.

He nodded. "Come on." He grabbed her hand and ran down the hall toward the bedroom, dragging her behind.

"Whoa!" she laughed. "Are we in a hurry?"

"Always." The skin around his eyes crinkled when he smiled, and she cupped his face in her hands for a moment, enjoying the closeness. "I'm always in a hurry to have you."

Zoey was about to point out that he'd only had her once, but he distracted her by sliding his hands under her sweatshirt to cup her breasts. She closed her eyes and sucked in her breath. Here we go again, she thought, but at the moment, with Scott unbuttoning her jeans and peeling off her panties, she couldn't think of a good, solid reason to stop him. Why was today any different from yesterday? It would just be sex—no commitment, no infringement on his karma or his life with his wife and kids.

Just sex . . . delicious, satisfying . . . "Mmm," she moaned as he dipped his fingers into the moisture between her legs. She finished stripping off her clothes while he undressed and put on a condom. This time they stood at the foot of the bed, and Zoey was able to watch Scott's reflection in the mirror.

"Pretty amazing, isn't it?" He moved up behind her and pressed his sex into her.

Intrigued, Zoey watched their reflections in the mirror: lines of silken flesh, his hard butt and sculpted shoulders, her own curved breasts with brownish nipples, like two sensual forms in a nude painting.

"Awesome," she whispered, suddenly realizing why Skye had installed so many mirrors.

Rocking his hips against hers, Scott caressed her breasts, then moved one hand down over her navel and slid it between her legs. She closed her eyes as he stroked her there, driving her wild with swelling sensation.

"No, don't close your eyes," he whispered in her ear. "Look at us. Look at you. I'm stroking you and it's so beautiful."

She turned her head to dart a look in the mirror, and he was right. They were so sexy together, his fingers driving between her legs, disappearing into her. She was awash with sweet sensation.

"Let's try a new pose," he whispered, taking Zoey's hands. He moved her hands forward, bending her over until her arms were resting on Skye's desk. Glancing at the reflection of her smooth butt in the air, Zoey knew what he was going to do, and she was ready.

She watched as he crouched over her and drove himself into her. He held her cheeks in the air with two hands and thrust into her again and again and again. His penis was long and thick, and he moved it in all directions, driving her wild. This time as her cravings increased she felt her abdominal muscles tighten around him, and their passion was reflected in the mirror, a vivid picture of sex.

That's me, Zoey thought, her eyelids drooping with lust as Scott touched her in all the right places. Her hair was falling out of its clip, and a few blond strands hung over her shoulders, covering her face in a demure veil. That's me, she thought, smiling at their reflection in the mirror—his hand following the curve of her breast, her back arched and legs open to take him in—before all conscious thought dissipated in the rising wave of sensation.

When the phone rang an hour later, Zoey was stretched out on the bed in front of the computer, still basking in the afterglow.

"Zoey, it's Skye," came the friendly voice that sent Zoey scrambling to an upright position. "Just wanted to call and see how the new carpenter is?"

"The new carpenter." Did Skye know she was sleeping with him? Zoey felt her face heat up with embarrassment at the thought. Yes, I'm not only using your apartment, I'm seducing your carpenter and screwing him big and bold so that we can watch ourselves in your bedroom mirror.

"Do you think he's someone I can trust?" Skye went on. "It feels kind of out of control, being here while the work is going on, but I really want that mess taken care of before I get back."

"The carpenter . . ." That was when Zoey realized that Skye was talking about Sheetrock and nails. "He's great, really great," Zoey said, twirling a strand of hair around one finger. "He's only been here a few days, but if you want my opinion? He does excellent work. Fast and neat, with lots of attention to detail."

23

"Are you joking?" Merlin's blue eyes glimmered as he lowered his menu to gasp at Zoey. "Four times in four days?"

She nodded, turning her head slightly to see who was sitting in the booth behind them in the coffee shop where they were catching a quick bite before Merlin's shift at the posh hotel across the street. She'd managed to work through some of the guilt, but she still felt uncomfortable advertising that she was having regular sex with a regular guy.

"You have been a busy girl," Merlin said. "And here we thought you were holed up to work on a book. Mouse is so mad that you've been missing the night shift at Vermillion. She seems to think we're obliged to keep her company while she pours navel shooters for the next generation of Young Republicans."

"I have been writing, but somehow I've had time to . . ." she shrugged ". . . to squeeze Scott in."

Merlin laughed. "Good for you. You've found a handy handyman."

"I'll say." Zoey thought back to that morning, when Scott wanted to make love on the floor in front of the living room windows.

The reflection of their naked bodies joined at the hips, together with that of the inspiring spire of the Empire State Building, had made Zoey feel a new sense of power in the act, which was probably enhanced by the fact that she wasn't afraid to take the initiative with Scott. She loved to massage his legs, place a chain of kisses over his chest, lick his ears, his fingers, his cock.

"Hello?" Merlin snapped his fingers. "Have I lost you?"

"Sorry." Zoey took a deep breath, shaking her head. "I can't believe I'm doing this. Pure physical sex."

"Again, you're saying it as if it's something naughty and forbidden. Didn't your mother ever have that talk with you? What's that song? Birds do it, bees do it . . ."

"My mother handed me a pamphlet from the inside of the tampon box. But you are so right about the guilt thing. I just can't get rid of these Victorian notions that sex is wrong before marriage, not to mention the fact that it seems wrong to enjoy it so much with a guy who's a virtual stranger. I don't know. I guess I was born in the wrong century."

"Whatever." Merlin closed his menu. "I'm having a raspberry smoothie and a veggie burger."

"How are the BLTs here?"

"Don't know. I've been a vegetarian for two years."

"When did that happen?"

"I don't know, it just sort of happened." Merlin touched the diamond stud in his ear. "I started liking beans and soy products, and it occurred to me that the slaughter and cooking of meat is so . . . barbaric. Uncivilized."

"I thought civilization was the fact that we cooked our meat," Zoey said, opening a packet of Saltines. "But out of deference to you, I'll get a veggie burger too. I hear bacon is so bad for you."

"And you have to stay in shape for the Olympic Intercourse Event."

Zoey shoved back a strand of stray hair and smiled. "Yeah, I guess I do. Which gives me no transition, so I'll just have to blurt out the reason I've been bugging you to have lunch." She reached across the table and touched Merlin's wrist. "Josh wanted me to talk to you about the partnership agreement." When Merlin rolled his eyes, she hurried on. "I know, I know, and I told him I am the very last person on earth to be giving out relationship advice right now, but he's so persistent. And I know he's crazy about you, and you two do make a great couple. So, why the hesitance? Do you love Josh?"

"There you go again." He pointed a finger at her. "Talking about love as if it's a tangible thing. I'm happy to be with Josh, yes. And I value our relationship, but I look at this whole thing with the same ambivalence most Capricorns feel toward every issue of life. I don't know that I believe in love at all, especially when you talk about falling in or out of it or giving your life for someone because you love them, or letting someone stamp their feet all over you like a doormat. Sometimes I think people mistake their dysfunctions for love—attachment, obsession, dependence."

Zoey nodded, wondering which category she fell under but not wanting to explore it too deeply. "Wow. I never thought of any of that stuff when I married Nick. Maybe I should have."

"Maybe. But it's not in your nature. You are so wrapped up in your own Pisces dreamworld, you don't understand resistance. Josh does. He's got duality in his Gemini personality. And I think my Capricorn is similar to a goat on a leash, always striving to get somewhere but never really moving."

"You are your own worst enemy," Zoey agreed. "Can't you just suck it in and go for it?"

Merlin ran a hand through the gold-tipped crest over his forehead. "I hate to ruin what we have, and I think when you try to put a name on it or proclaim it on an official government form, that overanalysis puts a strain on the relationship. On any relationship."

She nodded again, lifting her hands as the waitress slid the hot plates onto the table. "You're right, as usual. Your hesitance makes perfect sense, and I'm not sure why Josh is so determined to push you into something you clearly don't want." Zoey munched on a sweet-potato chip, then held it in the air. "But on the flip side, I understand Josh's desire to make your relationship real."

"You mean 'institutionalized,' like a deranged killer."

"Deranged though he may be, Josh is in love with you and he wants to make that official in the only way this city knows to do that. What's the big deal about a partnership agreement?"

"It doesn't stop there. He wants a big reception, with flowers and friends and tuxedos and a cake, just like a wedding."

Zoey winced. "Well, forget I said that. But, really, about the commitment—"

"The 'C' word again."

"Just hear me out, because I remember a Merlin who was so hot and intriguing and exotic, he could walk in the bar alone and walk out with any guy there. You were the guy to have at NYU, not just among the students, either. Remember that professor who took you to his house upstate?"

"Boring."

"Exactly. You could have had anyone, and I don't know if you realized how jealous I was at times, but you got bored with each relationship. It was so hard for a lover to . . . engage you before you met Josh. And since then, I don't know, have you even been with anyone else?"

"N-n-not really," Merlin said.

She pointed a chip at him. "Excuse me, but that's like being almost a virgin or kind of pregnant."

He took a bite of his burger, chewing carefully. "There was one time—a short fling with a guest at the hotel. Max Divine."

"No way!" Zoey said over a mouthful of food. "Maniac Max? Is he sexy or what? I didn't even know he was gay."

"Bi, I think. But it was just a short-lived celebrity thing. No, Josh is it for me. As I said, I value our relationship. I just don't want to jeopardize it."

"I understand that, but I think marriage would have the opposite effect. It could make your relationship stronger."

Merlin stared at her as he ate, his thoughts obvious.

"Okay, I'm not the poster child for happy marriages. But I do hate to see you lose Josh over this."

"He'll stick around."

"Okay, then forget we ever had this conversation. I'll tell Josh I did my best, and he'll just have to live in sin with you the rest of his life."

Merlin rolled his eyes. "You and your Catholic guilt."

After lunch Zoey let herself into the quiet apartment and found that Scott had already left for the day. She changed into sweats and jumped onto the bed, determined to write a few pages before depression and Tylenol PM sent her crashing back against the pillows.

Scrolling through the manuscript, she came to a row of stars—the place marked for the love scene—and paused. Maybe she was ready to write this. She started slow, closing her eyes to imagine how Armine would feel as Quinn touched her for the first time, his hand traveling down over her hair to her slender neck, dipping lower beneath her shirt to cup a breast.

Armine's sensual world was fertile territory. Zoey imagined the first touch of warm human flesh, the ticklish burr of a man's chest hairs, the melting power of a man's caress.

Yes . . . she was ready to write these scenes, thanks to Scott. She closed her eyes and sighed again. Yes, many thanks to Scott.

That night after midnight Merlin returned home and pushed his key into the lock. He hoped Josh was asleep. He'd heard people talking about the crash at work, and though he knew there had to be some truth behind so many rumors, he needed to confirm it for himself, alone.

He tossed his blazer aside, loosened his tie and turned on New York 1 for the news. He lowered the volume as commercials flashed by, then the weather. Then the headline news. It was true, a plane carrying Max Divine and his band had gone down, killing the two pilots and the entire band, except for the drummer who had flown home to see his wife.

Max was dead, just like that.

Merlin rubbed his hands together to make fire, then pressed the warm energy in his palms against his face, his tired eyes, the crown of his head. Despite the report he was still in denial, still finding it impossible to believe that Max was dead. How could Max, a man so full of life, a creative, outlandish spirit that had broadcasted itself through music to touch and move spirits all over the world, how could such a spirit die? If there was a God, or a master planner, in the universe, surely he would refuse to extinguish something so beautiful. Reincarnation? Merlin sank back against the cushions of the sofa. He certainly hoped so. It would be wonderful to meet Max's spirit again.

Not that he'd ever expected to have another encounter with Max. Their two days together were somehow enough—enough time to feel Max's passion for life, to block out the demands of the world and worries about the future and live for the moment. To drink and party and laugh and have sex and philosophical conversations about what it all meant to be a speck among millions of specks on a revolving ball of dirt. The sounds of moving sheets in the other room reminded Merlin that Josh didn't know about his affair with Max, and he would be pissed if Merlin spilled it all now. Josh would lash out and throw things and probably threaten to walk out. No, Josh couldn't share his grief, or denial, or whatever he was feeling.

Merlin collapsed against the arm of the sofa. What exactly was he feeling? A sense of loss for the universe. A yearning to catch the disembodied spirit of Max if it was flying in the cosmos somewhere, to jump up and catch that energy like a ballplayer with a fat, webbed mitt. And he also felt a desire to seize the moment and live the way Max had lived, with spontaneity and laughter and impulsiveness.

"Hey," Josh said from the bedroom. He sat on the arm of the sofa, his flannel boxers brushing Merlin's cheek. "You look beat. Why don't you come to bed?" He placed a gentle hand on Merlin's cheek.

Closing his eyes, Merlin pressed his face to Josh's hand and savored the warmth. Josh didn't know what was going on in Merlin's head, yet he knew that Merlin needed him. He was Merlin's partner, his warm sensitivity the perfect complement to Merlin's logical coolness.

What am I waiting for? Merlin thought as he stood up and

pulled Josh into his arms. He had been reluctant to make their relationship final, as if sealing it would paralyze it in stone. Only now he could see that he'd been reluctant to be in the moment, afraid to take the final step with Josh and accept the relationship for what it truly was. A perfect bond.

Merlin hugged Josh close, so tightly that Josh growled, "What are you doing?"

"I don't know," Merlin said happily. "I don't know anything anymore, and that's a good thing."

Josh cocked an eyebrow and said, "Whatever," before he reached up to kiss him.

24

It had been a long day, with two closings and three important clients in need of housing in the three-million-dollar range, and Jade was still in the office long after everyone had left. "It will work out," she told one of the three-million-dollar clients, an actress who was splitting with her actor husband and trying to find a new home for herself and a few children in Manhattan.

"I don't know," the woman said. Emily Turner was known for her chameleon-like voice on screen, and Jade wondered if the woman realized that her real-life speaking voice held a distinctly whiny quality. "I'm just so worried about my kids. They've never lived on the East Coast before and . . ."

Blah, blah, blah, blah, blah. . . . Jade rolled her eyes as she paced through the office with her cell phone. One of the other brokers had a jar of chocolate Kisses on his desk, and she strolled into the office and swiped one while Emily Turner droned on in her ear.

"I know," Jade said, unwrapping the foil. "This is a difficult time for you and the children, but Manhattan is the perfect place to start over, and I know people in admissions in all of the best schools here. . . ."

Sagging in Devlin's chair, Jade allowed herself to succumb to the hopelessness that had been gnawing at her lately. Oh, she'd gotten over the idea of ever seeing Taki again, and she'd taken Zoey's suggestion to pursue her own study of tantric sex. So far the big drawback was the need to teach Taki's technique to another man. While a willing partner for sex was no problem, she needed a partner who was also willing to learn, and so far two men had lost interest completely when she mentioned trying something a little different. One had thought she was trying to make a religious convert out of him; the other was just too damned lazy.

To each his own. Still, Jade was determined to find a student. Actually, she had no choice if she wanted to have awesome sex again.

Taki had really ruined her.

Blah, blah . . . Emily whined as Jade chewed on the chocolate and spun around in Devlin's chair. In her mind, she was saying, "Stop whining!" and, "Get a therapist!" and, "Do you think I care about your emotional stake in Los Angeles?" But she continued to coo as Emily complained.

Devlin had a recent copy of *Forbes* magazine on his desk, and Jade recognized the face of Donald Tarrant on the cover near the subhead, "Billionaires Top Ten List."

Billionaires! Really? Jade opened the magazine to the contents and paged right ahead to the cover story. Donald was on the list, but she had already dismissed him from the running. But what about these others? The article mentioned their marital status—good for starters. Hmm. This was worth looking into. The article included photos: men in sunglasses, fat bellies, greasy hair, goofy looks. Certainly not contenders for a Mr. America contest, but some of them had potential. A haircut at Marcellos and a trip to Brooks Brothers could do wonders for a man.

With magazine in one hand and cell phone shouldered against her ear, Jade headed back to her office and grabbed her briefcase. Might as well grab a bite with Mouse at the club. With any luck, Emily would be through griping by the time she got to Club Vermillion.

Jade was in a cab headed downtown when she felt a surprising compulsion. "Hold on, Emily," she said, then told the cabdriver to continue down Ninth Avenue to Chelsea. "I'm sorry," she told the actress. "But there's a place downtown I wanted to scope out for you tonight," she lied. "Yes, I'm on my way there now."

On my way to Grandpa's library . . . to Grandma's parlor, Jade thought as raindrops zigzagged down the cab's window. She hadn't been back to the Chelsea apartment since her walk-through with Zoey; she didn't have the desire to show it to a client for fear that they'd snatch it up and rob her of her dreams. It was way out of her price range, but she couldn't get it out of her mind. The place haunted her.

What the hell was wrong with her these days? She had never been one to suffer angst in any way, shape, or form. Now it seemed to rear its ugly head in every aspect of her life: dissatis-fied with her home, unfulfilled sexually, totally bored at work.

The doorman gave her the key to 10-G, and Jade let herself into the apartment, slipping off her shoes in the foyer. Again, it was like coming home to a place of warmth and security she hadn't known since her childhood visits to her grandparents' Boston home. Walking through the mahogany-paneled rooms lit by del-icately made brass wall sconces, Jade realized how much she'd missed the feeling of home found only at her grandparents' house. Not once in the rambling garden apartment in Fresh Meadows, Queens, had Jade sensed the same secure feelings: the assurance that she was loved and would always be well-protected, the notion that a comfortable place in the world had been cre-ated for her. With their arguments and curses and grumblings about each other's inadequacies, Enid and Aaron Cohen had had neither the warmth nor the sense of responsibility to make a safe place for their daughter to live.

Protection . . . she'd never had it. But considering her mother's upbringing, that wasn't surprising. Jade had never known her mother's parents, the Falkowskis, who had immigrated to Greenpoint, Brooklyn, from Poland only to die in a car crash on the Long Island Expressway on the way back from dropping their ten-year-old daughter at camp. Mama had said only that they were strict and very old-fashioned, but when Jade tried to get a true reading on them, her mother's eyes seemed cold and vacant, as if she had never really had the chance to get to know her own parents. Or, perhaps, in the interactions she'd had during those first ten years, Enid had not been able to extract enough warmth or reassurance to convince herself that her parents loved her.

As for Jade's father, he seemed to have inherited the worst traits of his parents. In Aaron, their ambition turned to self-absorption, their work ethic devolved into obsession, their persistence to stubbornness. And what was to become of the warm, nurturing qualities of Jade's grandparents? Somehow, they were lost in Aaron Cohen, a man who'd spent most of his time away from home under the guise of working. When he did make an appearance, he expected to be waited upon and indulged by his wife and daughter. Jade remembered one occasion when her mother was off at a meeting and she had been relegated to the role of cook and waitress for dinner. Jade had burned the frozen chicken and spilled applesauce on the dining room rug, and her father had managed to control his usual hot temper, grinding out a comment about what a terrible wife she would be.

A terrible wife, that's me, Jade thought, remembering the incident as she passed through the formal dining room into the kitchen. Well, she'd shown her Dad, hadn't she? Over thirty and not married. There you go, Dad. Once again you were right.

Her parents still lived in Queens, just a cab ride away, though Jade hadn't been there for at least a year. Enid and Aaron were not the most pleasant people to be around, especially for their daughter, who seemed to elicit constant criticism from Aaron, which only made Enid argue with him all the more in Jade's defense.

For years, Jade had been on her own, without a home. Of course, she had her co-op, but it was little more than a place to sleep, have sex, shower, and change clothes. And then she'd walked into this apartment, after touring thousands of apartments in New York City, and for some reason this place cried out to her. She needed a home, a place to wrap around her shoulders and soothe her mind, and this apartment was it, despite its rip-roaring price tag.

The windowed alcove in the kitchen held a built-in booth, and Jade slid onto the patterned chintz banquette, placing her Coach briefcase on the granite tabletop. She pulled out a notepad and pen, and Devlin's *Forbes* magazine slid out. "You lucky bastards," she said, winking at the photos of the billionaires. "Some of us have to work for a living."

She itemized her assets on the notepad: her co-op, her share in the Hamptons summer house, her stock portfolio . . . even her jewels, most of which had been gifts from wealthy boyfriends. When the list was complete, Jade tapped the pencil against the pad and shook her head. First, even if she cashed in the whole list of assets, she wouldn't come close to raising the down payment she needed for this place. And second, she couldn't bear to give up most of the things she loved. After all, she'd worked hard for her stuff—and that included the diamond bracelet from Lenny Pushkin, that egotistical bastard.

She turned back to the billionaire photos. "Why don't you just send me a check, boys?"

They stared back, some sleazy, some smiling, some total dweebazoids. Jade drew antennae on one of the nerdy guys. "Yeah, I'll bet you're a real slug in bed," she said. "But I could give you a few pointers." She laughed.

Nerd boy grinned back, antennae and all. Of course, the man stunk in bed. He'd been so busy developing his billion-dollar corporation, he couldn't have had the time to polish his sexual skills. But Jade could help him. And in return, she would have her apartment, her home, and a billionaire husband to share it with.

Now that was not a bad idea . . . not a bad idea at all.

25

"Well, I've weeded out billionaire number one," Jade told Zoey over the phone. "Elliot Van Dorne, CEO of Gemini Enterprises. I actually ran into him while having dinner at Elaine's with Emily Turner, and he seemed interested."

"Van Dorne? I've never heard of him, but don't you work fast," Zoey said, clicking the mouse to save her work before she dared to look away from the computer. She was inputting changes into her final draft, a stage which always made her paranoid that some brown-out or computer crash would happen, dissolving weeks of creative labor in a single electronic fizzle. "So, are you having drinks with him?" she asked Jade, who had told her friends of her methodical plan to marry a billionaire from the list. "Or are you going to dispense with the traditional dating ritual and just ask him to marry you?"

"Not this time," Jade said, sighing. "I'm crossing him off the list and moving on."

"Already?" Zoey was surprised. "What's wrong with him?"

"The man is way too fat and slimy. Not that I couldn't get him to a health club or invest in a bottle of shampoo, but this is a case in which the slime slips beneath the surface. Pervasive slime personality."

"That's a tough one," Zoey agreed. "You can lead a man to the altar, but you can't alter the man's personality."

"Exactly. But I'm not giving up. There are more on the list, and if I run through those, there's always a millionaire list. My needs are simple. Great sex and a three-million-dollar apartment."

"You always were a practical girl, Jade. So down-to-earth."

"That's me. Besides, I've got a date with Taki tonight. He's still hung up on his wife, but I've convinced him to be my guide into the Tantric World. At the very least I should be able to squeeze a few sessions out of him. How's the writing going?"

"Great. I'm hoping to read over the final copy once more, then send it off to Skye. Maybe even today. She hasn't seen an outline for this one, but it sort of rolled out in full-fledged story form before I could sit down and do a blueprint."

"Good thing you went for it, honey. I'm still pissed off at Nick for giving you writer's block."

"I'm not sure he's completely to blame." Zoey uncrossed her legs and leaned back on the bed. She was still wearing her bathrobe, having just showered and slipped into something skimpy before Scott arrived. The occasional thud of his nail gun told her he was hard at work in the living room.

"Are you still defending Nick?"

"No . . . actually, I haven't thought about him for the past few weeks, having been otherwise engaged." She turned toward the bedroom door. Were those were Scott's footsteps in the hall?

"Engaged is when he gives you a ring, honey. What you and Scott have going is good old-fashioned sex."

Adrenaline shot through Zoey as Scott stepped into the doorway. He was naked . . . naked except for his tool belt.

"Honey?" Jade's voice seemed so faraway. "Is he there now?"

"Mmm-hmm." Rolling onto her side, Zoey slipped the knot out of her belt and flashed the robe open. Beneath it, she wore purple satin panties and a matching push-up bra that held her breasts in a huge bouquet of cleavage.

Scott winced, as if burned by the sight. He rubbed his thighs seductively, then thrust his hips toward her. Zoey sucked in her breath, already feeling titillated. What was it about this guy, that he could turn her on in seconds? In the past two weeks of love-making they had nearly dispensed with foreplay, mostly because they were always ready to have each other. He seemed to have no trouble rising to the occasion at a moment's notice, and she felt herself creaming at the first suggestion of an encounter.

"He's really there?" Jade was saying. "In the room?"

"Mmm-hmm."

"Well, go for it, girl, and we'll finish this conversation later."

"Mmm-hmm." Zoey clicked off the phone, stood up and slid her robe off, tossing it onto the bookshelf with a seductive look. She had never done anything like this with Nick, but somehow the mirrored audience of this apartment brought out the actress in her, compelling her to play a new role with Scott.

"You dressed for me," he said. "I like that."

She nodded. "You undressed for me." She crossed the room, grabbed him by the tool belt and pulled him closer, until his chest brushed against her nipples, his erect penis against her smooth abdomen. "I like that."

26

Scott's naked appearance in the doorway made it into Zoey's novel. Not with a tool belt on, of course, but the idea of Quinn standing naked while talking to the innocent Armine had a certain perverse appeal for Zoey, and she had to work it into the book.

The next day Zoey stacked the pages of her new manuscript, *Pleasure Points*, then leafed through one last time to spot typos. She'd worried that Skye's printer wouldn't be compatible with her laptop PC, but it had worked beautifully. She smoothed over the pages, glad to see that a manuscript truly existed. There was something satisfying about the tactile feel of a printed manuscript still warm from the laser-jet printer—the fruits of creative labor. She read a passage and bit her lip. Was it rich and compelling, or did it suck? Ambivalence always hit her right around this time, which always drove her to pack up the damned thing and slide it onto the scale at the post office, getting it out of her hands by sundown.

Would the post office suffice for a mailing to Italy? Zoey wondered if she should use Federal Express, though the overseas fee alone might drain the last of her savings. On the other hand, Skye had no envelopes or boxes or mail packs here. The post office would have something. In the meantime, she wrapped a hair band around the manuscript and hurried to get dressed.

"See you tomorrow," she told Scott as she left the apartment in a loose black skirt, black boots, black leather jacket.

"Take care," he called after her. So civil. So polite. So hard to believe that three hours earlier he had been massaging her breasts with his green-fingered gloves, and in a fit of rebellion she'd tugged one off and wiped it between her legs, giving him something to remember her by.

The manuscript mailing ritual went off without a hitch. International Express Mail seemed the most expedient and inexpensive choice, made more palatable by the fact that the line at the post office was short, and the short Asian woman behind the counter actually seemed to enjoy her job.

Then it was off to Club Vermillion to celebrate.

"Here's to the end of the long, lean hermitage of Zoey McGuire," Mouse said, hoisting a glass of ginger ale with a tiny paper umbrella in it. The manager was pushing paper umbrellas these days, the latest in a series of publicity ploys to cover up the fact that the club was a haven for drug traffickers and their clients.

Jade toasted with her margarita, then dabbed her tongue over the salty edge. "Now that your book is done, what are you going to do with yourself?"

"Well, I plan to get out of the apartment at least once a day," Zoey said.

"If Scott will let you out of bed," added Mouse.

Zoey grinned. "And I just want to hang and relax and soak up New York again." She hitched her boot heel over the rung of the bar stool and leaned closer to Mouse. "You've been complaining about not seeing enough of me? Well, from now on you won't be able to get rid of me. I'll be here every night, eating those free nachos, scarfing down wings, and making a generally bad scene at the corner of the bar."

"You're going to start eating the nasty nachos at this place?" Jade cringed. "So you weren't kidding about running out of money?"

"No, but let's not go there now. Actually, I do have to call my lawyer and find out what's going on with the settlement, something I couldn't bear to do while my head was into a book. Nothing like a whammy from Nick to throw me off for a few weeks."

"Well, I'm glad your book is done and I hope it makes pots of money for you," Mouse said. "I've got an audition tomorrow, but I'm trying to play this one low-key. I think that maybe I've been psyching myself up too much, scaring people away during auditions."

"Interesting theory." Zoey nodded, tapping a Vermillion matchbook against the bar. "Who knows what's going on in the producers' minds. You could just strategize all night."

"Believe me, I have."

"I've got some good news, too," Jade said. "One of my billionaires is coming to New York next week for some Wall Street summit, and I've got a friend who's a secretary down there who's going to get me in to see him."

"Really?" Zoey patted Jade's shoulder. "You get bonus points for determination. I don't think I've ever seen you stick to a plan this way. Back in college, you changed your major every week."

"Back in college she changed boyfriends every week," Mouse muttered.

"Still do," Jade said proudly. "But yes, I feel really good about being focused on my billionaire. I don't know why, but I've got a really good feeling about this. Snagging a rich man, teaching him about the wonders of tantric sex, and letting him buy me the apartment. . . . I'm just sure all these things are coming together at this time in my life for a good reason."

"Yeah, it's called middle age," Mouse muttered.

"What?" Jade's black hair splashed through the air as her head whipped around. "What did you say?"

Sensing the rising tension, Zoey put a hand on Jade's arm.

"Jade . . . Mouse . . . we've all been through some rough times lately." She lifted her margarita glass again. "Here's to the beginning of wealth, health and happiness . . . for all of us."

"Here, here," Mouse said, clinking glasses. She sipped the ginger ale, but her brown eyes were full of rue as she stared out at the dance floor.

"I'll drink to that." Jade downed her margarita, then checked her watch. "I've got a session with Taki, and I don't want to keep him waiting." She tucked her purse under one arm. "Tomorrow, chicks?"

"Tomorrow," Zoey said, sitting back to lose herself in the pounding music and flashing lights and the sweet bite of Mouse's phenomenal margarita.

Over the next few weeks Zoey's life fell into a new pattern: coffee and sex with Scott, a run down to Union Square park and back, a shower, a walk through the streets of New York for research purposes, free dinner at Club Vermillion, then a night at the bar cajoling Mouse and trading jabs with Jade and sometimes Merlin. Occasionally she worked in a trip to a museum or accompanying Mouse to auditions, but generally her days were chock-full. After the sexual exercises with Scott by day, she was happy to send him home and head out to the club, then have the bed to herself for a good night's sleep.

Once, while in the throes of making love with Scott, she realized that she was really learning to let go of her former life. That was the hardest part—not so much accepting that Nick was a traitorous fool, but realizing that she had been in on the fantasy, coddling him, living in the bubble dream he'd created. Why this thought occurred to her as she was watching herself in the mirror, sitting on the edge of Skye's bed, legs spread in the air while Scott nailed her into the mattress, eluded her at first. Then she realized what she would be missing if she had remained "happily married" to Nick. All this ecstasy. All this sex. Even if it was emotionally lacking, it sure felt good.

Thank you, Nick.

27

"I'm washed and willing and ready to learn all about your tantric sex," Jade said, swishing her hair back seductively.

Taki nodded and she noticed the creases around his eyes. With pale skin, squarish mouth and a mop of straight, dark hair, Taki wasn't really that attractive. Why had she thought he was attractive? Maybe because of the way he made her feel. Well, she was about to learn his tricks.

"Did you empty your bladder?" Taki asked as he knelt beside Jade. She was stretched out, naked, on the soft straw mat that he had brought to her apartment.

"Yes!" She smiled, running her hands down over her perfect breasts and flat stomach. Sometimes Taki was so methodical, and she just wanted to get started. "Is that so important?"

"Tonight we will be focusing on your sacred spot, and my touch against a full bladder might make you want to urinate."

"Okay," Jade said, soaking it in. There was certainly no pretense of romance in Taki's tantra instruction, which was that much better for her mindset. "That's good. Give me the salient points, the key to big, fat, earth-shattering orgasms."

"Your mind should be focused not so much on orgasm as on sexual healing," he said. "Concentrate on feeling. Your mind is quiet and at peace. All that you need to feel is the sensation in your sacred spot."

Jade sat up, leaning on her elbows. "Honey, it's nice of you to call it sacred, but it's okay to say vagina. Or pussy. Or cunt. I'm not offended."

He shook his head. "This is different. That part we will call your yoni."

"Then you mean clitoris?"

"No, let me explain, please. The clitoris sits like a jewel on the top of your yoni."

A jewel? Jade lifted an eyebrow. What an apt description.

"Your sacred spot is deep within," Taki continued. He positioned himself between her legs and lifted her feet so that the backs of her thighs rested against his chest. "The first few times the sacred spot is touched, it can be painful or frightening for some women. For you, I think it is not a problem."

"You betcha, honey," Jade said, smiling as he gently slipped a finger in her vagina. It was an odd arrangement, sort of a cross between a gynecologist's exam and a high school guy copping a feel, but Jade didn't care. He pressed his other hand down from the outside, just above her pelvic bone, then rubbed the finger inside against the wall there, producing a gnawing, bittersweet sensation.

"Ooh." Jade heard her own moan, as if it came from some other woman on another astral plane.

"Tell me to stop if it is painful," Taki said.

"No, no . . . just different. I . . . I thought I'd done it all, but no one has quite touched me in this way." She took a deep breath, so conscious of her own body, her own sexuality. Each gentle stroke brought her deeper into this world of white light and spiraling energy.

"Do you feel the energy?" he asked, still stroking her gently. "See the white light come down through the top of your head. It moves like liquid energy through your brain, between your eyes, your face, your neck, and down through your body."

"Yes," she gasped, pushing against his hand for another deep breath. Amazing what this man could do with one finger. It was different from the times she'd felt her mind drift to a different place, apart from her body. Now she remained within herself, but her entire body was being transported, feather-light and floating through space.

"Feel the light bathing your body, renewing you with sexual energy."

She could feel herself holding him inside her. Was that a muscle or what? She knew all about the Kegel exercise, but this felt different. She closed her eyes and imagined herself as one cavernous ghost, a dancing ghost that had complete control over its visitor, gripping and stroking, and that control gave her a deep, overwhelming sense of pleasure. Jade could feel herself gripping him, stroking him, squeezing him. And the simple deft touch of his finger sent sensations seeping through her body, through her womb, shooting up to her chest and darting out through extremities.

"The liquid light will explode from within you," came his voice from a distance. "Watch it explode. Hold the vision. See yourself in all your radiance. There is a cosmic halo of energy over your head. Do you see it?"

"Yes!" she cried as tears rolled down her cheeks and sensation swept over her. "Yes, yes, yes . . ."

28

Today I am definitely, absolutely not going to have sex, Zoey thought as she turned off the shower and stepped onto the bath mat. She was toweling herself off in the bedroom when Scott arrived with coffee. She pulled on a pair of jeans and buttoned a white cotton shirt that she had swiped from Nick's closet, folding the cuffs up to her elbows. This morning she was determined to get out of the apartment before anything happened with Scott. Not that she didn't want to be with him anymore, but the daily ritual of sex (with weekends off) had become a little tedious. Unlike Nick, the guy wasn't even daunted when she had her period, and though she had to admit that those sessions in the shower left her feeling incredibly coddled and satisfied, the whole package was just beginning to be too much. Too predictable, too regular, too emotionless, too confining.

Hmm. She could probably use the exact same words to describe her sex life with Nick. No, not really. It was infused with passion, at least from her side. But now she wondered if Nick had really been along for the ride. Had he really loved her and felt the same passionate need to join with her, or had she only projected those feelings onto him?

She sat down at Skye's desk, working the buttons of her shirt. Nick had usually been the initiator when it came to sex, mostly because he usually thought of it first. Zoey did remember one time when she'd staged a seduction dance that failed. They had returned to the city one Sunday from a weekend in the Hamptons, and while Zoey was in the bedroom changing she noticed how the tan lines of her bathing suit played up her breasts and the triangle below her navel. Feeling impulsive, she grabbed a white silk shawl from the closet, slipped on a pair of metallic Candies slides, and sashayed into the living room where Nick was watching a baseball game.

"I've got the most amazing tan lines." She stood beside him, silently begging him to look up. The silk shawl teased her nipples as she swished it over her shoulders and turned to reveal some bare butt to Nick.

"Really?" He didn't even look at her.

"Nick . . ." She stepped in front of the television and posed for him, rubbing the satin fringe over her collarbone. "Don't you want to see?"

His face puckered in distaste. "I'll look at it later. Can't you see I'm trying to watch the Yankees?"

Zoey folded her arms and hugged herself as the memory faded. Okay, Nick wasn't always the perfect guy, but every person in the human race had their flaws, and they'd certainly engaged in plenty of lovemaking in the years they were together.

Or was it love?

Whatever it was, it was over, and today she was on a different track. Today she needed to assert her sexual independence from Scott, even if it meant coming up with a diversion to keep her out of the apartment. She could always have coffee with Jade, walk around the Museum of Modern Art for a while, or steal into the Museum of Broadcasting under the pretense of researching a book and plotz down in front of a video monitor to watch reruns of *Cheers* or *Seinfeld*.

"Or you could take your laptop to the library and start outlining your next book," she muttered under her breath. Swiping at a speck of dust on the lid of her computer, she pulled it open and checked her email. Nothing. These days, email was the only exercise this baby got, considering Zoey's nonexistent work schedule. But she had just squeezed out a book in record time, and her mind needed a rest.

Okay, forget the library. Try a museum or a coffee shop. Most places would let her sit over a cappuccino for hours, people-watching, a valuable experience even if the coffee did cost three dollars. Now that she was closer to broke, Zoey was learning ways to see New York on the cheap. Broadway shows and movies were out, but museums were in, thanks to Nick's compulsion to sign them up for memberships at nearly every nonprofit organization in Manhattan. Without the membership cards, even museum fees were too high for Zoey's limited budget.

Scott was out in the living room, mixing spackle, when she came out. "Good morning," he said cheerfully.

"Hey, thanks for the coffee," Zoey said, pulling the lid off one steaming paper cup. "How's everything? I've got to run in a minute . . . a meeting with my agent," she lied.

Scott nodded, glancing up at the ceiling. "I'm almost done here. There's still some taping to do in the bedroom, and the molding around the hall closets, but other than that, my job is done. I should be out of your hair by the end of the week."

"Oh." Zoey plunked down on the couch and took a sip of the black coffee. Usually she took milk and sweetener, but at the moment a bracing sip seemed the appropriate accompaniment to Scott's news. Finishing up and leaving? Well, of course, he wasn't going to keep rebuilding this apartment forever. "Have you got someone else lined up?" she asked, thinking about another job, then realizing how it might sound to him. Did you find another client to nail? "I mean, another job?"

"There's always more work. I spend most of my time juggling and scheduling."

"I'll bet you do," she said, her tone sassy but without malice. That was a funny part of their relationship; they never discussed the fact that they were having a relationship beyond that of a contractor doing work in the apartment where she was residing. Never an "I love you," never a moment of regret about cheating or a worry about being caught cheating, never a comment about how the previous day's lovemaking session had gone. Somehow, that had worked for Zoey, who had spent so much time evaluating her relationship with Nick that there seemed to be no room in her mind to fit in an analysis of her sex romps with Scott.

He sat beside her, opened his coffee, and took a sip. His blue eyes flashed over his cup, friendly, upbeat, sexy.

Oh, no, not today. She'd promised herself.

But that was before she'd known he was leaving. Now . . . now she felt a familiar tingling sensation between her legs, the instant arousal power that Scott had over her. Blood seemed to rush to her lips, swollen and ready for kisses, and her skin was suddenly supersensitive, yearning to be touched by him.

Oh, hell. He was only going to be here for a few more days.

She put her cup down on the table and kneeled on the floor at his feet. Grabbing a work boot, she hoisted it aside, separating his legs and moving into the space. "We've had some really good times together," she said, pulling his T-shirt out of the belt and hoisting it up. He put down his coffee and lifted his arms, a willing victim. She unbuckled his belt, unzipped his jeans, and pressed her fingers inside to get a solid handful. "I'm going to miss this," she said, gliding her hand over his erection.

He smiled, gazing at her through hooded eyes. "Me, too. You are so beautiful."

Zoey tossed off her shirt and leaned forward to rub her breasts against him. "I guess I'll just have to give you something to remember me by."

29

"I've got a meeting with my agent today," Mouse told Zoey over the phone. "I want to find out why he's been sending me out for these parts. An aging matron. A withering debutante. Hey, I'm an actress, not a morphing mannequin."

"Don't be too hard on him." Zoey sat on the bed in her sweat pants and sports bra, waiting for the motivation to finish dressing and go for a run around the park.

"I will be the incredibly charming Marielle Griffin, as usual, dahling. What are you doing today?"

"I don't know. Maybe I'll collect some bottles from the trash and turn them in for the deposits. Better yet, maybe I'll collect the trash, haul it up to Connecticut, and dump it on Nick's car. This budget thing is really starting to get to me, as in, I am broke."

"Poor baby. Do you want to borrow some money?"

"No, thanks, Mouse. I know you'll stop me before I check into the shelter, but in the meantime I refuse to take a loan. I mean, I'm a working writer. I've got royalties and a decent savings account—or at least, I would if that bastard hadn't frozen everything."

"Yeah, what's happening with that?"

"I don't know. I've been exchanging phone messages with my lawyer, Natalie. She's been in court, and his lawyer has been in court, and no one has been able to reach anyone. It's still an exercise in voice mail."

Zoey leaned back on the bed and stuck her feet in the air, remembering the position from a yoga class. Although she looked like an overturned turtle, it tightened the abs. "As soon as I get my banking privileges back, I'm signing up for a gym. Exercising with Scott kept me on my toes, but now that he's not around I'm beginning to feel like a slug."

"Do you miss him?" Mouse asked. "Tell the truth or don't bother answering."

"Do I miss Scott?" Zoey stared at a cobweb on the ceiling, considering the question. "No; no, I don't. It's sort of like he was a hired gun, here for vacant, mindless sex. Good sex, tremendous sex, but sex does not make a relationship."

"Don't let Jade hear you say that."

"Jade . . ." Zoey pulled her knees to her chest. "I think her meeting with the new billionaire is today, isn't it? I should call her to wish her luck."

"Jade doesn't need luck, she needs a lifetime supply of condoms."

"You are so bad."

"I know. Look, I gotta go, I'm going into the lobby of his building. Wish me luck?"

"Always," Zoey said, and she meant it. Mouse had been suffering a dry spell since Zoey returned to Manhattan, and Zoey hated to see her friend grow discouraged by the harsh realities of show business.

After she hung up, Zoey went online to check her email. There were three junk letters, along with an email from Skye titled "WRITER'S BLOCK OVER."

She'd read the manuscript! Zoey sat down and sank toward the screen as she clicked the mouse to open the letter.

Dear Zoey:

After our discussions about your artistic block and your philandering husband (or is that ex?) you can imagine my surprise at receiving a complete manuscript from you in the mail. Hallelujah! I can't tell you how thrilled I am that you've worked through that difficult period and found your muse once again.

I love this manuscript. I really do. Hell, this is far sexier than this Italian genius I'm trying to squeeze literature from. What's that expression about squeezing water from a stone?

Anyway, my dear Zoey, you have certainly come into your own as a woman's writer savoring the act of passion. *Pleasure Points* is an inspiring contribution to erotic fiction—absolutely delicious.

However, and I don't want to alarm you because you know that I am your biggest fan . . . however, as your editor I am not sure that the publication of this book as the next novel by Zoey McGuire is a good career move for you. The question is, do you really want to go into pornography? If you do, I will run this by the editorial board and fit it into our next list. On the other hand, if you want to protect your name and literary reputation, I suggest you put this aside for now and sink your toes into another concept. Something with more pathos, more edge and warmth.

No, no, no! Zoey raked her hair back with her hands. She couldn't write another book. She needed money now!

Skye's email contained one last piece of advice:

If you're interested in placing *Pleasure Points* under a pseudonym, have your agent shop it around. I'm sure someone is publishing this sort of thing well these days.

Zoey stared at the email, looking at the heading for the first time. Skye had already copied Robin Buckner, her agent; at least Robin would be forewarned about this manuscript. I need to print her a copy, Zoey thought, jumping up and checking the paper in Skye's printer. Yes, print a copy and get it over to Robin. Got to keep moving. Got to sell this manuscript. Can't think about what just really happened.

She brought up the manuscript file, clicked on "Print," then paced down the hall trying to escape the despair of the bedroom, as if the email message had zapped all the air around her. Why hadn't she sent Skye an outline first? She had written a story about characters she didn't even know, tried to bring Jade's sensual life into earthly terms. That voice wanted to rise up and whisper, "And you thought you could pull it off!" but she turned away and feathered fresh paper for the printer before it could catch her.

As soon as the manuscript was printed she pulled on her sneakers, a T-shirt and soft gray sweat-jacket and headed out. She was going to run this over to the post office, then run over to Union Square, then run down the meager paths of the parks, circling trees and sandbox and flower beds until she could get the ugly word out of her head . . .

Rejection.

30

"Tell Mel that I'm sorry we couldn't get together," Mouse told the receptionist, forcing herself to be polite. She wanted to grab the overly made-up girl by the ugly plastic ID tag hanging around her neck and give her a good shake and warn her never to wear blue eye shadow. She wanted to push through that glass door and march into Mel's office and remind him that she had an appointment and he would regret canceling out on Marielle Griffin.

But Mouse practiced restraint. All the way down the elevator and through the lobby, where she made eye contact with the man at the security desk and gave him her usual warm smile. Somehow she always felt the need to hold herself together, pretend things were going well, encourage the people around her even when she felt terrible inside. Did Zoey know that Mouse was getting sick of rejection and thinking of giving up acting? Did Jade realize that Mouse hadn't been with a man for almost a year now? And it wasn't just a lack of sex; there'd been no kisses, no dates, no warm bodies snuggled up beside her on the couch.

Mouse kept so busy trying to take care of other people's problems, she was losing control of her own life.

The echo of her heels in the lobby was irresistible, and she
took a deep breath and sang out, "Amazing grace! How sweet
the sound that saved a wretch like me. I once was lost, but now
am found. Was blind but now I see."

She riffed the last note, holding it and going up and down in
a jazzy ending.

Behind her the guard applauded. Two women in suits passed
by, staring icily.

Mouse pushed through the door and stepped onto the pavement, feeling frustrated. Oh, Lord, what am I doing wrong?
Jesus, help me through this time, because every time I try a door
it closes in my face and I'm getting really frustrated.

Jesus God, are you listening?

"Lord," she said, "I am beginning to get the feeling that we are
not tuned into the same frequency." Not that she would ever
abandon her belief in the Lord, but sometimes she had trouble
feeling God's presence.

The sun was hot, teasing at spring as she walked down
Madison and paused at the corner of 53rd Street. She hated this
neighborhood, full of towering office buildings and pricey boutiques. Two men in suits nearly mowed her down, and she
moved away from the center of the sidewalk and stared into the
window of a travel agency. There was a cardboard palm tree advertising the Caribbean and another cutout of the Eiffel Tower.
Maybe she should liquidate her life and tend bar on some island
beach. Maybe it was time to make a life change like that, time to
realize that she was getting too old to play Tiger Lily in *Peter Pan*
or a chorus kid in *South Pacific,* time to acknowledge that she was
approaching her mid-thirties and her career was going nowhere.
Time to become a responsible adult.

Mouse stuck her tongue out, then noticed that her long curls
seemed stiff in the reflection of the glass. An agent making a
phone call from a desk inside gave her a curious look, and she
waved, then moved on.

It was time for a change, and she knew of a fabulous salon in the fifties just over on Fifth Avenue. What was it called—Bijou's? Balto's? Something like that. She would know it when she saw it. She turned west on 52nd Street and trudged ahead past delivery trucks and cavernous buildings with a purpose. When all else failed, a haircut could freshen things up and put a new spin on life.

The receptionist at Becko's was a little flip when Mouse insisted on seeing Serge, a stylist who had done hair for the production of *Hair,* but Mouse persisted until Serge appeared, scissors in hand, shocking gold cap of hair dangling over the dark brown sides that were shaved short. "Hello," he said, friendly but curious. "I know that I know you . . ."

"Marielle Griffin, from *Hair.*"

"Yes, of course!" Serge embraced her, kissing both cheeks. "So good to see you."

Mouse smiled, pleased that he remembered her. "I need a haircut, something radical, and you were the first person I thought of. What do you think?" She flipped her head back so that her long curls whipped over her shoulder.

"Beautiful hair, yes. I would be delighted to work with you. But you want . . . today?"

"Absolutely. The sooner the better."

Serge went over to check the book on the receptionist's podium. "We are busy, of course, but I will fit you in if you would like to take a seat. Deirdre will get you something to drink." He reached out to squeeze Mouse's hand again. "A few minutes and we will begin."

As Serge disappeared behind a wall of glass brick, the receptionist turned back to Mouse with a warm look, as if Mouse were suddenly in on the conspiracy. "Can I get you something to drink?"

"I'd love some water." While Deirdre bent down to reach into a small refrigerator, Mouse sat on the upholstered bench. With a deep breath she took in the marble floor, the track lighting, the vaulted ceiling washed with a textured gold over copper, the New Age music. This was a good place to make a life change.

Her black skirt fell away from her brown suede boots as she crossed her legs. Yes, a haircut was just what she needed. What better way to transform a woman than to reshape the hair that framed all her features?

Yes, a haircut was just what she needed.

31

Stay in the moment, Merlin told himself as he waited in line behind Josh in the art deco lobby of the Empire State Building. Already his mind was leaping ahead to when he would face Josh, ask the question, and take the velvet box from the pocket of his leather jacket. Josh seemed a little irritated at Merlin's insistence on making the trip to the top, especially since he had a masseuse class in a few hours, but Merlin had persisted.

"Visibility is twenty miles today," the guard announced as the line moved up.

Fortunately, tourist traffic was light this late in the day and the line moved quickly. "I still don't get this," Josh said as the elevator began its 1050-feet ascent to the main observatory. "We could have waited until we both were free. Besides, we're New Yorkers. We're not supposed to visit the tourist traps."

A white-haired woman wearing a red visor that said LITTLE OLD GRANNY FROM PASADENA turned and gave them a skeptical look, but Merlin just smiled. He had purposely arranged the trip for a day that Josh had plans, knowing that if they both had off they would have celebrated afterward and tumbled into bed for some lovemaking. But he didn't want this to be about sex, not today.

Merlin felt his ears popping, and then the doors were opening to the watery light of twilight. They stepped out the doors into the brisk wind, and Josh walked up to the railing, his face suddenly opening up and relaxing.

"Geez . . . this is great!" he said, smiling like a schoolboy who'd won at lacrosse.

Merlin smiled back, feeling his hair blowing in the breeze. He had been here on class trips, but the sights held new excitement now that he was a part of the energy of this city. Manhattan stretched out below them like a toy city of steel and glass, the streets lined in neat grids bordered by the rivers and crowned downtown by the harbor.

"Look at Central Park!" Josh grinned at the rectangular patch of green. "It's enormous. The way it's cut into the center of the city. . . . I can't believe they haven't taken a bulldozer to the place and put up more skyscrapers."

"It's a beautiful city," Merlin said, his fingers closing over the box in his pocket. "And I want it to be our city." He took the velvet box out and opened it to reveal the ring inside, a gem-cut gold band with a round diamond in the center. Josh's face went white and Merlin had to plunge on before he lost momentum. "I want to be with you forever, Josh. I love you."

"Oh my God!" Josh's hands flew to his face. "I can't believe you . . . and up here. Isn't this the ultimate proposal place for couples? I don't believe . . ." He pressed his fists to his eyes, then took a deep breath.

Merlin wanted to cry himself. He had never seen Josh so elated, so giddy.

"Wait . . . aren't you supposed to get down on your knees?" Josh pressed Merlin's shoulders to push him down, then pulled him close to hug him. "Oh my God, I love you too." He leaned back and grabbed the velvet box. "Now let's get a look at this rock, and don't tell me you settled for less than the Hope Diamond."

"The Hope Diamond is cursed."

"Whatever." Josh slid the ring out of the box and slipped it on his finger. "It's very nice, and it looks spectacular on my hand."

Merlin realized he was still smiling; it was as if his whole body were locked in a happy position, like one of those drippy Dr. Seuss characters who dance across the pages. "If you don't like it, I can turn it into an earring for you," he said, reaching toward Josh's hand.

"Don't—" Josh made a show of slapping his hands away. "It's everything I always wanted." He held out his hand to admire it, showing it to a tourist couple nearby. "Isn't it beautiful? We just got engaged."

"Congratulations," the woman said. The man nodded politely, a little confused, but Josh didn't seem to mind.

"We're gay," he explained. "Did you ever see *La Cage Aux Folles*?"

The man snapped his fingers. "Right. Gene Hackman, right?"

"Exactly."

The couple went over to check out the east side, and Josh went back to admiring his ring. "I've half a mind to call Fitzroy and bag out for tonight. What's one class? I mean, this is the day of our engagement!"

"No, don't cancel," Merlin said softly. "You should go. It's important to you, and you're so good at it, but you won't get anywhere with it if you don't make it through the program."

Josh held the ringed hand to his heart, his face so full of love. "There you go, campaigning for me again. You've always believed in me."

Merlin felt his throat tighten with emotion, and though all his instincts told him to squash it down, this one time he let himself feel it. He thought of his mother, a cool brisk woman, unemotional not because she didn't favor emotion but because deep, textured feelings were not part of her nature. When Merlin cried as a child or stayed up late at night worrying through an existential crisis like the discovery of death or the fear that the giant, saucer moon would certainly fall from the sky and crash into the earth, his mother had tried to calm him not with a soothing hand to his head but with a logical explanation. And his father, strict and old-fashioned, always suspicious of western ways. Between the two of them, there was no place for emotion in the Chong house. No time for tears even when a toe was stubbed or a heart was broken, no tolerance for anger even when injustice had been dealt. And somehow, Merlin had managed to swallow back his own emotions, keeping them quiet and hidden under so many layers of intelligence and wit and bravado. He'd maintained that safe, solid repression through unsteady high school years and decadent college years of one-night stands in the face of AIDS. Then Josh had come along and reached beneath his steel-riveted facade.

Josh had made him feel happiness, anger, jealous rage, and love. So much love. Watching him now, he wanted to feather Josh's hair back with his hands and run his hands over his beautiful earnest face and cry on his shoulder. Somehow, the sum of emotions threatened to come out in a torrent of tears, and Merlin had no idea how he'd explain that to Josh. "Oh, God . . ." He put a fist to his mouth and swallowed back a sob.

"Stop it! Stop it now," Josh said lightly. "You're going to make me cry, you bastard." Josh pressed his temples, as if to stop the tears from forming. "Oh, Merlin, I can't believe you've finally come around, but now that you have, I want to savor this moment. You're everything I've always wanted. And I am going to make sure you spend the rest of your life in delicious, tortured ecstasy."

"Thanks, I guess."

Josh took Merlin's hand and squeezed it, hard. "No more guessing. This is when we say 'I do.' A sure thing."

Merlin felt tears sting his eyes at the sight of this man he loved. "A sure thing," he said, swallowing hard against the knot in his throat.

"Oh my God, we need to start planning a wedding," Josh said, turning back to face the uptown view. "Something lovely and intimate."

"Small, I hope."

"Oh, yes, small and classy." Josh nodded. "Just a few hundred of our closest friends."

32

Zoey pushed through the crowd at Club Vermillion, wondering if it was worth the effort. Thanks to this place, her clothes smelled of smoke, the soles of her shoes were tacky from the sticky floors, and she was beginning to suffer indigestion for the first time in her life, probably due to a steady diet of Vermillion wings and nachos. Still, Mouse was here, and Jade thought she'd stop by ("Unless I sweep the Wall Street billionaire off his feet and spend the night inflating his stocks.") and Merlin had agreed to come later; it was a central gathering place for her friends, and with Mouse behind the bar the price was right. Looking for her friends, she slid off her black blazer and pulled her white shirt away from her throat. Already the air was thick with body heat and smoke.

Where was Mouse? Elvis was behind the bar, along with a short blonde with . . .

Zoey blinked, then cut straight over to the bar. The blonde was Mouse.

"Oh my God, look at you!" She reached across the bar to hug Mouse. "Your hair!"

"I got it all chopped off," Mouse said, tugging on a strand by her ear. "Chopped and bleached. What do you think?"

"I can't get over it!" Zoey shook her head, a little shocked and not quite sure how to tell Mouse how much she had adored her dark, thick hair. Somehow Mouse's round, waif-like brown eyes, stunning cheekbones and sweetie-pie smile looked over-animated under this superwhite cap of hair.

Mouse was expressionless as she popped the tops off two bottles of Corona, shoved lime wedges onto the narrow necks, and pushed them toward a patron. She took his ten-dollar bill, then paused to face Zoey. "You hate it."

"No, I don't!"

"You hate it, because it's awful." Her mouth puckered and she blinked rapidly. She turned to the register to hide the tears.

"Mouse, don't worry," Zoey said, wishing she could jump over the bar and pat her friend's back. "It's just such a different look for you. I didn't even recognize you when I came in. But maybe that'll work for you. Maybe this will be the thing that gets people to see you differently. This could make casting directors change their limited view of your scope."

"Do you think so?" Mouse was unconvinced.

"You never know. I think this is—" Zoey was saying as someone pushed into her, cutting her off.

"I need a round, pronto," said the wiry woman with a big head of red hair and gold glitter on her face.

"Excuse me?" Zoey glared at the woman. Granted, Club Vermillion was getting a rowdy reputation, but etiquette still prescribed that you didn't barrel into someone else at the bar.

"I should think so. You've been standing here hogging the bar while my friends have been waiting for drinks." The redhead didn't even get her skinny butt off Zoey's knee as she turned to Mouse. "Do you work here? Or are you just trying to impersonate Little Richard?"

Mouse blinked, obviously stung, but quickly rebounded. "Easy, Tinker Bell. Give me your order—or do you want to run into the ladies' room first and wash up? Your hand must have slipped when you were spreading your fairy dust."

Red sneered, but she was obviously more interested in drinking than arguing. "We need two Buds, a white wine, Wild Turkey on the rocks, and three peach daiquiris."

"We don't have peach daiquiris. Strawberry or lime."

Red rolled her eyes. "Make them strawberry."

Zoey swung her knee away from Red, who was obviously still in her twenties, obviously a little slow on getting the personal-space lesson. As Mouse made the drinks, Zoey tried not to stare at her friend's wiry new haircut with hair the texture of fine nylon thread. Oh, well, it had been a bad day all around. She'd gotten the rejection from Skye, and a hesitant phone call from her agent, Robin Buckner.

"It's a very specific market, something I don't know much about," Robin had told Zoey. "We might be able to soft-pedal it as a very sexy romance."

"Anything you can do to sell it," Zoey had answered. "The thing is, I'm strapped for cash. Not to go into the sordid details, but I'm going through a divorce right now, and my husband's got me on a tight allowance."

"Really? Then this could actually be good for you. If you write this book under a pseudonym, your husband might not even have to know about it."

It would be fun to pull one over on Nick, but at the moment Zoey was in a panic over finances, and also worried that she had lost her creative spark forever. Somehow a sale, even as a series release under a pseudonym, would validate her, assuring her that she could still support herself by writing. "I'd appreciate it if you can sell it, anywhere," Zoey had told her agent. "I'll revise . . . expand or delete. Whatever it takes."

"Will do," Robin had said brightly. "I'll let you know."

"What are you drinking?" Mouse asked, having gotten rid of Red and her loud friends.

"A Cosmopolitan, please," Zoey said. "One in a long line of drinks I'll be consuming tonight."

Mouse squinted at her friend. "It's been a long time since I saw you drinking with a vengeance."

"Well, I have good reason. Skye rejected my manuscript today."

"That hurts." As Zoey explained the details, Mouse went back to the vodka bottle and added more. "I think I'll join you tonight. It's been a bad day all around. My agent canceled our appointment at the last minute, which just threw me." As she was mixing the drinks, Jade appeared, looking radiant in a black beaded camisole over raspberry silk shantung pants.

"Make that three of whatever you're drinking, golden girl," Jade said, slamming her beaded black bag onto the bar. She took a moment to study Mouse's hair. "I like the look. Didn't Tina Turner have something like that going on for awhile? Anyway, I've had a very disappointing day."

"Oh, no! Your billionaire?" Zoey asked as Mouse poured three Cosmos into lovely v-shaped glasses.

Jade nodded. "There's a reason why these men are single, girls. My friend got me into the offices where Alphie the billionaire was meeting, and I managed to talk my way into his presence. I told them I was a broker and had a wealthy investor interested in the building they were in. They bought my horseshit excuse, and I started working the men, pretty well, I might add. They were having some sort of catered dinner, and I could have had Alphie eating off my cocktail plate."

"But . . ." Zoey prompted her. "What happened?"

"Halitosis," Jade said, her eyes squeezed shut. "I got within two feet of the guy and I was afraid I'd lose my lunch all over his silk tie."

"A fire-breathing billionaire." Mouse shook her head. "Some people stink so bad and nothing they do will stop it. I got a cousin, he drank mouthwash for breakfast. Breath sprays, garlic pills, baking soda—he tried everything, but it didn't work. Lucky for me, he's still in Rhode Island."

"Maybe Alphie had a bad day," Zoey said. "A spicy lunch? An upset stomach?"

Jade lifted her Cosmo. "No, you can tell the smell of habitual bad breath. And his secretary confirmed it. Alphie actually uses his breath to intimidate business associates. And believe me, if I were across from him at a conference table, I'd back down in two minutes." She sipped her drink and sighed. "I can't imagine kissing those festering lips. So . . . another bachelor bites the dust."

"Join the club," Zoey said, lifting her glass for a toast. "We all had days from hell. To us . . ."

Jade clinked her glass against the other two. "May our lives suck less tomorrow."

"Amen," Mouse added as the three tossed back the drinks in one swallow.

With a sigh, Jade placed her glass on the bar. "Another round, please, Mouse. I need some liquid sedation before I hit the dance floor and drag one of these sweaty junior entrepreneurs into the alley behind the kitchen."

"Oh, leave the children alone tonight," Zoey said, slapping Jade's hand like a parent correcting a child. "I thought we were going to commiserate together."

"You're not the only one who's had a bad day, Jade," Mouse said as she mixed another round of Cosmos. "Zoey got a rejection from her editor, and she's running out of money. And I had this important meeting lined up with my agent to reevaluate the direction of my career, and the jerk canceled. Which is worse than it sounds, only I'm not going to get into the details of it now, because if I talk about it, that might make it real. Besides, we never really talk about my problems anyway. So why don't you cross your legs and hang with your friends, just for tonight?" She shook the second round of Cosmopolitans.

"I could do that," Jade said, a look of disappointment in her eyes as she scanned the dance floor, "but they're such easy targets." She nudged Zoey. "Why don't you pick one up, too? It's great for the self-esteem."

Zoey's hair swung as she shook her head. "Not for me, thanks. I've decided to live like a nun for awhile. I mean, Scott was a great lover, and I'm glad he got me past all the anti-male feelings I was harboring because of Nick. But I think I need a little time to myself, time to grieve. I mean, I went through hell with Nick, and it's still hard to let go of him and of my dreams. Besides, I've realized that sex isn't everything."

Jade laughed. "It may not *be* everything, but it certainly makes everything better."

"I wouldn't know," Mouse said, taking a sip. "I haven't been with a guy since the fall of the Berlin Wall."

Zoey and Jade looked at her.

"Okay, I'm exaggerating, but my nonexistent love life is just one more factor in my failure of a life. I'm supposed to be out there, sharing my talent. Instead I spend my days singing my guts out for producers who are looking for the next Bernadette 'white-girl' Peters, and my nights waiting on spoiled grad students. Oh, Lordy, my life does suck." Mouse took a long swallow of her drink as her cell phone started beeping. She finished the Cosmo, then grabbed her phone from her belt. "Excuse me, that must be Hollywood calling."

She flipped the phone open and said hello, while Zoey and Jade spoke softly behind their raised glasses.

"Mouse is losing it," Jade said.

"I wish she would just land a great part." Zoey took a sip, thinking how much more smoothly the second and third round went down. "No one deserves it more."

Mouse's eyes opened wider in surprise, then her face grew fierce. "And who the hell is this? His assistant? You mean the man doesn't have the balls to call me and tell me himself?"

Zoey squeezed Jade's wrist. "Prepare for meltdown."

Jade nodded. "The fur will be flying."

They couldn't help but listen to Mouse's conversation.

"Well, listen up, Tiffani. You can tell Mel that he can't drop me, because I was going to fire him, anyway. And you can also tell Mel that any pansy-assed agent who can't make his own phone calls doesn't deserve to represent me. And you can tell Mel that I will see him in the audience of my next Broadway show. And don't call me for house seats, because you're not getting them!" Mouse flipped the phone shut and grunted at it.

Zoey took another sip of her drink, looking for wisdom and

strength in the clear pink elixir. She knew Mouse was already feeling bad and this phone call was going to push her over the edge.

"Oh, honey . . ." Jade's voice was sympathetic. "Your agent?"

"My former agent." Mouse shoved the phone onto her belt and clasped her hands together in front of her chest. "Oh, Lord, what am I doing wrong? Don't you want me to be an actress anymore?"

"It'll be okay," Zoey insisted, though she was beginning to hate the eternal optimist inside her who was always saying kind, pat little phrases. "Maybe this is for the best. He hasn't really been doing his job lately and—"

"We need shots." Mouse set up three shot glasses. "What is it? Johnny Walker? Stolies? Or some nasty schnappes? I'm sticking with vodka." She poured herself a clear shot and tossed it back.

"Make mine Courvoisier," Jade said.

Mouse took down a squat bottle of brown liquid. "Excellent choice."

"Mouse, aren't you going to get in trouble for that?" Zoey asked quietly.

"Yo!" The abrasive male voice was followed by a solid push at Zoey's side. "One of these drinks is wrong."

It was a heavyset guy with a short ponytail, one of Red's friends. Pushy, rude, and now snagged on Jade's beaded camisole.

"Watch it," Jade said, unhooking Ponyboy's jacket zipper.

But instead of apologizing, he slopped a half-empty red drink on the bar. "One of the daiquiris was supposed to be lime. You fucked this one up."

"I gave your friend what she asked for," Mouse said, her words clipped with restraint,"but I will make you a lime daiquiri if you like." Methodically, she started pouring liquor into the blender.

"If I like?" Ponyboy held his arms out dramatically. "I would like you to say that the customer is always right and that you're sorry for fucking up the order."

Mouse didn't respond, but Zoey could feel the tension in the air as the blender whirred.

"What's the matter?" he persisted, looking around to see who was watching. He was the kind of guy who got off on starting a riot. "Your mother never taught you how to apologize? Or are you PMSing or something."

Mouse poured the frozen foam into a class and leaned across the bar, her face just inches from his. "Apparently, your mother never taught you how to be a human being," she said sweetly. "But don't worry about the drink. It's on me. Or, actually, oops . . ." She tipped the glass, pouring the drink down the front of his shirt. "Looks like the drink is on you."

"Whaddaya . . ." He threw his arms out, knocking into Jade and clocking Zoey in the chest.

"Oooh." Zoey slid off her chair, then stepped away to rub her breast tenderly and to finish off her Cosmo in relative safety before fleeing. Maybe it was the liquor, but she had the feeling she was watching a barroom brawl unfurl in slow motion. So far no one had responded to Ponyboy's holler, but it was only a matter of minutes before this bar would be far too hostile for Mouse and friends.

"You little bitch!" he growled, waving a fist at Mouse, then grabbing a wad of napkins from the bar to dab at the front of his shirt and pants.

Mouse stood behind the bar, tears in her eyes. "Oh, I'm sorry. Was that the wrong drink again?" Her voice cracked, but Zoey knew this wasn't about a daiquiri or an irate customer. Mouse was falling apart.

From the periphery, Zoey saw the crowd begin to react: Elvis moved down from the other end of the bar. Ponyboy's friends were rushing over, the guys with balled fists, the girls with hands over their mouths as if they had never witnessed such an atrocity. Two bouncers were pushing through the crowd.

"Mouse . . ." Zoey said, wishing she could reach out and hug her friend.

Suddenly, Jade was at Zoey's side, her beaded bag under her arm. "Marielle, should we meet you by the back door?" she asked, suggesting that Mouse sneak out the rear exit.

"Nope." Mouse cleared the bar by scooping two empty beer

bottles off, sending them crashing to the floor. Bracing her hands on the bar, she vaulted up. Her black boots made a clacking sound on the lacquered wood. From where Zoey stood it looked as though she were going to walk right over Ponyboy. Instead, Mouse pulled off her apron, balled it up, tossed it into his arms and jumped to the floor, looking like a little Ninja in her black tank top and leggings. She stepped between Jade and Zoey and threw her arms around their shoulders. "Let's get the hell out of here."

They stepped forward and were met by a burly bouncer.

"Don't worry, Bear, we were just leaving," Mouse said pleasantly. As if she instigated a barroom brawl every night.

Zoey's head was reeling but her limbs felt loose and graceful. Her pulse raced from a mixture of adrenaline and booze. "This is just the best ending to the worst night," she said, slurring a bit.

"A stellar performance from our little Mouse," Jade said as they reached the edge of the cavernous club. When the receptionist gave them a curious look, Jade turned to her and said: "Oh, we'll be sure to trash you in the *Zagat's Survey.*"

At the door, Mouse broke away from her friends, turned to face the main room, and bowed dramatically, her hand sweeping the floor. "Goodbye, Club Vermillion. So long, drug-abusing brats! I swear, on the worn carpeting of this lobby, I will never suck up to a rude patron again!"

"Adios, free nachos," Zoey lamented. "Thanks for the killer Cosmos!"

"Farewell, steady paycheck," Mouse called as Jade tugged her out the door.

Outside the night air was cooler, fresher, far more forgiving. Zoey had a feeling that the party had just begun. She stepped back, wavering a little as a yellow cab pulled up to the curb.

"How's that for an exit?" Jade said, smoothing the edge of her camisole.

"You guys were great!" Mouse punched the air.

Zoey felt herself grinning. "We were!"

"Hey!" The cab door slammed and Merlin came over to join them. "What are you ladies doing out here?"

"We got bounced," Mouse said proudly. "Bounced, rejected, dropped, and disappointed." She smoothed the lapel of Merlin's navy shirt affectionately. "Jade's millionaire had bad breath and I quit my job. Oh, and I haven't had sex for the longest time, though we really shouldn't go there."

"What?" Merlin smiled at the other two women. "Anyone care to translate?"

"We all had days from hell," Zoey tried to explain. "But somehow our luck has changed. Either that or we just don't care anymore. But I'm glad you came, Merlin. So glad you came, because we don't see enough of you. Probably because you have Josh. Ironic, isn't it? Out of the four of us, only the guy has landed a steady guy. What does that say about the future of feminists in America? Or am I just talking too much?" She covered her mouth and giggled. "Am I babbling?"

"You are, but somehow it makes sense," Merlin said, taking Zoey by the elbow as she wavered on the pavement. "But I have exciting news, actually about Josh and me. I proposed tonight, and he accepted." His eyes were full of light as he smiled. "We're getting married."

"Oh my God!" Zoey turned to clap him on the shoulder. "Congratulations!"

"Attaboy!" Mouse said, fist in the air. She jumped into Merlin's arms and gave him a bear hug.

"Ugh, I can't breathe," Merlin said. "Have you guys been power-drinking, or was there a chemical spill from a nearby alcohol refinery?"

"Let's have a drink to celebrate," Jade said. "Anywhere but here."

"Good idea," Zoey shouted before she realized she didn't need to shout. "Grab that cab. Or should we walk? I'm way too drunk to drive."

"The truth?" Mouse asked. "You always sucked behind the wheel of a car."

"Did not!"

"Did too!" Mouse pranced toward the street, her arm raised to flag down a taxi.

Zoey screwed up her face, thinking. "When did you ever see me drive, Mouse?"

"What's going on?" Merlin studied the three women, as if trying to get a handle on the situation. "What exactly happened tonight?"

"We realized that we're all going to die," Jade said seriously. "But in the meantime, we need to find a new place to party."

He rolled his eyes. "Thanks, Jade. That explains nothing." Linking arms with Zoey, he said, "Catch me up here. I think I missed a few important segue aways."

"Revelations," Zoey said. "We all had revelations, but I don't remember what they were exactly." She pressed her eyes closed and giggled at the memory of Mouse leaping onto the bar. "You know, Mouse, you were like a superhero back there." She stared up at Merlin. "The thing is, we all saw the end coming today, but we can't let it be the end, can we? I mean, what if I never write again. I can probably run groceries past a scanner or something."

"Don't you think that noise would drive you nuts?" Mouse asked. "Bleep. Bleep. Bleep . . ."

"Anyway . . ." Zoey patted Merlin's arm and snuggled close for a moment.

From the curb, Mouse continued, "Bleep. Bleep . . ."

Jade clapped her hands over her ears. "Oh, shut up and find us a cab."

"The thing is," Zoey told Merlin, feeling suddenly wise, "sometimes you just have to shut down your mind and enjoy. Didn't Einstein say you can never understand everything?"

"That sounds right," Merlin said. "But I don't think he referred to trying to decipher the evening chronology of three wasted women."

"Whatever." Zoey shrugged. "You know, sometimes you read into things too much."

Merlin smiled. "So I've been told."

Part Three

The Mouse That Roared

33

"Oh, the morning after." Zoey moaned on her way into the kitchen. She opened the refrigerator and hung on the door handle as she surveyed the empty shelves. What did she expect? That the elves her father always used to talk about had come during the night and stocked the fridge with coffee, milk, and juice? Add to that a fat, spongy bagel to take the edge off her rocky stomach.

"Don't wake me up till after dark," Mouse called from the living room where she had crashed early this morning on Skye's couch. When they'd abandoned the third club after four A.M., neither Mouse nor Zoey were in any shape to go home alone. Merlin had packed them into a cab together and given the driver Skye's address, as it was closer than Mouse's apartment on Riverside Drive in West Harlem. At least, that was the way Zoey remembered it, though the latter part of the evening seemed like a fuzzy sequence of scenes shot through one of those misty lenses, the characters' dialogue not quite matching up with the movement of their mouths.

"No, don't wake me up until Thursday," Mouse added. "Actually, I don't have anywhere to go. Friday will be fine."

Zoey pushed her hair back and twisted it over her head as she padded out of the kitchen and sat on the coffee table near Mouse. "Are you okay?"

"I will be. Just as soon as I figure out what to do with my life."

"You sound like a grown-up."

"Coffee. I need coffee."

"I'll go," Zoey said, holding her head as she walked back into the bedroom. Why couldn't she drink the way she used to? She'd gotten up around nine to gulp down two glasses of water and three Tylenol, and still, her head felt like it was encased in a cushion of watery pain. She managed to pull a baggy white T-shirt on over her jeans, but her head ached when she leaned over to tie her high-top sneakers. "Oh my God, I am getting old."

"I heard that," Mouse said. "And shut up."

"Better be nice to me. I'm the one making the Starbucks run."

Outside the air was damp and sunny, smelling of bleach from the cleanser the custodian was using to scrub the steps of the building. Zoey scooted around him, sensing spring in the air. The corner market was a burst of colors, with its tall stacks of oranges, apples and lemons and entire shelves covered by blossoms. The towering mound of lemons reminded Zoey of a trip she'd taken with Nick once, driving up in New England past a New Hampshire farm where horses grazed in a field of buttercups. Past postcard-perfect village greens, church spires, stone walls, wooded hills and tiny harbors.

They had done a lot of driving during their time together, Nick always restless to move on, get somewhere, explore, hit the road—never content to simply *be* somewhere. Perhaps he'd never experienced the sweet, deep breath of arrival, that moment of success and satisfaction. That field of buttercups had stuck in her mind. Zoey had longed to stop, pick a few, walk along the edge of the field, sit down for a moment on the grass and maybe roll in the huge patch of lemony sunshine. They had driven for hours, and the leather smell of car with its low-slung sporty seats was closing in around her. She was trapped in a sleek hunk of metal and steel while beautiful villages and fields and farms flashed past her window, still distant and inaccessible. Untouchable.

They had argued that day, bitterly. Nick finally stopped a few miles down the road, but by then the scenery had changed and Zoey was unable to get past the tightness in her chest and commune with nature. He had argued that he was going places and she liked to stand still. He was aggressive, restless, eager for change. She was passive, meditative, happy to spend a day contemplating the mythology of a buttercup.

He had laid out their opposing qualities like a lawyer presenting two profiles in court. "Let's face it, we're incompatible," he'd finished.

Incompatible. The word had surprised her. She had known all along that their natures were different, but she had thought those differences would help them stay together. She had thought they complemented each other.

That night a storm had rolled in and they'd been forced to get off the road and spend the night in a small bed-and-breakfast somewhere in New Hampshire. And although Nick had not apologized for snapping, and he did not rescind his argument for their incompatibility, when he pulled her onto the bed, she'd slipped her arms around his shoulders and kissed him willingly. They'd had some of the wildest, rawest sex of their relationship. He'd forced her to beg for him, he'd threatened to hurt her if she didn't come, and she had played along with him, driven by a sense of need and desperation. It was as if their relationship were also being ravaged by a storm, and as water splattered the window screens and beat against the tin roof of the barn outside, their love was being tested with equal force.

This may be our last night together, Zoey had thought as he ground into her savagely. It's okay, she told herself. It's our dismal good-bye. I am losing this man that I love because he doesn't understand that we belong together. And I will mourn the loss of him for the rest of my life, but for now, I need to be joined with him in whatever way he will take me.

The next morning, Nick woke up and pulled her against his

naked body. "Last night was great," he said. "So when do you want to get married?"

And that was his proposal. No romantic buildup, no transition, just a statement of fact. Just a question voiced in a tone on par with, "So what's for dinner?"

And I said yes, Zoey thought as she stepped into Starbucks and put her hands to her temples. Her headache was getting worse, though she wasn't sure if it was from the hangover or the memory of Nick. He'd proposed with all the charm of a business merger. And like a fool, she'd accepted.

Twenty minutes later, Mouse and Zoey sat on the floor, heads against the couch, hands cradling warm paper cups of coffee.

"I need a shower and some clean clothes." Mouse lifted the black tank top she'd slept in and took a sniff. "I'm in bad shape."

"I'll get you something to wear. Just as soon as the jackhammer in my head dies down." Zoey held the warm cup to her cheek. "We can't drink like that anymore."

"At least, not tonight."

"So . . . what are we going to do with ourselves?"

"Tonight?"

"I meant our fledgling careers." Zoey took a sip of coffee and closed her eyes. "I always feel the need to purge the morning after a wild night. As if I can make up for bad behavior by getting my life back on track."

Mouse tugged on a few strands of short blond hair. "Well, I've got to get another job. You know me, with Nelly Griffin's work ethic engraved in my brain. An honest day's work. Gotta earn your way." Mouse's mother, a retired teacher in Rhode Island, had pushed all her children to take on part-time jobs as early as junior high. Mouse had almost gotten cut from high school shows when she'd missed rehearsals because she was baby-sitting or scooping ice cream at the local shop.

"Maybe I'm being a prima donna," Zoey said. "I could get a real job and focus on my writing at night."

"Oh, there you go with the grocery store plan again. Bleep! Bleep . . ."

Zoey swatted at her friend. "Stop!"

"Make me spill my coffee and I'll whop you, girl."

"I would never waste good coffee." Zoey scratched her nose. "I'm just trying to be realistic. I need money, I should get a job."

"But you'd be a terrible cashier. I'm telling you, you'd be fired in a week."

"In any case, it's time for a major rehab for the two of us. Not giving up drinking, just . . . I don't know, some fun, uplifting activities that will boost our morale."

"Field trips?"

"Exactly. We need to have pedicures and dinner at Lotus. We should see a taping of the Rosie O'Donnell show and have high tea at the Helmsley Palace."

Mouse cocked an eyebrow. "We can't afford any of those things, except the taping, and with that you need luck, which we're not having."

"Well, we can get cheap pedicures, and forget dinner at Lotus, we'll just go for drinks. Watermelon Martinis. We've got to squeeze some life out of this city, something to pull us out of this funk."

Mouse was nodding. "Let's start with the pedicures tomorrow, my feet are a mess." She wiggled her tiny toes. "Oh, and you got a call while you were out. Natalie something. I wrote it down by the phone."

"Natalie? My lawyer. Oh, God, maybe she talked Nick into a settlement." Zoey pulled herself up to her knees, hobbled over to the cordless phone, and dialed the number Mouse had written there. The line rang twice, then:

"Natalie Rodriguez." Zoey's lawyer answered her own phone, a fact that would leave Nick unimpressed.

"Natalie, it's Zoey McGuire. I heard you called. Did you reach a settlement?"

"Well, not exactly . . ." Natalie went on to describe Nick's latest demands and quibbles. Zoey tried not to get upset as she took notes, but when Natalie got to the part about the house, she couldn't restrain herself.

"He wants to sell the house for a loss? Why should we take a loss? I got an estimate from a realtor before I left, and he said the place is worth a million at least, and the market is good now. Did the market change in, what . . . two months?"

"Nick and his lawyer seem to feel that a quick sale at a reduced price is preferable to a prolonged situation in which you would have to carry the mortgage."

"Oh my God, I don't need a divorce, I'm going to kill the man first. A quickie sale is what he wants? When we've got at least $300,000 collateral in that place?" Zoey felt her cheeks heating up. "Well, you can tell him that's impossible; we are not taking a loss. And I wouldn't share the loss even if I had the money, because *he* was the one who wanted that damned house in the suburbs of Connecti-fucked."

"You go, girl," Mouse said quietly.

Natalie wasn't cheering quite as loudly. "Zoey, you don't have to agree to his offer on the house. But you should know, he has a buyer who is interested right now."

"Oh, and is her name Eileen?"

Silence. "It very well might be a friend of his, so I agree, it's wise to turn down the offer. Let's go over the other terms. . . . "

By the time Zoey hung up, her headache was worse.

Mouse had finished her coffee and was massaging the back of her neck. "Sounds like Nick the Prick is living up to his name."

"He's waging a war." Zoey looked over her scrawled notes. "Besides the mess with the house, he refuses to divide his savings, but wants half of mine. And he wants half of my royalties, past, present and future. Maybe that's why I'm feeling so blocked; I can't stand the fact that he thinks he owns me and all my books."

"Wait until it's time to divide up your possessions. I had a cousin who went through a bitter divorce, and he actually slashed her clothes. Can you imagine? There are some real psychos out there."

Zoey sighed. "This is so unfair. His salary is four times my monthly 'allowance,' but I'm not allowed to touch the money I earned on my books because of him. It just feels so . . . so anti-artist. Anti-female, too."

"At least you got a female lawyer."

"But it's just a job for her; for Nick, cheating me out of my earnings is a passion. Don't think he's not the one behind his lawyer's new proposals. He probably stays up late thinking up ways to screw Zoey."

"At least you know he's thinking of you." Mouse stood up and stretched. "I'm gonna shower and get my ass over to the newsstand for a copy of *Backstage*. Looks like I'm going to have to be my own agent for the time being."

Zoey got up and went inside to find something for Mouse to wear. "Call me a wide-eyed optimist," she called from the bedroom, "but I'm still seeing this as a silver lining. With Mel out of the picture and your new hip hair, who knows what doors will open up for you."

The shower was already running as Mouse leaned down the hall and shouted: "You're a wide-eyed optimist. But nobody's perfect."

"That's right," Zoey said, leaning against the windowsill to take in the downtown view. Eww, the sun. She went to the desk, slid on a pair of sunglasses and returned to the window, where the gorgeous view belied her new predicament. Her marriage was over, and yet she couldn't make it be over, not when Nick insisted on dicking around with the settlement. Damn it.

But wait . . . She bit her lower lip. Progress had been made. Because now she wanted the separation agreement. She was willing to say good-bye to the marriage, instead of moping around about how and why and what if it went awry.

She touched the yellowing leaves of one of Skye's plants, which she kept forgetting to water. "Yes," she said under her breath, "progress has been made." Even if it was at a snail's pace.

34

Jade kicked off her snake-embossed Charles David heels under the desk and tucked one leg under her butt. It was ten o'clock and she had never been in the office this late, though this wasn't exactly business. She was wading through websites on the internet, trying to collect information about the men on her Most Wanted List, but the computer was slow at times and some of the links led her to dead ends, providing boring information about the billionaires' corporations and stock offerings—some pretty tedious stuff. She clicked on a link that sent her to yet another site about a corporation, this one with photos of smiling young people that reminded her of an army recruitment poster.

"Okay, that's enough," she said, trying to close the site, though the computer continued to download it. On her desk was a printout of some information that might be helpful, a biography of Reese Hilliard, a man who had started with a family vineyard and turned it into a multimillion-dollar corporation. Okay, he wasn't a billionaire, but she'd realized a few days ago that she might need to drop below that list since the candidates were dropping like flies. Since she'd compiled her Most Wanted List she had learned that two of the single men were gay, and one of them had gotten married last week in a much publicized ceremony at the foot of a Hawaiian volcano. Frankly, the guy was a weaselly little shrimp, but Jade hated losing another candidate from her shrinking list.

Beside the printout was a stack of half-read books—Jade's newest reading material on tantra. She'd been amazed to find that a number of books were available on the subject, some written by swamis and full of spiritual voyages and messages, others written by clinicians who could spell out specific positions and sensual areas of the body and describe what finger went where to produce various sexual awakenings. She had learned that tantra was actually a series of ancient Hindu writings that described sexual rituals, disciplines, and meditations. The original tantra was written as a dialogue between Shiva, the Hindu god with powerful energy, and his lover, Shanti, who represented the female creative force. There was information about breathing technique, meridians and chakras, yin and yang. At first Jade had considered a lot of the philosophy to be so much hogwash, but the more she read the more she began to see a connection between sexual feeling and some sort of spirituality. Hadn't she always felt herself going off to a distant place in order to forget the details of the man she was with and just seize the pleasure? There was definitely something of value in this ancient practice, although it wasn't the quick fix she had hoped for; this was going to take some study, consideration, and, although most authors prescribed practicing with a dedicated partner, Jade was determined to practice with any and every healthy male she could get her hands on.

But somehow, she'd been having less sex lately. She'd been spending most evenings curled up with her tantra books, considering philosophies and meditation technique, and getting horny as hell. It had been a week since she'd had sex, and that was a rather perfunctory exercise with Chuck on his kitchen table. Yes, she'd had two orgasms, but they seemed so small and hollow compared to the way she'd come with Taki. With Chuck, it was like a sneeze, a physical reaction to a physical stimulus. Satisfying? Fulfilling? Hardly. And afterward she couldn't wait to get untangled from his arms and rinse away the tension in her own shower downstairs.

She clicked on "Shut Down" and reached for her shoes as the phone rang. Ugh. What idiot was calling at this hour, desperate to find a cheap studio for a lazy daughter or a two-bedroom in a "nice" neighborhood for a couple with a newborn baby? She was tempted to let the machine pick up, but couldn't stand the thought of missing the call.

"Carter Cantrell, this is Jade speaking."

"Hello, I'm calling from the West Coast, looking for a place for my boss to relocate," said a shy male voice. "You're the first person I was able to reach, and I hate those machines."

"Well, it's a little late here, but if you'd like to leave your name and number I'll be sure to get back to you tomorrow."

"Oh, okay. I wasn't sure how these things worked, but, the thing is, my boss will be in New York in a few days and he wants to find a place immediately. He hates to waste time, and if you don't have anything to show him, I'm going to be in big trouble." He sounded sweet and desperate, his vowels with that midwestern roundness that was so warm and appealing.

"Honey, we always have something to show," Jade said, scribbling idly on a pad. "What's your boss's name."

"Mr. Chenowitz." As he spelled out the name, Jade's eyes flitted from the notepad to the open magazine beside it. There it was, under billionaire number 6—A.J. Chenowitz. No, it couldn't be.

"And his first name?" Jade asked.

"He just goes by the initials A.J."

Jade stood up, phone pressed to her ear, and did a little dance around her desk. Yes, yes, yes! Yes, yes, yes!

"Hello?" the voice sounded lost. "Are you there?"

"Yes, I'm here." Jade stopped dancing and held the phone with both hands. She didn't want to lose this nibble.

"So you'll call back tomorrow? Because your morning is still our night, and . . ."

"Don't worry about that," Jade said in a soothing voice. "If you like, I can take all the information now so we can get started looking as soon as your boss arrives in Manhattan."

"Oh, wow, that'd be great, Jade. Really, it'll be a big load off my mind to know that this is being taken care of. We're out here in Oregon—Portland, Oregon—and though Portland's a city we're actually out in the suburbs, and things around here don't really compare to places like Manhattan or Tokyo. Though we're not far from the Silicon Valley. If you drive down the coast, they're . . ."

Jade listened intently as he babbled on, a little amused by his fresh view of everything from cities to weather. She managed to steer him back on track, covering pertinent details and trying to decipher exactly what type of place A.J. Chenowitz desired.

While the assistant talked, Jade glanced back at the photo of Chenowitz in the magazine. His hair was light, hard to tell whether it was sandy brown or slightly graying, but it seemed full and thick, a nice frame to his square face and wide smile. He wore thick black glasses that cried out "NERD!" but Jade could work on that.

She flipped open her date book. She would have to reschedule showing Mrs. Langley around on Thursday . . . and another broker would have to take over the Friday night open house on East 54th Street. Otherwise, commitments could be easily shuffled.

"I can clear the next few days for Mr. Chenowitz," Jade told the assistant. "It will be no problem at all."

35

"And *he* called *you?*" Zoey did some situps on the floor, phone to her ear as Jade filled her in on the latest billionaire. "That's amazing. Maybe he's meant to be the future Mr. Jade Cohen. Face it, Cohen is better than Chenowitz."

"Fingers crossed," Jade said. "I'm meeting him this evening. . . . Wish me luck."

"May you fall in love, marry, and have a whole brood of little Chenowitzes."

"Please! I said luck, don't curse me. But I gotta run, my seven-thirty turned into a five. I'll call you after I meet him. Bye."

Zoey peeled herself up from the floor and returned to her perch in front of the computer—the blank square of a screen. It was framed by toolbars that were supposed to make writing easier. Perhaps they did help when the writer had something to write, but she found herself studying the little icons and widgets, one like a paintbrush, two shaped like squiggly arrows, another like an open book. . . . On the upper left corner of the screen the cursor blinked, beckoning, mocking. "Write something! Write something! Put some words down! What's the matter with you, have you totally lost it?"

Yes! she admitted to the cursor. I am suffering a temporary lapse in creativity and judgment, and it would be enormously helpful if you would simply choose some letters and get moving on your own. Let me slide for awhile, and I promise, I will have my brain back in a few months.

Of course, the cursor didn't cooperate. It blinked. It laughed. It beat her between the eyes with its incessant rhythm. Somewhere in a cubicle in Silicon Valley, couldn't just one computer genius come up with a writing software that didn't mock the writer? She would have to email the software companies about that . . . just as soon as she finished off an outline for her next novel.

Sighing, she rested chin in hands and stared at the books scattered on Skye's desk, books she had gathered from the New York Public Library using Mouse's library card. She had read articles and books written by writers and writing "experts," people who should understand what she was going through. But all of the pieces were laced with cheerful advice, positive, aggressive thoughts about rewrites and choosing the perfect word and programming yourself to dream about characters. Most annoying was that old nugget she'd first encountered in grade school: "Write about what you know!" Yeah, right. Hadn't she done that when she'd incorporated her sessions with Scott in *Pleasure Points?* And look where that had gotten her—nearly booted out of the literary world with a quick, firm kick.

She glanced at the calendar, wondering what was happening with *Pleasure Points* right now. When she'd called her agent last week, Robin had said that it got a positive first read at one publishing house, and that no one had had a chance to it yet at the second place. Closing her eyes, she sent out positive vibes. Please— read it, love it, buy it!

When she opened her eyes the computer still hummed before her, the cursor blinking like crazy. This was ridiculous. She had plenty of stories to tell. As a kid she used to fixate on an object around her and make up a story about it, a talent that had come in quite handy on rainy days or during boring birthday parties or around the fire at summer camp.

So what was her personal story? Thirtyish divorcee sits in Manhattan apartment within the glow of computer screen as twilight falls over the city. Fascinating stuff. Film at eleven.

She took a deep breath and tried to look deeper, at the woman inside. Close your eyes and what do you see?

A blank. A void. The black vortex of a soul.

"Grrr!" Frustrated, she stood up to search Skye's kitchen. Surely the woman must have something with chocolate tucked away in the corner of a cupboard. She was crouched on a counter, sifting through boxes of dry pasta, when the phone rang. She jumped down and snatched it up halfway through the first ring, glad for the diversion.

"Hello?"

"You busy?" Mouse asked.

"Yes . . . no. I wish I were." Zoey raked one hand through her hair, entangling her fingers in a knot. "What's up?"

"I was wondering if you could come up and help me shift the furniture around in my apartment."

"Now?" Zoey frowned. "I'm supposed to be writing."

"How long have you been at it?"

Zoey sat on the window ledge, watching the cars move below. "I don't know, since this morning."

"Sounds like you need a break." Silence.

"I agree, I really do, but it's hard to justify taking a break from accomplishing nothing."

"Mm-hmm. You need food, fresh air, and an infusion of life. Take the number one train up to a hundred and twenty-fifth street. Actually, if you come now you can meet me at my future employer's operation. My cousin Sarah set the whole interview up. It's a new club, still under construction. I'm sure I got the job, but I have to meet with the owner today, and I hear he's a cutie pie. Sounds like a pansy-ass to me, but I'll show him what's what."

"A construction site . . . I think I'll pass."

"It's going to be a tremendous place—with an outdoor garden and waterfalls and live fish and birds. Come on."

Zoey lifted one leg and dug her nails into the tough skin on the sole of her foot. "No, I'm not showered or anything."

"So get off your butt and jump in the shower!" Mouse ordered. She gave Zoey the address of the club, then hung up before Zoey could protest again.

"Alrighty, then." On her way to the shower, Zoey remembered one of the pearls of wisdom from a writing book. "In order to write, you must first live!"

Okay, life, here I come. Instead of spending the evening writing I'm going to spend the evening living. "Whoopee," she said flatly, lifting her face into the hot stream of water.

36

Mouse tugged open the temporary plywood door and walked straight into the old West Harlem building that used to house a school. Her sandals scraped over the paper-covered floor of the foyer as she went up to the dark wood balcony and waved down at the construction crew of nearly a dozen men in hard hats. "Hey, guys. How's it going today?"

"Hey, Marielle." Shouldering Sheetrock against a wall, one guy nodded.

Another man pointed his nail gun toward the side, where there used to be a schoolyard. "Kenny's here today . . . out in the garden."

"Thanks." When Mouse stopped by the day before to speak with the manager, she'd chatted up all the workers, trying to get a feel for the type of club they were building. The plans sounded impressive, though she found it hard to believe the place would be up and running in little more than two weeks.

A quaint bridge over the main dining room floor and balcony level led her to an arch of May sunshine. Stepping into the light,

Mouse noticed three men seated on overturned crates, their
heads bowed over a fourth crate. The old schoolyard was now
surrounded by ten-foot walls. The asphalt and basketball hoops
had been removed for a maze of ruddy brown paths that swirled
and curved around patches of dried dirt—future flowerbeds,
she imagined. She followed the twisting path toward the men,
eavesdropping as she strolled.

"We'll need to get the inspectors in here within the next
week," one man was saying. "Rainforest will open on time, but I
don't want to cut any corners. I'm paying for the best, and I will
have it, gentlemen."

"Absolutely," said Jake, the head contractor and the only man
of the three who was wearing a hard hat. Mouse had met him
yesterday. "I've got the landscaper coming in tomorrow, but we
won't be planting for at least another week. The retractable roof
is . . ."

Glancing up, Mouse lost track of Jake's words as she caught
sight of the man at the head of the triangle, a large African-
American man wearing a fine moss green suit and black shirt
that surely had to come from one of those Big and Tall Men
shops. He lifted a pantleg to cross his legs, and she realized that
the suit had to be tailored. It fell gracefully over his bulk, accen-
tuating his wide shoulders and flat abdomen. His shaved head
was smooth and shiny, reminding her of an eggplant at its peak
of ripeness. Something about the man made her just want to run
over and rub his head and snuggle against his shoulders, as if he
were a big brown teddy bear.

Mouse stared down at the path to hide a grin. What's the matter with you, girl? Is it the fact that there's been no booty call? Or
maybe you're just sick of those sleek, slender dancers' bodies
that surround you on stage. Lithe and spry, lean and thin, skin
and bones. After a while, it was hard to tell one from the other,
equally hard to imagine raw sexuality exuding from those upright skeletons. All the gyrating and fanny-wiggling in the world
couldn't begin to come close to the warm, sensual aura that surrounded this man.

"I think that's it for now, gentlemen," the large man was saying. "And it looks like we're wrapping up just in time, because we have a visitor. Can I help you?"

Glancing up, Mouse realized the three men were watching her, and suddenly she wondered why she hadn't worn something nicer than these denim shorts and black top. Of course, the top did provide a tantalizing peek of her navel, but maybe that wouldn't be considered too professional in this forum.

"I'm Marielle Griffin," she said, coming forward to shake their hands. "Jake and I met yesterday, and I also met Dee, the manager. He told me to come back and meet you, Mr. Aragon." Her hand was lost in his, like a child's hand in a bear paw.

Kenny Aragon squinted against the sunlight. "You're the new hostess?"

She cocked her head, wondering if he was testing her. "You seem surprised."

"No, it's just that, watching you wander the path in the sunlight, I thought you were one of the children who used to play here in the schoolyard. I . . . I didn't realize you were a grown woman."

Was this man for real? His voice was so gentle, Mouse realized he was being earnest. He certainly hadn't come from New York.

"You're just not used to normal-sized people," Jake said, easing the moment. "What do you expect after sharing a locker room with seven-foot giants. Do you miss that? How's life after pro football?"

A football player? Of course. Mouse followed the conversation with a polite smile, tickled that her new boss was a former football player. Imagine that. Not that she'd know if he was good or not, as most male-oriented sports merged together in her mind. Now why hadn't cousin Sarah mentioned that when she'd told Mouse to call him? Well, at least the girl had remembered that he was single and sweet, but she'd painted him as a tender little lonely hearts mama's boy. What was wrong with that girl?

The meeting broke up and Mouse lifted her chin to smile up at her new employer. "Where should we start?"

He wove the fingers of his large hands together. "I guess we should have gone through a more formal interview process, but I've been tied up in Atlanta opening the first Rainforest Club. I expected to be here weeks ago, and consequently I need to hire a hostess immediately, and your cousin swears that you're perfect for what I have in mind."

"Cousin Sarah is always right," Mouse said.

He laughed. "And she's almost as persuasive as you are."

Just then Zoey called out, hurrying along the stone path to reach them. "Hey, hi! I was banging on the door, but no one answered, and some guy in a hard hat told me to just go in. So . . ." She joined them, swiping back a lock of hair that had fallen from the twist. "Here I am."

"This is Kenny Aragon, the owner of Rainforest," Mouse said cordially. "And this is my best friend, Zoey McGuire. She's a novelist. The novelist."

"Really? Welcome." Aragon shook her hand. "I'd be proud to have a novelist of your stature join us at Rainforest."

"Thanks," Zoey said, smiling but obviously embarrassed. "It looks like you're really transforming the place, but I'm trying to swear off late-night partying."

"I hear ya." Kenny's gaze swept across the garden to the wall covered in bright blue tarps. "I'm not a drinker myself, and that's one of the reasons I'm determined to open a place where people feel comfortable without having to drink or use drugs or tolerate too much smoke. Not that we won't serve liquor, but I prefer to think of Rainforest as a casual supper club where friends can gather to enjoy each other and listen to good jazz at its source here in Harlem. I'm talking about relaxation and communion with friends. We'll be a throwback to the elegant night spots of the past, before the music got too loud and the air became too toxic."

"Trying to make New Yorkers relax . . ." Mouse folded her arms. "That's pretty ambitious, Mr. Aragon." Oh, why did she sound like a two-year-old?

"Call me Kenny, please. Come, let's take a tour."

The women followed him as he explained the architect's plans for the building. There was to be a retractable roof over the garden, and the wall between the garden and club was going to give way to a waterfall and wide-open space. "That way, we'll have a year-round garden, stretching into the club, providing a hideaway for guests who want privacy as well as the gentle ambiance of a quiet retreat." There would be live exotic birds, a small brook of fish, rest rooms with free toiletries and no attendant hovering over guests, warm mists, furniture designed by the architect, and a four-star chef.

Mouse paced the foyer near the entrance, trying to get her bearings. "Let's see. This area will get crowded as people line up, so you might want to get rid of that divider and let the traffic spill into that small bar area there. The coatroom is a good spot, doesn't block the flow. . . . But I'll need some kind of station here. Maybe just a podium. It's a subtle way of telling people not to wander past this point without being seated."

Kenny studied Mouse, his arms folded, finger pressed to his chin. "That's a good idea. Yes, I like the way you think, Marielle."

"Get out!" She slapped his elbow playfully. "You sound like you just stepped into this business like, yesterday."

"Actually, I did. That's the bad news. The good news is that I'm willing to take good advice when I hear it, and I'm a quick learner."

Zoey smiled. "That's convenient. Mouse—I mean, Marielle—has plenty of advice to give."

Mouse continued with a series of questions about the menu, the menu design, the club's hours, the staff training. "And you're opening in two weeks?" She frowned. "So . . . who's coming to the opening?"

"Lots of my friends have promised to be there. My father was hoping to make it up from Atlanta, but unfortunately he has a previous commitment."

"Yes, but . . ." Mouse spun her hands in the air. "Who's coming, as in, celebrity guest list?"

Kenny shrugged.

Mouse let her mouth drop open for a dramatic gasp. "Don't tell me you didn't invite celebrities?"

With an embarrassed grin, Kenny pointed to Mouse. "See,

that's why I knew enough to hire experienced people such as yourself." He pulled a notepad from the pocket of his jacket. "Who should we invite?"

"Well, I could shoot off a few hundred names, but that won't help you without addresses. Look, I've got a cousin who works for a PR firm, and she probably has access to a list of Manhattan notables and their contacts. Right now we need to design invitations and get them to the printer. Something classy but a little bit funky, I think."

"That's right, with the rainforest theme." Nodding, Kenny took notes. "Maybe just a parrot . . ."

"Or a palm frond . . . something simple." Mouse was on a roll.

Kenny's cell phone rang. "Excuse me." He answered the phone, asking the caller to hold on. "If you ladies can stick around, I can use your help making some final menu choices. Michael is in the kitchen whipping up some entrees as we speak. Michael Donatello, do you know his work?"

"Donatello." Mouse put her hands on her hips. "Wasn't he one of those Mutant Ninja Turtles?"

Kenny laughed. "Can you spare the time for a tasting?"

Mouse knew that Zoey was always up for free food. Her friend nodded, but Mouse checked her watch, making it look like she was torn. She didn't want the man to know that her only plans for the day were to move furniture in her apartment and split a pitcher of margaritas with Zoey. It wasn't good to look too available. "We can squeeze you in," she said.

"Great." He smiled, and the warm glow in his brandy eyes melted the icy frosting around Mouse's heart.

As he went back to the phone call, Mouse and Zoey wandered off along the balcony area that ringed the main dining room. It was wide enough to accommodate two rows of tables, Mouse thought, pacing to measure the width. She was starting to get excited about all the possibilities of this building and her new boss.

Mouse turned to her friend. "So . . . what do you think?"

Resting her arms on the fine mahogany rail, Zoey tilted her head to one side. "Not too shabby. I won't mind hanging out here."

"Not that! What about him? Isn't he something? A real moun-tain of a man. I'd love to get in his bloomers."

"He is a hottie. But he's your boss, and you have that vow of chastity when it comes to your employers."

"That's just producers and directors and artistic people. When I'm a famous actress, I never want anyone to say that I slept my way to the top," Mouse said vehemently. "But this is dif-ferent. It's a job, not a career."

"So he's excluded from the rules?" Zoey nodded. "Remind me to make an addendum to the contract." She checked her watch. "Speaking of contracts, I wonder how Jade is making out with her latest billionaire."

"Probably another bust. That Most Wanted List is totally fried. You can't make a man fall in love with you."

"I don't think love is what Jade is looking for," Zoey said. "Actually, love has nothing to do with it."

37

For her first meeting with A.J., Jade tried to anticipate every possibility. She picked out restaurants near each property, wanting to have a romantic place lined up in case he wanted to stop looking and grab a drink or dinner. She decided to meet him at the first property, assuming he would have a limousine ferrying him around. That way they could ride together, a cozy interlude in the back of his car. She was wearing a Calvin Klein suit that framed her butt beautifully in cherry red taffeta, with her Manolo Blahnik heels—killer heels—and she carried a slender briefcase containing a few listings, perfume, breath spray, and a supply of condoms.

Hey, you never know.

Her heels clicked as she paced the lobby of the Imperial Plaza, her stomach a mesh of anxiety. This Most Wanted List should be so easy, but she was steadily striking out, and that was not like her when it came to men. Was she being too picky, applying the impossible standards of women's self-help magazines to mere mortal billionaires? Naw. These guys were hopeless mate material, each case completely incapable of being shaped and molded into an adequate husband.

She heard the door open and there he was, looking goofy and youthful in his black glasses and green baseball jacket with white leather arms. Oh, God, she was trying to snag a teenager!

But as he came closer, she saw a few signs of his forty years. His thick hair was streaked with silver, and there were those friendly creases at the edge of his eyes when his face screwed itself into a giant smile, as it was now.

"I hope you're Jade Cohen," he said, extending his right hand. "Otherwise you're going to think I'm some geek who tries to meet women in the lobby of posh buildings. Which I very well might be, but let's not go there now."

Cornball, but genuine, Jade thought. She fixed her standard professional smile on her face. "I'm Jade, Mr. Chenowitz, and it's a pleasure to meet you."

"Is it, really? I mean, has it been a pleasure so far? People always say that but personally I'm not . . ."

He was making her nervous, suddenly aware that she'd had nothing to eat since noon and that was just a bagel.

"Though, actually," he went on, "I can say it's a pleasure to meet you because that color you're wearing just makes me want to smile. Do you ever feel that way about a color, Jade?"

Her smile slipped a bit. "Well, yes, I think I do. Some shades of blue." The doorman was eyeing them now. "If it's all right with you I'd like to take a look at the apartment upstairs for starters, and you can feel free to tell me what you do and don't like about it. That way I can steer you toward something that's right for you."

"That sounds great."

She gestured toward the elevator, and he followed her there, craning his neck to study the lobby. "It's such a beautiful day out there, and no one seems to notice. Maybe it's because we don't get a lot of sunny days in Portland, but I don't know how people can make it down the block without just looking up and saying . . . 'Wow.' "

Was he kidding? Jade turned toward the elevator and walked into a wall.

"Ow," she yelped, rubbing her shoulder.

"They must have moved that recently," he joked.

"I guess," she said, wondering how that had happened.

"Are you okay?" He paused in front of the open doors, as if all the elevators in the world could wait for answer.

"Yes, of course." Jade felt a moment of panic as she followed him onto the elevator. She had dealt with cool CEOs, international ambassadors, without missing a beat. But this guy was throwing her off her game. Why? Because he was genuine?

"Do you like sunshine, Jade?"

"Yes, of course," she answered, realizing she sounded snappish as she hit the button for their floor. "Actually . . ." She faced the doors and took a moment to think about a winning answer. "One of my favorite things in the world is to be on a quiet beach with the sun warming my skin. They say the sun is so bad for us, but I'm convinced it has healing properties." She turned toward him, feeling suddenly shy as she met his gray eyes.

"Healing properties?" He seemed intrigued. "That's an interesting theory, certainly worth a study or two. I'll have to make a note of that." He took out a Palm Pilot and started keying something in.

He liked my answer. Jade turned back to the elevator door and tried to ignore the sweaty feeling at the nape of her neck. Why did she feel like a six-year-old wearing Mommy's makeup? It wasn't just his unpredictability that threw her off balance; she was miffed by her own reaction to him, the fact that she cared about whether he liked her.

She wanted him to like her. How ridiculous was that?

38

Zoey and Mouse sat at a portable card table set on the balcony, overlooking the workers as they picked at the remains of a sampling of food that Zoey had called "Ambrosia." The chef enjoyed their ecstatic responses to his entrees, savory combinations such as veal with chestnuts in a sherry glaze, or chicken breast with pear and gorgonzola, or monkfish medallions in a chardonnay sauce, or salmon *meunière*. Sensing his pleasure, Zoey had trumped up the enthusiasm until she and Mouse were rolling their eyes and searching for adjectives to top each other.

"It's better than sex," Zoey had finally said, and though Michael gave an appreciative grin, Kenny seemed embarrassed by the comment.

"I don't know if I'd go that far," Mouse said, turning to Kenny with a flirtatious look.

Holding up his hands, Kenny excused himself from the table to make a phone call. "You northern girls are too much. My mama would be blushing."

"Oh, aren't you sweet," Mouse told him as he walked away. "Tell Mama our bark is worse than our bite."

While Mouse discussed the rest of the menu with the chef, debating the merits of salad with wildflowers and whether or not anchovies must be obvious in a good Caesar salad, Zoey slid her chair closer to the rail so she could rest her head there and watch the guys work and let her mind wander. After having Scott around, the noise of nail guns and power tools soothed her. Maybe that was the problem with her new block; she needed to get a tape of carpentry sounds to play on Skye's stereo while she waxed creative to the whine of a power drill or the thud of a hammer.

She tipped her head to the side, cheek against the back of her hand as she watched two guys huddle together to move a large piece of Sheetrock to the wall. Twenty-first century gods, she thought, seeing images as a collage. The way their T-shirts stretched over their shoulder blades, taut as they lifted the heavy piece. Solidly planted feet in steel-toed boots. And then there was the row of men facing away from her to work on the wall, their blue-jeaned butts like a cancan line, one flat, one round, one ready to pop the seams, one high and proud. *Vive la variété.*

At the end of the line, in the shadows, was a turquoise shirt that caught her eye. It was the same color as . . . and, yes, there was the printed logo: Scott Peterson Carpentry. She lifted her head. "Oh my God."

"What? What is it?" Mouse looked up from the menu list she was scribbling on. Chef Michael had already returned to the kitchen.

"It's Scott—he's working down there," Zoey said in a stage whisper. "He must have been hired to help renovate the building."

"Which one?"

"Last butt on the left. Turquoise shirt."

Mouse leaned against the rail and glanced down casually. "Mm-hmm." She smacked Zoey's shoulder. "Mm-hmm! That is one nice-looking hiney. Why don't you go down and say hello?"

"Me? No!" Zoey turned away from the rail, panicking at the thought that he might see her.

"And why not? Are you afraid he might pick you up, throw you over his shoulder, and spank you in front of all those macho men?"

"No, of course not." Zoey crossed her arms, realizing that Scott would never be so demonstrative. The guy was a married man. But what if they sneaked off together? The coatroom was empty. Certainly the ladies' room was abandoned, though unfinished. They could pull each other's clothes off, and he could do that teasing thing with his hands, running his fingers over her body, dipping lower, lower. He could press her against the newly set tiles there, or maybe she would bend over and grip the counter while her ploughed her from behind. She crossed her legs. She could do it right now.

Or could she? Yanking a guy from his coworkers and going at it in a rough construction site was not quite the same thing as seducing a man in the privacy of a safe apartment.

Mouse smacked her shoulder. "Well, here's your chance, girl. He's coming up the stairs."

Snapping back to reality, Zoey sat up straight and glanced over at the men climbing the stairs. When Scott's head rose to eye level she quickly turned away and walked to the table, pressing her fingers on the surface till the knuckles turned blue. But she knew he had seen her, and he was approaching.

"Hey, there," Mouse said, glancing at someone behind Zoey.

Zoey turned, suddenly startled by the electric quality of his blue eyes. "Scott . . . hi."

"Hey." He seemed casual, distant. "What are you doing here?"

"Just hanging out. My friend Marielle is going to be working here."

"Great." He nodded. "It's going to be a nice place."

Zoey nodded back, wishing he would leave so this awkwardness would disappear. She wasn't going to seduce him here, not now. Not ever again. And he didn't really seem interested anyway. The prime opportunity for their wild, shameless lovemaking had expired along with Skye's service contract.

"Well, I'm off," he said. "Heading home. Take it easy."

"You too." Zoey nodded, watching him walk out. Actually, watching his butt, one of his better angles.

Mouse was watching, too. "Oh, Lordy." She bit her hand and rolled her eyes. "If he was in my apartment, I'd do him too. Actually, I've been wanting someone to build me a bookcase." As soon as he went out the door she scurried over to the beveled glass windows to watch him out on the street. "You are a cutie, Mr. Hammer. Hey, get a look at this."

Zoey joined her. Outside, Scott climbed into a shiny van angled right in front of the club. He slammed the door, the sun glinting over the name and logo painted on the side.

"Yes, he puts his name on everything," Zoey said, recalling how he'd once scratched it onto her midriff during a rough session.

"Look at the names painted on the front."

On the chassis, were three names: Cindy, Jason, Alexa.

"Must be his wife and his kids," Zoey said. "He never disguised the fact that he's married."

"I wonder if his wife knows he plays."

Zoey shrugged. "I never thought about it too much, but I guess he covered his tracks. He always jumped into the shower after sex. I don't know for sure, but I doubt that I was the first . . . or the last."

"Are you kidding? Honey, if he jumped your bones on a regular basis, you can bet he's finding somewhere else to make a booty call now."

"So I shouldn't feel guilty about sleeping with a married man? Merlin gave me a hard time about it last time I talked to him. Said it's okay to have sex, but bad karma to screw around with a married man. He's worried that I've messed up my karma. Or maybe he just wants to be sure I find someone more eligible next time."

"Really?" Mouse turned away from the window. "Bad karma. Well, that's all fine, but what about the married man who's doin' the screwin'? With a womanizer like Scott, I'd say his karma must be shot to hell. Or don't they apply the same standard to guys when they're giving out karma?"

Zoey laughed. "I don't know. Who gives out karma, anyway? The karma king?"

Mouse smiled. "I'd love to know who makes up the rules, because some of them need to be rewritten." She looked toward the garden area, where Kenny had already disappeared to make his phone calls. "You know what he told me? That he doesn't believe in dating employees. Wouldn't want me to feel that he's taking advantage of me."

"Really?" Zoey glanced at the door. "And you've already covered all this ground after you just met him today? You work fast, Mouse."

"Why wait around? Anyway, I've got to talk him out of his straight-laced, southern ways. I mean, come on, people must have sex down there. Get down in Dixie."

39

"Welcome to Zoey McGuire's Pot-Less Dinner," Zoey said, holding the door open for Merlin and Mouse. Now that Mouse was out of Club Vermillion and waiting for Rainforest to open, it was becoming way too expensive for the group to eat out and party at clubs with their usual frenetic pace. So Zoey had decided to invite everyone over, specifying that she would provide beverages as long as they each brought something to eat.

"Jade's inside already, and she brought Thai dumplings and spring rolls, so I hope there's no duplication. Something smells good." Zoey reached for the bag in Mouse's arms, but she snatched it away.

"Hands off," Mouse said. "Chef gave me a freebie but made me promise to do the presentation correctly. And you know I wouldn't dare undermine that man's creative sensibilities."

"Help yourself to utensils or plates," Zoey said, gesturing toward the kitchen. "I still don't know where anything is, but what do you expect? I spent the past three months living on coffee and take-out."

"Well, I just slaved in my closet-sized kitchen to make eggplant balls, and they're delicious." Merlin put his tray on the kitchen counter and rolled up his sleeves. "If I hear one person tell me they taste just like chicken, I swear I'll throw a hissy fit."

"God, I wish I could cook," Zoey said, watching them unwrap the dishes. "Actually, I take that back. It's too artistic and engrossing, and too many calories. I already have one artistic, engrossing, time-consuming passion."

"Sex?" Jade called from the living room, where she'd been calling her own cell phone from Skye's line to make sure it was still working. "I thought Scott was gone."

"I meant writing," Zoey said, "Though that's as good as gone, too."

"Oh, poor baby. Still blocked?"

Zoey groaned. "Is the pope Catholic? Is the mayor an art critic?"

Jade patted her shoulder. "It'll pass."

"We're going to show you how to put up a pot of spaghetti, Ms. Zoey," Mouse said. "That way, you'll never starve. Right, Merlin?"

"Right." He blinked, hands on hips. "But how do you make spaghetti?"

Mouse placed chicken cutlets on a plate and started squirting green sauce around the edges from a baggie that had been tied into a pastry bag. "Spaghetti, rice and beans . . . all the cheap staples. You'd be surprised how far you can go on yogurt and a can of soup with crackers."

Jade shuddered. "You guys are scaring me. The real way to avoid starvation is to have lots of take-out menus by the phone. If you call them, they will come. Some of them take charge cards now. Can we eat?"

Zoey handed out plates and beers, and they all served themselves. This time they sat around Skye's dining room table, "Like grown-ups," as Merlin said.

"I am just so sure this thing isn't working," Jade said, placing her cell phone beside her dinner plate. "I'm going to turn it in tomorrow for a new one. I just can't afford to miss calls."

"I never got cozy with my cell phone," Merlin said thoughtfully as he dipped a squash dumpling into hot sauce. "Usually I forget to carry it. I guess I'm just not a technology person."

"We know," Mouse said. "It took you years to get an answering machine." She smiled as she thought of something. "I just called Kenny and left a long, long, long message about the outfit I'm wearing at the opening. This costume is hot, but I breathed it all heavy and nice onto his machine, trying to work my magic."

"This is the boss?" Merlin asked. "The one who doesn't want to fish off the company pier?"

"That's the one." Mouse wiped her mouth and pushed her hands to her breasts. "It's got this shiny copper bikini top that pushes my boobies into happy mounds. And feathers on the shoulder. And the skirt, the way it hugs my curves." She pursed her lips, as if in pain. "I'm telling you, the man is going down."

"Let's hope so," Jade said distractedly, picking up her cell phone. "Let me check my voice mail a sec."

As Jade pressed the phone to her ear, Mouse went on. "I've been working on Kenny, just a little every day, and it's taking hold, I think. His lips are still saying no, no, no, but I've got his body saying, yeah, uh-huh, I am liking this. I make a point of touching him. Smoothing down his lapels, or massaging his shoulders a little or squeezing his arm when I get excited about something. We work so well together, it's incredible. We designed these invitations together, and took them to the printer, and I got this mailing list from my cousin, so lots of the celebrities in town will be invited to the club's opening night. You all are invited too, and it's going to be a night to remember. Anyway, I am working my charms on Mr. Kenny Aragon, burly bear of a man, and just you wait. When I'm done with him, he won't be able to resist me."

"I should say not." Merlin smiled. "And if he tries, just talk up a blue streak like that and he'll have no choice but to give in."

Mouse tossed her balled-up napkin at him. "Go on and tease. I know you love me."

Merlin dodged the napkin and spoke without looking up from his plate. "An overinflated sense of self-confidence, but then you need that in your business."

"When is the opening of Rainforest?" Zoey asked. "Not that I have anything else on my calendar for the summer, but I've begun to look forward to the prospect of discounted food."

Mouse gave her the date, and Merlin marked it on his calendar, too. "Josh has class that night, but I think I can be there. God, I can't believe summer is nearly here." He looked up at Zoey. "Any success in getting money out of your rich husband?"

Zoey let out a breath. "Don't ask."

"That bad?" Merlin asked sheepishly.

"My career is stumped again and my sex life is zilch and my husband is trying to screw me royally in the divorce. Can you believe he wants some kind of payment for the emotional support he reportedly gave me that contributed to the literary magnificence of my novels?"

"What the hell does that mean?" Merlin asked.

"Oh, I don't know, I guess it's a backhanded way of saying that I would not have had a best-seller without him." Zoey pointed a fork in the air. "Which isn't true. You all know that. If anyone inspired *His Daughter's Keeper,* it was my father, God rest his blistered soul. Damn it, look at the title."

Jade flipped her phone shut and turned to Zoey. "Nick the Prick is just playing the lawyer game," she said. "Annoying though that is, you've got to separate yourself from it and let your lawyer deal with him."

"I'm doing that!" Zoey insisted, gesturing at the walls and the apartment around her. "Isn't this all about moving on?"

Silence.

Zoey looked down at a plateful of food—potluck delicacies, courtesy of her friends. "Oh, guys, I'm sorry. It's not your fault, and you're right, I've got to get him out of my life, out of my psyche. Completely out of my head."

"I think you're doing a good job trying," Merlin said sympathetically. "Really, Zo, you're doing everything right, but it takes time to make a life change. Give yourself a chance."

"You are so wise," Zoey said. Then she shoved an eggplant ball in her mouth.

"A real wise-ass Yoda," Mouse said, pointing her long-necked beer at Merlin. "So wise, Grasshopper, that we don't know a thing about your walk down the aisle with the man of your destiny. What's with the wedding plans?"

"Things are in motion," Merlin said, biting his lower lip nervously.

Zoey noticed Jade tapping her cell phone and wondered what was wrong. Usually Jade didn't stress over business calls.

"Of course," Merlin went on, "all the planning seems to be falling in my lap since Josh hates obsessing over details, and he's so busy with school that he really doesn't have time, anyway."

"School?" Jade blinked. "I missed something. Did Josh go back to finish college?"

"It's a masseuse school," said Merlin. "He's so good with his hands, the guy has a natural healing energy in his fingers. So I pushed him to do something with that talent, and he finally agreed to go for it. He started back in September, and he and his partner are doing well with it."

"And Merlin is footing the bill," Zoey said, pointing at him across the table. "You always manage to forget that part, you modest boy. Oh great benefactor of scholarly massagers."

Merlin turned to Zoey and squinted. "Shut up."

Zoey started laughing over a mouthful, and Mouse waved her hands at the two of them. "Oh, stop fighting, children, and tell us about the wedding, Merlin. What are you wearing? What kind of flowers . . . music . . . food? And promise me you won't be inviting that asshole."

That asshole was Leo Milewski, a friend of Merlin's who'd dated Mouse in college before coming out of the closet. Zoey wasn't sure of the precise details of his relationship with Mouse, but everyone knew there were some hard feelings from both parties.

"Leo is on the guest list, yes, but I hear he's going to be in England for the next six months so your pride may be spared."

Mouse raised her hands to the heavens. "Oh, thank you, Lord! Please detain him overseas for as long as possible."

Jade tapped her cell phone against the table.

"Jade, you barely ate anything." Zoey handed her the platter of chicken, but Jade waved it away. "Honey, what's wrong?"

"It's the absolute worst thing in the world," Jade said.

Zoey braced herself for the worst possible scenarios that might rock Jade's world: Bad lab tests, a worthless IRA portfolio, fire at the summerhouse, swindler at the brokerage. She reached across the table and placed her hand over Jade's, which seemed cold and pale. "Oh, honey, what is it?"

Jade's blue eyes sparkled with pooling tears. Her voice cracked with emotion as she answered, "I think I'm in love."

40

Silence hung in the dining room as Zoey tried to recover from Jade's bombshell. It was an innocuous announcement, really, but no one had ever expected to hear those words from Jade Cohen. At least, no one who knew her well.

"Oh my gosh." Zoey patted Jade's hand. "That's great, honey. Tell us all about him."

Jade's face was pale, a white mask framed by her silky black hair. Her lipstick had been chewed off to reveal bluish lips. "I . . . I don't know where to start."

"His name might be good," Merlin said. "From there you can do birth sign, where you met, his favorite position in bed, you know . . . the regular *Cosmo* crap."

"He was on my Most Wanted List," Jade began. "A.J. Chenowitz. I think it stands for Alfred James, but he's just A.J. It was a lucky coincidence that we met. I mean, his office called the agency to look at listings in Manhattan, and I answered and . . ."

"Wait a second," Merlin interrupted. "You've fallen in love with A.J. Chenowitz, the computer nerd. The dot com guy?"

Jade nodded.

Zoey looked from one to the other. "Do you know him, Merlin?"

"He's a regular guest at the hotel, a very nice guy, but . . . really, Jade, I don't see it. I mean, are you sure you've got the right man? Silvering hair? Round midwestern twang? With a gosh-golly-jeepers attitude about everything?"

Jade nodded so vehemently her dark hair bobbed. "Why? What do you know about the man? Oh, Merlin, tell me he's not gay?" she said, sounding suddenly panicked.

"No . . . I don't think so. I've never seen him with anyone, male or female. I always thought he was a loner, a little idiosyncratic. Likes vodka martinis and peanut M&Ms. Tries to keep things simple, doesn't go for frills or lavish dinners or limos. The guy's a billionaire, but he rides the group vans in from the airport."

"Exactly!" Jade nodded again. "The first night we met, I assumed we'd be riding around in his limo or car service, but he turned up on foot. Told me he came on the subway, can you imagine? A man worth billions and he rides the subway." Normally Jade would have scoffed at such frugality, but tonight she sounded mystified, as if she were describing an innovative guru.

"Whoa, whoa, whoa," Mouse said quickly, snapping her fingers in front of Jade's face. "What's up with you, girl? You're in love with the man and you want to know if he's straight? You mean you haven't slept with him yet?"

Good point, Zoey thought as she studied Jade. She couldn't imagine her friend spending an hour with a man she was attracted to and not trying to get in his pants.

"No," Jade answered innocently. "No, we've only been together twice, and somehow it just didn't seem right. I mean, I get so *nervous* around him. For some reason I really want him to like me, and when we're together I pump all my energy into trying to connect with him. Trying to understand him, I guess. The man is so corny and quaint, but he's genuine and I'm not used to that. Give me icy, jaded cocktail party conversation and I'll peel away the layers and figure out whether you want to head over to my place or have a quickie in the storage room. But earnestness, I can't take. It just throws me. He throws me."

The three friends exchanged looks of surprise and amusement.

Merlin began to sing: "This girl is a woman now . . ."

"Call the paramedics," Mouse said, "she's lost her mind." She sneered at Merlin, who was still singing. "You lost yours years ago."

"Don't tease her." Zoey defended her friend. She patted Jade's hand, which was still poised beside the cell phone. "I think it's wonderful, Jade. Really. Falling in love is . . ." Her mind raced back to the early days with Nick, when he seemed to be a god casting brilliant light and sexual energy into her exceedingly normal world. "This could be your once-in-a-lifetime, honey. I'm so glad it's happening for you."

"But so far nothing is happening." Jade's face was shadowed by fear, like a child who'd just run downstairs because of a noise from her closet. "I mean, he came to town and I showed him around twice, on two evenings, and that was it. Since then he hasn't called or emailed or anything. No messages on my machine, nothing on my cell phone, which I'm getting totally paranoid about because if he did call and can't get through . . ." She sighed. "I can't stand to think about it. Because if my cell phone *is* working, that means he hasn't called, and that he doesn't feel the same way about me. Both options are devastating."

"Oh, honey." Zoey pushed her chair back and went behind her friend to rub her shoulders. "He'll call."

"Or maybe he won't, if he doesn't have a clue that you're interested," said Merlin. "Did you give him any hints? Any indications or invitations?"

Jade's expression drained to a vacant panic. "I don't know. Probably not. I was so busy trying to keep the conversation going without sounding like a jerk." She slapped her hand against her cheek. "Oh, no, do you think . . ."

"Call him," Mouse said. "Don't you usually do follow-up calls to clients anyway?"

"Yes, but I didn't want him to think I was pushing him. I wanted him to call *me*. I want him to want me."

Merlin got up from the table. "This conversation is beginning to remind me of things I overheard in the schoolyard in seventh grade, and that was not a good year for me."

"See, that's where Jade is different from the rest of us. Back in seventh grade you were a geek, I was trying out for school productions, Zoey was captain of the goddamned dodgeball team, and Jade was letting some boy feel her up in the science lab."

"And liking it," Jade added sadly.

"Oh, get over yourself, Jade," Merlin said briskly. "You can handle this. You are the Queen of Cunts, and I mean that in the best possible way. Strut your stuff. Wiggle your ass. Whisper in his ear. Let your body brush against him. Just try the usual with Chenowitz and if he's got a scintilla of testosterone in his body, he'll go for it."

"I can't help it." Jade stared down at her plate, pushing an uneaten dumpling until it toppled over. "Whenever I think about him all my normal instincts dry up and I get paralyzed. A total brain freeze. This has never happened to me before." She felt her forehead. "You know, yesterday I started wondering if it wasn't about A.J. at all . . . if I was coming down with the flu or something, but no such luck."

"God, I remember that feeling." Zoey finished massaging Jade's shoulders and began clearing the table. "Although that was quite awhile ago. But then, I've shot my chance at true love. My star-crossed love crossed over to someone else." She straightened, holding a stack of dishes away from her white blouse. "All that's left for me now is sex. The exercise of mutual orgasm. Sort of like naked aerobics with a partner."

"I've lost that, too," Jade said sadly. "Since I met A.J. I haven't had sex with anyone. No sex at all, for at least, I don't know, a week . . . ten days. It just doesn't seem appealing, now that I know so surely that I want him. It would just be a waste of time."

"I can't believe you're finally in love," Mouse told Jade. "This is going to be good, girlfriend. Don't be looking like somebody died."

"I just feel so lost. I need help. Coaching. Counseling. I actually bought a woman's magazine last week and took the 'How to Know If He's into You' quiz. And I failed." She put her head on the table. "No one ever told me this was painful. Or if they did, I certainly didn't believe them."

"It'll be okay," Zoey assured her. She brought the stack of dishes into the kitchen, thinking about how Jade should proceed. "I say you call Dot Com Guy right now, and do your standard follow-up routine."

"Right," Mouse agreed. "But add in a little something extra. Like, how you keep thinking of him. That he's a special client. That you'd love to have him as a neighbor in New York."

"That's all part of the standard bullshit."

"Tell him you'd like to rub his balls," Merlin called from the living room. "Or is that in the broker's manual, too?"

Jade lifted her head and stared at the ceiling. "I am so lost here."

"No, you're not." Zoey handed Jade her own cell phone. "Make the call. Give him the standard bullshit. Then add something special. Something from the heart. If he's a genuine guy, he'll understand the language of truth."

Jade flipped open the phone and paced off to the bedroom nervously.

"The language of truth?" Mouse screwed up her face. "What kind of crap is that?"

Zoey shrugged. "I know, I know. But it sounded inspired when I said it."

"I like the poetry of it," Merlin said. "I don't know what it means, but perhaps that's what makes it poetry."

41

"You look gorgeous," Kenny told Mouse as she stepped out of the ladies' room for the opening night at Rainforest. "Thank you." Since no one was watching, she rose up on tiptoe to place a kiss on his smooth cheek, making sure to rub her breast against his arm on the way down. His resolve was melting, she could feel it. Despite the ringing of his cell phone and the employee calling from the kitchen, the man couldn't take his eyes off her.

She wore a two-piece costume, yes, a costume, rented from a theatrical costume house. Mouse knew she couldn't afford to buy a gown for this evening, and she also knew she would need something stunning and dramatic: A bikini top made of shiny copper lamé that perked up her breasts like a Wonder Bra. The straps of the top were covered with darker brown feathers that teased the air with her slightest movement. The skirt, which dipped below her navel with a hint of naughty, was made of clingy fabric adorned with silk appliques and shiny beads. The warm coppery tones complemented her brown skin and the combination of bare skin and feathers made her feel almost like an exotic creature found only in the depths of this wondrous Rainforest habitat.

Kenny took her hand in his, gazing into her eyes. "I know tonight is going to be hectic, so I wanted to take the time to thank you for helping me get everything off the ground here. You've done a lot more than most employees. I mean, a regular hostess would just show up tonight and start pointing people to tables, but you've been a strong source of guidance for me. A real friend."

Mouse smiled. "And you're just realizing that now?"

"I'm a little slow on the uptake." He pointed to his head. "Too many tackles on the football field."

"Get out!" She reached up to stroke his head, then swirled her hand around his ear playfully. "I am your friend. But I want to be so much more."

"I know, but—"

"Don't say it!" She pressed her fingers over his lips. "Didn't I tell you a million times, Kenny Aragon? I am going to win you over. So you can keep on saying no, and resisting, and telling me you're a man of ethics while you undress me with those big, hungry brown eyes of yours."

"What . . . me?"

"Mm-hmm. I see you, lover. And don't think I'm not doing the same." She lowered her voice as someone walked by with a tray of exotic flowers in vases. "But right now, we'd better get down to the nightclub business. After that, we'll take care of booty business."

Kenny folded his arms with an embarrassed smile. "You are naughty, woman."

"I never said I was an angel. Listen, Mr. Aragon. You are going to walk me home after we close tonight," Mouse said, turning to open the reservation book. "Now go, take care of those frantic people in the kitchen. Guests are going to be arriving soon."

"Yes, ma'am," Kenny said, swaggering away.

Flipping through the giant leather-bound book, Mouse felt her hands tremble with a nervousness that reminded her of first-night jitters. They were nearly booked solid with reservations, many from the celebrities on the guest list. The evening had the potential to be a success, barring a sudden thunderstorm, or an accident by the waterfall, or an outbreak of food poisoning. "Fingers crossed," Mouse whispered to herself as Crash, the jazz band, began to set up on the stage.

Once the first party arrived, Mouse clicked into performance mode, playing a cordial, charming hostess. She forced herself to memorize guests' names and faces as if they were lines in a script. Like a hawk, she kept a close eye on available tables, quietly directing staff to clear away dishes and put on fresh linens so that guests wouldn't have to wait. Her voice sounded warm and hospitable as she greeted and cajoled guests. And within an hour of opening, the lobby was crowded with various celebrity guests, people from politics, television, stage, and film. Mouse approached them with the same warmth she lavished on any other guests, but inside her heart was beating with excitement at meeting these extraordinary men and women.

"So good of you to join us this evening, Mr. Koch."

"Did you enjoy the show at the Apollo, Mr. Powell?"

"Enjoy your evening, Ms. Winfrey. Oh, if you insist, Oprah. And I'm so glad you made it to New York for our opening. Mr. Aragon will be sure to thank you."

"Yes, Mr. Newman, our owner insisted on locating the Rainforest in Harlem. Would you and Ms. Woodward like a table on the balcony or closer to the main dining room?"

"Right this way, Senator Clinton."

Although Mouse had always pictured herself among celebrities, she hadn't expected it in this venue. She'd imagined these people coming backstage to congratulate her after that big show. She had seen herself laughing with them over drinks at charity fundraisers or socializing with them at parties after the Tony or Drama Desk awards. Still, this sort of exposure couldn't hurt. Now, when she became a star, these celebrities could smile and say, "I knew her when . . ."

Throughout the evening, Kenny circulated, greeting people at their tables, a relaxed hand on their shoulders as he spoke softly, always engaging them, never interrupting or imposing. The

man had such a natural charm, a light sense of humor, a genuine warmth for friends and strangers. It was as if Rainforest
were his home and every guest there his extended family.

When her friends arrived, Mouse was able to set them up at a
prime seat on the balcony. "No freebies tonight," she said, speaking softly over the table, "but enjoy the view. You've got Alec
Baldwin to your left, and Tom Hanks with wife Rita on your
right, fresh from a film shoot on location in Central Park." She
nudged. "I hear Mr. Baldwin is available these days."

"That's lovely," Jade said, picking up a menu. "But I only have
eyes for A.J."

"I hate to say something nice, since it's not in my nature,"
Merlin admitted, "but this place is really lovely." He lifted his
martini glass containing a lemony yellow liquid spiked by
pineapple leaves—"a pineapple and sage martini," the waiter
had said. "It's going to be this summer's drink."

Sticking with champagne, Zoey punched Merlin's shoulder.
"And we've got an in. Our little Mouse has landed in a hot spot."

"Better start calling her Marielle now," Merlin said with mock
pomposity. "Marielle Griffin, a new power player in the Manhattan Club Power Game. Is this the best revenge on those NYU
brats, or what?"

Zoey lifted a champagne glass, loving the feel of the smooth,
thin crystal against her lips. "We can get a table without a fifty-
dollar tip. And I've been invited to sit at the bar anytime I want."

"Really?" Jade seemed surprised. "What's that about? Have
you been sleeping with Kenny on the sly?"

"Of course not!" Zoey raised her chin indignantly, then realized how overpronounced the gesture was. Okay, she was a little
tipsy, but this was a big night, right? "If you must know, Mr.
Kenny Aragon realizes that I am an important writer. He wants
me to be the bar's literary muse, the way Hemingway and Fitz-
gerald breathed life into those bars and bistros in Paris." Zoey sat
back in her chair, and smiled, really enjoying the air and the exotic flowering plants and the company. And perhaps the alcohol
in her veins. Yes, life was good.

"Sort of a literary mascot," Merlin observed.

"Exactly." Zoey glanced down toward the stage, where the band was taking a break. It took her a moment to locate the cute guitarist, but there he was. . . . "And I think that guy from the band is going to come right over to this table. Right here. Oh, no, maybe not. No, he's going to talk to a friend. Oh, well."

All night long she'd been watching the jazz guitarist in Crash, waiting for his keen dark eyes to wander her way. She liked the way his brown hair feathered back over his high cheekbones. Once, when he'd made eye contact, she'd been so tickled she'd felt like a junior high girl who'd been felt up for the first time under the bleachers. Absolutely tickled. Or maybe it was the champagne. Or the Cosmopolitans. Or the wine. Did she have wine tonight? She was losing track.

Jade pointed to the champagne glass in Zoey's hand. "Is this your first night out with the drinking license? Not to be a noodge, but those things are going down fast and furious."

"But Zoey's loosening up," said Merlin. "This is the most re-laxed I've seen her in months. Maybe years."

"I am the epitome of loose." Zoey held her glass up so that the lights from the ceiling hit the popping gold bubbles. "Loosey goosey."

Mouse passed by, seating guests, and on her way back Zoey snagged her to ask about the hottie. Zoey loved to watch his body move, stretching over his guitar in his leather pants and deep blue shirt like a thick bungee cord. His fat bottom lip gave him a permanent pout. Mouse said the guitarist's name was Jonathan Prescott, though everyone called him Snake.

"Snake?" Jade said. "Well, there's your answer about how he is in bed."

Zoey slapped her arm. "I'm not interested in a sexual rela-tionship again. You know that." But that was a lie, of course. She was dying to have sex again, perhaps only because the prospect of steady sex had disappeared when Nick had stopped coming home. There was no turn-on for the libido like a cheating hus-band.

"Okay, I want sex," Zoey admitted. "I mean, sex can be good. It was very good with Scott. Scott the handyman. Sort of regular-guy sex, but after a while I realized that something really important was missing. It was just a lot of sex for the sake of sex." Her voice was getting loud, she suddenly realized, and she smacked a hand over her mouth and looked around. "Oops! Do you think Alec Baldwin heard that? I can't believe I'm talking about my sex life in public." She took another sip of champagne and added in a stage whisper, "And talking about it in front of Alec Baldwin."

"Like Alec Baldwin never had sex," Jade said, waving a hand at Zoey. "I realize you're a private person, Zo, but it kills me that you still haven't come to realize that everyone has sex. Everyone. If they're not doing it with a partner, you can bet they're doing it on themselves. I don't even believe that priests are celibate."

"Easy, Jade," Merlin said. "Please, don't ruin my image of those monks in Tibet. Some things should be sacred."

"Sorry, honey." Jade patted his hand. "You just hold tight to your dreams."

"What was I talking about?" Zoey put her fingers on her temples, trying to concentrate. "Oh, yeah, sex without emotional attachment. Sex with Scott. Our bodies worked well together, but our minds never connected. There was a definite brain void between us."

"Much as it frightens me to admit it, I know exactly what you're talking about," Jade said. She sipped her Cosmopolitan and frowned. "That's the way sex has always been for me. A physical connection. I never expected more than that and I wasn't disappointed until . . . Well, Taki started me thinking. And A.J. epitomizes the need for an emotional connection. Goddammed love. I could just kill him."

"Did you ever hear from him?" Merlin asked.

Jade nodded. "He came back to look at places again, and I think he's settled on one. I also went to dinner with him, and I think he's getting the message that I've got a thing for him. Though we're moving at a snail's pace. At least he's coming back to town. Day after tomorrow."

Merlin nodded. "I knew he was in town. He still stays at the Royale. But I didn't want to mention it to you, just in case he didn't—"

"Get out!" Jade slapped his shoulder. "Next time you even see his name on the reservations list, you call me. Do you understand?"

"Just don't use my name," Merlin said. "Some customers are hinky about their privacy."

"I'll show you privacy," Jade said. "Next time he's visiting, you can deliver me to his suite on the room service cart."

Zoey laughed. "That's precisely why Merlin never talks about work, and never tells us who's staying at the hotel. He knows we can't be trusted."

"Actually, I have the opposite problem around A.J. I still get so flustered and nervous around him. Totally unlike me, but yes, whenever he's near I am a total buffoon. When we went out to dinner I lost the grip on my roll and it went flying onto another table. Then I put my elbow in the butter. When I'm showing him places I walk into walls and stub my toes on furniture. I get so freaked that I can't calculate the trip for a cabdriver, which I can usually do in my sleep."

"Oh, my gosh, you're losing your cool around him!" Zoey smiled. "That is so sweet."

"Hardly." Jade tipped back her Cosmo glass and drained it. "I feel like an oaf around him, and yet I can't wait to see him. What the hell am I going to do?"

"You're in love!" Zoey announced giddily. "Enjoy! Be yourself. We know there's a warm, kind person under that bitch exterior."

"Thanks for sharing that, sweetie." Jade rolled her eyes. "The odd thing is, I can't even be bitchy around him. He has this way of turning me into a quivering adolescent who walks into walls and loses her train of thought."

"See." Zoey nodded. "He brings out the true you. Definitely love."

"I am in deep shit," Jade said. "Let's get another round of drinks."

"Jade, Zoey may be looped but there's a grain of truth there," said Merlin. "Just be yourself. You can be endearing at times. If he's going to fall for you, he might as well know the real you."

Jade nodded sadly. "Don't take this personally, guys, but I hate advice."

Their waiter brought a tray of desserts to the table and presented it with a flourish. "Our dessert selection, compliments of Ms. Griffin." He placed an ice cream sundae in front of Zoey, cheesecake for Jade, key lime pie for Merlin.

"Oh my gosh!" Zoey grinned. "She knew exactly what we like."

"Not that it's the mystery of the new millennium," Jade said, lifting her fork. She and Merlin thanked the waiter as Zoey contemplated her sundae.

"Nuts. I love nuts," she said, lifting a walnut on her spoon. "I never appreciated them as a kid, but now I've just got to have them. I need nuts every day."

A hand touched her shoulder gently. "How lovely for your boyfriend." The voice had a British accent and a lively timbre. Clever. Playful.

Zoey turned around to face the smiling face of the jazz guitarist from Crash. She hadn't known he was British; she'd always had a thing for British accents.

"Oh, I don't have a boyfriend," she said. "But, I mean, I was talking about nuts that you eat."

He smiled. "Mm-hmm."

She put her spoon down as her friends laughed under their napkins. "Oh, you're all enjoying this, aren't you?"

"Immensely," said the guitarist. "My name's Jonathan, but they call me Snake."

He held out his hand, and Zoey shook it. "My name's Zoey, but they call me nuts." She delivered the line without flinching, stunned at her own brazenness. "Or nut lover."

Everyone laughed, but Zoey just smiled as she looked into Snake's brown eyes. There was something there—an intelligence. Humor. A connection.

Houston, we have touched down.

42

As the last guests were leaving, Kenny came up to the reception area and slid an arm around Mouse, his fingers gently stroking her bare lower back. "I don't need to ask how you're holding up, because you look as warm and sexy now as you did when the doors opened a few hundred hours ago."

"I'm doing just fine." Mouse leaned against him for a moment, not wanting anyone to see them cuddling, but not wanting to resist him. She patted his back, but noticed the guests at table seven standing up to leave. "There's the Washington party," she said, stepping away from him.

"I'll let you do your thing," he said. "Which you do so well. It's been a great night. We were a success, I think."

"You don't have to be modest with me," she said as the guests came up the stairs. "You rocked." Mouse took her time talking with the guests, asking them about the food and seeing them out the door. When she turned back to her podium, Kenny was there, tapping on the book with his gold Cross pen.

"Time for me to walk you home?"

She nodded, wondering if she'd finally broken down his resolve. "Let me get my cape."

When they reached Mouse's apartment Kenny was hesitant to come in, claiming that he knew Mouse was tired. She put her hands on her hips, refusing to let him go. She had spent two sessions rehearsing for this with her dance instructor. She was wearing a very sexy thong under this costume. She had even cleaned her apartment.

"Listen to me Kenny Aragon, and listen good. I am *not* tired and you are coming upstairs with me *now.*" She dragged him upstairs, got him a beer, and pushed him onto the sofa. He sank down onto the cushions so easily, like a giant, pliable teddy bear. Kenny Bear. Passing behind the sofa, she paused to rub his shiny shaved head, enjoying the slight bristles on the surface. Oh, she was going to enjoy being in his arms, this big, gorgeous, gentle man. Over the past two weeks she'd grown fond of him, and his evasiveness was getting downright silly. For a while she'd worried that he was gay or married—why else would a guy put off sex?—but some research and friendly advice had convinced her otherwise.

No, he was straight, single, and definitely attracted to her. It was time to show him how good they could be together.

"Did I tell you how beautiful you looked tonight?" he asked, putting the beer bottle on a coaster. "Everyone noticed. And that outfit . . . you are really a knockout in that."

"I'm glad you like it," she told him. She turned on the stereo, programming the CD to play the song she'd practiced choreography to. "Because when I picked it out; I was thinking of you." A drumbeat began, and she swung her hips left and right, the beaded skirt shimmering over her legs.

"Whoa, now." A huge smile lit Kenny's face. "Don't tease me like this, girl."

"Oh, I'm not a tease," Mouse said, lowering her feathered shoulder straps. She strutted over to Kenny and arched her back, leaning over him so that her lips were inches away from him. "I never promise what I can't deliver."

His dark eyes flickered with interest, but she snapped her head up and danced before him, wiggling her hips wildly.

"Oh, girl. You are killing me with that body of yours. You don't know what I want to do to you."

"Oh, you think so?" Still facing away from him, Mouse reached down to her ankles and rubbed her hands up along her legs, lifting her skirt sensuously over smooth calves, curved knees, tight thighs, and round butt.

"Marielle, Marielle, you can't do this to a man and expect to walk away!"

She turned toward him and dropped a strap completely off, letting a firm brown breast pop out. "Who's walking away?" She loved the tortured expression on his face as she stroked her breast, making the ebony nipple harden to a peak.

He shook his head. "What am I going to do with you, girl? You know I can't resist you, but I don't want to take advantage."

"So let me take advantage of you." She stepped up to him and unfastened the hooks in her skirt. In a soft jangle of silk and beads, the skirt swished to the floor, leaving her before him in a high-cut bronze thong and her elegant silk heels. "Forget that you're the boss, forget what your mama told you about ethics, and hear me now." She took his hand and he stood, towering above her, his broad chest and beautiful shiny head begging to be touched. "You're a man, and I'm a woman, and if you haven't noticed, I've been trying to seduce you."

He sucked in his breath. "I have noticed."

"So . . ." She slid her hands around his waist and ground her hips against him. He was hard and large inside his pants. "Oh . . . I guess you have noticed," she said, stroking him through his slacks. "Well, you wouldn't want to disappoint a nice girl like me, would you?"

"No, no, girl, I don't want to let you down." He stared down at her in wonder, then outlined her shoulders and arms with his enormous hands, as if he couldn't believe she were there. "But you know I respect you. And I have a moral code here that's flying right out the window. God, you are bringing me straight to hell."

"Well, wherever we're going, we're going to enjoy the ride," she said, covering his large hands with hers. She guided him down to smooth her hips and cup her buttocks, then wriggled in his grip. "Ooh. That feels nice."

Next his large palms moved over her breasts, and she swooned against him. She had never known a man to be so hesitant or gentle, a gentle giant. And his reluctance made her want him that much more. Every time he'd turned away from her or made an excuse or gently reminded her that it wasn't right for them to be together, she'd felt more charged up, determined to undo his determination. Because of his hesitance, she'd pushed harder and faster. With an interested guy, she might not even be up to the lovemaking point yet. And she had never, ever staged a striptease for a man before.

"Come on, baby," she said, taking his hand and sliding it under one cup of her top till his warm fingers teased her nipple. "It's time to show me some good loving."

"How could I say no?" he asked, unbuckling his belt and sliding down his pants to reveal black silk boxers.

Mouse stood back, hands on hips, and watched as his body was revealed: beefy shoulders, narrow hips, smooth stomach and muscled legs with thick thighs that reminded her of pictures of lumberjacks.

"Oh, you are one gorgeous hunk of man." She unclipped her top, and her breasts sprang loose as she pulled it away. Lifting her arm, she swung the garment over her head and let out a happy yelp. He was watching her, mesmerized, loving her body with his eyes.

She gyrated her hips toward him, and he groaned, reaching for her breasts. Stepping into his arms, she slid her fingers under the waistband of his boxers and slid them down.

Praise God! she thought, seeing that his erection matched the size of his body. He was large, probably the largest man she'd ever been with, and though size wasn't as big a deal as some of the magazines said, it couldn't hurt.

She cradled him with her hands, stroking him, then pushing his large body back onto the couch so that she could straddle him. "We are going to have some good times together, honey," she said. He kissed her neck and shoulders as she straddled him, sitting on his lap. She felt wet and open, but the head of his penis was large, and he wasn't going to fit in without a squeeze.

"Oh, my, you are so big."

He sighed. "I know. I'm sorry, baby. I don't want to hurt you."

"You'd better quit apologizing and take care of business here," she said firmly. "First of all, you are one fine specimen of large, beautiful manhood. And second of all, you're not going to hurt me, and any woman who told you she couldn't stretch to take on a man like you is full of steel magnolias."

Resting on his thighs, she moved forward until the tip of his penis touched the lips of her vagina. She took his rod in her hands and slowly began moving it along her clitoris, stroking herself with his firm flesh.

They moaned together.

Although Mouse was already turned on from her own striptease, she always liked good clitoral stimulation before intercourse. It never hurt to grease the pan before frying up the main course.

"Wassup, woman?" His eyes were half-closed, weary with wanting her. "Are you making me wait?"

"Mm-hmm. And you love it." She kept rubbing his penis over her jewel, using firm pressure and a steady hand until the sweet heat rose within her.

"I do love it, I do." His eyes rolled back as he groaned. "But you are driving me crazy, woman. I can't take this."

"You can't?" she asked, swiping his penis through her wet lips once more. The sensation was sweet and thrilling, a wellspring of pleasure rising from between her legs, shooting through her whole body. "Then we'll have to do something about that." She pressed forward, hard, pushing her vagina over the head of his penis. She had to rotate her hips and bounce over to him to squeeze him in, but it was fun work, rocking onto him.

He moaned as she jostled on his lap, teasing him into her moist opening.

"Oh, woman, oh, yeah, that's right," he whispered as she nudged herself against him.

At last, she slid down onto him, sighing as he filled her deeper and deeper. His penis seemed to expand everything inside her, thoroughly massaging her, pummeling her G-spot, over and over and over again. She felt like she could ride his rocket into the sky, his super-powered express ship. They were staring into each other's eyes, and the intimate contact made Mouse that much hotter.

"Oh, we are going to have some good times together," she told him, writhing up and down on his firm rod. "Some very good times."

43

"It seems that each person has a very different idea of what would constitute the perfect wedding," Merlin spoke over the rumble of the Uptown number 4 train rocketing into the Bronx. He had talked Zoey and Mouse into joining him for a Wedding Expo held at a Bronx Hotel. "Someone mentioned a castle in Tarrytown, and there's an old mansion on Long Island that's supposed to be quite elegant."

"But you have to watch out for those wedding factories," Mouse said. "The places where they have six or seven affairs going on at the same time, separated only by accordion pleats. The last time I went to one of those the wedding sucked, and we ended up next store at a bitchin' bar mitzvah. There was a Candy Store Cart with make-your-own sundaes and giant lollipops and caramel popcorn. Very cool."

"I was with you," Zoey said, pinging her shoulder. "We brought cotton candy back for every member of the bridal party."

"Mental note," Merlin said, writing in the air, "Candy Story Cart is in." He unfolded the wrinkled brochure for the Wedding Expo and frowned. "Why are we doing this? The World's Largest

Collection of Bridal Attire and Accessories Under One Roof. Gowns, Tuxedos, Flowers, Photographers, DJ's, Chocolatiers. Sounds like a dream I once had. A nightmare."

"Doesn't your friend Emily swear by this thing?" Zoey asked.

"My friend Emily also loves revolving restaurants and Teddy Bear Grams."

Zoey winced. "Oh, *that* friend Emily. The hairstylist?"

"Yes, and the other Emily had a mouthful of advice, too. Everyone has their wedding stories. A woman at the hotel keeps asking me who's going to do the videotape, as if this is going to be a Francis Ford Coppola film available at Blockbuster. And then there's favors. What does she mean by favors? Sexual or otherwise?"

"Otherwise, unfortunately." Zoey scrunched up her face. "I remember that. You're supposed to give each guest a token gift— you know, something useless and tacky and ridiculously expensive. When Nick and I got married we gave away china picture frames. Ugly white things that cost a fortune. It killed me, since I wasn't working at the time, but Nick insisted, spurred along by his mother. Oh, and as if the picture frame wasn't enough, each one had a little net bag of candied almonds attached. I hated, hated them. Fortunately, by the time the reception rolled around I was too freaked about trying to pronounce all those Armenian names to notice."

"But you had a forceful mother-in-law to make all your wedding decisions, you lucky girl," Merlin pointed out.

"Right. She chose the place, though it didn't hurt that Nick's uncle was the Armand in Armand's Lake Club."

The doors opened at 86th Street, and people got on and off, but Zoey barely noticed. They had to ride this train to the end of the line, to the serene surroundings of Greenway Manor, wherever that was.

"Did you know that my friend Gerald and I went skinny-dipping in that lake after the reception?" Merlin asked.

Zoey gave a mock gasp. "God, you should have told me. I would have joined you."

"No, you wouldn't."

"You're right, but I should have. It would have been better than partying back in the bridal suite with Nick's law school buddies. Such titillating talk of torts and probable cause."

Mouse crossed her legs and toyed with a purple crystal ankle bracelet. "Yeah, well, I never told you guys, but I tossed my cookies in that lake during the reception." She turned to Merlin. "I hope you had all your shots."

"That explains why I was sick for weeks after that. I blamed the shrimp cocktail, but now I know it was you." He glared at Mouse, who stuck her tongue out at him. Merlin swiped a hand over his spiked hair and sighed. "Weddings . . . Big groan. I wish Josh were interested in helping me plan this thing. I just don't know where to begin."

"Ah-ha!" Zoey said, unzipping her backpack. "That's why you called in your trusted friends for consultation. Behold." She held up a glossy paperback book with a soft-focus photo of huge white orchids on the cover. "A Wedding Planner."

"Voila!" Merlin's smile held a trace of embarrassment. "Wow. Thanks, I guess." He opened the book and started paging through it.

"It covers every detail, totally anal," Mouse said, "but you can use it as a guide."

Merlin nodded. "Actually, it's perfect. I can brush up on etiquette and tradition while checking out all the incredibly tacky things to avoid." He flipped ahead, but Zoey stopped him.

"No, go back . . . right here. Check this out: 'Your Wedding Time Line.' It's a list of things to do at various intervals."

"Let's see if I'm on target," Merlin said.

"Let me read it," Mouse said, snatching away the book. " 'Twelve months before the wedding: Bride . . .' "

"I guess that's me," Merlin interrupted, "since I'm doing all the work."

" 'Bride, start planning! Use a notebook or file to keep track of every detail."

"Okay, I guess this book is a start."

Mouse read on: " 'Pick a date for the ceremony and reception.' "

Merlin nodded. "That's a problem. We're going to register down at City Hall, but that doesn't really mean much to either of us and we're not going to bother having friends come along for that. I do have a cousin who's an excommunicated priest, who's agreed to say a few prayers that sound wedding-like. And the date . . . Josh is hoping for July or August, but people say it's impossible."

"This summer?" Mouse asked. "Do you know how hard it's going to be to get a place?"

"I know, but Josh says he always wanted to be a summer bride."

"I thought you were the bride," Mouse argued.

A man in soiled coveralls and work boots lowered his newspaper to glance over at the three of them curiously.

Mouse was shaking her platinum blond head in disgust. "Well, if you're planning a shotgun wedding, we'd better move ahead on the list. Let's see. . . . 'Decide on a color scheme. Decide on a florist. Decide on your accessories: the shoes, the bag, the lingerie, the make-up.' "

"Now that's right up my alley. I say no on the mascara, yes on the eye cream. And I love shopping for shoes, though they may be the most expensive item of the whole damned affair."

" 'Three to four months before: Coordinate the mothers' outfits, if possible,' " Mouse continued.

Merlin rolled his eyes. "You mean I have to invite my mother!"

Zoey laughed.

" 'Two months before: Get yourself a facial, massage and pedicure—you deserve it!' "

"That sounds like a great idea right now," Merlin said, checking his watch. "Why don't we blow off this Wedding Flea Market and head back down to Elizabeth Arden on Fifth Avenue?"

Zoey held her hands up, stopping him like a crossing guard. "Let's just check this thing out. If it's really awful we can leave."

Merlin tugged on the book in Mouse's hands. "Do they mention the appropriate time to start popping Valium in there? Xanax? How about Klonopin?"

"Don't see any prescription drug references," Mouse said, yanking the book back. "No, wait. They do remind you to get a refill on those birth control pills before you leave for the honeymoon."

"The honeymoon! Oh, girls, what am I getting myself into!" Merlin buried his face in his hands and let out a theatrical wail.

The construction guy in the dirty overalls looked over with concern. Zoey tried to hide her grin as she patted Merlin on the back. "Don't worry about him," she told the man, adding, "Cold feet."

44

Jade was not surprised when she opened the door to the Chelsea apartment and A.J. reacted with a hoot. He wasn't one to temper his reactions, and she had suspected he would fall in love with this place just as much as she had.

"This is fantastic!" He danced up and down the first few stairs of the circular staircase, then spread his arms wide and looked up at the ceiling. "It's just what I had in mind when I told you I wanted a place with history, a place that felt like it was home already. Though, of course, I'd never envisioned anything so remarkable."

Jade nodded, swallowing hard over the knot of emotion in her throat. She had never taken a client to this space, for fear that they would take it off the market. A few weeks ago another agent had found a client for the apartment, and when Jade saw the contract pop up in the listings, it had put her plans into a tailspin. She couldn't bear to think of someone else living in her dream home.

Fortunately, the deal had fallen through, and the listing was available again. Still, she had debated about bringing A.J. here, reluctant to share the apartment with him, as if offering up a piece of her life to him.

"Woo-hoo!" A.J. kicked up his heels and clapped the soles of his sneakers together in the air. "Do you mind if I wander around for a few minutes? I'd like to soak up the ambiance."

"Of course," Jade said, extending an arm toward the spiral staircase. "Now that I know you, I won't even try to sell you on the features."

He rubbed the shoulders of her navy Anne Taylor linen suit—a friendly gesture, though she felt his touch right down to her toes. "Thanks, thank you for that, Jade. You've learned that I don't need the pitch. I know what I like and what I don't like, and that's enough for me." He bounded up the first few steps, then paused to take in a deep breath, his chest expanding as he savored the air. "Can you smell that? History. Human experience. And knowledge. An inquisitive mind must have lived here."

She nodded, not certain how he knew these things, though she, too, had sensed them. The ghosts in this apartment were friendly spirits, quiet and playful and astute. This apartment still reminded her of her grandparents' Boston home, where Grandma used to claim that the spirits helped to lighten the load of daily tasks by helping to fold the laundry and dusting. Back then Jade had tried so hard to see the ghosts, squinting her eyes and peering into the dark closets, sitting in the corner between the croquet set and Grandma's fur coat, watching and waiting. Funny, she had never seen a ghost back then, but now that she wasn't trying she could feel them all around her.

As he disappeared from the upstairs landing she walked into the kitchen and dropped her briefcase onto the table. A.J. was going to take this place; she could feel it. And that certain knowledge should have made her the happiest woman in the world, as it was the fulfillment of her master plan to snag a billionaire and lure him into buying this home of her dreams.

But she wasn't happy. In fact, the tightening of emotion in her throat was beginning to feel like a physical pain.

"It's in your head, all psychological," she said quietly. She ran her hand over the grain of the wood cabinets and noticed a built-in spice rack shaped like a wooden house. Subtle but quaint. So lovely, this place. This place that had seemed so important in her initial scheme, but now paled in comparison to something she had discovered that was far more valuable. That man upstairs.

She sat down hard on the upholstered cushion of the booth. She wanted that man upstairs, desperately, but for the first time in her life she wanted something different from a man, and she was at a loss as to how to achieve it.

And she had thought that she knew everything about men. She had thought she understood their behaviors—animal; their needs—sexual; their patterns—predictable. "You have no respect for men," a therapist had once told her. She had argued that it wasn't true, that, in fact, she understood them more than most women, and that the therapist was simply annoyed that she refused to rank his testosterone-laden species on the same level as women. They had argued the issue for months, but Jade had walked away with the same sure knowledge that men were good for amusement—physical comfort and playtime. Beyond that, the species could not be trusted.

She had refused to invest emotions in a relationship because, let's face it, an emotional commitment with a man almost always turned out to be a bad investment. Men didn't want it, and neither did she. At least, not before A.J.

But now she wanted more, partly because she found A.J. so genuinely compelling, and partly because she felt that he deserved to have an emotionally fulfilled relationship. She felt as if they had been friends forever, but at the same time there was a fresh quality to each moment they spent together. And her feelings toward him were strong, almost palpable. She wanted to care for him and mother him and amuse him and cower under his protective arms. She wanted to be the woman who made his life complete, and yet, she had no idea how to get there from here.

She pounded her fist on the table. It was so frustrating. Here she was a successful, mature woman and nothing in her life had prepared her to deal with a real adult relationship. Oh, she'd fucked like a bunny all her life, but in the realm of mature relationships she was truly a virgin.

Pushing away from the table, she strode into the next room to find A.J. She felt driven by the need to confess, the need to tell him something. But what? What?

What had her friends said? Hands pressed against her chest, she thought back desperately to the brief conversation at Rainforest. What had Merlin and Zoey said. Oh, right. Be yourself. That old pearl. Although around A.J. her "self" was a klutzy broker who never seemed to know what to say.

She found A.J. in the library, sitting in a lotus position on the floor before the old fireplace with its porcelain tile imported from Holland. He looked so at home there, with his eyes closed, a gentle smile on his face. But telling him that would sound like another sales pitch, and she wanted to save her words for more important things.

"Hi." Her skirt slid up her thighs as she kneeled on the floor beside him.

"This is it. This is the place." His eyes twinkled, and she could feel his excitement.

"That's great, I'm really happy for you, but I need to talk to you about something else."

He cocked an eyebrow. "Shoot."

"I am . . ." She was about to say "so in love with you," but stopped herself. That would scare him, as it would any man, and it wasn't necessarily true, at least, not yet. She shook her head. "I don't know why this is so hard for me, but it is. I guess, it's hard because I value our relationship. The thing is, I hope I've been a good realtor for you, but I want to be more, A.J. I am very, very attracted to you." He tilted his head to the side with a coy look. "And I don't mean sex. I mean, sex would be great, but I feel more than that. Affection, I guess."

"I'm flattered," he said. "You're a beautiful woman, but I had no idea that . . . that . . . I didn't know. Usually when a woman is after me she makes it so obvious. Or then again, maybe it's just obvious that she's after me for my money." He squinted behind the black glasses, assessing her. "Do you know what I'm worth?"

"I do." She squeezed her eyes shut. "I do, I do! I know you're wealthy . . . extremely wealthy. And that was certainly an initial attraction, both as your broker and as a woman. But that's not what I'm seeing when I look at you right now."

"Really? What do you see?"

She leaned forward, eye to eye, and placed her right hand on his knee. "When I look at you, I see a man who is happy to wake up in the morning. A man who still sees the sky beyond sky-scrapers. Someone who looks people in the eye and tells them what he really thinks without a trace of animosity, even when it's something they don't want to hear. Someone who jumps up to apologize when my dinner roll clocks another diner, then makes sure the waiter brings an extra basket to the table so that I don't feel bad. I see a man who checks his email every hour because he doesn't want other people to feel ignored, and in this day and age that is so . . . so . . . ."

Her voice caught and she realized that tears were forming in her eyes. "I've never known anyone as kind and genuine as you."

"Jade . . . you're crying." He took a plastic pack of tissues from the pocket of his jeans and handed her one.

"I can't help it." She sniffed, pressing the tissues to her eyes, sure that her mascara was running down her face in disastrous streaks. "What I'm trying to say is that I'm crazy about you, A.J., and I don't know how to begin to deal with that. You are so out of my league and I act like a . . . a total . . . you know."

"A klutz? A knucklehead?"

She waved the tissue at him. "I don't know why I act that way around you, but I do, I can't help it."

"Maybe it's a subconscious need to be saved," he said. "To put me in the role of savior or hero?"

"That sounds good." She tried to swallow, but the lump in her throat was tighter, and the motion came out as a pathetic sob, which made another round of hot tears well up in her eyes. "I just felt that . . . that I had to tell you the truth. I had to let you know how I felt, even if there's no hope that you'd feel the same way. Because I . . . it's just that this is the first time I've ever felt this way about a man, and it's . . . it's difficult for me."

"Oh."

It was the shortest answer he'd ever given.

She glanced up and found an unfamiliar wariness in his gray eyes.

He nodded, pursing his lips together. "I'm glad you told me the truth, because I had absolutely no idea about your feelings for me." He shook his head. "You are one cool city slicker, Ms. Jade Cohen. I mean, whoo! Not a clue!"

She swallowed again, pained by the way his corny overreaction appealed to her. He was so damned cute.

His eyes were intent on her. "Yessiree, I am totally taken by surprise, and loving it. You see, I've liked you since I met you, but guys like me do not date women like you. Nosiree. Of course, unless those women are just going out of their way to snag a fortune, which doesn't work out in the end. I mean, how could I stand to spend time with someone who is only tolerating me?" He waved his hand. "No good. That wouldn't work at all."

Jade took a whimpery breath as his words sank in. "You mean . . ."

He grinned. "Yeah, yup. I like you."

"You do? Really?"

"And why is that so hard to believe?"

"I don't know. . . ." Suddenly she worried that A.J. was the kind of guy who was happy to be with any woman. Had he ever been in love, or did he fall in love on a daily basis? She wanted to be more than just a fling, but she wasn't sure how to say that without making a jerk out of herself.

She slipped off her heels and lined them up neatly at the edge of the Chinese rug. "Have you ever been in love?"

He adjusted his glasses, a tick that Jade had learned was an indication of nervousness. "Yes. Once. But she didn't love me."

"I'm sorry."

"It happens. I met her at a charity fundraiser. She's from a political family, and they all have this turned-up Irish nose. Cute as a button, she was . . . is. She would have married me, but not for love. For a while I thought that it would happen in time, that she would just see the light one day and fall head over heels, but it didn't happen, and being with her became too painful when I realized that my feelings were unanswered. It's the strangest thing. You reach out to grasp a hand, and there's no one there. Just your own hand, flailing through time and space."

She reached forward and gave him an awkward hug. His chin hit her shoulder and her nail snagged on his shirt, but the embrace was real and warm, and Jade closed her eyes, wanting to kick off her heels and dance around the room.

Usually, this would be the moment when Jade and her man would roll back onto the carpet and begin writhing against each other, pulling off garments and seeking pleasure in the stroke and kiss and pump of a good, solid fuck, a chance to christen the new apartment with a happy memory.

But tonight, with A.J., there was just an awkward kiss, a fleeting touch of his lips. When they parted, she put her head in his lap and tugged her skirt down awkwardly.

"Can you just hold me for a while?" she asked quietly.

"Sure." He began stroking her hair, gently, lovingly.

She wrapped her hands around one of his knees, loving the softness of the worn blue jeans. He likes me, she thought, flabbergasted that the language of junior high could matter to a thirty-five-year-old woman. She felt a tug on her scalp, then realized his watchband had gotten caught in her hair.

"Sorry," he said.

"That's okay," she said. They were not the model couple; not the subject of perfume ads in magazines. But they were real, this was real. The beginning of a real relationship.

It was a wondrous thing.

45

"Rainforest is a rare dining experience, reminiscent of the old supper clubs! Jazz is right back at home in Harlem—and a beautiful home it is!" Mouse read the headline from the *Daily News* and dropped the newspaper onto the bar in front of Zoey. "Are we a hit, or what?"

"You're a hit, my dear, though I don't think you need any of the critics to tell you that. You've had a line out the door since the night you opened. The only reason I have a seat here at the bar is because I know *the* Marielle Griffin." Zoey finished scribbling on her notepad and tucked the pencil behind her ear. Over the past two weeks she had taken Kenny up on his offer to haunt the bar, and spent most evenings sitting at the end stool, scribbling down behavior observations, nursing a club soda with lime and gazing longingly at Snake whenever there was a break in the crowd allowing her to see through to the stage. So far, she had a casual thing going with Snake, and two notebooks full of chicken scratch. Not that her notes weren't fascinating, but she hadn't yet found a thread to tie them together.

Mouse leaned back against the bar, resting her arms on the wooden edge. She looks like a queen on a throne, Zoey thought. Even in repose, Mouse presided over her kingdom, scanning the balcony to see who was paying the tab and getting ready to leave, monitoring the foyer to greet any new arrivals. It was late for a Tuesday—nearly one in the morning—and the line was gone, the patrons wined and dined. Those who remained were here to party and enjoy the jazz music from Crash, which would be finishing their final set momentarily.

"You never stay this late," Mouse said, turning to Zoey suspiciously.

Tapping her pencil against her pad, Zoey grinned. "I've got a date."

"At one in the morning? You're dating a night-shift worker?"

Zoey nodded toward the stage.

"Snake?" Mouse's mouth dropped open. "You go, girl. I love his accent. And with the way that guy makes love to his guitar on stage, those fast-moving fingers? Mm-mm. You know what I'm saying."

"One can only hope," Zoey said, chewing on her pencil. So far, she and Snake had stolen a few kisses outside the club while his band was on break. Slow, sexy kisses with a spark of something when their lips met and a nice tingle as his hands passed over her shoulders, arms, and butt. She loved the press of his thick lips against hers, though once there Snake seemed a little laid back, as if his mind were elsewhere when her tongue was teasing his or tracing his smooth teeth. And although it felt nice to snuggle in his arms, he wasn't nearly as aggressive as Scott. There'd been no grinding of hips, no stray hands reaching for bosom or crotch. Snake seemed content to let the physical progress slowly, which was exactly what Zoey had in mind, too.

But tonight he had asked her to stay until the show was over so they could leave together. Leave together. Was that the new lingo for sex? Instead of the tired "Hang out at my place" or the ancient "I'll come up for a drink"? Hard to say, but she'd been out of the dating scene for years, and her relationship with Scott wasn't any help since they'd never done anything socially.

"You sound like you're nervous," Mouse teased her. "You'll be fine. It's like riding a bicycle."

"Thanks, Mom. Now that you're back on the old ten-speed, you've become an expert again."

Mouse grinned. "A ten-speed with a banana seat," she said, laughing. "That's a great analogy. A big banana seat."

Zoey shook her head. "Now, that's more information than I want to know. And I like Kenny."

"So do I! I like him late at night, and then again in the morning, just after I wake up and have that first cup of coffee. He is fine, and right now I would hate to spend a night without him."

"You guys are getting cozy fast."

"I know. I was thinking about moving into his place, save us both a little on the rent, but do you think it's too soon to push? He's been so tied up with opening this place, I'm afraid his head is spinning."

"I wouldn't give up your own place just yet," Zoey said. "You two are great together, but it's a big move. Some guys totally freak over the mere mention of it, even when you're spending all your time together, anyway. Besides, your apartment is rent-stabilized, right?"

Mouse put her hands on her hips. "Oh, now you're sounding like Jade!"

"It's one of the realities of life in the city." Zoey slid her pencil into the spiral binding of her notepad. "A harsh reality. I'm going to need a place to live soon. Skye isn't going to be off cajoling that reclusive novelist forever."

"The woman still hasn't booked her flight back. For now, that apartment is a great gig. And you're getting off the subject at hand." She grinned. "Me. What about me and my needs? My career? My boyfriend?"

"Excuse me, did I slight the ego of an up-and-coming star?"

"Thank you." With a lift of her chin, Mouse tossed back the orange chiffon scarf that draped her bare shoulders. Tonight she wore a shimmering, shoulderless sheath accented by sequins that covered the fabric in gradations of color starting with burnt orange at the top and ending with lemon yellow at the hemline. "I was just about to tell you about my next gig. Not that I've had time to audition much lately, but my dance teacher, Teddy, showed me something the other day that gave me an idea, and I ran it by Kenny and, what do you know . . . I am going to be on that stage next week. I'm rehearsing two Broadway tunes, with choreography and costumes and everything. A one-woman show, starring Marielle Griffin, though it's just two songs right now. But it's a start."

"That's great." Zoey realized this job was turning out to be just the lift Mouse needed for her career and her love life. "You'll have to let us all know when you debut the act. We'll throw you a little party."

"She's going to be spectacular," Snake said from the foyer, where he'd suddenly appeared, beer in hand. Looming in his sleek black duster, he reminded Zoey of a thick-lipped vampire, dark and sexy. "We've only had one rehearsal with the band, but this woman has a fabulous voice."

"Thank you!" Mouse curtsied. "I'm looking forward to it." She patted Zoey's shoulder and stepped away. "Excuse me. I'd better see what's holding my man up. He's probably scrubbing pots in the kitchen or pruning one of the plants. I'm telling you, if he could run this place singlehandedly, he would."

Zoey learned that "leaving together" meant taking a cab to Snake's apartment in the west thirties—Hell's Kitchen, as she remembered it. He had commandeered a six-pack of beer from the bartender and downed two before they made it to his place. Still, he didn't seem to be drunk as he keyed open the door of the third-floor walk-up, flicked on the light, then quickly flicked it off.

"The place is a mess, as I remember." A match flared, and he lit three candles on a rough wooden coffee table. An unfinished table, Zoey thought as she sank into the futon couch in front of it. "So we will sit in the dark and have a memorial service for the dearly departed roommate who used to tidy up here. Me mum. She left for England last week. Just visiting."

"Good for her. Was it nice having her here, or do you have a normal mother-son relationship—strained and manipulative?"

"Mum puts the fun in dysfunction, so she supplies a hefty amount of nagging and bitchering while I adore her takes on celebrities. And no one makes curried chicken like her." He tossed off his duster and sank down beside her. "Now that's charming. You've learned that I'm a slob and a mama's boy. Shall we move on to my negative qualities, then?"

Zoey laughed. "I like to watch you perform."

"Trying to suck up to me, are you?" She watched his back bend as he leaned forward, her eyes moving down to his ass. He was wearing a black shirt tucked into black satin pants with tiny mirrors inset amid looped stitches. She liked the pants. At the moment, she was curious to get inside them. He opened two beers and handed her one.

"Some people just can't take a compliment." She took a swig of beer, letting her hand move to his thigh.

He laughed. "Do you like my mirrors? You know, I'm very vain, an absolute narcissist, so these shiny ditties come in handy. Yes, I can be walking down the street, wanting a good look at my beautiful self, and all I need do is just bend down like this." He doubled over, pretending to preen in one of the tiny mirrors on his knee.

It was Zoey's turn to laugh.

"I like that sound," he said. "Like a waterfall, smooth and powerful."

"My laugh?" Zoey took another sip of beer. "I've been told it's a bit forced."

"By whom—a masochist?" He stood up and crossed into the darkness. "Let me put some music on. I can't think straight without it." He made some motions in the dark corner, and thick, lush jazz music filled the small room.

"You must have an expensive sound system," she told him.

"It's the only thing of value in the room," he said. "Which you would readily detect if I allowed any light in this space." He sat beside her again and turned his face, his lips just inches from her. "Are you nervous, then?"

"A little."

"So let's just break the ice, shall we?" He kissed her quickly, then came back again with moist open lips. Zoey pressed against him and let her tongue explore his even teeth, his open mouth. She reached for his shoulders and moved her hands over them, stroking his back. His hands held her back firmly.

It felt good, soft and nice. Almost unsexy.

After a moment Snake ended the kiss and smiled. "Feel better, then?"

"Mmm. Not nervous anymore."

"That must mean my diabolical plan is working." He reached for his beer and she nestled against him.

"How long have you been in New York?"

"How long?" He took another swig of beer. "How long, you ask? Perhaps you would like the story of the life and times of Snake Prescott."

"I have a feeling I'm going to get it whether I like it or not."

"Exactly. Didn't I tell you I was a narcissist?"

She pulled her feet onto the futon and stretched out, so that her head was resting on the overstuffed pillow at the end. "Okay, okay. I will listen, but only because I find you fascinating as a person."

"Of course you do." He tickled her ribs and took another drink of beer. "Now, then, how to begin? I was born a poor— No, that's too far back. Let's see. In primary school I was voted most likely to pick my nose while meeting the Queen of—no. You don't want to hear about—"

Zoey smiled as he rambled on. He was quite entertaining. If only she could stop thinking about what was inside those pants. . . .

46

A warm, tingling sensation across her abdomen woke her. Someone was stroking her, his hands sending warm sensations radiating through her. Nick.

No, wait . . . it couldn't be Nick. It took her a moment to realize that she must have dozed off on Snake's futon. He had talked for quite awhile about growing up in Nottingham, a pub town about two hours away from London. He told anecdotes of coming to the United States as an exchange student and using that connection to return years later, living with old friends' parents in Northern New Jersey, and commuting into the city for gigs. He was a delight to listen to, and Zoey had found herself giggling as she leaned against the couch, and teasing him back.

The candlelight had widened the hollows of his eyes, making his dark eyes darker and giving him a haunted, poetic look. She loved the set of his brow, the strong line of his nose, framed by his long dark hair.

Somehow, they'd gotten onto the subject of the jazz trio, and Zoey learned that Snake wrote most of the lyrics for their songs. They talked about classic poetry and avant guard and "the ridiculous pomposity of Poetry Slams," as he put it. It turned out he was educated at Cambridge, although when Zoey heard his year of graduation she cringed. She was the class of 1989; he was in the class of 1998. Okay, she had realized he was a tad younger, but by nearly a decade? She had told him she was robbing the cradle, and he'd handed her another beer and asked about her field of study at university. He started quoting Keats, and Zoey grabbed him and kissed him, hard. Then she'd tried to initiate a little cuddling, but he had pulled away to recite a few of Shakespeare's romantic sonnets.

At one point, she told him she had to close her eyes for a second . . . which was probably when she'd dropped off to sleep.

His hand was still moving, stroking provocatively. Ordinarily it would have been a welcome overture, but right now sleep seemed a better option. "I'm so tired," she said.

He hushed her, sliding his hand beneath her panties, then back to her tummy.

His body was a heavy weight pushing her into the cushion. His breath was warm on her cheek, and it smelled stale, of beer and sour mouth. She felt tired and wished she were at home, in a clean, comfortable bed.

She shifted her foot, causing the clang of glass. Beer bottles? Votive candles? Hard to tell in the darkness.

"Mmm. I must have fallen asleep," she said.

"Shh. Don't say anything." His hand moved in circles over her tummy, then dipped beneath the waistband of her black spandex skirt, cupping her between the legs. He held her tight for a second, then pulled his hands out. There was a whisper of material as he slid off the couch. Now she could see enough to know that he was kneeling at her feet. His fingers pulled at her skirt, and she lifted her hips to help him remove it. He moved industriously, peeling off skirt and panties in one motion.

She started to sit up, thinking she would undress him, but he pushed her back onto the couch, lifted her legs and shifted her so that she was facing out. The mound of darkness before her eyes must have been his head closing in between her legs.

She flinched at the sensation of his mouth on her. He began

licking the folds voraciously, and she realized she must be completely dry, still half asleep.

Should she stop him?

Resting her head back against the couch, she thought of Snake, his sexy pants, his thick lips, his amusing stories. Already she was warming to his touch, starting to feel the familiar pangs of desire. Yes, she could rise to the occasion, though this wasn't quite the way she'd pictured this when she'd fantasized about making love to Snake. Somehow her own version had him singing and stretching languidly, naked and smoky-eyed, as she danced naked around him.

He moved close to a sensitive spot, and she whispered: "That feels good." She hoped that, with a little encouragement, he might linger there.

"Quiet!" he warned her.

What is this, fifth-grade assembly? And he was missing the mark down there. She wanted to call out when he got near a sensitive spot, but apparently he had a thing for quiet sex. Hmm. Zoey glanced up and tried to make out shapes on the ceiling, hoping that the main event would be better than this. She thought about her most recent effort at an outline for a novel, the story of a successful stage actress who lost the ability to speak. Was that too much like her previous porno effort?

Hello—some guy's giving you head! a voice shouted from within. Maybe you should pay attention to him instead of juxtaposing plots and characters?

But the random licking wasn't getting her anywhere, and she felt stifled by his order of silence. The only sound was the smack of his lips and tongue against her. She wondered if he'd be mad if she stuck her hand down there and did a little stimulation on her own. It was frustrating that he kept missing the spot, but since he seemed to be freaky about being in charge, she didn't want to undermine his approach.

She felt coldness as he pulled away. She sat up to help him undress or to cuddle against him, but he pushed her back again. "No, stay there," he ordered. He was slipping off his mirrored pants when she thought about protection.

She lifted her head. "I have a condom in my purse," she said.

"I got it." There was the sound of rustling foil, and she could see his dark form fumbling near his crotch area.

She flopped down again, then felt him pressing against her. Okay, I can do this, she thought. I can make this fun and worthwhile for both of us, even if I can't shout and moan.

He pulled her legs high, placed her feet on his shoulders, and entered her with a hard thrust. It hurt a little, and she touched her breasts, massaging the nipples, trying to keep the mood going.

And then he was in again, and out. And suddenly he was pumping against her hard and fast, a desperate man. Zoey wanted to get into the movement, to rock with him or hold him inside. She wanted to stop and cuddle or kiss, but he was working so fast and furiously, like a runner finishing a race.

She turned her head to watch him, a dark form writhing in rhythmic fury. He was working so hard, so unnecessarily. It was as if she didn't even need to be here. She could send out her vagina to date Snake and stay at home for a good night's sleep.

Not a bad idea. At the moment, sleep was definitely preferable.

47

Merlin awoke with a vague feeling of warmth and satisfaction. He was spooning Josh in the glorious canopied bed of the Westminster Suite, and for a moment he didn't move, content to listen to the steady wisp of Josh's breath against the ivory linen pillow.

It was so unusual for them to fall asleep in the middle of the day, especially during an interlude at the hotel, but they had both been somewhat sleep-deprived lately. Josh was having trouble dividing his time between work and masseuse school, and Merlin had taken to spending most evenings after work with the Party Girls, who usually graced Manhattan's new hot spot, Rainforest.

He ground his hips against Josh's bare ass, feeling a new rise of desire, but the dark-haired boy was lost in a deep sleep. The room smelled of sex and the hotel's standard cinnamon potpourri, and Merlin took a deep breath, finding the scent somehow comforting. They had needed this rendezvous. With all the wedding plans tugging on Merlin and the school demands on

Josh's time, Merlin had begun to sense that they were drifting apart. "It's too easy to let daily demands pull us apart," Merlin had told Josh. "So many relationships disintegrate because of job stress and arguments over money, and we can't let it happen to us." "Yes, oh wise one," Josh had answered with a mocking bow.

He noticed Josh's hand curled on the ivory sheet and wondered if Josh would wear a wedding band. He hoped so. A ring exchange could be an important part of the ceremony, and Merlin thought it was an important symbol, a sign to the world that they were committed to each other. He would have to ask Josh about it.

So far Merlin had managed to settle the most important wedding details. The Wedding Expo had been a true education for anyone planning to pour mega-bucks into a single day. Merlin, Zoey, and Mouse had walked past booths with open mouths and eyes popping with horror: booths featuring chocolates with the faces of the bride and groom etched upon them; headpieces with sprays of netting and fake flowers and glitter and fake gems; photos of catering halls, low-ceilinged affairs lit by tacky chandeliers, gardens studded with quaint Astroturf bridges and white latticework gazebos.

From that day forth, Merlin had decided to keep everything human, normal, and in Manhattan. With those guidelines, he had managed to book the upstairs room of a small restaurant on the upper west side, where the eggplant parmesan was heaven and the nonvegetarian dishes were said to be quite good as well. The only snag was that Venus was retrograde for all of July, the only month when the restaurant was available, and retrograde Venus was not a good time for romance. Venus was the planet of love, the planet that ruled attraction, cohesion, gentle persuasion. While the planet was not moving in its usual course Merlin was sure that any union that transpired would be fraught with self-indulgence and dissonance. No, he would not be married during such a discordant time.

At first Merlin had insisted on choosing a different date, but Josh had worn him down with talk of his romantic dreams. Then

Josh contacted another astrologer, who thought the chosen date was appropriate, that Merlin and Josh had enough crossover in their two charts without having to rely on Venus for cohesion.

Now, they had a date—a July wedding. Merlin was still working on flowers and clothes, but he felt more relaxed about making choices now that the important decisions had been made.

The electronic purr of a cell phone split the silence, and with a sigh Merlin rolled away from Josh to find the phone. After two rings he located it in the pocket of Josh's shorts. "Hello?" he answered quietly. He sank down on the edge of the bed, trying not to disturb Josh.

"It's me," the woman said. Her voice was flat and annoying, like a squeegee on a dry window. "I wanted to let you know that your sister is going to be visiting next week. Not that you should join us or anything. I told your father you wouldn't come. That you think you're so much better than us. That's what I said."

"Hello?" Merlin squinted. The woman sounded like Edith Bunker. "This must be a wrong num—"

"Oh, now you're going to pretend you don't know me?"

"But I don't," Merlin said. "You must have the wrong number."

"This isn't Josh." The woman sounded angry. "Where is he?"

And now Merlin was the one at a loss. She was looking for Josh—not a wrong number. This woman was giving him a bad feeling. He wanted to hang up, but didn't seem to have the power. "No, it's not Josh." The bed moved as Josh stirred behind him.

"Then where is he?"

"He's here," Merlin said, tempted to add, "sleeping naked behind me." But somehow his usual wit didn't seem appropriate. The bad feeling was getting worse.

"Don't play with me, mister, okay? Just put him on."

"And whom should I say is calling?" Merlin asked in his best butler imitation.

"His mother."

Merlin felt a stab of pain and horror. But Josh's mother was dead. He'd figure stepmother, but Josh hadn't heard from his father in years, not since he'd run away from his Minnesota home in high school.

"Josh . . ." Merlin turned and touched Josh's hip bone.

He swatted Merlin away, then turned his head on the pillow. "What is it, lover?" he murmured, his eyes closed, his face still peaceful.

Merlin swallowed hard against the rising fear in his chest. "There's a woman on the phone who says she's your mother."

Josh's eyes opened quickly, dark with panic. "Oh." He frowned, rubbing his eyes briskly. "I wonder what that's about." He sat up and took the phone from Merlin.

"Yes?" The sheets slid away as Josh rose and paced, holding his other hand to his ear as if to concentrate. "No. No, not really."

Merlin studied his beautiful naked body as he walked away, pronounced shoulder blades, arched back, the gentle curve of his spine down to a high white butt. Strong legs, with thigh muscles bunching above his knees. Josh still had the lithe, lean look of a high school runaway, the combination of youth and danger that Merlin had always found so attractive. But somehow that body seemed alien now, a source of disorientation and fear as a result of the phone call. Who was Josh talking to . . . this woman claiming to be his mother.

Josh's end of the conversation was fairly closed . . . a string of one-word answers. When he hung up, he didn't turn to Merlin to explain, but went to the chair and pulled on his shorts.

"Who was that?" Merlin asked.

"Some woman. She's crazy." Josh pulled on his polo shirt and tucked it in. "Don't worry about her."

"But I am worried when you get a call from some bitch and you can't tell me anything about it. What's going on, Josh? I thought we had no secrets."

Josh turned around to face him, his face tight. "I didn't want to upset you, and now you're all pissed off."

"What?" Merlin demanded. "What's going on?"

Josh gazed across the room, as if the answer were hidden beneath the paisley window drapes.

"Tell me."

Letting out a sigh, Josh answered: "She's my mother, although I never knew she existed until recently. I thought she died when I was younger but . . . I guess that was one of my father's lies. Anyway, she managed to locate me recently. She's lives upstate. And apparently I have a sister, too. Some suburban blimp with three brats."

Merlin swallowed over the knot in his throat. It was disconcerting to imagine Josh connected to that shrill woman, even more upsetting to realize that he had kept it a secret.

"Why didn't you tell me? If you have a family, I want to be involved with them, too. We're going to be lifetime partners; we should know all these things."

"I didn't think it was important. I don't feel any connection to her."

Merlin sat down on the bed and crossed his arms in front of his chest. "I should probably meet her."

"Be my guest," Josh said. "You can let me know what she looks like, because I'm not going anywhere near her. Putnam County, Merlin. That's in the boonies. Land of K-Mart and pumpkin patches. Right now they're probably getting ready to crown Queen of the May."

"You can't pass the whole thing off as one big joke, Josh. You lied to me about something important—your family. It's scary from this side, and I'm having a lot of trouble understanding it." He was also wondering if Josh had lied about other things, but right now he didn't have the composure to go there without totally losing it.

"I think it's a big hoot because it's not that important, sweetie. So some old hag pops up and claims to be my mother. The truth of the matter is, she was never a mother to me in any sense of the word, and at this point in my life I have absolutely no use for her. I don't know how she got my number, but she'll eventually stop calling, given the cool reception I just gave her. Listen, lover . . ." He jumped onto the bed, kneeled behind Merlin, and started massaging his shoulders.

Merlin felt his anger begin to melt at the warm touch of Josh's fingers.

"It's you and me. I'm sorry if I upset you by not telling you about her, but to be honest, it's a little embarrassing. To be related to white trash, even distantly . . . I had to tell myself she's not really my mother, and she's not. You've been more of a mother to me than she has."

"Thanks, I guess." Josh's hands were soothing and magical. Merlin could feel the warm energy radiating from his shoulders, down his back and arms.

Josh leaned forward and planted a kiss in the smooth hollow behind his ear.

Merlin sighed. "If I were really your mother, I'd ground you right now."

"Don't be mad," Josh pleaded, pressing between Merlin's shoulder blades. "You can't stay mad at me for long. You never do."

"I know," Merlin admitted. "I'm a real sucker for you."

"Thank God. Just think, you saved me from that loudmouthed bitch in Putnam County. Without you, I'd be a suburban mall queen."

"Instead, you're just a flaming queen."

Josh bit Merlin's shoulder and pulled him back on the bed, growling, "Oh, you're going to pay for that one, lover."

Merlin smiled. He loved it when Josh played rough. "Go ahead and make me."

48

"Okay, ladies and gent, what will you be drinking tonight?" Mouse asked as Zoey, Jade, and Merlin settled at a table on the balcony.

"I'm surprised to see you playing hostess tonight," Zoey said. "Kenny couldn't give you the night off to do your performance?"

"He would have, but we're both nervous about letting anyone else handle the door all night. Ellie is sweet, but she just doesn't know the etiquette yet. Besides, Kenny is paying me for hostessing plus actor's scale to do the performance." She covered her sweetie-pie smile with one hand. "I'm making out like a bandit."

"Can't wait to see you on stage," Zoey said encouragingly.

Mouse patted her shoulder. "I can get you a pitcher of anything for free, but if you want one of Anton's designer drinks it'll have to go on the tab. And please, don't get wasted before my act. I need you guys to be sober so you can leap to your feet and applaud like crazy."

"Remember the old days when we had to be stoned to appreciate the show?" Merlin leaned back in his chair. "God, I feel old."

"Soon to be an old married man," said Zoey. "I'm up for margaritas tonight. Anyone want to share a pitcher?"

"Bring it on," Jade said, waving her hand. "I definitely need something to take the edge off. Falling in love is a very trying business." She set her cell phone on the table gently, then looked up at her friends self-consciously. "Yes, I'm waiting for him to call again."

Zoey frowned. "Jade, why don't you just call him?"

"Because I did, and I'm waiting for him to call back. The only problem is that he operates on a different plane than most people. He'll answer an email within minutes, but won't interrupt a day-long symposium to return a phone call."

"Then maybe you should email him," suggested Merlin.

"Oh, right, then we'll have an electronic relationship."

Hi, honey, are you free for dinner tonight? No, but how about breakfast tomorrow? Sorry, got an A.M. meeting, but I can squeeze you in for an early lunch.

Jade shook her head. "And I had to fall for a dot com guy."

"Listen, Jade." Mouse pointed to the phone. "I know you're in love for the first time, but let me warn you, if that thing rings during my show you will be dead meat, sister girl."

Jade gave Mouse a wry look. "I'll switch it to 'vibrate' and hold it between my legs."

Zoey laughed. "What's wrong, Jade? Doesn't dot com guy deliver? Or are you still having virtual sex?"

Jade gave a tight smile. "We haven't actually done it yet—"

"No way!" Mouse pulled out the fourth chair and sat down. "This I gotta hear."

"Just calm yourself down," Jade told Mouse. "There's been a lot of heavy petting, heavy breathing, heavy sighing. He seems content to snuggle and kiss, and I don't want to push him. I worry that if we move too fast . . . I don't know, I hate to jinx the relationship. Not that I'm not dying to get in his pants, believe me. But for now it's okay to be where we are, getting to know each other. And I can't believe how wonderful it is just to have someone hold you at the end of the day."

Zoey rubbed her arms, remembering the early days, when Nick first moved into her apartment in the city. It had been wonderful to know they would hook up at the end of the day for dinner or drinks or a movie. Sometimes they would just sit together and watch television. But always, always there was the night when they would share a bed. They didn't always make love, but in the beginning they held each other every night. It got to the point where Zoey could not fall asleep without Nick's arms around her. Feeling a twinge of envy, she glanced over at Jade. She missed that feeling of security.

Mouse looked around the table and grinned. "It just occurred to me, every one of us is getting regular sex these days."

Merlin nearly choked on a sip of water. He put down his glass and coughed.

"What's wrong with that?" Mouse asked.

"It's just the way you announce it so blithely," he said. "As if we've all achieved black belts in karate."

"Well . . ." Zoey toyed with the hem of the burnt orange tablecloth. "There's sex and there's sex."

Jade squinted at her perceptively. "Meaning?"

Zoey shrugged. "Not to whine or anything, but Snake is not . . . well, he's just not the best lover."

Mouse blinked in surprise. "That gorgeous boy sucks in bed?"

"Sucking would be a welcome change," Zoey said. "As it is, he just goes through a standard routine. A little limp cunnilingus followed by some major pumping action."

"Can you believe it?" Jade interrupted. "Zoey just said one of the 'C' words and she's not even blushing. Our little girl has grown up."

Zoey thought about it. "Yeah, I guess I've made some progress. It's just so frustrating because it could be really great, but it never is. There's no talking allowed. And he has to do it at, like, five in the morning."

"You stay up that late?" Mouse asked.

Zoey shook her head. "No, we usually doze off at two or three.

I think he's too drunk when he gets off work, too drunk to perform. But he wakes up with this hard-on during the night and has to have sex right away, and for me . . ." She shrugged. "I'd rather sleep. I guess we're all getting old."

"I used to date a guy like that," Jade said. "Nocturnal intermissions."

"Obviously, you have to talk to him," Merlin pointed out.

"I have." Zoey glanced down at the stage, wondering if Snake was in the building. She certainly didn't want him overhearing this conversation, but she didn't see him. The equipment was set up, but the band wasn't slated to begin for another hour. "And believe me, I chose my words carefully, since I know how delicate our egos are about performance in bed. Twice, he's agreed to have sex before we go to sleep or even in the morning. But when I've tried to entice him, he just keeps talking. And one night I . . ." She glanced down, feeling a little embarrassed. "I stroked him for a few minutes and he didn't get hard."

Merlin nodded. "Sounds like a nocturnal performer. His conscious mind censors his actions, inhibiting him from getting aroused unless he's in the semiconscious sleep state. Of course, the alcohol doesn't help his ability to be aroused or his sensitivity."

Zoey threw her hands out. "How do you know these things?"

He shrugged as if it were no big deal. "You read a few books, screw a few guys."

"The prognosis is not good." Jade shook her head. "You and Snake will have to work really hard to have fun in bed, and it doesn't sound like he wants to work."

"Thanks, Doctors Jade and Merlin." Zoey smoothed the tablecloth down. "Believe me, I wouldn't still be seeing him if we didn't have so much fun out of bed. When we're together alone, it's like a true meeting of minds. Did you know he writes most of the lyrics for Crash? And lots of other bands have recorded his songs. The other morning I woke up and found him stretched out on the floor, writing song lyrics down on a paper towel."

"A paper towel?" Merlin smirked. "In case the lyrics suck, he's got something to wipe up kitchen spills?"

Zoey thought back to that morning, finding Snake stretched out, naked on the parquet floors. It was the first time she'd been able to get a good look at his body in the light, and he was slender and lean, though a little bony around the hips. He reminded her of a naked model for a Michelangelo statue. His penis had dangled over one thigh as he'd scratched away with a pencil, humming and crossing things out.

"I have paper," she'd murmured, watching him from under the sheet.

"This roll of paper is perfect," he said. "Did you know that Jack Kerouac wrote *On The Road* on a continuous scroll of paper, probably paper that architects left behind in the Village loft where he lived."

Zoey yawned. "Yup. I read somewhere that they're auctioning off the original."

"This will be my scroll," he said proudly. He lifted the roll of paper towels and brought it to Zoey in bed. "What do you think?"

Snake's penmanship was awful, but she was able to follow the words:

Sunstreaks in Zoey's hair.
She speaks of hidden desire,
Indigo fire.
On a city street you never know
Who you'll meet. You never know.

Sunstreaks in Zoey's hair.
Sparkling words in her dark eyes,
Her light so wise.
On a city street you watch her go
With a city beat. You watch her go.

The air was still for a moment as the words resonated around her. "This is beautiful," she said. "And you used my name; that's nice." She turned and kissed his cheek.

"You inspired it, my muse!" He unfurled the roll of towels and danced it around the room like a banner, his genitalia bobbing.

She yawned again. No, their sexual relationship wasn't on fire, but intellectually there was definitely something there.

Back to reality, Zoey said, "There was something charming about it."

"And you guys always seem to hit it off when you hang out together here," Mouse said, matchmaker that she was.

"We do. He makes me laugh, and think. It's like dating a rock 'n' roll lit major. We're great together, as long as we stay out of bed."

"Oops." Someone was motioning to Mouse from the front foyer. "Gotta run before it gets busy and Ellie gives the prime tables away to peons. I'll send over those margaritas and some appetizers."

Zoey scratched her nose, recalling the old adage about "scratch your nose, kiss a fool." True in her case. "So I'm having vapid sex, Jade is just at the petting stage . . ." She turned to Merlin. "How's your love life going?"

"Why does that question make me feel so defensive? Sometimes I think you women have impossibly high standards."

"You didn't answer the question," Zoey persisted.

"It's okay, I guess."

Jade flipped open her menu. "That's a rave."

"Sex is fine. It's just that I had a little scare with Josh this week."

Zoey and Jade listened carefully as he explained about Josh's mother.

"He insists that he's never met her and has no interest," Merlin went on. "He says she's remarried an obnoxious man, but the woman called the man Josh's father. And if Josh never met her, how does he know this guy is obnoxious?" He squeezed his eyes shut, truly tormented. "I'm not sure what to believe. And I don't know whether to push or back off. I mean . . . we're getting married in July. Call me crazy, but maybe I should invite his mom to the wedding."

"You're crazy," Jade said.

He turned to Zoey. "What do you think? I mean, this is a once-in-a-lifetime thing, and I'd hate for Josh to get to know her and then eventually regret that she didn't share in our wedding because he's so stubborn. Should I invite her?"

Zoey screwed up her face. "You're asking me? I think the woman sounds like a nightmare, but I was never a fan of my own mother-in-law."

Disappointment darkened Merlin's blue eyes.

"Oh, God, did you really want me to say yes?" She folded the menu and tucked it under her chin. "It's a tough call, I know, but it's a decision you have to make. I guess the bigger question is do you want to open this Pandora's box for Josh? There's a chance that he'll never bond with this woman, and by inviting her to the wedding you might be humiliating him, exposing a part of his life that he's not at all comfortable with."

"I didn't see that." Merlin shook his head. "Oh, God, why didn't I see that? I've lost my usual logic. My edge is gone. This wedding frippery is turning my brain to mush."

"Don't worry, sweetie." Jade winked at him. "With friends like us, you can't fail. We'll keep you in the game."

49

Mouse knew they were important even before the man in the gray suit with the darker gray shirt and the woman in the black dress and linen blazer worked their way up the line.

"Danny Edwards," the man said quietly, handing her his card. "And this is Sheryl Villanova. We do A&R for Metropolis Records."

Mouse turned away from the podium and looked him in the eye, wanting him to remember her well. She wanted to jump up and down and shake their hands and squeal, "Metropolis Records? That is the absolute best record company, and I would give anything to get a recording contract with you guys, and I'm going to be on stage in about thirty minutes—yes, me!—and would you like a copy of my demo CD?"

Instead, she said, "Good evening, Danny. Would you and Sheryl like a table on the balcony or closer to the stage?"

"The best place to hear the band," he said.

"I've got a lovely table downstairs, very private," Mouse said, standing erect on the first step and lifting her hand ever so slightly. "Right this way, please."

As she seated them she put in a good word for Crash, chatted about the success of the club, assured them that they were always welcome at Rainforest despite the long wait for reservations. "My name is Marielle Griffin, if you ever need anything," she said, thinking, Remember the name, you'll see it in lights.

Danny and Sheryl thanked her. Then Mouse put Ellie in charge of seating the guests, while she ducked into the dressing room beside Kenny's tiny private office to change into her costume. Crash was on a break, but Mouse saw the drummer talking to Kenny in the wings. She told them about the A&R people in the house, and the drummer hurried off to find the other guys in the band, saying, "We are going to blow them away!"

Kenny stepped into the dressing room and smiled down at her. "Nervous?"

"Always," she admitted. "I have to be a little nervous to have an edge." She smoothed the lapels of his jacket, wishing he could show a little affection in front of the staff and acknowledge that they were a couple.

But he just patted her hand, then stepped back, ducking through the doorway. "You'll be fine, Marielle. Just fine."

The club lights dimmed and a spotlight swept the tables in the main dining room, zigzagging until Mouse felt the white circle fall over her. God, she was nervous! Dear Lord, she prayed, please let this be good. Really good. A knockout performance. The purple sequins of her bikini top shimmered as she moved slowly toward the stage. Her body mike was in place, hidden in her elaborate headpiece of purple and silver satin decorated by sequins, rhinestones, and feathers. With her skimpy bikini top and low- slung raspberry satin pants, there was no concealing it in her clothes, but her dance teacher, Teddy, had told her the headpiece made her look like a cross between Cleopatra and Dame Edna.

Kenny had wanted to announce her formally, but Mouse had thought that entering from the audience would be a little more fun. People loved impromptu performances, and if they thought she was sneaking onto the stage they'd be more likely to be on her side.

Snake started up the music, and Mouse leaned down to the diners beside her. "How's this table working out for you?" she asked. When the men nodded, she continued. "Oh, good. You know, I love my job, but sometimes, when I hear music like this, it just makes me want to burst into song."

Tossing back her feather boa, Mouse danced up the stairs to the stage and glanced out at the audience in mock shock, thanking them for their polite applause.

"I don't know what I'm doing here! But then again, neither do you!"

"Hey, lady," Snake called. "If you're going to be on stage, you'd better shut up and sing."

"He's right," Mouse told the audience. "More music, less talk." She put a hand to her cheek to speak confidentially. "I wish my therapist would go for that." Then, as laughter rippled through the audience, she spun around, stretched her feathered wings and started singing.

The nervousness bubbled in her chest, then flowed out of her in song. Singing was her thing, her means of expression, and she was so comfortable with the basics of vocal performance that it allowed her to wax artistic, flourishing a bit, holding the notes and syncopating the beat when it moved her. She breathed deeply, opening her chest, and belting out the melody when it needed belting.

In the second chorus she began to move with the steps she'd worked out with Teddy—nothing elaborate, just enough to keep the momentum of the song flowing, the eyes of the audience moving. The stage was sparse, just the three musicians in Crash and a glitter-covered star dangling from a rope. At one point she pretended to be singing confidentially to Snake, and he nodded knowingly to the lyrics of the song.

Applause burst out when the song trickled down to the final notes. Mouse bowed deeply as Snake lit into the introduction to the second song. She jumped in right on cue and strolled down into the audience, singing directly to people. She passed by the A&R people and crooned to an elderly man, who beamed in delight.

"Or would you like to swing on a star?" she sang. "Carry moonbeams home in a jar." Back on stage, she hooked her high-heeled foot into the back of the star and Snake gave her a push that send her sailing over the heads of the people in the main dining room. Air brushed her skin and rippled her satin pants around her legs—a thrilling sensation. The swing gained momentum, and she felt as if she could reach out and touch the balcony.

Flying over the heads of the surprised and delighted people, Mouse felt like a stage star. This was theater at its best, when music, atmosphere, and visual spectacle came together. She leaned down from the swing, dipping low. She was probably displaying some major cleavage, but she didn't care. A little peak would only make the act that much more tantalizing.

Feelings gushed through her—power, vulnerability, and affection for the audience. She loved performing. These potent moments, these feelings . . . if only she could hold onto them forever.

When the second song ended, applause exploded throughout the house. Mouse hopped off the star onto the stage, surprised that it could be over so quickly. She bowed before them, exhilarated by the cheers and shouts, the swelling noise of clapping hands. They liked her. She straightened, and it hit her. This was no longer polite applause: they loved her. She blew kisses to the crowd, then ran through the main dining room to the dressing room beside Kenny's office.

"Great show!" "Very nice!" Guests called along the way.

She was exhilarated with a capital X!

"Love the swing thing," a waiter said as he passed by with a tray of drinks.

Kenny stood in the short hallway by the dressing room. His arms were folded, and he was leaning against his office door, bent in an odd stance. "I need a moment with you in my office, Ms. Griffin," he said coldly.

Mouse's elation waned slightly. "Okay, honey. Just let me get changed."

"Immediately," he roared.

"Oh, okay." She had never seen him in a grouchy mood before. What could have happened to upset him?

Wiping a touch of perspiration from her forehead, she led the way into his small, windowless office, facing the bookcases as she heard the door slam behind her. Oh, please don't ruin my one night of success with some awful news, she prayed.

"I need you now." She felt his fingers pressing into her satin-covered hips, savoring the tantalizing richness of her butt, his hands caressing her thighs.

Her first response was a soft moan as his hands slid in front of her, grabbing her by the crotch. "I was afraid you didn't like the show," she whispered.

"I loved it," he said. "Every second of it. And now I've got a raging hard-on that won't go away. Not until you put out the fire, woman."

She reached back to embrace him, loving the feel of his erect penis pointing through his trousers. To make love with Kenny while still high from performing—she couldn't think of a better way to celebrate. "I'd be happy to do another show—just for you," she teased. Stepping away from him and turning around, she shimmied her shoulders and slid her feather boa over her shoulders.

He moaned with pleasure, his arms folded self-consciously as he leaned back onto his desk.

"You need to relax," she told him, dancing closer. She made a show of unbuckling his belt and opening his pants, wiggling her hips as she pulled everything down, exposing his enormous, pulsing hard-on. "Let me give you a little taste of what's to come." She slid down to her knees and pressed the head of his penis between her breasts, letting him caress and love her curves. Then she licked him and sucked him deep into her mouth while stroking his shaft.

Then, she got up, slid off her satin pants and pulled her G-string to the side. She pushed him back onto the desk, and climbed atop him, straddling him with her knees on the desktop until she was poised with his head near her slit. "I'm glad you liked the show," she said, grasping his penis and rubbing it vigorously over her clitoris. "Ooh . . ." She moaned, losing momentum as the thrill began to swell between her legs.

"Here, let me help you." He took hold of himself and repeated the motion, sending sweet sensation through her body.

"Mmm. That's nice." She could hear the wet lips smacking against him, and that tug inside her told her she was ready, ready to have him. They were going to do it right on his office desk. This was a first for Mouse.

"I needed to touch you," he said quietly, dragging his penis toward her opening. "There were hundreds of people out there, looking at you, lusting for you, wanting your body. But I want to be the only one who can touch. You belong to me." He pushed himself into her, then pulled her down until he probed deep. She moaned, sure she was coming already, coming on sheer impact of his enormous cock.

Kenny straightened, holding her in place. Clinging to him, she rested her head on his shoulder for a moment as he turned and swung down to the floor. He lowered her to the carpet, then sprawled his body out so that he could do push-ups over her, thrusting her into the floor. She let her head roll back, loving the feeling of being a tiny doll at the mercy of his cock.

From outside, jazz music filtered in, and Mouse recognized Snake's voice, singing "Sunstreaks in Zoey's hair. She speaks of hidden desire, indigo fire . . ."

Ha, that had to be the song Snake wrote for Zoey.

Nice background music, she thought. Great music for fucking.

50

That night the A&R people left a card for Crash, with a note scrawled on the back saying: "Give us a call." They also asked a lot of questions about Mouse, wondering what sort of background Marielle Griffin had and did she have a song album available.

"With the way you can burn CDs these days, I must be the only Broadway actress without one," Mouse complained later that night as the evening was winding down.

Jade and Merlin had already left, and Zoey and Mouse were nursing Cosmopolitans at the bar with Snake, who was powering down the beers like there was no tomorrow. "This is a full-scale celebration," he'd told the bartender as he'd asked him to line up two cold beers at a time. Zoey glanced at the amber liquid, realizing that it meant there would be no private celebration later at her apartment. At least, not until the early hours of the morning when Snake woke up in a horny haze. She bit her lip, thinking that she might be better off sending him home on his own tonight.

"You want a song album?" Snake asked Mouse. "I'll help you

do one. Thatcher has a studio in his basement, and we can back you up." Thatcher was the drummer in Crash, a stout stub of a man with a girlfriend named Dolores who sometimes hung late at the bar, waiting for him. Zoey had spoken to her a few times, but the woman gave off such a groupie vibe, with a vernacular that didn't reach beyond Thatcher, that Zoey had learned to avoid her. "Only drawback is you have to travel out to Brooklyn. End of the earth, if you ask me. The subway doesn't even go there."

"You're full of it," Mouse said, rolling her eyes. "I used to date a guy from Brooklyn, and plenty of subways go there. The only problem with Brooklyn is, once you live there it's hard to get out. Did you ever notice that? But really, would Thatch do it? We could probably put something together quickly, and I'm very easy to work with."

"I'll talk to him tomorrow," Snake promised. "He'll do as I say."

Zoey noticed Mouse eyeing Snake's Metropolis Records card on the bar. "That'd be great. I'd love to have something I can send out." She lifted her glass to Zoey, who toasted her in return.

"To a twist of fate," Mouse said.

"The turn of the screw," Zoey added, "and the rising career of an actress not daunted by a lousy agent or a bad dye job."

"Ha!" Mouse took a sip, then touched her platinum page boy. "You know, I'm sort of getting used to this hair."

"I think it's smashing!" Snake raved, puckering his fat lips to assess Mouse's look. "You're the chocolate Marilyn Monroe."

Mouse giggled. "I think I should resent that. No, actually, I sort of like it."

Zoey smiled. Snake could be so much fun in situations like this. If only he could be as playful between the sheets. As he gulped down another beer, she made a final decision. She would not bring him home tonight. Savoring another sip of the chilled Cosmo, she realized it was enough to enjoy his company here at the bar; lovemaking could wait until they were both sober.

* * *

One hour and two Cosmopolitans later, she sank into a cab beside Snake and wondered if her declining moral character was caused by the consumption of three stiff drinks in one hour; or was it the opposite—that she had consumed the drinks due to a lack of moral fiber? It was the endless chicken-or-egg conundrum: Which came first—the moral decline or the excessive drinking?

In either case, she found herself in Snake's dark apartment where the electricity had been cut off for the usual reasons, and the bedsheets smelled of sweat and body odor even worse than the last time she'd been there, probably due to the fact that they hadn't been laundered since long before her last visit.

"Did I ever tell you how I crave your incredible curves?" he asked as he pulled her onto the musty bed. He ran a hand over her bottom and gave a gentle pinch. "Thou flea, thou nit, thou winter cricket thou." He kissed her neck.

"Thou bastard, thou Shakespeare-quoter," she said, recognizing the lines from "The Taming of the Shrew." He nuzzled against her, breathing heavily.

"Snake?" She saw that his eyes were closed. He was asleep. Well, wasn't she the fool to expect that he would be capable of altering his behavior tonight? She couldn't have really expected him to perform—especially after he'd tossed back more than a six-pack of beer.

She rolled over, avoiding the lump in the mattress and trying not to press her nose too close to the pillowcase.

"It's over," she murmured. This would be the last night she would spend in this flea-bitten apartment. She was out of here . . . just as soon as she slept off the vodka haze.

The gentle sweep of fingers across her abdomen was startling at first. Zoey opened her eyes and found herself peering into the warm brown eyes she had come to love. Nick smiled, the tiny lines on the outer corners of his eyes revealing his regrets, his realizations, his apology.

"I never thought we would do this again," she whispered, and he brought his hands up to massage her breasts. As if to say, I'm here for you. I was always here. Chase the darkness from your mind; it was all a bad, nonsensical dream.

"Ohhh . . ." she groaned, moved by the growing pang of passion and the incredible relief. Her dreams hadn't slipped through her fingers. Nick was here loving her, teasing her body to a climax. Her brilliant, fierce, headstrong husband was back in her arms.

The world was right again.

Her head rolled back against the pillow as his hands moved down between her legs, stroking her clitoris, then dipping down into the wetness there.

"Ooh!" she moaned again as the warmth began to rise and spread through her abdomen. She was hot and wet for him, wanting him so.

"I missed you," she whispered. "I missed this."

He stroked her harder and faster, the heat mounting as his motions became frenzied. She squeezed her eyes shut, savoring the mix of sexual craving and love. Oh, God, she loved this man. She loved it when he touched her.

His hand pulled away for a second as fabric whispered, and she realized he was undressing. A gentle smile curved her lips as she opened her eyes to unfamiliar darkness.

"What?" This place . . . this man . . .

It wasn't Nick at all.

Snake.

The emotional beauty of the moment shattered, a plate-glass window caving in to reveal a man and a woman having sex in bed. The exquisite love scene was a dream. There was no Nick. But her body betrayed her, still frenzied and hot and wanting completion.

For the first time, she was ready as Snake entered her and began pumping against her. She felt her muscles closing around him, embracing him, wanting to squeeze something out of this moment, even if it was all the shadow of a dream.

Close your eyes, return to the illusion, make it last.

She knew it was a cheat, but she had to let her mind fill in the emotional cracks in the scenario. Squeezing her eyes shut, she lifted her hips and rocked against Nick. She held his cock inside her with each shattering thrust. She savored the sound of his breaths, the heat of his skin against hers, the feel of his balls slapping against her.

Yes, Nick. This is love. Physical, soul-wrenching love. Star-crossed lovers.

And when she felt him shudder in orgasm, she let herself come, too, spiraling through the sky in physical release.

This was it—the perfect union.

She bit her lower lip, stopping herself from whispering, "I love you, Nick."

51

"**I** am in deep doodoo," Zoey told Merlin as they sifted through a rack of bridal gowns, examining white lacework and beads and gathered net skirts and chiffon pleats, all delicately preserved under clear plastic covers. Mouse was at the other end of the shop browsing through the rainbow array of bridesmaid gowns, but Merlin could not resist exploring the epitome of bridal fashion—the bridal gown.

"Such a charming way you have with words," Merlin said, not looking up from a spare sheath in an icy hue of pale blue. "No wonder you're a writer. So, what cow patty have you stepped in now?"

"It's Snake. And Nick. Snick. They're like one big evolving monster." She shook her head, wishing she could control her thoughts and feelings.

"Nick?" Merlin blue eyes flashed at her. "He's back in the picture?"

"Only in my deluded little mind. I had a dream the other night while Snake was having one of his nocturnal intermissions." Zoey looked over her shoulder to make sure they weren't being stalked by an aggressive salesclerk. "Snake was trying to have sex with me, only I thought it was Nick. To make a long story short, it was the best sex we ever had. The only good sex we ever had. I mean, it was as if—"

"More information than I need to know," Merlin said, putting up a hand to stop her.

"The scary thing is, what am I doing thinking about Nick? I thought I was over him. I really thought I'd moved on. Damn it!"

"It's okay to revisit fond memories. Maybe not okay to do it at Snake's expense, but he doesn't seem to be too worried about your feelings if he's trying to jump your bones as you sleep."

Zoey pulled out a gown with a beautiful vee back of sheer rosette lace, so much like her own bridal gown when she'd married Nick. "The memories," she said, suddenly breathless. How did you wash the memories from your mind? "I had so many plans and dreams. We had the house. I guess I assumed a baby would be on the way in a year or two. It's not like I just lost a husband; I've got to stand by and watch as a whole beautiful bundle of plans and dreams crashes onto the shoreline. Here I am, middle-aged, starting over again from the ground up."

"How old are you?" asked Merlin.

"Thirty-three."

"You've got time. Didn't you read about that woman in California? In her sixties, I think, and she had a healthy baby."

Zoey winced. "Are you trying to console me or frighten me?"

He took a gown off the rack and showed it to her. "How about this? Halters are big. Did you see the gown Jennifer Aniston wore when she married Brad Pitt? A halter covered with sparkling beads. Plunging back." He nodded at her. "You still running in the park? Or should we look for something more . . . forgiving?"

"You're trying to distract me."

"Exactly. Now the ballroom skirt is making a big comeback. And flowers are being used more and more as embellishments. Did you see what Sarah Jessica's Carrie was wearing in *Sex and the City*? Something like that, with a tiny bouquet of flowers pinned on the shoulder or sleeve."

"Someone's been doing their wedding research," Zoey said.

"It's genetic. A gift among my people." Merlin returned the gown to the rack and studied her. "You're going to be okay," he said earnestly. "I think you're doing a fine job of getting over Nick the Prick. These things take time."

She forced herself to smile, though she didn't feel so good about anything right now. Her career was in the toilet, she was dating a sexual dud, she was running out of money, and she'd begun to fantasize about a man she couldn't have. Beyond that, life was one big fucking party.

"Find anything?" Mouse asked, joining them.

"Just the big gaping vortex that is life," Zoey murmured.

Mouse scowled at Zoey. "What the hell is wrong with you, girlfriend?"

"She's having one of those days." Merlin raised one hand to shield his mouth, as if speaking confidentially. "I suspect the bridal couture is producing painful flashbacks."

"Why do you think I made a beeline for the bridesmaid section? One look at these frothy white cream-puff gowns and any girl has visions of wedding cake dancing in her head." Mouse pulled out a chiffon gown with bell-shaped sleeves. "I'll bet Kenny is the kind of guy who would like a traditional wedding."

"Kenny?" Zoey asked. "I didn't know you two were talking about getting married."

"We haven't discussed it; I was just speculating." She held the gown under her chin and preened in the mirror. "He is a great guy, isn't he? Attractive in a cue-ball head sort of way, and loaded."

Zoey nodded. "We all like him, and you know how particular we are when it comes to approving mates for our friends."

"But you could never wear that shade of white," Merlin said, taking the gown from Mouse. "It's got way too much gray in it. Try something like this, with a hint of ivory or gold."

He handed over a gown with a dramatic empire waist, and Mouse nodded at herself in the mirror. "That's it." Holding the gown in place, she pretended to greet guests. "So happy you could make it. Isn't it lovely? Oh . . . thank you!"

"Oh, God, I can see it all before my eyes," Merlin said. "You in a brownstone with Kenny and two point five little Kennys. You're dragging them out of the house, trying to get them to their dance lessons on time."

"Let's not skip ahead too far," Mouse said, returning the gown to the rack. "Kenny is definitely a find, but I'm not into kids right now. At least, not until my career takes off and glides for awhile. Did you hear about my next gig? Starring in a music video."

"Metropolis Records offered Crash a recording contract, and part of that includes doing three videos," Zoey filled Merlin in. "Snake asked Mouse to star in the first one."

"We're already working on the concept," Mouse said. "Something about me dancing behind a screen that changes colors. You don't see me till the end, when I emerge like magic through a veil." She lifted the spray of a bridal veil and pretended to dance behind it.

"Could be a great break for you, Mouse," Merlin said. "Imagine turning on VH-one and seeing Mouse."

"Her career is really exploding," Zoey said, noticing that a salesclerk didn't seem too happy with the veil dance.

"Are you sure you don't need help?" the clerk called.

"We're fine!" Zoey and Merlin answered in unison.

"We'd better get down to business." Merlin turned to Zoey. "And that means finding you a maid of honor gown."

"I'd rather be best woman. Can't you make Josh's friend be man of honor?" Zoey said, reaching for a Vera Wang gown and holding it under her chin. She looked in the mirror, at her long hair pinned into a twist, her sunglasses tucked up there, her banged copper earrings dangling. How had she gotten so pale? Definitely in need of blush.

"Who's standing up for Josh?" Mouse asked.

"His masseuse partner, Fitzroy. He's from the British Virgin Islands. Very quiet around me, but apparently he works well with Josh. The teacher often has them demonstrate for the class." Merlin checked his watch. "I have an appointment with the florist at three."

"You've been planning this wedding single-handedly," Zoey said. "Doesn't Josh care about anything?"

"He's just so busy, and I have to admit, I'm enjoying some of it."

"That's good, but Josh is paying his half." Zoey's sunglasses slid down so that she looked like a punk bride. "Isn't he?"

"He will. We're going to divide everything up after it's over, but right now, since I'm doing the legwork, it's just easier for me to put things on my card."

Zoey swayed back and forth, letting the gathered skirt of the gown billow over her legs.

"No way, sweetie," Merlin said, shaking his head. "Next time, you're wearing blue."

"Or black." Zoey replaced the dress on the rack. "At Nick's funeral. That's after I kill him for ruining our marriage and then trying to cheat me out of every penny and potholder."

52

For the first time in her life, Jade was afraid to have sex.

Not that she thought her practiced talents wouldn't hold up in bed with A.J. She was confident that she still knew all the right moves, even if she hadn't practiced them lately. Over the past few weeks all her energies had been soaked up by the overwhelming task of learning how to build a relationship. She'd had some of the basic framework from the relationships she'd established with her friends. Notions of honesty and loyalty and dependability certainly rang true in any context, and although these factors had never come into play with her previous relationships with men, it wasn't too difficult to incorporate them with A.J. Looking up into those earnest gray eyes, she thought she would never have the heart to lie to him, never the need to deceive him.

But the daily stress of thinking about him constantly, playing phone tag, and managing a long-distance relationship pressed down upon her. "How do people live through this?" she'd asked Zoey during one emergency phone call. She felt like an idiot, calling her friends constantly, asking stupid questions like 'How long should I wait for him at the restaurant?' or 'Do you think he's really working late?' or 'Should I push for a commitment or play hard-to-get?'" She was thirteen years old all over again and hating it.

When he was in town, she got the feeling he wanted to spend every available minute with her, but she had unavoidable job commitments, and he was always being held up in meetings, software emergencies, phone conferences, and brainstorming sessions with clients, financial planners, investors. Jade had developed a strong phone relationship with Hank, A.J.'s right-hand man, the friendly voice who had called her initially to show A.J. properties in New York, but much as she reminded them both that she worried when A.J. was late or incommunicado, neither man thought to call her when A.J. was detained. Men! They really were from a different planet.

So she wasn't surprised when she appeared at A.J.'s apartment on Thursday night to find he wasn't there yet. "I'll let you in," the doorman said, reaching for the keys. "Mr. Chenowitz is definitely in town, but not here at the moment."

"Yes, I know that much," Jade said, disappointed, not bothering to tell the man that they'd had a quick lunch together at Café La Soup, a small midtown eatery with simple French fare. Not the sort of place she'd expected her billionaire baby to dine in, but it wasn't surprising now that she'd come to know A.J.'s personality. He loved a bargain, he loved simple pleasures, and he loved discovering things on his own. Gone was the notion of becoming a heavy hitter at power places in the city; A.J. hated inflated prices and pretension. But somehow, it didn't seem so important to see and be seen at Nobu or Lotus or Le Bernardin. Jade just wanted to be with her man, even if it meant fries and sandwiches at Chicken One.

"What's happened to my life?" she muttered as she kicked off her shoes under the gilded dome of the vestibule and padded into the library. It was one of the few rooms that A.J. had found the time to furnish, with two brown leather sofas and a desk from an antique auction they'd attended one Saturday. Jade had enjoyed closing the deal with A.J. and helping him shop for his new home. With each acquisition—a Waterford crystal vase for the ledge along the stairs or a Persian runner for the hallway—she felt that another paving stone was falling into place, cementing their relationship.

She sank onto the sofa, loving the buttery feel of the leather under her fingertips. These days she could use a sensual thrill. Not that she didn't love making out with A.J.—kissing and stroking each other for hours, always dressed, and always stopping at the petting stage. He never pushed beyond that, and she was afraid to go there, afraid that somehow the act of sex would ruin the delicate emotional ties she'd worked so hard to weave between them. Superstitious? Maybe, but she'd never had a relationship in which both the emotional and sexual worked, and she doubted that it was possible.

But this was getting ridiculous.

She loved the man, and she knew he was growing attached to her. So why were they acting like adolescents in the back seat of Daddy's buick? Her phone rang, and she got up to pace while she talked to Mr. Bettlemeyer, a client in need of an office suite.

She was still on the phone when the door opened.

"Jade . . . ? Honey, I'm home," he joked.

She held up a finger and pointed to the phone.

He mouthed "Sorry" and slipped off his Keds. He was wearing jeans and a Portland Blazers T-shirt, a large part of his wardrobe. At first she'd thought he was a fan of the team. Later she'd learned that he was a part owner, though A.J. had never mentioned it. He wasn't one to throw his weight around.

She stood at the window, talking with the client. Magically, a frosted martini with a curl of lemon appeared before her eyes. She took the drink and nodded to A.J., who sat with his on the rug, his legs crossed in the lotus position. Halfway through the drink, she finally finished with Mr. Bettlemeyer and turned to him.

"Hey, you!" She knelt beside him. "Thanks for this."

"Hey yourself." He leaned up to kiss her. "Sorry I was late."

"The doorman is going to stop letting me in," she said. "He probably thinks I get here early to go through your underwear drawer or pilfer your collection of baseball cards."

He gave a mock gasp. "You wouldn't dare touch my cards."

She tilted her head, admiring the line of his jaw. "What do you want to do for dinner?"

He sighed. "I was thinking of a quiet meal here? Maybe order in Thai food? How about you, what would you like?"

She bit her lip, feeling a sting of adrenaline. "You want to have sex?"

With a look of shock he rolled back, his feet flailing in the air as if she'd just blown him out of the water.

She laughed. "No, seriously. Would you like to?"

"I'd hate to be negotiating a tough deal across the table from you. You don't play around with small soldiers. Just bring out the big guns, why don't you?" He sat up again, facing her, taking her hands in his. "I would love to make love with you, Jade. I've been thinking and dreaming of it since . . . well, since we first met, and I hope you don't think I'm a pervert for admitting that. I was afraid to push, though. You seemed hesitant, and I don't want you to think I'm one of those guys who's just out for physical pleasure. I'm not like that." He pulled one hand away to push his glasses up on his nose. "The question is, do you want dinner first?"

She rose on her knees to stretch toward him. "I don't think I can wait," she said, leaning down to kiss his cheekbone, his ear, his neck. She lost her balance and teetered against him. He fell back against the rug, and she landed on his chest, but the motion tipped his martini glass. The remains of his drink splashed on the rug, and the glass rolled away toward the mantle.

"Sorry," she whispered.

"It's okay, mostly vodka and gin. It'll dry clear, and should act as a disinfectant, too."

"You're so practical," she said, trailing kisses along his collarbone. "I love that about you."

He sighed. "That feels wonderful. But if we're going to make love, there's something I want to tell you first, and please, don't be frightened."

She lifted her head. "What is it? HIV positive? Transexual? Got to wait for the Viagra to kick in?"

He laughed. "What a fantastic imagination you have! None of the above, but, well, you know I practice yoga, and I've been studying this form of ancient sex for years—mostly through book research, I'm afraid, but I'd love to try it with you. Anyway, it's called tantra, and I think you'll find it quite lovely."

"Tantric sex?" She felt her mouth drop open. Bingo. She had hit the lottery of love. "Yes, yes, I've been studying it, too," she said, grabbing his shoulders and shaking him excitedly. "Oh, A.J., honey, this is unbelievable."

He smiled. "A dream come true."

53

Zoey paced the living room in her nightshirt, waiting for the water to boil in the kitchen and wishing she could think of a way to get Snake out of her bed.

It was 6:42 A.M., and she was pissed off at being up so early but hesitant to return to his nocturnal gropings, which had started about an hour ago. She'd managed to fend him off, wanting sleep, but he'd started again a few minutes later. Finally, she'd decided to get out of bed and make some coffee. Skye didn't have a coffeepot, but Zoey had created a contraption which balanced a plastic coffee filter holder over a thermal carafe with the help of chopsticks and two tall pasta boxes. Ingenious. She'd even invested in a pound of Starbucks Sumatra, deciding that if she was going to go bankrupt on the tiny allowance from Nick, she might as well do it on a caffeine high.

The kettle whistled, and Zoey stomped into the kitchen in her bare feet, angry with herself for tolerating this relationship. The old Zoey wouldn't have put up with Snake. The nights of sleep interrupted for perfunctory sex; the late nights sitting at the Rainforest bar, waiting for the guys in the band to unwind, waiting for Snake to power down a six-pack of beer; the nights spent flopping in his grungy apartment because it was closer to the club.

"What is wrong with this picture?" she asked aloud. It was all about nightlife, all about Snake's life.

Meanwhile, she spent very little time at the computer these days. She had started a few chapters of a novel loosely based on Mouse's struggles and rising success, and though she liked the material, she just never seemed to get to it these days. Probably because her days were simply a prelude to her life at night. Hey, she had to catch up on her sleep sometime.

Were her standards slipping? She wouldn't have put up with this behavior from Nick. Although she'd rarely had to give Nick sex tips in bed. He seemed to know where and when and how to touch her, how hard to stroke and how fast. At least, he did in the beginning when he cared. Those magical days spent exploring each other's bodies in bed, kissing and talking and kissing and making love. Back rubs and foot massages culminating in passionate sex, followed by pasta and red wine in bed.

Oh, God, there she went again . . . strolling down a prosaic memory lane. Why did she torture herself like this?

Perched on the rug at the foot of the couch, Zoey hugged her mug and tried to focus on the here and now. She contemplated the copy on the decorative wrapper of the Starbucks coffee. The choice of words was so visual, so suggestive. She turned over an envelope and started scrawling words:

savory
smokey
rich, deep, dark

She smiled. Even "mountain grown" sounded exotic in this context. As she drank the coffee she toyed with the words, trying to find a structure to accommodate them. They had all the texture and funk of a jazz piece.

Two cups of coffee later, she let her head fall back to the couch and closed her eyes. She'd come up with a simple lyric.

"Good morning, luv." Snake bustled in looking athletic and ridiculous in his black jockey shorts and shiny green tank top. "Ah, coffee, don't mind if I do." He lifted her cup and took a sip. "What's this?" Picking up the envelope, he read her lyrics:

> *Smokey room, dim the light.*
> *Seize the gloom. It's your night.*
> *Your night for savoring,*
> *Tasting every flavoring*
> *In your mountain grown mind.*
>
> *Smokey room, dim the night.*
> *Seal your tomb. It's your right.*
> *Your night to devastate.*
> *Your pain will radiate*
> *In your mountain grown mind.*
> *Can't you leave those thoughts behind?*
> *Never know what they will find*
> *In your mountain grown mind.*

"What's this again. You're writing lyrics?"

Zoey nodded, bracing herself for his cutting criticism.

"And bloody good ones, too." He toasted her with the coffee cup. "We'll have to get you up every day at dawn now, so that you can hear your muses." He glanced back at the envelope and winced. "Fuck me, these are brilliant."

Zoey felt her anger melting away. Snake did have some good qualities. Maybe they just needed to spend some time together outside of bed and the bar. "I called it Coffee Copy," she said, feeling her face warm with pride. "Inspired by the Starbucks label."

His eyes went back and forth from the label to the lyrics then back to the label again. "Well, not quite sure how you got one from the other, but who's to argue with genius?" He gave her a fat kiss on the cheek, then turned away. "Got to run. Meeting with the Metropolis people today."

"Really?" Zoey stood up, stretched, then followed him down the hall. "How's that going?"

"Excellent. We should be ready to begin shooting the first video in two to three weeks. I hope little Marielle can squeeze us into her schedule. I understand she's rehearsing yet another act for Rainforest, though I've not seen it yet." As he spoke he stepped into his Lycra pants and pulled on his boots. Reaching into his pants, he scratched his butt and rearranged his balls without a trace of self-consciousness before zipping up.

Arms crossed, Zoey made a notation of the behavior. More proof that men and women should be classified as different species.

After Snake left, Zoey turned on her computer, hoping to work. She yawned as the machine grunted quietly. It was only nine-thirty, but she felt exhausted, certainly not up for writing. Plopping down at the desk chair, she decided to check her email and return to bed.

As she started to rest her head on the desk for a moment, her eyes lit on the rough draft of the first few chapters of Mouse's story. She sifted through it—almost six chapters. Maybe she should send it to Skye and get some early feedback. Hadn't Skye advised her not to send a completed manuscript this time? Advice she usually ignored, being a compulsive control freak, but perhaps it was time she matured and listened to her editor for once.

She clicked on the "Mail" icon, determined to send it off today. If nothing else, it would help her realize that she was making progress, even if that progression was slower than desired.

The mail folder opened, revealing an email from Robin Buckner, her agent:

Good news!
Got an offer on your manuscript from a small house that specializes in erotica. They offered 5000 but I think I can get 6000. You need to decide and come up with a pseudo-

nym pronto if interested. Quick money for you, since it's complete. Waddaya say, kiddo?
–robin

Zoey blinked as her pulse raced with joy. Or maybe it was caffeine. In any case, the offer was good, which she immediately told Robin in an email response.

She stood up and did a happy dance across the bedroom. Snake had admired her lyrics, Robin had sold her novel. Maybe Skye would like her latest effort, too? Wasn't there a saying about good news coming in threes?

54

"I love doing cosmic breathing with you," A.J. said. Behind his thick glasses, his gray eyes flared with passion as he pressed his ring finger into the sacred spot deep within her yoni. His other hand rested lightly between Jade's breasts, "Over the heart chakra," he explained. It was a serene moment in which the lovers maintained eye contact and breathed together.

It was one serendipitous moment of many over the past day and night.

After a night of tender, perfectly paced lovemaking, Jade and A.J. had cleared their schedules for the next twenty-four hours to spend an indulgent day loving each other.

Last night, after a playful cleansing in the spacious double shower, A.J. had wanted to start by massaging and awakening her sacred spot. Jade had felt so at ease in his arms, so comfortable making love with him, that her body had responded quickly to his touch, and A.J. had been delighted when her yoni had released amrita, a light liquid. "It's called divine nectar," he'd told her, "and it's considered to be a joyful explosion of energy when it occurs." He'd licked it from his fingers, savoring each drop.

Watching him, Jade had felt immense pleasure at his wonder over her sultry body and its responses.

She had met her match.

Last night A.J. had held his orgasm, twice. Jade couldn't believe it. She'd read about it, but still wasn't quite in tune with the theory. "Isn't that painful?" she asked.

"Actually, it's empowering. I'm controlling my energy, building it up. You see, women are energized by orgasmic love, because a woman's shakti is negatively charged to begin with. Upon orgasm you discharge your negative energetic field, and become lightened by its release. However, it's the opposite for a man. When I discharge my positive yang energy, I feel depleted. By containing the ejaculate, I am able to build up more positive energy, to sharpen the yang element."

"Really." Jade smoothed her palms over his chest. "I have to admit, I didn't bone up on that principle too thoroughly, but if you feel strongly about it . . . okay." She did like the positive effect of A.J. holding his orgasm: he became aroused very quickly when she wanted to make love again.

Now Jade let out a cry of delight and stretched out on the floor, never losing eye contact with him. "Let's try one of the visualization techniques," she said softly. She reached down to find his erect penis, and slid her fingers around the thick, solid bulk. "The position where I hold your lingam inside me and stroke it with my muscle. I think it's called rings of light?"

"Mmm . . . the tower in rings of light." He stretched out beside her and leaned down to lick a nipple.

She took a moment to savor the sensation at her breast, then pushed him down onto the bed. "Let me sit on top of you, okay?"

"Yes," he whispered eagerly.

She mounted him, thrilled at the sensation of penetration. "I'm going to massage you inside me. I'm picturing my yoni as a cylinder made of rings. Rings of white-gold light, and I'm opening and closing my rings to give you a cosmic massage." As she spoke she contracted her PC muscle, trying to start near the clitoris and make the muscle contract up through her abdomen, creating a ripple effect.

"Exquisite embrace . . ." he murmured. "I'm envisioning the white-gold rings of your yoni . . . I feel them clasping me. . . ."

"The rings are transferring their energetic field into your tower," she said, seizing hold of his cock and squeezing as she inhaled. Jade had always enjoyed talking dirty during sex, but now, with this new lingo, the talk was somehow mystic and pure, as if they were performing a divine rite. And she could see it all—the rings inside her vagina, the golden white light of her femininity gripping A.J.'s spirit, stroking him in a sexual dance.

"You're receiving my powerful sexual juices," she whispered. "Do you feel it? Do you feel the energy?"

Breathing out, she released her muscle.

And he roared: "Yes!" He sucked in his breath, his face a study in ecstasy. "I'm drawing your energy in, up to my highest chakras."

She saw the white light dancing from her body into his—the cosmic energy of sex and love entwined in one playful flame.

Wait till the girls heard about this.

55

With the prospect of a few thousand dollars coming her way, Zoey was in the mood to party.

She called her friends to share the good news. Merlin was ecstatic and promised to help her celebrate, though he couldn't make it to Rainforest that evening. "But I'll see what I can work out," he said cryptically. Mouse was about to go into rehearsal for her next cabaret act, so her response was a bit restrained since Teddy looked down upon the use of cell phones in his studio. And Jade wasn't answering her cell. Very unusual. Zoey left a message, changed into her sweats, and went for an extra long run around Union Square. If she was going to look halfway decent in the gown Merlin wanted her to wear, she had better keep in shape.

After a shower she treated herself to a grilled shrimp Caesar salad at the Bluewater Grill, then walked home past the boutiques along Union Square, turning left up Park Avenue. Two dresses in one shop window caught her attention, glittering affairs decorated with beads and crystals. She went inside to inquire and learned that the decorations were real jade and Swarovski crystals, the dresses somewhere in the four- to five-thousand-dollar range. Zoey faked an interested smile, thanked the clerk, and headed out, rolling her eyes. Five thousand dollars! Would she ever have the money to afford a dress like that?

Even if she did, she wasn't sure it would seem worth it.

She settled for a coral tank top with rhinestones scattered over the shoulders from a boutique on 23rd Street. The color brought out the peach in her complexion, the cut accentuated her toned biceps, and the shirt was a bargain at $39.95. She slapped down her plastic charge card and signed her name, suddenly glad that she hadn't taken Nick's name when they married. Imagine having to go to court to change it, or to carry it around for the rest of her life, a constant reminder of an unfortunate mistake.

That night she was wearing the coral tank top with a black linen miniskirt as she walked into Rainforest. Mouse greeted her with a huge smile, her eyes glowing beneath the black netting of a sexy red Eugenia Kim hat.

"Here's the famous author, come to celebrate the sale of another book," she said. "Congratulations, honey." Amid the crowd of guests waiting to be seated, heads turned as Mouse gave Zoey a hug and took her elbow to guide her through the pack.

Behind her, Zoey heard someone ask: "Is that Danielle Steele?"

"Oh, God," Zoey muttered to Mouse. "Do I look that old?"

"Obviously the comment of someone who hasn't read a novel for years," Mouse said, leading her over to the bar. "First drink is on me. What are you having tonight? A Cosmo? Or how about one of Anton's specialties?"

"I've been in a summer mood," Zoey said. "How about a watermelon martini?"

As Anton moved down the bar to make the drink, Mouse squeezed Zoey's arm. "I'm so glad about your porno book. Did you pick a pseudonym yet?"

"I'm torn between Lotta Levine and Paige Turner."

"As in Lot of Loving? Ha!" Mouse laughed. "I think I like the other one, though. Having a little financial cushion will take a load off your mind for a while."

"I can't believe how freeing it is to be earning money again. I took myself to lunch and went shopping and even allowed myself a little nap without feeling guilty about it."

"Good for you. Oh—I almost forgot! Merlin called, said he couldn't reach you on your cell but he's got a surprise for you. He's working tonight and can get you and Snake into one of the posh suites at the Royale. I know, Snake isn't exactly the man of your dreams, but maybe if you get the room for free he'll rise to the occasion."

"That Merlin. He comes off as a cold fish but inside he's one big mooshball." Zoey smiled as Anton slid a drink in front of her, a lovely y-shaped glass with a pink cloud beneath its frosty gleam.

"Mazel tov," Anton said.

Zoey lifted her drink, feeling sophisticated and worldly in her new tank top with her new pseudonym drinking a cool drink.

Life was definitely a party—if you could afford it.

Snake came up to visit with Zoey while the band was on a break, and she told him about the suite at the Royale. "Isn't that sweet? He wanted us to have our own little place to celebrate tonight." She leaned forward, trying not to sound as if she were bragging. "I sold a book today."

"Good for you." Snake lifted his glass of beer to toast her. "Another best-seller, I'm sure."

"I tend to doubt it, though it could be one of my most timely sales." She slid off her barstool and nuzzled close to him, sliding one hand onto his thigh. He was wearing the mirrored black pants again. God, she loved those pants. "Promise me you won't get totally soused, so we can enjoy the suite together?"

He frowned. "Something tells me you're trying to get in me bloomers, luv. But I'll behave myself. Scout's honor."

"Good." She kissed him, and he reached down to cup her bottom. He could be so sexy when he was sober and she was awake. A few times she'd been tempted to drag him out of the club during one of the band's breaks and screw him in a phone booth or an alley or something. But in the end, it just wasn't Zoey's style.

After the break Mouse went on stage for another blockbuster number that brought the house to their feet. She had changed the two songs, but her routine was still basically the same, starting from offstage and ending on the swinging star. As Mouse finished up, Zoey went to the balcony railing surrounding the bar and applauded loudly, shouting and whooping along with the audience. What a difference Rainforest was from Club Vermillion. If Rainforest was the Broadway of Clubs, Club Vermillion was the Senior Prom, complete with gaudy stretch limos and puking patrons. It was clear that Mouse's luck had changed. Maybe luck is changing for all of us, thought Zoey.

As the crowd settled back into their seats, Snake introduced a new song. "I just put this together today and we haven't had much time to rehearse, though you may think that of all our pieces," he joked. "But this is new, and I do hope you enjoy the 'freshness' of it all. It's an upbeat little ditty called 'Suicide.' " The bass and piano spilled out a whimsical intro, then Snake sang:

"Smokey room, dim the light . . ."

"What?" Zoey nearly fell off her barstool, catching her skirt on the edge. She went to the balcony, tugging down her skirt.

"Seize the gloom. It's your night. Your night for savoring . . ."

"That's my song," she said aloud.

Another woman at the bar scowled at her, then turned back to her friend, as if Zoey were one of those weirdos who haunted bars in search of a listener.

"Damn it, that's my song." He had stolen the lyrics and called them his own, the cute British bastard. Well, it was time for the big talk. It was one thing for him to be a narcissist, quite another to be a thief.

56

By the time Snake had socialized with every funky musician type and packed up his amp and stowed away his guitar and grabbed one last beer for the road despite his promise to stay sober, Zoey was beginning to think that a stay at the Royale was not such a great idea. Or at least not a stay with Snake, the poisonous python plagiarist. Perhaps she should monopolize the suite and celebrate on her own, letting the Jacuzzi tub and room service be her faithful companions.

The air was humid and still as they stepped out of the club to hail a cab, and the thought of getting close to another sticky body had no appeal. Her hair felt heavy on her shoulders, and she lifted it and wiped away the perspiration behind her neck. "I hate this weather," she told Snake, wishing she had something to pin up her hair with. Could romance happen so late on such a dismal night? But despite her attempts at being realistic, Zoey was that eternal optimist who could always spin a positive scenario from the most dire circumstances. A yellow taxi pulled up to the curb, and Zoey climbed in after Snake.

They arrived at the Royale, and Snake led her in through the marble foyer and across the elegantly furnished lobby with rich carpeting of cabbage patch bunches of flowers that made her want to jump from one to another.

Merlin was not at the front desk as she'd expected, but the woman there, looking like a flight attendant in her concierge uniform, gave Zoey the suite number and told her that her friends were upstairs.

"Friends?" Zoey said, tapping the plastic key as the elevator took Snake and her up to the twenty-fourth floor. Okay, maybe Merlin was there. Had he gathered Mouse and Jade for an impromptu surprise celebration? She shook her head. No, that would be way too much . . . but he'd been so thoughtful lately.

When she and Snake trekked down the hall and found the door to their suite open, music blaring, Zoey realized she'd been wrong. "Definitely not my friends," she said, pushing on the door suspiciously.

Inside, she spotted the bass player from Crash dancing with his shirt off. Merlin sat like a sentinel in an upholstered chair, arms folded, face stiff. A couple Zoey didn't recognize lay prone on the majestic bed, kissing and grinding.

"What's going on?" she asked.

"I invited over a few of the guys," Snake said, pushing past her. "Hey, hey!" he called to them. "You beat us to it, mates!"

Plodding into the room, Zoey felt alienated. The band and its extended entourage was here, along with a few unfamiliar faces, and everyone seemed to be having a fine time, drinking and laughing and dancing.

"Wait till you see the tub!" Dolores shrieked. "We filled it with ice to keep the champagne chilled." She jumped up and down like a two-year-old, pointing toward the bathroom.

Snake clapped Thatcher on the back. "Champagne! Now there's a party! How did you haul that up?"

"Didn't need to." Thatcher smiled proudly. "Room service."

Zoey felt her chest tighten. "Room service? Who's paying the bill?"

"Relax," Snake told her. "Don't worry about that now." He went into the bathroom suite with Thatcher, laughing about something.

Zoey turned toward Merlin, who looked as out of place as she felt. Behind him, a very thin guy in black bike shorts, tank top, and boots was tugging on the drapes. "How do you get these things closed?"

"Don't break them," Zoey said, going over to find the cord. By the time she found it, Bike Pants was gone. She went over to Merlin and sat on the arm of his chair. How had her night of bliss disintegrated into this chaos? "This is so over."

He nodded. "Sorry it didn't work out, but this was not what I had envisioned."

"No, I'm sorry. I should have cut off Snake a long time ago. I just kept hoping that . . . I don't know what I was hoping for, but we are definitely not compatible."

"Hey, hey!" Snake emerged from the bathroom with a bottle of champagne that bubbled over, splashing puddles of foam onto the carpet. "Who wants some of the good stuff."

"Snake!" Zoey stood up indignantly. "You're making a huge mess."

"Oh, sorry, luv." He handed her the bottle. "Ladies first!"

She put her hand on his, gently pushing the bottle down. "We need to talk. This party isn't going to work out."

"Of course it is! You need to chill, luv. Have a drink, or go talk to Dr. Derrick about some pharmaceuticals. Your head is definitely in the wrong place." He touched her cheek, as if patting a pet.

"No! Listen to me, Snake. This is over. Tell your friends it's time to go."

"Oh, come on, now!" Frowning, he placed the champagne on a table, closed in on Zoey and hoisted her into his arms.

"Put me down!" she demanded.

People were laughing, though she couldn't see Merlin's face. "Put me down, now! I—"

Her words were cut off when he pressed his mouth over hers for a forceful, wet kiss. Zoey squirmed in his arms, though she could feel the motion of him walking, crossing the room with her. She stopped kicking, afraid he would drop her. Then the light changed and they were in the bright white bathroom. Snake pulled his head back to end the ugly kiss. He laughed as he lowered her . . .

Into a tub full of ice and champagne bottles.

"Oooof!" Cold hard lumps pressed into her bottom, chilling her back as she sank in. Her feet sank in but her bare knees stuck in the air, like tan mountains over the snow. She pressed her hands between her legs, holding down her miniskirt demurely, as if dignity still mattered. The ice bed closed around her uncomfortably, but the sight of Snake's pompous grin was more chilling. "You bastard!"

"That's the way to chill!" He laughed, his dark eyes smug and mocking. Cold and cruel.

She grabbed a handful of ice and threw it at him.

"Ouch!" He lifted a hand to his face. "Bitch!"

"Get your sorry ass and your sick friends out of here!" she screamed. "I'm sorry I ever met you."

"Oh, go to hell," he answered. "You'll get over it in the morning. You always do." He was a stranger, a distant, predatory creature staring down at her. She couldn't believe she'd ever let him touch her.

"I hate you!" she shouted.

He grinned. "You loved it." He left the room, still smiling and chasing the party.

Zoey slung more ice after him, but it hit the wall and skittered across the floor.

Shifting in the ice, she tried to pull herself out of the tub but slipped when her foot slid under a bottle. Giving up, she dropped her head back into the rocks. Giving up. It was so over.

57

Merlin appeared, extending a hand toward her. "Come on. I'll call security."

She grabbed on to him and climbed out, too numb to formulate an emotional response like anger or tears. They left the suite and went down one flight so that they would be out of sight while security chased out the revelers. Merlin put his blazer over her shoulders, and she began to warm up as he radioed the security team with the details.

Twenty minutes later Zoey and Merlin returned to the suite to find further damage. Someone had pulled down the curtains and sprayed the windows with foam from a fire extinguisher.

"Oh, God! This is going to cost a fortune." She stared at the damage, suddenly overwhelmed and exhausted.

Merlin rolled his eyes. "Let me call downstairs and see how security resolved it."

As he spoke on the phone, Zoey puffed up the pillows on the gloriously plush king-sized bed and fell against them. The sun was rising, casting a metallic orange glow over the room, dispelling the darkness, reinforcing the ennui that filled her. It was the beginning of a new day, and she was less prepared to face it than she had been the day before. She rubbed her eyes, feeling a glob of eye shadow rub onto her fingers, as Merlin hung up the phone and checked the damage to the curtains.

"I feel so hopeless," she said. "How could he do that to me?"

"It should work out okay. Apparently when security spotted the damage and threatened to press charges, Dr. Derrick pulled out a wad of bills. Nine hundred dollars. That should pay for the room service bill, the fire extinguisher, and the drapes. The broken glass will clean up. The ice will melt. Do you want some champagne?"

She shook her head slowly, like a zombie. "No, thanks."

He sat down beside her on the bed, stretching out his long legs and crossing them at the ankles.

It felt good to have him by her side. Her friend. Without him she would have melted down hours ago.

Zoey turned her head into the pillow, trying to escape the crushing pain in her chest. She was so angry with Snake, the bastard. He was mean-spirited, cruel, far too intelligent for his wicked ways. He hadn't been kidding about the narcissist crap.

But she couldn't let go of the pain. How had she let him hurt her? And why did she care? She wasn't in love with him. She'd never even pretended to be. So why was he hurting her like this—so far under her skin.

The answer, when she dug deep in her heart, was even more crushing.

"How could he do that to me?" she blurted out again. Only this time it came out as a hot, tearful sob.

Merlin turned to her. "Oh. So we're not talking about Snake?"

Zoey shook her head, unable to form the words. It was Nick: Nick under her skin, Nick haunting her dreams, Nick destroying her sense of self. Merlin put his arm around her shoulders and she rested her face on his chest.

"It's okay to cry," he said. "Sometimes it's the only thing you can do."

"I should be beyond this. I'm such a baby."

"No, no, you're not. You're brave and smart and trying to handle this in a logical way, when it's not a logical thing at all. Sometimes these things don't make sense."

She squeezed her eyes shut as a tear trickled down to her nose, making her face itch. She swiped it away with her hand. "How could he leave me? I just keep going back to that question in my mind and I'm afraid that I'll never have an answer that doesn't point to my own inadequacies as a partner."

"It wasn't about you, was it? Did Nick ever say that he was leaving because you're a rotten cook or a slut in bed?"

She shook her head, sobbing. "No, but if I was enough, he wouldn't have left, and that just kills me. I'm afraid he never loved me, that it was all in my head, that all the emotion was on my side and he just played along because we looked good together, or because I *was* a slut in bed, or some mystical-male reason that's just as banal."

"I don't know, Zoey. The truth is probably something that involved Nick's world more than it involved his life with you. But you may never know the answer to that question. Why would anyone leave you?" He hugged her close for a moment. "I really don't know. You're a beautiful person. A good person."

His momentary lapse of cynicism brought on a new wave of tears. Her body trembled as she sobbed against him.

"I could tell you a story about a couple I knew once upon a time. They seemed very happy together. They didn't argue, at least not in public. They actually seemed good for each other, and when you spent time with them you got the sense that they enjoyed each other's company. They married and fled the stress of urban life for a slower pace. But as they grew and approached the dreaded thirties, they began to change. She missed the frenzied pace of the city and found she was spending far too much time waiting at traffic lights and running to the cleaners for his suits. He became engrossed in his work, and in the off moments when he saw his wife he felt that they weren't connecting anymore. He didn't care about the traffic lights and the cleaners. Furthermore, he could see their relationship steam rolling down the traditional road—marriage, house . . . and then the inevitable kids. Suddenly, that path seemed stifling. He wanted to hold on to the reckless, exciting life of his pre-married days. Even if that just meant holding on to it through quickies in the office. The quickies extended to weekends, and at last he became torn between two worlds, unsure where he wanted to be."

"Don't tell me you're taking his side." She sniffed, realizing how hostile her comment sounded. But she wasn't angry . . . just defending herself.

"I'm just trying to give you a reasonable scenario to hold on to. Personally, I don't know Nick's motivations and I don't care to. What was the appeal with him, anyway?"

She lifted her chin defensively, swallowing hard over the tears in her throat. "Didn't you think he was gorgeous?" She sobbed. "And smart?"

"Oh, okay, we'll tackle that issue at another time and place."

Sunlight washed into the room, pointing out the gauche quality of the decor: the fancy chairs, the bold designs, the satinesque wallpaper. The luxury suite seemed so cold and fabricated in this light.

Zoey closed her eyes, trying to find some release from the pain. "He's ruined my life," she croaked through her tears. "He really has. He's destroyed me."

"Naw," Merlin growled fiercely. "He's not that good. He doesn't have the power to squash your spirit. Not the real Zoey." He pressed his knuckles to the center of her chest. "She's still there. Deep down inside, she's there. And she'll emerge again."

"Not today," she insisted. She sniffed, annoyed that her nose was running now. The sun was up now, the day begun, and she was already miserable before breakfast.

"Okay, you stubborn girl, not today." Merlin checked his watch. "But how does Thursday look for you? Or better yet, Wednesday night? I'd like a few days with the old Zoey before I go off and get married."

Tears squeezed from her eyes as she snorted a small laugh. "We'll see," was all she could say. "We'll see."

58

"So what happened?" Mouse asked Zoey the following after-noon when she stopped by Skye's apartment. "Kenny told me that Crash quit, effective immediately. He's in a panic over getting a band for tonight. And then he called back to tell me that Snake had a message for me—I'm fired from the video." She held out her hands, as if baffled by it all. "What the fuck is going on?"

"I am so sorry." Zoey hadn't realized her breakup with Snake would have such far-reaching effects. Mouse stood in the kitchen doorway as she made a pot of coffee and recapped the disastrous party. "I was ready for Snake to be angry with me, but I didn't real-ize he would be so vindictive. Especially to quit the gig at Rainforest. I can't believe the whole band went for that." She squeezed Mouse's arm, then reached for the sugar. "God, I'm sorry."

Mouse shrugged. "I told Kenny I know tons of pit musicians who have their own bands on the side. I've already lined up some guys for tonight, and they'll have no trouble backing me up for my cabaret songs."

Zoey poured the coffee and handed a mug to Mouse. "But the video. It would have been a great break for you."

"Yeah, but it was still their thing, their music, their recording deal. I'm more into the performing I'm doing at Rainforest. My new act is going to blow people out of the water. I won't even let Kenny see it until opening night. You're coming, right? I open three nights after the wedding."

"Definitely. Aside from the wedding, I have nothing on my calendar for the next twenty years." She blew on her coffee. "God, I'm depressed."

"Now just wait! You are not allowed to feel sorry for yourself. I know you got a raw deal with Nick, but look at yourself. You have a great place to live. You've had two boyfriends in the last four months. You just sold a book and you're working on another. You're bright and cute and . . . you could use a haircut."

"What?" Zoey raked her hair out of her eyes.

"Just a thought. My roots are growing out, and I was thinking about getting a touch-up today. Why don't we go together?"

"I don't know." Zoey ran a hand through her hair, swirling the ends around her fingers. "No one but Magdalena has touched this for years. And I want to use her again, as soon as I have the nerve to go back to Connecticut."

Mouse rolled her eyes. "Like there are no decent hairstylists in Manhattan."

"I don't know." Zoey put down her mug and stretched. "I'm still stressed about money. Though I sold the book, it'll be a few weeks, maybe months until the advance comes in. I'm behind in my rent deposits to Skye, but I'm hoping she'll barter with me and let me paint the place in lieu of one month's rent. And my lawyer is supposed to be arranging a face-to-face with Nick to resolve the divorce agreement once and for all, but that hasn't happened yet, and the very prospect of seeing him again throws me into such a tailspin that I hope it doesn't happen anytime soon. Meanwhile, I'm broke and depressed."

"Let's go for a haircut," Mouse said, pulling her out of the kitchen. "Throw some clothes on and I'll call my guy."

"Weren't you listening? I have no money."

"Put it on a card. Come on, girlfriend. Get your rear in gear."

Feeling twenty pounds lighter, Zoey unlocked the door to Skye's apartment and immediately checked her reflection in the mirrored hallway. A woman with a bronze-red page boy stared back at her. She smiled. She tilted her head. She ruffled the bangs, then smoothed them out again.

Julia Roberts? Maybe not. But close. It was definitely a smarter, more sophisticated look than she'd worn in years. So many years . . . Nick had loved long hair. Yes, this haircut was definitely liberating.

She strolled into the bedroom, watching her hair swing and bob slightly as she moved. Eventually, her obsession with the haircut would fade, but for now it had proved to be an amusing distraction.

Mouse had gone red, too. She had also gotten a gentler cut so that her hair fluffed around her face, replacing the platinum avant-guard style with a natural, innocent look. "Aren't we just adorable?" Mouse had said as they left the salon together.

Thank God for Mouse.

Spotting the emerald green "Best Woman" gown hanging outside the closet door, Zoey picked up the phone to call Merlin. He would want advance warning about her new look for his bridal party.

"Oh no!" he yelped when she broke the news. "Does it clash with the green?"

"Of course not. Bronzish, reddish, copper doesn't clash with green. In fact . . ." She held the gown up to her chin. The dark green sheath had a glimmering translucent layer of beaded fabric over the opaque silk. "I think it's a better complement than my old hair color. And the cut will leave my shoulders bare." She flung back her head, letting her hair angle back. "Ooh, sexy."

"Don't get too excited. Most of the wedding guests are gay or in committed relationships."

"Believe me, I am not looking for it anymore. No more men.

No more sex. From this day forward I'm taking a vow of chastity."

"Thank you, Sister Zoey. Speaking of chastity or the lack thereof, have you heard from Jade? I keep missing her and I'm afraid she's going to blow off the wedding."

"She'll be there, I'm sure." Zoey sat down and turned on her computer. "We've been exchanging phone messages, but my understanding is that she finally got into A.J.'s pants and they've been fucking like animals ever since."

"This from the nunnery. Well, if you speak to her, remind her that it's Saturday night. And Zo, are you okay about last night?"

"I'll live," she said, clicking to open an email from Skye.

"Okay, then. I'm supposed to go to the restaurant to finalize the menu. Can you come with?"

Zoey tuned him out as she read Skye's email.

Ciao, bella!

I'm just about ready to wrap things up here, so yes, it would be great if you could do the painting yourself. I loved that wash technique you used in your powder room, so let's try it in the bedroom. The hallway should remain white, as should the living room ceiling.

Which leads me to the next question. Where are you going to go? Have you lined up another place yet? I'll let you know when I have a definite arrival date, but we're chugging toward the finish here.

"Hello?" Merlin sounded impatient. "Earth to Zo."

"Sorry, I'm just reading an email from Skye. She's going to let me do the painting, which will save me some bucks, but she's coming back soon and I haven't got any leads on another place. Do you know anyone who's subletting?"

"Not offhand, but I'll ask around."

Zoey scrolled down to the bottom of the email.

Thanks for sending me the chapters of your latest effort. So glad you gave me this advance sample; it will save us both time. Here's my take on it: Can't tell where this is going, but it reminds me of that old TV show with Marlo Thomas. I'm sure you've seen the reruns. Anyway, got anything else in mind?

"Ah!" Zoey pushed her laptop computer back and banged her head on the desk.

"Zoey?" Merlin sounded concerned. "What's going on."

"I've been rejected! Another rejection. Oh, God."

"Oh. Sorry."

Silence.

Then Merlin spoke quietly. "I don't know what to say."

"I do." She lifted her head and frowned. "Bring on the plagues."

Part Four

Table For One

59

"Oh, my God! You look so handsome!" Zoey rose up on her toes to give Merlin a kiss on the cheek. She had arrived at the restaurant to find Merlin waiting in the downstairs lobby, calm and sedate despite the fact that his wedding was less than thirty minutes away. "I think I'm more nervous than you are."

"That's because I took a Valium," he admitted, squinting at her. "Nice hair."

"Thanks." She grinned. "Julia Roberts?"

"I was thinking Susan Sarandon, but . . . yes, maybe a touch of Julia."

"Susan Sarandon? God, I must be getting old."

"We're not on the sunny side of thirty anymore."

"Don't remind me," she muttered.

"Have you seen Jade and Mouse?"

"They'll be here any minute." She spotted the mark on his cheek. "Looks like I got you." She used the butt of her palm to wipe the lipstick from his cheek. "Sorry."

"That's okay. By the time today is over my face will probably be ringed with various shades of lipstick." He straightened, smoothing the lapel of his black tux. They had chosen a black Bill Blass tuxedo with a square-cut jacket that was long, hanging just above his knees. Beneath it he wore a sapphire blue square-cut vest with a matching necktie. Josh would be wearing the same thing with a gold vest, and his friend Fitzroy had been assigned an emerald green vest to match Zoey's gown.

Merlin pushed the jacket open to put a hand in one pocket, and Zoey was struck by his broad shoulders and the long, lean line of his body.

"Aren't you the *GQ* man?" she teased.

He took out a watch. "Josh is late, as usual. Why am I not surprised? I haven't seen him since yesterday; we decided to spend the night before the wedding apart."

Zoey smiled up at him, feeling her hair bob around her ears. "You guys are true romantics at heart. Have you been upstairs to check out the room?"

"Yes, and everything looks fabulous. The florist arranged the centerpieces—fragrant orange blossoms, and they look lovely. Orange blossoms have been a favorite of many White House brides, and legend has it that Juno, the Roman goddess of marriage gave these fragrant flowers to her groom, Jupiter, on their wedding day. There's a trellis for the ceremony, and I had it decorated with lilies of the valley—that was what Princess Grace carried down the aisle in Monaco. They also snuck in a touch of rosemary for remembrance and dill for lust, but don't mention that to my parents. They're such cold fish. Sometimes I wonder how they ever had sex to conceive me."

"Not a word," Zoey promised.

"I hope my Aunt Annabelle doesn't drag out her new boyfriend. And then there's Josh's mother. We didn't invite her, but somehow she found out about the wedding and threatened to show up." He ran a hand over his brow and paced over to a window. "For a man who isn't nervous, I'm certainly chattering a lot."

"It's okay, Merlin." She tried to think of something to distract him. "Oh, hey, where are you guys going on your honeymoon?"

"The Virgin Islands," he answered. "Josh booked it. His friend

Fitzroy is from Tortola, I think that's in the British Virgin Islands, but anyway, all the islands are supposed to be beautiful. Tropical and lush."

"Sounds great." Zoey leaned against the wall to peer out to the lobby. A group of guests climbed the stairs, and she could picture the room filling up, becoming animated with voices and laughter.

Merlin spotted someone down the hall, and lifted his hand to wave. "Hey, Fred," he called, then explained to Zoey, "Josh and Fitzroy spent last night at Fred's place."

The young man came down the hall, his blond hair still damp, slicked back behind his ears. Fred was dressed in jeans and a polo shirt, and for a moment Zoey wondered that he'd dress so casually for a wedding, but then in New York City anything was plausible. One ear had been pierced many times, and Zoey watched the row of silver rings twinkle as he passed by.

"Merlin . . ." Fred's voice seemed heavy, weighted down by regret. "I've got some bad news, man."

Merlin didn't flinch; he seemed unwilling to let any mishaps spoil his well-planned day.

"I . . ." Fred winced. "I'm not sure how to tell you, but Josh isn't coming. He left for the Virgin Islands last night. With Fitzroy."

"You're kidding . . ." Zoey swung around to face this Fred guy. "Right? Is that a joke?"

She swung a look at Merlin, whose face went slack as he fell back against the wall. He slid down, down, until he was sitting on the carpeted floor, staring into space.

"I'm sorry, man, I . . ." Fred said, fumbling over the words. "Josh promised me he would tell you himself. He was supposed to call you as soon as he got there. But . . . I guess he didn't."

Merlin raised a hand, as if to dismiss and absolve the bearer of bad news. A glaze had come over his face, a sodden weariness.

Hitching up her dress, Zoey sat down beside him and grabbed his arm. "It'll be okay, Merl. I know this is awful right now, but you'll be fine."

He took a deep breath, then let it out through his teeth. "I don't think so," he said quietly. "I don't think I'll ever be fine again."

"You will," she said.

He shook his head and patted his tuxedo jacket. "I need my Valium. More Valium." Not finding the vial, he covered his ears with his hands and let out a painful sigh. "I need to be alone."

"No." She squeezed his arm. "Not drugs. You need your friends."

Fred gazed down at them awkwardly. "It's starting to fill up upstairs. Do you want them to just go on and start the party?"

Merlin shook his head. "Whatever. I . . . no, no party. Send them home. What's to celebrate? Tell them to leave."

Fred winced at Zoey, clearly not sure what to do.

She spotted Jade and Mouse at the end of the hall, and motioned them to join her. "Don't worry, Merlin." She stood up and straightened her beautiful gown. "We'll take care of everything."

Half an hour later, Zoey and Mouse helped Merlin into the back of a cab and scooted in behind him. Jade took the front seat and turned to the back. "Where to?"

"Someplace quiet," Zoey said, suddenly remembering an old haunt. "The Beatrice Inn, down in the Village. I think it's around Eighth Street."

As the cab pulled away from the restaurant, Zoey closed her eyes, thinking of how sad the empty party room looked. Jade had stepped under the trellis to make her blunt announcement: "Thanks for coming, but the wedding is off. Enjoy your evening!" Zoey had made a deal with the caterer to refund as much of Merlin's money as possible. The appetizers that were already cooked were to be picked up by a society that provided meals for the homeless. The flowers would be sent to an AIDS hospice. The gifts would be returned. The honeymoon plane tickets would not be refunded, because Josh and Fitzroy had used them to fly standby to St. Thomas, the rats.

"I need to call Kenny," Mouse said, taking out her cell phone.

"I need a drink," Zoey said, swallowing hard. Her throat was dry and sore.

"I need a new life," Merlin said blandly.

They waited for Jade to follow suit, but she remained silent.

"Jade," Mouse prompted. "Aren't you going to tell us you need a good poke in the whiskers or something."

Jade laughed. "No . . . not today. For once, I am . . . okay." She nodded, staring ahead. "I'm really fine."

Zoey's jaw dropped. "Oh my God, she's fallen in love."

Jade nodded. "Yes, yes I have. And now that I know what all the songs are about, I, I just . . ." She shook her head. "Phew! What can I say?" She turned back and gave Merlin a pained look. "I'm sorry, honey. Do you hate me? I won't talk about it any-more."

"Go ahead," Merlin said, waving her on. "Coming from you it's a true novelty."

"How was the sex?" Mouse asked.

Jade faced forward again and shuddered. "Spectacular!"

The cabdriver flashed her a quick look, and she wagged a finger at him. "Eyes on the road, please." She turned back to her friends. "I'll tell you all about it over a jug of wine."

60

The theme of the night was failed relationships. As if it were an unspoken rule, Merlin was exempt from telling a story, as his example was painfully fresh and obvious.

Jade was spinning a yarn about a boy she had shadowed in high school—a jock from the football team. She had really liked him and he seemed to like the things she did to him. But he had refused to take her out in public, let alone ask her to the prom. "He had that stereotypical notion that girls who are knowledge-able about sex don't make good social partners. And so he ended up going to the prom with a cheerleader who wouldn't know a hard-on if it smacked her in the face." She shook her head. "God, he broke my heart, the big-shouldered bastard. If I could get my hands on him now, I'd teach him a thing or two."

"I'll bet vengeance is yours," Zoey said. "He's probably fat and bald and arguing about who has to pick up the kids from soccer camp."

Jade hoisted her wineglass. "Here's to the fat, bald men of the world, may they always be attracted to someone else."

"Amen," Mouse said, toasting her.

Zoey and Merlin clinked glasses, and the friends drank together. Afterward, Mouse refilled everyone's glasses from the pitcher of red wine. She spilled a little near Zoey's hand, but Zoey was able to mop it up with a napkin. Not that anyone would really notice here. The dimly lit basement restaurant was casual and quiet, containing only a dozen or so tables, and only three of them were currently occupied. Zoey had eaten most of her baked ravioli, and Jade and Mouse had split salads and chicken piccata. Merlin had only picked at his fettuccine with eggplant, but that was to be expected.

"We need another pitcher of red wine, please," Mouse told the waitress. The older woman picked up the pitcher and disappeared into the kitchen. Mouse swirled the wine in her glass. "Is it my turn?"

"You already told us about Steve Wilbert, the most gorgeous boy at Providence Central High School," said Jade.

"Oh . . . right." Mouse sighed. "I'm telling you, that boy was hot, makeup and all. I couldn't believe it when he told me he was gay. And when the two of us were backstage together in the dark green room? Mm-mm. I'm telling you, for someone who wasn't interested, he sure knew where to put his hands."

Zoey smiled. "His passion for Broadway musicals didn't tip you off? How about the fact that he had no girlfriends throughout high school?"

"I thought the boy was discerning!" Mouse insisted. "Just waiting for the right woman. And can't a straight boy like musicals?"

Merlin wagged a finger at Zoey. "You are perpetuating a stereotype there."

"Sorry." Zoey shrugged. "I don't know, I probably would have fallen for Steve, too." She scratched her head, loving the way her new hairstyle fell back into place. "You know, that's a good question. Are there any straight guys who love musicals?"

"To Broadway musicals," Mouse said, raising her glass. "Let's hope somebody else learns to write 'em."

"Cheers," Zoey said, drinking her wine quickly. Maybe a little too quickly, but she liked the warm feeling running through her veins. Her shoulders felt relaxed. Actually, as she looked down at her body couched in the elegant emerald sheath, she felt nimble and soft, like a graceful marionette. An independent woman, relaxed, in control, and slightly buzzed.

"Your turn, Zoey," Jade prodded. "Tell us about Mr. Wrong."

"Well . . ." Zoey put a finger to her chin. "That would have to be Nick, a.k.a. the Prick. But where do I begin? Was it the fact that his mother choreographed our entire wedding? Or maybe we should discuss the law school days, when all energies had to go into Nick and his study group and his briefs and his bar review. While Zoey was wasting her time on a writing career that would surely amount to nothing, since writers make—what is it now?—five hundred dollars a year?"

Mouse tapped a spoon against the table. "Very nice examples, but weren't we focusing on sex?" She leaned closer to squint at Zoey. "Give us some of the dirt on Nick's prick."

Zoey laughed out loud, then put her hand over her mouth to compose herself. "It was nothing special. I mean, a prick's a prick. Actually, when you really look at it, a penis is a comical organ. Dangling there in the hair, all wrinkled and pink, with the sad little sack behind it."

Mouse nodded. "I know what you mean. Out of the context of what it can do for you, that thang is hardly attractive."

"Not that a vagina is so beautiful," Zoey admitted. "I mean, what is it? Lots of folded flesh and a hole? A nostril is a hole, and you know what people think of that."

"You guys . . ." Jade shook her head. "You know, when you study tantra you come to see the beauty of sexuality, the grace of our sexual organs."

"Looks like Jade has found religion," said Merlin.

Mouse and Zoey looked at each other, then started giggling. "Sorry, Mom," Mouse teased.

"I think it's all ridiculous," Merlin said quietly. "The sex drive. The way people ruin their lives over sex."

The group was silent as Merlin's reference became obvious. Josh had abandoned his partner of six years for another lover. Zoey realized that Josh had probably been motivated by sex.

Or was he? "You know," she said, "when Nick first left, I thought it was all about another woman. Other women. Whatever. But now I see . . ." She shook her head. "It wasn't about her. She was just an excuse, the catalyst for him to make his move. I guess he was looking for a way out. I think he had . . . issues. The girl in the office was just the simplest means to an exit."

Merlin met her gaze, and for a moment she felt that they shared the same pain. Together in rejection. But at least they were together. Zoey blinked. Was the room rocking slightly? She flattened her hands on the table. No, it seemed to be steady. "I think I'm getting wasted," she announced with a little laugh.

"But you still didn't tell us a sex story," Mouse said, nudging Zoey's arm.

Zoey took another sip of wine, draining her glass. Mouse refilled it as Zoey thought hard.

"Well, there was this one time when I was trying to seduce him." She pushed back her chair and stood up. "He was watching something on television. Some sports. And I did this little dance. Duh-duh-duh . . ." she sang lightly, gyrating.

Jade and Mouse laughed.

"Oh, right, that's sexy," Merlin teased.

"I *was!*" Zoey insisted. She slipped out of her shoes and picked up a napkin. "Wait, wait, I didn't explain it right." She climbed atop her chair and held the napkin demurely over her crotch.

"Ooh! Don't fall, sweetie," Jade warned.

"I have per-fucked balance," Zoey insisted, teetering a little. The two couples at the corner table were watching now, but she didn't care. She rubbed the napkin over her breasts, then swung it down to her butt. Nick would come unglued if he saw her doing this, she thought, smiling. All the more reason to play it up."Oh, I forgot! I had a great tan. And I was naked. Completely naked. And I was dancing around with a teensy weensy silk shawl." She wiggled her hips, sliding the napkin across her neck. "But did Nick want to have sex with me? No, he didn't. He wanted to watch teller-fission. Unbull-leafable."

Mouse clapped, standing up beside her. "Oh, honey, be careful. But that is just the cutest dance. Nick was a bigger asshole than I realized."

Zoey felt the room begin to spin. It was spinning around her. "Wasn't he?"

For some reason Jade was on the other side of her. "I think it's time to call it a night," said Jade.

"Oh, no!" Zoey insisted. "The night is young. I've only just . . . just . . ." The room was spinning faster, and she grabbed her head. She felt firm hands on her arms, helping her down, down, down to rest.

But she was smiling. Zoey felt her whole body smiling over Nick, the big fool. He had lost the best thing in his life, and he didn't even know it. What an idiot.

61

"Are you sure you're okay, honey? We haven't seen you at Rainforest since the night of the aborted wedding." Mouse covered the mouthpiece of the phone and blew a kiss to Kenny, who was stretched out across her bed, zebra print sheets draped around his beautiful brown form. The room smelled of sex and scented candles, and Mouse felt exhilarated both from her session with Kenny and from the prospect of debuting her new act at Rainforest tonight.

Sitting on the floor, Mouse lifted the hem of the red silk robe she'd thrown on when the phone rang. She held the phone with her shoulder and started rubbing lotion into her thighs. A girl could never moisturize too much, and she had learned from experience that this activity drove Kenny wild. They'd settled into a nice pattern lately, alternating between staying at her place or at his. His apartment was definitely tonier—a spacious two bedroom with a view of the Hudson River and New Jersey—but Mouse's place was closer to Rainforest, and definitely cozier.

"I felt like I was hung over for days," Zoey admitted. "But somehow it seemed worth it. I don't remember how the evening ended, but I have this vague sense that I was trying to purge Nick right out of my alcohol-laced veins."

"That's right, girl. And that boy needs to be kicked right out of the guy club after you did the dance of the seven veils right in front of him and he stayed on his butt to watch some football game or something."

Zoey groaned. "I told that old pearl again?"

"It's a good story, a perfect example of why you're better off without him," Mouse said, hearing Kenny stir behind her. "Look honey, I'd better run. But I'll see you at the club tonight, right? You remember it's the debut of my new act?"

"Of course. I've been on an alcohol fast since the wedding night. Only seltzer and coffee, trying to clear out the toxins so I can start all over again."

"Good for you. I'll reserve a table for you and Jade. Merlin, too, I hope."

"I'll call him," Zoey promised.

Mouse hung up the phone and stood up, rubbing her thighs seductively.

Kenny sat up in bed and reached for her hand. "You come here, woman." He pulled her onto the bed and they giggled as he cuddled her in his powerful, thick arms. "You know that lotion thing drives me wild."

"Mmm-hm." She ran a hand along his jaw and up over his smooth scalp, loving the shape of him. "You know what I'm thinking?"

"I bet I do. You want me to touch you some more, don't you?"

"How'd you guess that?" she teased.

He shifted her back on the bed, so that her head rested on the pillow, her knees up, exposing her cunt. It was a routine they'd worked out, since Mouse loved to have multiple orgasms and Kenny could only manage one good erection a day. After sex, he usually returned to the scene of the passion to massage her, and she loved the feel of his fingers inside her, the flow of his hot seed mixing with her juice and spilling out again all over his hand, onto her thighs.

I have the perfect man, she thought, watching him stroke her.

He was so kind, so bighearted, so gentle and strong. She had found the perfect man, and there was no way she would ever let him go.

"What are you thinking?" he whispered, smiling at her. "What's in your mind when I touch your most private places?"

"You," she whispered, feeling her arousal begin to peak. His hand was making her hot again, hot and tingling. "I'm thinking about you and your big cock."

He groaned and worked her even harder until she couldn't take it anymore. Adrenaline shot through her and her heart raced. She arched her back, rubbing against his hand, then thrusting it deep inside her, and holding him there for another moment of ecstasy.

He let out a breath, kissing her bare shoulder. "I love you," he whispered.

There he was, saying those dangerous words. He'd started doing that during sex a few days earlier, and at first Mouse had figured it was just what some people say when they're getting down and dirty. But no, Kenny had repeated it a few times.

It was scary territory, but, hey, they were there.

"I love you, too," she whispered for the first time.

Kenny's eyes seemed unusually shiny, and she wondered if there were tears forming, but he hugged her so hard she couldn't see his face anymore. She hugged him back, loving him. Yes, she had found the perfect man, and she loved him.

They cuddled and laughed for a few minutes. Then Kenny rolled over and looked at the bedside alarm clock. "Is that thing right?" he asked.

"You always ask me that, and the answer is always the same," Mouse responded.

"It's five minutes fast."

"Aw, man, I've got to run."

"What for? We're not due at the club for hours."

"I've got something to take care of. It's a surprise."

"Really?" She sat up in bed. "When will I find out this surprise?"

"Tonight," he promised, kissing her one last time. "I'll see you tonight."

"Why not now?" She pulled the sheets to her lap. "Oh, I can't stand to wait, honey. Tell me now."

"Tonight. Look, you're opening up your new act tonight, and I don't want to throw you off or make you more nervous. I'll see you at the club." As he let himself out, Mouse considered what the surprise might be. Of course, there was only one possibility.

She flopped back in bed and kicked her legs in glee.

An engagement ring!

62

When Zoey arrived at Rainforest that night, she could tell that something was up with Mouse and Jade. They stood at the bar, their heads huddled together, their faces pink with giddiness. Beside them Merlin sat on a barstool, staring off into the distance with a meditative look.

Zoey walked directly to Merlin and put her purse on the bar. "Hey, you. What's up with those two? They look like they're conspiring to form a coven."

"They're basking in the glow of love." Merlin lifted a magazine from the bar and handed it to Zoey as Mouse gave an excited little shout. "Jade made it into *New York Magazine* with A.J. Chenowitz. The article is really about him, but Jade is mentioned as his steady companion."

"Really?" Zoey grinned. "Jade! That is so exciting."

Jade clasped her hands to her heart. "It is. But mostly because I'm so thrilled to be shown with him."

As Jade moved something flashed on her wrist. White sparks. Diamonds.

"Jade!" Zoey reached for her arm. "What is this?" The white

gems winked and glittered, picking up colors and bouncing light with such intensity, Zoey knew they had to be real diamonds.

"It's a gift from A.J." Jade touched the bracelet fondly. "Isn't it lovely? I was so moved when he gave it to me."

"And it wasn't even your birthday. Where did he get it?" Zoey asked.

"Harry Winston!" Mouse answered. "Can you believe it?"

"He said it was a token of love." Jade pressed her eyes closed. "I know it's so corny and old-fashioned, but I'm right there, so into him. He's brought out a brand-new me."

"Which is a statement in itself," Merlin said. "The old Jade would be out having the bracelet appraised and certified for authenticity."

"Not to mention bragging about this," Zoey said, waving the *New York Magazine* in the air. "Your dot com guy has made you famous, but you're so focused on him you don't even care anymore. Looks like our little Jade is a woman in love."

"She's not the only one," Mouse said. "Guess who's going to pop the question tonight?"

Zoey gaped. "Kenny?"

Mouse's head bobbed. "I am so excited, I'm worried about my concentration on stage tonight. News like this could totally blow my timing on stage."

"You'll be great," Zoey reassured her. "We'll cheer extra loud."

Mouse looked around, then lowered her voice. "I almost forgot—I'm not supposed to know about the ring, because he said it was a surprise, so don't say anything."

"Our lips are sealed," Zoey promised.

"We'll wait until tomorrow to give the *Post* the scoop," Merlin said sardonically. Then he cocked an eyebrow. "Actually, the *Post* might run something. I mean, Kenny is the owner of Rainforest, and you're a hit here, too. Wow, my friends are becoming famous."

"You bet, sweetie." Mouse winked. "Did you see the write-up the *Times* did on Rainforest two weeks ago? Featured a photo of moi."

"I did." Merlin snapped his fingers. "I remember thinking at the time that the woman on the swing looked familiar."

"Well, ever since the story broke I've been getting calls from agents. But this time I'm going to be picky. I can afford to take my time. But we'll always remember who our friends are."

"Yes, don't forget us little people," Merlin teased.

"Little, my ass," Mouse responded, grabbing a stack of delicate menus printed on unbleached parchment. Looking sexy in a shoulderless black sheath draped with brightly colored African cloth, she showed them to a table. "I'm going to seat you in the main dining room tonight, because you need to be part of my new act."

"Oh, please!" Merlin groaned. "I will not let you saw me in half."

Mouse grinned. "It'll be fun."

As drinks were ordered Zoey sat down and skimmed the article about A.J. Chenowitz. It was the first time she had really paid attention to the man's looks, and she had to admit he seemed healthy, solid, but quite nerdy for someone with Jade's sophistication. Still, Jade had managed to look past his physical appearance to the man inside, and that was what mattered.

"So Jade, when are we going to meet this man of yours?" asked Zoey.

"Soon, I hope." Jade sighed. "He's trying to sell off some of his holdings so that the business will demand less of his time. If that happens as planned, he'll be able to lead a more normal life, with some semblance of a social life."

Zoey turned to Merlin. "How's your social life?" she asked.

"Sucks. And yours?"

"Double sucks. Nick is coming to town for a big face-to-face meeting, probably with an entourage of lawyers. I'm thinking of it as the fleecing of the innocent wife."

"Just stand your ground," Jade advised. "He may be a hotshot lawyer, but in most states you've got to divide things fifty-fifty."

"I know." Zoey toyed with the cherry in her whiskey sour. "It's just that I don't know how I'm going to react when I see Nick.

What if I burst into tears? What if he wears me down and I start sobbing at the conference table. I've even fantasized that I jump up on the table and place a karate kick right in his face, though that is probably the least likely scenario."

"Sounds like you need some moral support," Merlin said. "Do you want me to come along to the meeting? I can't give legal advice, but I can back you up if the attorneys come at you with some Ninja moves."

Zoey smiled. "That would be great. It's Friday morning. Do you think you can get off work?"

"No problem," Merlin said as Kenny passed by, leading an older gentleman. The white-haired, African-American man moved slowly but steadily to the table beside them.

"Good evening, everyone," Kenny said, smiling at the group. "How's everything going tonight?"

"Excellent," Jade answered. "We're looking forward to Marielle's new act."

"Me, too," he admitted. "She didn't even let me watch the rehearsals for this one." He dropped a hand onto the older man's shoulder, stopping him. "Dad, I want you to meet some friends of mine. This is Merlin Chong, Zoey McGuire, and Jade Cohen."

Zoey felt impressed that Kenny knew all their last names, but it was probably an essential tool for someone who ran a club like this. "It's a pleasure, Mr. Aragon."

"That's Reverend Aragon," Kenny corrected her politely. "Dad is the pastor of a Baptist church in Atlanta."

Kenny's father reached forward to shake their hands. "Very nice to meet you all," he said, and Zoey liked his warm, firm handshake.

"Your son has built a lovely club here," Jade told the reverend. "It's quickly becoming a Manhattan landmark."

"Glad to hear it," the reverend said. "I'm very proud of him."

"We'll be sitting right over here, Dad," Kenny said, guiding his father to the next table. "Enjoy your evening," he added, before turning away to join his father.

"Mouse is so lucky," Merlin said quietly. "If I'd seen Kenny first, *I* would have married him."

"You were otherwise detained," Zoey pointed out. "Besides, I don't think the reverend's son would swing both ways."

"You never know," Merlin said. "You just never know what's going on in someone else's life."

"Isn't that true." Zoey knew he was referring to Josh, but she couldn't help thinking of Nick, of the lies about working late, working on litigation out of town, losing his neckties, buying himself a new shirt at the airport shop. Such a string of lies . . . even now she wasn't sure what was legitimate and what was a fabrication. "You just never know."

63

Mouse was so sure she had a crowd-pleaser of an act, she could barely contain her smile when she joined her friends at the table, sitting in the fourth chair.

"Mouse?" Zoey squinted at her. "Is that your costume?"

She nodded, pulling the black duster closed over her knees, which were covered in an ankle-length black satin skirt. White gloves covered her arms up to the elbow, giving a very formal look to her attire, and making her feel warm already.

Jade cocked an eyebrow. "It's rather subdued for you."

"Sort of funereal," added Merlin.

Mouse sat back in the chair, waiting for her cue. "You'll see."

The band returned to the stage from their break, and the lead singer went to the center-stage mike. "Ladies and gentlemen," he said, "this is the portion of our evening when we like to show-case talent from the audience. To be honest, our manager doesn't agree with this policy, but if there's anyone out there who would like to . . ."

Mouse raised her gloved hand.

"I see we already have a volunteer. Would you like to come on stage, miss?"

Mouse shook her head, hunching her shoulders self-consciously.

"Oh. Ladies and gentlemen, I think she's shy." He took the microphone down into the audience until he was standing beside Mouse. The houselights had gone out, and the edge of the round table was spotlighted. "But you wanted to sing a song?" he asked.

She nodded. "Do you know 'Lullaby of Broadway'?" she asked in a tiny voice.

He handed her the mike. "You start, and we'll join in." He stole back onto the stage as Mouse held the spotlight and looked around the room, suddenly appearing frightened as she noted the crowd on the balcony.

She stood up, covered her eyes, and began to sing in a meek, strained voice: "Come on along and listen to, the Lullaby of Broadway."

The band started in, and she turned to them, as if startled. The band leader nodded encouragingly, and she sang on, her voice gaining strength. Mouse let the transformation unfold as she sang on with increasing confidence, skipping through the audience, then dancing onto the stage. She picked up a top hat that was lying near the drum set, and she strutted across the stage, pumping it over her head.

Toward the end of the number she went to center stage for a tap dance routine, then finished with a series of high kicks arm-in-arm with the guitarist.

The song popped along to its end, and the crowd roared with delight. Taking a quick bow, Mouse noticed that Kenny was seated at the table next to her friends with another man. How perfect! That would work well for her next number.

The band started up "Let Me Entertain You," from the musical *Gypsy,* and Mouse turned and waved her arms at them, stopping them. "Oh, no! I can't do that song!" She turned to the audience. "My Mama would never forgive me if I did that song. But you know . . . it's very warm up here on stage."

She started to peel off a glove, and the drummer did a striptease drum roll. She frowned at him. "Now cut that out!" Delicately, she removed the second glove and accidentally dropped it to the stage.

Laughter rumbled through the audience. "Oops!" She bent over to pick it up, making her jacket pop open at the bodice. "Oh my!" When she stood up, the coat billowed open, revealing a peek of her black silk skirt and sequined green bikini top. She looked down and sighed. "It's just too hot."

The lead singer tapped her shoulder and she turned. With a smile, he handed her a hanger. "Oh, thank you," she said. She slid off her jacket and hung it on the hanger. The lead guitarist took it from her and she thanked him again. He nodded, then flung it off into the wings.

"Hey!" she shouted.

He shrugged and turned to strike up the band again. They played the same song, and this time Mouse grabbed the microphone and started singing. She moved gracefully to the first chorus, starting to feel the beat and drive of the song. Now she used a few of the steps she'd done in her first striptease for Kenny, turning her back to the audience as she swung her hips, bent down and lifted her skirt up, up, up over ankles and thighs and knees and hips. With one bold yank, she tore the velcro tab and removed the skirt from her body.

The crowd roared.

The shiny green G-string bottom showed the best of her butt, and she gave an extra wiggle before turning to face the audience. She swayed, stroking her breasts, then giving them a jiggle. Teasing the straps of her green bikini top down one shoulder, then the next. She popped out a breast, then popped it back in. Actually, under the stiff green bikini top she was wearing a sheer brown bra with gold pasties over her nipples, but it was difficult to see that from the audience.

People cheered as she gave them a peek . . .

And she loved it. She loved knowing that men and women were looking at her body, admiring her tight, round butt and her graceful breasts. She knew what the men wanted to do to her

. . . she could imagine them lining up backstage to bend her over and stick it in her. The thrill made her tighten her Kegel muscles in anticipation of having Kenny inside her after the show.

Finally, Mouse whipped off her green bikini top and came into the audience, her gold pasties bobbing. She was still singing as she went to Kenny's table and made eye contact with the other man. He seemed a little hesitant, but she couldn't back down now.

As she sang, "And if you're real good, I'll make you feel good . . ." she lifted a leg and flung it over his knees, straddling him. She flashed him a seductive smile, but he looked down at the table. Pumping her hips, she gave him a seductive little lap dance. Her breasts jiggled right in his face, and she gave him a pouting look, but he seemed so mortified, poor baby. His reaction made other people laugh harder. Even Mouse had to smile in amusement as she hopped up and rubbed Kenny's head before climbing back onto the stage.

People were clapping before she'd sung the last note. A roar filled the cavernous room, and as she looked out, most people were on their feet, cheering and smiling.

Oh, Dear Lord, I'm a hit!

She blew kisses to the audience, then bowed deeply. She waved a hand back to credit the band, but the lead singer gestured right back to her.

Thank you, Jesus! They loved me! Her heart pounded as she ran backstage, bypassing the small changing room and going straight to Kenny's office for his own form of appreciation. She sat poised on his desk, one knee bent to reveal a lovely glimpse of crotch, as the door swung open.

"What the hell was that about?" Kenny asked, his eyes burning with fury.

Mouse's grin faded as she swung her legs down. "What do you mean? It's my new act."

"I had no idea you were working on something so . . . so tasteless," he exclaimed.

A pain cut through her as she realized the level of his anger. "It was cute. The audience loved it."

"Not everyone in the audience." He pointed a beefy finger toward the door. "Do you realize that you just did a lap dance on my father? He flew in this morning from Atlanta. I was going to surprise you, but ... he is a man of God. Do you know what you've done?"

"I'm a Christian, too," she said. "Doesn't mean God doesn't want me to use my talents."

He shook his head, glancing away, as if he couldn't stand to look at her. "Get out of here." The way he said it made her feel all used up, like a cheap pair of pantyhose you wore once then tossed out.

She slid off the desk and straightened her back. Holding her head high, chin up, she walked out of his office ... and out of his life.

64

"How was I supposed to know it was his father?" Mouse complained to Jade, who was pacing the office with her cell phone at her ear, waiting for A.J. to return her call. He was supposed to fly in this morning at ten, but it was already four and she hadn't heard from him yet.

Jade sat down and propped her high-heeled feet on her desk. "So how do you feel now? Embarrassed, or just angry?"

"Of course I'm embarrassed. I mean, I wouldn't tease my guy's father like that, let alone a minister. But how was I to know? And really, I don't think the act was tasteless, do you?"

"I thought it was PG, but don't use me as a gauge. In the meantime, are you still the hostess at Rainforest?"

"No way." Mouse was silent for a moment. "Damn, I loved that job. I mean, the hours and the pay and the perks, it just worked for me. But I am not going to subject myself to such a nasty, judgmental, bigheaded . . ."

"I get the picture. Well, this is your chance to get out to auditions again. You've been so busy working on your cabaret act, you've dropped out of the loop."

"And it's time I picked an agent. I'll be okay."

Jade sighed. "Where *is* he?"

"Still no word from A.J.?"

"No. Let me call him again."

"Okay. If he doesn't show, come over to Zoey's. We're having a painting party."

"He'll show," Jade said confidently. She was trying to stop being so nervous and unsure about her relationship with A.J., trying to let herself have faith in their commitment to each other. "Talk to you later."

She hung up and hit the speed-dial for A.J.'s corporate headquarters in Portland, Oregon. She was on hold for Hank when Omar, one of the other brokers, poked his head into her cubicle.

"Hey, Jade, did you see this?" He slapped a tabloid magazine onto her desk. "Your boyfriend made the papers again."

She nodded, not bothering to take her feet off the desk. Omar Ascobar was an aggressive big-mouth who didn't know when to back off. More than once, he'd scared her clients away from the office. "Yeah, thanks, Omar," she said, turning away before he felt encouraged to hang out.

Hank came on the line and apologized about A.J.'s change of plans. "We had something developing in Boston this morning, so he flew up there and delayed his meetings in New York," Hank explained. "I'm so sorry, Jade. A.J. was to notify you personally, but I guess he's been waylaid longer than expected."

"Okay, Hank," she said, feeling relieved that everything was okay. "I'm sure I'll talk with him later."

Hanging up, she glanced over at the magazine Omar had left for her. From the thin paper and blurred print, she could see it was a cheap tabloid, but it was open to an entire spread of photos of A.J. and . . . and another woman.

She checked the date . . . it was this week's. The woman was a redhead with a turned-up Irish nose—a member of the Kennedy clan, according to the captions. There were so many shots of them together—in swimsuits at the beach, playing football on a green lawn, A.J. holding her in his arms, her ball gown covering his legs, his smile so blissful.

He had talked of falling in love once before. What had he said? Something about her cute nose—and that she was from a political family.

Oh, God. And where was he now?

Boston. Jade covered her mouth, feeling sick.

She shoved the magazine into her bag and streaked toward the door, trying to get out of the office before tears filled her eyes.

65

"Is this stuff intoxicating?" Merlin called from the hallway. "I think I'm getting a buzz."

"It looks like cake batter," Mouse observed. "Really. It's making me hungry. Do you have any muffins, Zoey?"

"I figure we'll order out when we get the base coat done," Zoey yelled from the bedroom where she was trying to read the directions on the sand-wash technique Skye wanted. She'd done it once in the Connecticut house and the process had seemed therapeutic, but now that she read the directions there were so many things that could go wrong, with clumped paint, uneven textures, and uneven colors. Well, at least she'd finished the bottom coat. The wash would have to wait until another day. She went to the hall to check on her friends. "How's it going?"

"Almost done," Mouse said from the ladder. Her nose and cheeks were speckled with superwhite paint.

"I think we're a good team," Zoey said. "Maybe I should forget writing and just paint people's apartments."

Merlin swiped the roller over the corner of the ceiling, then lowered it and stretched his back. "Count me out. The ceilings kill your neck."

"Let's have a beer first, then we'll decide what to order," Zoey said, rubbing the sweat from her forehead. "By the time we eat, it may be ready for a second coat."

"Slave driver," Merlin said, plodding out to the living room.

Zoey covered the sofa with a drop cloth in case they had paint on their jeans and white shirts, and Mouse and Merlin plopped down.

"Payment for your services," Zoey said, handing them each a beer.

"There's nothing like hard work to help you forget your problems," Mouse said, scratching her nose. "Look at us! Three wonderful people. Three recently rejected people. Right now, listening to Jade, I get so jealous."

Merlin nodded. "As do I."

Zoey took a sip of beer and looked out at the jagged Manhattan skyline. "And when I look ahead . . ." She shook her head. "I don't see any relief in sight."

Merlin frowned at her. "You know, that's not true. I was looking at your chart last night." He had drawn up Zoey's chart years ago, when he started studying astrology. At the time he'd told Zoey a few things about her personality, but she was too frightened to hear about the future.

"Really?" She pressed the cold bottle to her cheek to cool off. "And you actually saw something good?"

"Well, for one, I could see your breakup with Nick. And some delay in getting money, but ultimately your money problems will go away by the end of this year."

"That would be nice," she said.

"And there's romance coming."

Zoey and Mouse exchanged a look of wonder.

"You're kidding, right?" Zoey asked.

He shook his head. "There's a love interest coming your way any day now—definitely this month. With significant potential. It's probably someone new, though it could be the reappearance of Nick as a mate."

Zoey winced.

Mouse patted her shoulder. "Don't worry, honey. I'll kill you before I let that happen again."

"Thank you!" Zoey hugged Mouse.

"No problem," Mouse said, patting her shoulder.

The doorman buzzed and said that Jade was here. Zoey thanked him and left the door ajar.

"Oh, good, she can help on the second coat," Mouse said. "Now, Merlin the magician, what about my chart? See any hotties coming my way?"

He smiled. "I haven't looked at your chart recently. Last time I tried to check, you were into major reborn-Christian mode, and astrology was the work of the devil."

Mouse shrugged. "I got over that."

"I'll have to take a look when I get home," Merlin said. "But you have to promise not to argue when I tell you what I see."

"What?" Mouse slapped her chest. "Me, argue?"

The door clicked open, and Zoey looked over and gulped as Jade's heels clicked on the parquet floor. Jade looked ill, with pale cheeks and sunken eyes stained with mascara.

"Oh, honey, what happened?" Zoey jumped up from the couch and went to slip an arm around Jade's slender shoulders.

Jade pulled a wrinkled magazine out of her bag and handed it over to Zoey. "Dot com guy is dot com dead."

"Let me see," Mouse said, getting up from the couch. Merlin joined them, too, and suddenly the three of them were huddled around the paper, staring in disbelief and disappointment.

"She's a Kennedy," Jade said, her voice hoarse with pain. "A Kennedy! How am I supposed to compete with that?"

"Oh, Jade, take off your shoes and sit down," Zoey said gently. "Let's talk about this. Maybe it's a misprint. Doctored photos or something."

Jade shook her head. "This is real. This is the girl he was in love with. He told me about her." She let her head fall back, her hands forming fists. "God, was I an idiot!"

"Don't give up the ship," Mouse insisted. "Okay, what if the man made a mistake. So he thought with his dick for a weekend or something. Can't you forgive him? Maybe not this minute, but, you know, in a week or so, after you yell at him some and he sends you nice gifts and talks sweet on the phone?"

Jade shook her head stiffly. "He loves her. This is more than an affair. I can see it in . . ." She pointed to the tabloid, her face crumpling as her voice caught. "In the look on his face in those photos. He's happy there."

Zoey squeezed Jade's arm. "But he loves you, too, and you're selling yourself short, Jade. You're a very special person. You *can* compete with a Kennedy."

Her eyes filled with rue, Jade shook her head again. "I already called his personal voice mail and left a scathing message. It's so over." She bent her head and wiped her eyes. "I'm sorry. You guys were . . . and I just . . . I'd better go."

"No . . . No! We were sitting here in a funk, and I think we all need something to snap us out of it." Zoey looked around, thinking fast. "Let's just cap up the paint and head out. Someplace noisy and wild and very distracting."

Mouse ran down the hall and pressed the round cap onto one half gallon. She threw a rag over it, then tapped it down with the hammer.

"But look?" Merlin said, tugging on his white T-shirt. The three of them were wearing faded jeans and white undershirts.

"I've got something in black." Zoey raced into the bedroom. "Black shirts all around!"

66

They took a cab to Diamonds and Spurs, a large, dark, rowdy dance hall on the East Side. The friends sat quietly at a table, eating ribs and fried catfish and corn on the cob and spicy shoe-string fries. They were already on their third pitcher of margaritas, and Zoey was starting to feel a relaxing buzz.

She noticed that Jade still looked haunted, like someone who'd just survived a fluke car accident. She was going to ask about A.J., but realized the wounds might be too fresh to probe right now.

Forget conversation. "Let's dance," she said, pulling on Jade's arm. Jade got up, and Merlin tossed down his napkin. Mouse jumped up and thrust her fists in the air.

"Do you know how to do the Texas Two-Step?" Zoey shouted over the music to Mouse.

She shook her head. "I just get out there and pound my feet and wiggle my butt, and no one seems to care!"

Hands on her hips, Jade looked skeptical, but Zoey pulled her along as she sidled up to a man in fancy tan and black boots, watching his moves. He smiled, and she tried to copy him, lifting her feet, stomping and clapping. Merlin banged into her, and they both stumbled and laughed. Mouse was already working her way into the center of a circle of dancers, looking more like an Irish step-dancer than a Texas hoofer, but no one seemed to care.

"Riverdance!" Merlin shouted, and the people close enough to hear him laughed.

Zoey was glad to see Jade making an effort, clapping and stomping, making eye contact with a guy who had a cute mustache and a fancy western shirt.

The music changed, and they started a new dance, and Zoey found herself following along, smiling despite herself. God, she was so clumsy! But with the bristling music, and all the stomping and clapping, no one seemed to notice, and she began to feel like the real points were gained by stomping loudly, hooting, and howling.

After a few minutes, she wiped her forehead and headed off the dance floor for another drink. Merlin was already at the bar, talking with the bartender, who handed him a pitcher of margaritas and a tray of glasses. Merlin lifted a twenty from his wallet, but the bartender waved it away. "It's on me," he said, reaching across the bar to shake Merlin's hand. "My name's Seth."

Trying not to be too nosey, Zoey twisted around slightly to get a glimpse of Seth as Merlin introduced himself. Dark hair that curled at the collar, prominent nose, nice smile, and cheekbones to die for.

Merlin poured two drinks as Seth headed down the bar, where a pack of women in suits—probably an office party—were pressing into each other to get drinks from another bartender.

"Don't look now, but I think Seth was flirting with you," Zoey said.

"Flirting? No one flirts anymore. They go straight for the pickup." Merlin handed her a glass and held his up for a toast. "Here's to moving on. To the thrill of being hit on for the first time in three years. To the prospect of freedom."

Zoey straightened. "Here, here! I like this toast." She clinked glasses with Merlin and tossed back the frosty bittersweet drink.

Merlin was glancing down the bar, checking on Seth. "You know, I've been out of the dating loop so long, I feel like a dinosaur. What if I don't understand the lingo or know the right moves anymore?" His blue eyes met Zoey's, and she blinked.

"Well, I was out of the mainstream for a while, too. I thought Nick was, too, but boy was I wrong on that. Anyway, I guess the answer is . . . there is no answer. I mean, jumping into bed with Scott helped me realize that most of the moves are still the same. But ultimately I think sex and relationships are so personal, they need to be personally tailored to the individuals involved."

Merlin's eyes were serious as he nodded, then refilled Zoey's drink. "You are making way too much sense. Drink up, my dear."

Mouse came over, dragging another woman by the arm. "This is my friend Carla," she said. "We were in *Hair* together, and we both study dance with Teddy!"

A thin, tall woman with wispy blond hair and an enormous smile, Carla nodded. "We used to room together, and for a while we were dating the same guy. Have you seen Bobby lately?"

Shaking her head, Mouse grabbed a few napkins to mop the sweat off her neck. "He dropped off the face of the earth, but . . . ."

"Pour me a drink, Merlin!" Jade interrupted, bouncing off Carla. "I need one of those." She was tilting, holding on to a beer, which sloshed out of the bottle as she tried to regain her balance.

"You already have one," Merlin pointed out.

"Don't argue with a woman in despair!" Jade ordered.

"I wouldn't dream of it." Merlin poured her a margarita, while Zoey steered her onto a stool.

"I've made an important discovery," Jade said. She paused to take a sip of the margarita, then lowered it to the bar slowly. "Men make the worst partners."

Mouse clapped, saying, "You said it, sister."

"Men suck," Carla volunteered.

"Men suck!" Jade repeated fervently.

"Such wise words from someone so inebriated," Zoey said. "But definitely true."

"You don't count, though." Jade reached out to touch Merlin's shoulder. "I propose an amendment. Or an addendment. No, wait—an exclusionary clause for Merlin. Because you understand. You know how men can be."

He bowed. "Thank you, ladies. And I stand here as living proof that you speak the truth, Jade. Men can be such big babies."

"That's right!" Mouse shouted.

Merlin finished off his drink. "And to think I paid for Josh to go to masseuse school."

"That boy was a user and a loser," Mouse said. "And you know what else? Men never grow up. They could be thirty, forty, and they're still hanging on to Mama, or worried about what Daddy thinks, or running home for Christmas or Easter or Sunday dinner because they're scared to do their own thing."

"Big . . . bad . . . babies . . ." Jade managed to get out. She shook her head. "Useless . . . the whole species."

Zoey knew the drinks were having their effect, but suddenly the noise and commotion of the room beyond seemed to fade in the background, and looming before her were the faces of her friends: Merlin, cool and composed; Mouse, indignant and spirited; and Jade, the pissed off Jewish-American goddess. They filled her world with humor and warmth and solid sense. Men might come and go, but her friends were her friends forever.

"Oh, God, I love you guys!" she said, rushing forward in an attempt to embrace them all.

She spilled some of her drink by Merlin's shoe, and he gave her a stern look. "If that was supposed to be a group hug, I'll have none of it."

"I'm sorry, but I just felt it was a bonding moment and . . . I don't know." She straightened and sipped her drink. "Guess I lost my head."

"We love you too, honey." Mouse hugged her, then reached for the margarita pitcher.

"I think I want to dance again," Jade said, suddenly noticing the beer in her hand. "Where did you come from?"

As the tight circle was broken, Zoey noticed someone on her right. There was the intense feeling of scrutiny, then a shower of warm feeling as she realized he was kind of cute. She turned for a better look, and she liked his pale brown hair, longish on top but clipped at the sides. Very nice haircut. And his chin—a strong chin. And a nice smile. And eyes that were looking right back at her . . .

Quickly she turned away. She'd been caught looking. And she realized a goofy drunken grin was pasted on her face. She straightened her mouth. No, that was a pucker. Suddenly her body wasn't responding to brain commands.

"You guys looked like you were having a club meeting there," the guy told her.

Zoey turned to face him again. A sunny glow seemed to surround him. Or was that a drunken haze?

"Can I join the club?" he asked.

"Only if you hate men," she told him.

He laughed. "That wouldn't be too good for my self-esteem." When she didn't respond, he added, "I try not to hate myself, though sometimes it's inevitable."

She nodded, squinting to see if the aura around him faded. Nope.

"Maybe I'd better go so you can get back to your club," he said. "You seemed to be having fun."

"We try," Zoey said seriously. "But you guys don't make it easy."

He laughed again. "I'm Sam. And you are . . . ?"

"Completely wasted," she admitted, immediately realizing it wasn't exactly what he was looking for. "My name is Zoey."

"Zoey. Okay, that's a start. Do you like country music, Zoey?"

She hoisted her drink. "It's great for drinking and banging your feet. How about you?"

"I was just thinking how much it's changed in the past few years. Not so much country anymore, but country mixed with pop and rock and even jazz. Sort of a fusion in music. I was involved in something similar in San Francisco. A mixture of graffiti and folk art and installations. Sort of a fusion thang," he said, twanging the words.

"A fusion thang." Zoey nodded, not following the meaning behind his words. What with the bouncing golden white aura around him, how was she supposed to concentrate? She did pick up graffiti and San Francisco, but overall his words had the connection of an e. e. cummings poem. She liked Sam. Yep, that golden aura sure sparkled. But he was death. "You know," she said. "You seem like a nice guy, but I can't talk to you anymore."

"Really?" He squinted at her, a squinty smile. God, he was cute.

"It's your species," she said, slurring the "s" sounds. "You can't be trusted."

He nodded. "You're probably right."

"I'm sorry," she said earnestly. "But even gay men cheat on each other."

He studied her closely. "Not following that, but why don't I just give you my number, and you can call me someday when . . . when my species evolves in your mind?" He took a matchbook from the bar and scribbled on it.

As he wrote, she realized he was flirting and felt compelled to ask him some questions. It had been so long since she'd done this; she felt stale. "What do you do, Sam?"

"I'm a painter," he said. "I've been living in San Francisco, but I just moved to New York."

She nodded, suddenly thinking about the unfinished work in Skye's apartment. Then she realized that Sam was wearing jeans and red high-top Keds. "Where are your cowboy boots?" she asked.

"My friends dragged me here," he said, nodding across the room. "And it looks like they're ready to go. So call me . . . or just use the matches at a great rock concert."

Zoey nodded as he smiled and headed off.

"Who was that?" Mouse asked, staring after him.

"I have no idea," Zoey said. "But . . . check it out. Is he glowing?"

Mouse studied the man, then swatted Zoey's shoulder. "Girl, you are more snockered than I am!"

67

It was the noon of the next day by the time Zoey felt adequately recovered to turn on her computer and log on. There was an email from Skye. With dread, she clicked it open.

> Big news! I just booked my plane ticket and I wanted you to be the first to know: I'll be returning to New York next weekend! Big sigh. I finally squeezed the manuscript out of eccentric author who will remain unnamed (I know you know) and he's just touching up a few scenes right now. Must admit, am sick of the hills and the charming lilt of speech here. Craving a fast-food burger and Ben and Jerry's. How are your housing prospects?

"Bleak," Zoey answered, talking to the monitor. She walked away from the computer and threw herself over the bed. How she'd hate to leave her new home. But she'd only gotten this place through luck and Skye's act of pity. It was time to face reality. She crawled across the bed and grabbed the phone to call Jade.

"I need a place to live," she yelped.

Jade was not encouraging. "Oh, honey, I've been watching for you, but the good, cheap places get snatched up in a flash. Do you want to look at something today?"

"Today and every day until I find something. Skye is coming back next weekend."

"I'm not going to say it's impossible, but the chances of finding something in your income bracket in such a short time . . ." Jade paused. "Can you ask Nick to increase your allowance?"

Zoey felt like a nine-year-old. "I can always try. Should I meet you at the office?"

"Sure. One of the agents keeps raving about Inwood, though I haven't been there in years."

"Inwood? Is that in Jersey?"

"Might as well be. It's upper west side. Upper, upper. I'll show you."

That afternoon they covered Inwood and parts of Harlem, without success. Zoey wasn't thrilled about being so far from midtown, though she would have taken two of the apartments if they had still been available. They decided to stop into Rainforest for a late lunch since they were in the neighborhood. Mouse's former assistant Ellie greeted them at the door and showed them to a table. The cool, tropical atmosphere was a welcome relief after hours spent walking up humid stairwells and crossing streets aglow with heat waves. Still, the club seemed odd and empty without Mouse.

"We'll keep looking," Jade promised as they dug into Tiger Shrimp Salads.

"Thanks," Zoey said. "I know this commission is nothing compared to most of your deals."

Jade waved her off. "I'm not charging you a commission, honey. You'll be putting out enough money—first and last months' rent—if we do find a place." She nodded to someone behind Zoey. "There's the man."

Zoey turned to see Kenny sitting on a barstool, hunched over a plate of food. "He looks lonely."

"He does. But we're projecting."

Ellie passed by with a new party. On her way back, Jade summoned her closer to the table. "What's with the Thinker? Is he having a bad day?"

Glancing toward the bar, Ellie spoke quietly. "Kenny's been a wreck since Marielle left. Personally I think he's in mourning. Totally lost without her. But he'll never admit it."

"Very interesting," Jade said.

Zoey nodded at Ellie. "We'll spread the word."

When Zoey left Jade, she went downtown to a photographer's studio in Chelsea. She had an appointment with Apple Sommers, the photographer who had taken the author portraits to run in the back of her books—but not for a session. The woman had agreed to give her five minutes of time for research.

Apple and her assistant were setting up for a shoot when Zoey arrived. "No, no, take some of the flowers out, it's too busy, and put some gels on those lights," Apple ordered judiciously before turning to Zoey. She raked her red curls off her forehead and scrunched them. "Hi, how are you?"

"On a mission," Zoey said, getting down to business. She showed the photographer the spread from *National Scout*. "Can you help me find out the real story here? I know you're not the photographer—they're by Andre Robbins—but I need to know if these were doctored or something."

Apple took one look at the spread, then pulled her cell phone from her belt. "Andre's a friend of mine. Let's see what he says."

Five minutes later, she had the answer. "The photos are legit," Apple said. "The lie is in the date. They were taken more than two years ago, a fact that the *Scout* forgot to include in the piece. Andre says he sold them to the *Scout* and forgot about them, but now that A.J. Chenowitz has become a hotter news item, they're running them."

"Two years. And they almost ruined my friend's life." Zoey blinked, feeling relieved. "Thank you so much."

Apple smiled. "No problem." She tilted her head to study Zoey. "This red hair is a new look for you, isn't it?" When Zoey nodded, she added, "Come see me soon and we'll update your author portrait."

"Definitely," Zoey said, thinking, "Just as soon as I manage to produce another novel worthy of publication."

As soon as Zoey hit the street she took out her cell phone and called Jade.

"Oh, no! I mean, that's great. But after the way I blasted him, I . . ." Jade paused. "I'd better call him. Thanks, Zoey."

Next, Zoey called Mouse, who had already heard from Jade about Ellie's comment at the club. "Boo-hoo, poor, poor baby!" Mouse said dramatically. "Meanwhile, I am going on with my life. I spent the morning at an audition, and let me tell you, it was hard to get out of bed this morning and I think I'm a little hoarse. But maybe my hangover paid off, because they liked me. I've got a callback for tomorrow. It's a supporting role, a gutsy siren. I'll bet they saw my cabaret act and realized my potential."

"Great!" Zoey said, faking her enthusiasm a little. She couldn't believe Mouse wouldn't try to work it out with Kenny. If she loved the guy, couldn't they get beyond a few misunderstandings?

You're just a pushover, she told herself. If Nick came running back now, you'd hightail it out of the city and jump right back in his arms. God, what she wouldn't do to fulfill her romantic dreams. Poor, pathetic Zoey. Note to self: Get a life.

68

Three days later, Zoey felt sure she had seen the sordid insides of every dark, dingy studio walk-up from the Bronx to the Battery. Acting on a tip from Jade, she was checking out a one-bedroom in Hell's Kitchen that had just been listed. Spotting the address, she crossed the street, running from a speeding cab as she realized why the address had sounded familiar.

"Snake's building." Although she had no desire to chance running into him on a daily basis, she had to check the place out. In the tight world of Manhattan real estate, you did not give up an apartment because someone else in the building was a jerk. She buzzed for the super, but over the intercom he told her people were upstairs, the door should be open. It turned out, when she went upstairs, the apartment for rent was Snake's. An Asian girl was in the living room, measuring the room with footsteps. "I'm taking it," she told Zoey, a competitive gleam in her eyes.

Curious, Zoey went into the bedroom, where two guys waited, one talking on a cell. The place was vacant except for the sad mattress of his bed, which had been turned on its side to droop against one wall. The place brought back ambivalent memories, and she was glad it was gone. Glad, but still homeless.

Merlin had left her a message to call, but his hotel was just uptown from here. Deciding to drop in on him, she walked uptown fifteen blocks and over two avenues, working up a sweat that frosted over as she passed through the revolving doors of the Royale. Merlin stood behind the main desk talking amicably with a guest. He nodded at Zoey, and motioned for her to wait. When he finished with the woman, he called to one of the other clerks to cover for him and emerged from a door to the side of the lobby.

"I'm due for a break. Let's go down to the locker room," he said, leading her to the service elevator. Zoey followed him down into the basement of the hotel, where there was a large, cool locker room and a simple but comfortable lounge area. A Latina woman said hello as she finished tying on an apron. Someone slammed a locker door. Someone else came in behind Merlin.

"This isn't bad," she said.

"It gets tired quickly." Merlin sat down on the sofa and leaned his head back. "I've sort of been living out of this place since Josh left. Usually I manage to get a spare room to sleep in, but I've spent a few nights right here on this couch."

"Really?" Zoey sat down opposite him, folding one of her legs under her. "Why? Are you working double shifts?"

He shook his head. "I just . . . dread going home. The apartment is uncomfortable for me now that Josh is gone. His mother actually came and picked up his stuff, which I thought would make me feel better, but it's just that much emptier."

"I didn't know you felt that way. God, it's like he died or something."

Merlin sighed. "It's lucky for me that we didn't file the business partnership with city hall before he left. That would have really been messy. Instead I just have to sort out the past, wondering what was real and what was part of the fantasy world he concocted. Turns out Josh never lived in Minnesota, and he didn't have an abusive father. Just a boring life in the suburbs."

"Oh, God, how awful." Zoey winced, understanding how a partner's deception could be devastating.

"But I'm trying to move on, and it's working in most places. Just not the apartment. There he haunts me, and rather than contend with his ghost, I avoid the place." Merlin closed his eyes.

Rubbing his arm gently, Zoey imagined his empty apartment. She'd felt that way about the Connecticut house, that the walls and floors possessed memories too potent to ignore. "I have an idea, though it may be disastrous. But what if I moved in with you? It might change the tone of the place. Besides, I am getting desperate. Yesterday I saw a hearse and wondered if the dead person had left behind a rent-stabilized one-bedroom in a doorman building."

"You're beginning to sound like Jade."

"The apartment hunt is warping my mind. But you have two bedrooms, right? And I don't have much stuff. And except for the wild parties I throw for my friends, I'm a very quiet person. The only sound you'll hear will be the patter of my fingers on the keyboard—if I ever start writing again. So . . . what do you think?"

"Of course you can move in," he said, opening one eye. "With the understanding that if we start to hate each other, you're out of there."

"Then I'll move in with Mouse."

"Well, I wouldn't do that to you." He took a deep breath. "Having you around might help. God, I'd love to have my apartment back."

"You have saved my life," Zoey said gratefully.

"I always do." Merlin lifted his head. "And I have a plan for saving Jade's ass, too. Although it goes against my usual work ethic of keeping my guests' private lives private."

"You know something about A.J.?" Zoey asked. Her discovery about the photos had come too late. A.J. had received all of Jade's poisonous messages and, apparently, he took them to heart. He refused to take her messages, and his staff members were not even allowed to speak to her. "I blew it, big time," Jade had told Zoey. "And all because I love him. If I didn't love the guy, I wouldn't have flown off the handle when I saw those photos."

"Mr. Chenowitz is coming to town this weekend," Merlin explained. "One of our banquet rooms is booked for a big affair, some charity thing, and Mr. C is involved. I can sneak everyone in, but we've got to make sure Jade gets there."

"Oh, my God, I can't believe you're matchmaking, Merlin!"

He pointed a finger at her. "Tell Mouse to keep this thing quiet. And if Mr. C asks, Jade is not to use my name."

"I'm sure she'll protect you," Zoey said. "This is a really nice thing you're doing."

Merlin frowned. "I just hope it doesn't backfire."

Before she left, Merlin promised to be on time at the law offices the following day. He also promised to bring a key so that she could start moving her things. As Zoey let herself into Skye's apartment, she saw the place in a new light. It had been a temporary home, a place for experimentation both in her work and her personal life, a place for healing. She also saw that the paint job was not complete, and she was running out of time.

She bit her lip, remembering the cute painter she'd met at Diamonds and Spurs. What was his name? Sam, and he'd left her a number. She fished through the clothes she was wearing that day and found the matchbook in the pocket of her jeans. Never one to pursue a man, she felt hesitant, but then she *did* need these walls painted. She picked up the phone and punched in the number.

"Sam Watson." The voice was bright, way too cheerful for New York.

"Hi, this is Zoey McGuire. We met at Diamonds and Spurs the other night?"

"The rodeo bar! Yes, Zoey, how are you."

"I'm great," she lied. "I'm calling to see if you'd be interested in a paint job. This apartment I'm subletting needs some work done quickly, before the owner gets back. Do you want to come over, or could you quote me a price on the phone?"

Silence.

"A paint job?" he asked. Then he laughed.

"Something funny?"

"I'm not that kind of painter," he said. "I paint on canvas, not Sheetrock. I'm an abstract artist. I've got a show coming up at the City Arts Foundation."

"Oh . . ." Zoey squeezed her eyes shut, held a finger to her head, and pretended to shoot. "Do I feel stupid, or what?"

"No, don't, it's my fault. I just hate the glaze people get in their eyes when I tell them that I'm an artist. Somehow painter sounds less pretentious."

"Right," Zoey said, dying to hang up and escape further humiliation.

"Listen, why don't we get together sometime for coffee?" he asked.

"Okay," she lied, "how about if I call you as soon as I find a real painter? Or, I mean, take care of all this stuff. I've got an insane deadline."

"No problem. Give me a call."

"Okay, bye." She hung up and tossed the matchbook into Skye's kitchen drawer, realizing that some relationships were just not meant to be.

Another note to self: Do not flirt with cute guys when you're drunk. Better yet, easy on the margaritas.

69

"Nervous?" Merlin asked her the next morning as they waited in the reception area of the law offices.

"Very nervous. I think my knees are shaking."

"You'll be fine."

"I'm just afraid I'll fall apart, and I don't want to do that. I want to stand my ground and fight, but I've never been able to do that with Nick."

"I hope your lawyer will take care of the fighting," he said. "You just need to look him in the eye and let him know that you're fine without him. That he can take away half of everything except you—he can't touch you. You will remain whole and intact."

"That's incredibly Zen of you," Zoey said, closing her eyes. "I'll try to remember it."

A few minutes later her lawyer, Natalie Rodriguez, arrived and brought Zoey and Merlin into the conference room. After a few minutes of water pouring and idle chitchat, Nick appeared with his lawyers.

The lawyers shook hands, but Zoey kept her arms crossed, refusing to touch her ex. His eyes swept over her and he smiled. "You got your hair cut," he said, infuriating her.

She wanted to stick her tongue out and say something snotty like, "Well excuse me for living," but she managed to restrain herself and just shrug.

"It looks nice," Nick said, nodding his approval. As if she wanted or needed it. Well, it didn't hurt, but Zoey didn't want to go there. He looked surprisingly normal, his dark eyes held their usual sparkle, and his suit looked smooth and crisp, as if he'd just ironed it during the ride down from Connecticut. How did he do that? She wished she could hate him, but she couldn't deny that he was attractive. She wondered who was ironing his shirts and picking up his dry cleaning these days, but she couldn't let herself go too far down that road.

The lawyers started talking, and Zoey felt like a little girl, sitting on the porch overhearing grown-up conversations. Nick made a few comments, and she realized the level of pride that fueled his every move. Nick cared about Nick, and she'd never seen that before. She used to think they were equal partners, but now she realized that Nick had called the shots all along.

Merlin kicked her under the table, and Zoey realized it was a cue. They were talking about the market value of the house, which was probably close to a million dollars.

"I'll give you the house," Zoey said.

Natalie touched her arm. "Let me handle this . . ."

"No, I mean it." Zoey felt nervous, but she pushed herself to keep her voice calm and low. "I'll give you the house if you take my savings and royalties out of escrow and back away from my future royalties. Come on, Nick. I wrote the books, I deserve the money. You can live happily ever after in the million-dollar house with your fat salary and your freedom. It's probably not the most equitable distribution for me, but I don't care, I want this to be over."

Nick's attorney looked at his client and nodded. "With that point agreed upon, I think we can move swiftly to a conclusion."

"There's one thing," Nick said, holding up one hand. He was staring at Zoey as if hypnotized by her. "If we could take a break and clear the room, there's something I'd like to discuss with Zoey. Alone."

The lawyers stood up, sweeping their legal pads from the table. Merlin mouthed "What?" to Zoey, and she just shrugged, assuming Nick wanted to get in his last licks. Some vindictive "I won" or "I told you so!"

After they filed out Nick closed the door and leaned against it. "Zoey . . ." he said in a low voice. "What did you do to your hair?"

"I shaved it off, Nick. This is a wig."

He sat at the head of the table and laughed. "Still have that biting sense of humor. I missed that. I miss you."

She shrugged. "You should have thought of that when you started playing grab-ass in the law library. You'll get over me."

"No," he said quietly. "I don't believe that I will, Zo. There's no one else like you out there. And just now, when you made your demands . . . you had this fire in your eyes. I can't tell you how turned on I was by that."

Zoey bit her lip to keep from smiling. God, he sounded so cliché!

"What do you think, Zo. Should we send these guys home and try it again?"

Unable to believe what she was hearing, she looked up to take in his expression. There were tears in his eyes—real tears. Well, at least real saline, even if the emotion behind the tears was questionable. Was he the best con artist in the world? How could he imagine that their marriage would work now, after it had been ripped down the center, the two sides tossed to the wind.

"It's over," she said aloud, without thinking. And as she said it, she believed it herself for the first time.

"I don't think so," he insisted. "I think we are destined to be together."

She stood up, feeling suddenly giddy.

"You'll never find anyone else like me," he said sternly.

Thank God! she thought, suddenly laughing. "It is so over, Nick," she announced, feeling frisky with liberation. "You know, I used to believe in that destiny bullshit, too. But now I see . . . actually, I don't see it anymore at all. What did I ever see in you?"

"We were good together," he insisted.

"Past tense," she said. "Way past." Laughter gripped her again as she headed toward the door. Her shoulders were shaking with laughter as she left the conference room and dragged Merlin toward the elevator.

"Wait!" Nick called. "What about this? The negotiation?"

"Talk to Natalie," Zoey shouted as the elevator doors whooshed shut.

Merlin grinned as she laughed all the way down. He held her hand as she pushed open the glass doors to the noisy air of Park Avenue, buses humming, street construction chinking.

"Didn't Nick look ridiculous in there?" she asked.

"What happened?" Merlin seemed confused. "What did he say?"

"He wanted to get back together, but when he opened his mouth, I don't know, somehow I saw what a jerk he is and the whole thing seemed so ludicrous, so insane that I've been pining over an idiot all these months. Was he a jerk all along and I just didn't see it?"

"I'm not sure," Merlin admitted.

"Well, he's a jerk now." Zoey glanced down toward the buildings of Grand Central and took a deep breath, trying to suck in the traffic and haze and congestion. "The man I fell in love with doesn't exist anymore, except in my memory. Suddenly, it's all so clear: It is so over between Nick and me. So over. And suddenly, I realize that's a good thing."

70

"Ladies and gentlemen, I give you Cleopatra!" Merlin pronounced, bowing before Jade as the elevator took them up to the banquet level.

Jade ignored him, checking her makeup in a compact mirror. "Has A.J. arrived yet? Does my hair look limp to you? Maybe this eye shadow is too shiny . . ."

"You look fine," Zoey assured her. Jade wore a shimmering Bob Mackie gown covered with sequins. The front was a simple square cut, navy with silver around the border. The back was cut devastatingly low, revealing buttery skin delicately arching down. Zoey straightened her own gown, the green sheath she'd bought for Merlin's wedding. "For once, I got a bridesmaid dress that I could wear again," she said, smoothing the bodice. "Who knew that I'd be in it so soon?"

"Who knew," Merlin agreed. Since he was working, he wore his blazer and a tie, a uniform that Zoey always found hopelessly preppy. "The benefit is for some art foundation that Mr. Chenowitz is involved with," Merlin explained. "I managed to get your names on the guest list, so don't feel you have to sneak around."

"That's good, because I'm nervous enough without having to crash the party." Jade held a hand to her breast and closed her eyes. "Oh, jeez. I've got butterflies." Her blue eyes flashed with fear. "I never get butterflies."

"You're on a mission to win back your man," Zoey said. "You should be nervous."

Merlin escorted them to the ballroom, where a woman at the door greeted them enthusiastically, as if they were, indeed, very important people. Once inside Zoey was impressed by the beautiful flowers, sparkling bar setup, and food tables with an array of platters on tiered shelves and silver chafing dishes with hot hors d'oeuvres.

"Nice party," she said.

Jade was silent, her lips pressed tight, her eyes moving rapidly, scoping out the crowd of guests. "There he is . . . oh, God." Her eyes misted and she fanned herself with her hands. "No, wait, I can't fall apart. I can do this. I have to."

"You go, girl," Merlin said. Zoey and Jade gave him a skeptical look, and he shrugged. "It seemed like the right thing to say."

"Do you want us to come with you?" Zoey asked.

Jade considered, then shook her head. "No. I need to do this alone." Lifting her chin, she set out across the ballroom, gliding toward a graying man with distinctly large, black-rimmed glasses. His face caught as he noticed her, and though he didn't turn away, his reception was less than warm.

"Oh, God, I feel like a chaperone at the senior prom." Zoey grabbed Merlin's arm. "What if he doesn't take her back?"

Merlin watched quietly. "It's very difficult to say no to Jade."

"But this guy is a billionaire entrepreneur. He says no at all the right times, in all the right places."

"Sometimes you just have to leave it up to the stars, I guess."

Zoey heard laughter at the corner bar. "Isn't that Mouse?" she asked. "And Kenny?" She gasped. "That little sneak. Come on." Zoey and Merlin went over to the bar, where Mouse and Kenny were engaged in conversation with two men Zoey didn't recognize. Mouse wore a shoulderless red gown that accentuated her curves.

"You look stunning, my dear," Zoey said, giving Mouse an air kiss.

"Thank you, dahling!" Mouse joked. "Kenneth was just talking about his golf game."

Zoey linked her arm through Mouse's and tugged her away. "What's going on with you? Seeing a man behind your girl-friends' backs. You're going to get yourself kicked out of the girl association."

"I know, I know, I'm sorry," Mouse said. "I started seeing him again after you and Jade tipped me off that he couldn't live with-out me, and after that it was just hard to eat crow."

Merlin picked up a silver fork from the buffet table and handed it to Mouse. "Dig in, toots."

"I brought him here to try to get our relationship back on a more social track again, but I still have my doubts. Kenny has is-sues. Things about religion and his father and what a nice girl should and should not do. He thinks that only bad girls enjoy sex, and I am not about to extend my acting career to the bed-room." Mouse lifted her champagne glass thoughtfully. "I'm crazy about the man, but he does torment himself."

"At least he's working on it, and he's honest with you," Zoey said.

"That's good, right?" Mouse's brown eyes were full of con-cern. "Sometimes I think we are so good together. So good for each other. Other times I just want to kill him."

"Sounds like love to me," Merlin said.

As the party was winding down, it became clear that Operation Snag a Billionare had been successful for Jade, who brought him around and casually introduced him to all her friends. Zoey liked the man's earnestness, and he seemed im-pressed by her choice of career.

"A writer!" He shook his head. "I just can't imagine coming up with all those words. Three, four, five hundred pages worth? That's just amazing to me." He scratched his chin and adjusted his thick black-rimmed glasses. "How do you come up with your stories?"

Zoey swallowed a bite of shrimp and licked one fingertip. "I try to get them from real life. Not actual accounts, but inspired by life. I've fashioned a heroine after Jade, here." Zoey wondered if Jade realized she was referring to the woman in her porn book, but Jade seemed to be busy basking in A.J.'s attention. "And recently I wrote about Marielle."

"Get out!" Mouse slapped her shoulder. "You didn't tell me."

"Well, it looks like your story might not make it to print," Zoey admitted, thinking of her most recent rejection from Skye. "But I certainly found it inspiring."

"Fascinating," A.J. said. "And what about yourself? Do you ever write about Zoey?"

The old autobiography question. How much of this is you? "I guess the closest I ever came to portraying my own situation and feelings was when I wrote *His Daughter's Keeper*," she admitted. "But I haven't tread that territory for awhile."

"And why not?" A.J. asked innocently.

Zoey shrugged. "Too painful. Too much exposure."

A.J. reached out for her hand and squeezed it hard. "But it was a wonderful book. Thank you, for taking the risk. Your pain is shared by others, and somehow, when we encounter it in a book, it's reassuring to know that someone else is trying to untangle the same conundrum."

Emotion choked Zoey's throat as his message hit her. She had been skirting the truth, dancing around the pain and disappointment, sanitizing the infestation. She nodded, and the conversation went on to another topic as Zoey tried to sort it out. Had she been avoiding her true authorial voice? God, maybe that was the source of her writer's block; she wanted to write without true pain or emotion. Nick had broken her heart, and while healing she'd been unable to lay her torn and tattered soul upon the literary table.

As Zoey ruminated, a new arrival caught her attention. Sam the painter entered the room, trailing another man and an older woman. Hmm. Now that she was sober he looked even more attractive to Zoey, though the aura that she'd seen the other night no longer existed. No, he was not aglow, simply a flesh and blood man. An attractive man with a winning smile and a clean-shaven jaw that cried out to be touched.

Mouse grabbed her elbow, and whispered: "Look who's here."

Zoey nodded.

"Do you think he would do a few touch-ups on the stucco walls at Rainforest?" Mouse teased.

Zoey pinged her shoulder. "As if I'm not tortured enough? Go see what you can find out about him."

As Mouse slipped away Zoey watched him for awhile, kicking herself. Sam was cute but probably gay from the way he seemed to be "with" the other guy.

Mouse reported in: "The woman with the two guys is a powerful art dealer, and the other guy is an artist, too."

"Two artists." Zoey nodded. "They're probably together. He must be gay."

"I think this is a situation that requires closer consideration," Merlin said, glancing across the room. "Excuse me."

While Merlin scoped out the guys, Zoey hooked up with Jade and A.J. again. "You've got to see the apartment," A.J. told Zoey. "You're all invited over soon for dinner. Casual, because I don't have a dining room table." He turned to Jade. "Do I have a dining room?"

She nodded, laughing easily. "You have a dining room. Maybe two."

"But it's so boring to put dining room furniture in. How about a pinball machine? Or a pool table? Jade helped me pick out the best stuff." He turned to Jade. "You'll come shopping with me again, won't you?"

"Yes, of course," she said confidently. "We can go this weekend."

We, she'd said. Remembering when she'd been a happy part of a "we," Zoey sighed. That was long ago and far away. Now I'm learning to live for the moment, Zoey thought. She watched

Jade rub A.J.'s back to scratch an itch he couldn't reach, and felt glad that she and Merlin had intervened. Sometimes meddling paid off.

Across the room, Merlin had made progress. He seemed to be hitting it off with Sam.

Damn.

Okay, so Sam *was* gay, and probably not with the other artist. Well, good for Merlin. Zoey reminded herself to chastise him for moving in on her territory, only she hadn't really established Sam as hers yet. Oh, well.

A.J. and Jade said goodbye, and once again A.J. raved about his good fortune in finding Jade. Zoey was glad to become friendly with Jade's new boyfriend, but she didn't have the heart to tell him she couldn't bear to hear about one more happy ending that did not involve her. Mouse and Kenny had left a half hour ago, and suddenly Zoey found herself standing alone in a ballroom where the action was fizzling. Forcing a confident smile, she found her way to the lobby and out to the circular drive, where most guests were piling into private limos.

Beyond the overhang, rain cascaded down in wavering sheets. The storm had brought a cool wind with it, but now that it was raining Zoey was going to have a hard time finding a cab. The doorman came over and blew his whistle. "I'll get something for you ma'am. Eventually," he promised.

Zoey nodded, hoping he would understand when she didn't whip out a twenty-dollar tip.

"Ooh, look at that rain," Merlin said from behind her.

She turned to see him standing alone. "Where's Sam? I noticed you two hit it off."

"Meow," he said. "If you can retract your claws a moment, you'll learn that Sam and I *did* hit it off. Mostly because we both wanted information. I wanted to know about the other artist he was with, who goes by the name Marlon Jefferson. Gorgeous, wasn't he? Marlon is gay, and he is available, much to my delight."

"Oh."

"Close your mouth, Myrtle. And Sam wanted some information about you."

"Like what?"

"Everything. Which I revealed, of course. I told him you drool in your sleep. I told him to go read one of your books, starting with the porno one first."

She swatted his shoulder, laughing. "You know, I've realized that my theory about love was completely wrong. That notion that we're two stars who cross in the heavens, that two people, and only those two people, are right for each other?"

"Total garbage," Merlin agreed.

She looked up at him. "I'll be moving in as soon as I finish the painting."

He nodded. "Good. It'll feel good to have a home again."

She gave him a hug, and he actually hugged her back for a moment.

"I feel so free," she said, spinning around. "I think I'll head out to the street and find my own cab."

"You're crazy. You're going to ruin your bridesmaid gown."

"I know."

"Wait!" Merlin called. "What if I meet someone and plan a quickie wedding?"

Zoey turned back to add, "I'll find another dress," before she gamboled over the concrete to the wet street. The rain tapped her face and bare shoulders, but she enjoyed it, feeling purged of her old life and her old faulty theories with each drop of rain.

She made it to the avenue when she heard someone calling. "Hey!" Turning, she saw Sam running, his umbrella stretched out to her. He caught up with her and held his umbrella over her head. So chivalry wasn't completely dead.

"You left in a hurry," he said, struggling to hold the umbrella and keep up with her. "Are you under a deadline?"

"Yes. I have an apartment to paint, remember?"

"Oh . . ." He dashed around a mailbox and met her on the other side. "You know, I've been known to be pretty handy with a brush."

"So I've heard." She couldn't believe he was following her with an umbrella. She stopped walking and grabbed hold of his hand on the umbrella. "Do you want to come over, Sam? I'm a terrible cook and I really do need to paint, but there's a bottle of wine in the fridge and my friend has a pretty good CD collection."

His eyes revealed so much, open, honest, inquisitive. "I'd like that," he said. "And I really will help you paint."

Zoey laughed. "My friend is so lucky. Bedroom texture by Sam Watson. Her apartment will become a national treasure."

"Oh, now you're bullshitting me."

"Maybe. I'll have to see your work to know for sure."

He tucked his arm through hers and held the umbrella over their heads as they faced the street. "There's a cab," he said, waving it down.

The cab veered close, its tires hitting a puddle. Muddy water rose and sprayed Zoey and Sam as the cab sped past. They were left, dripping and sputtering.

"I've got an idea." Sam closed the umbrella and held his arms out, as if to catch the raindrops.

Zoey glanced at the soggy man beside her and burst out laughing, thinking that this would be a great opening scene for a novel. The story of two people who had just come to New York City. He was an artist, she was a novelist in the throes of a treacherous divorce and . . .

Her mind wandered over story possibilities as they walked, kicking through puddles, licking the rain off their lips. She could even see the first few lines:

Some things never change. Like New York City.

Thank God.